ABOUT THE AUTHOR

Awais Khan is a TED speaker and a graduate of the University of Western Ontario and Durham University. He has studied creative writing at Faber Academy.

His debut novel, *In the Company of Strangers*, was published in 2019 to much critical acclaim, subsequently reissued in 2022 by Hera Books with Film/TV rights going to Pikchur TV. His next book, *No Honour*, was also published to similar critical acclaim in 2021, getting featured in *Woman and Home, BuzzFeed, Heat* and other leading publications. Romanian rights for *No Honour* were sold to Tritonic.

Awais Khan has been longlisted for the Short Story Dagger and shortlisted for the Dead Good Reader Awards. He has served on the judging panel for the Cheshire Novel Prize and the Gwyl Crime Cymru First Novel Award. He regularly appears on television and radio and also teaches a popular online creative writing course. When not working, he has his nose buried in a book.

He lives in Lahore, Pakistan and *Someone Like Her* is his third novel.

He is represented by Annette Crossland.

Follow him on Twitter, Instagram and Facebook @AwaisKhanAuthor.

Someone Like Her

PRAISE FOR AWAIS KHAN

'This book centres on the terrible price paid to protect a family's honour. With gripping twists and turns, your heart will go out to women who are persecuted for being human.' - ***Woman and Home***

'*In The Company of Strangers* is a moving tale of love and loss and human frailties set amidst starkly contrasting sections of society in Pakistan.' - ***Khaleej Times***

'So powerful!' - ***Heat***

'The author's portrayal of deplorable, unpardonable reality is brutal, but he handles the subject with empathy and compassion. A gripping novel.' - ***Dawn***

'Inspired by a real-life story of honour killing in Pakistan, this is an important and powerful read.' - ***Buzzfeed***

'Gripping from the first page, Khan paints an at-times terrifying picture of a world where a woman's worth is measured by her fertility, domesticity and obedience.' - ***The National***

'Captivating and social inspired, Awais Khan's debut novel paints Lahore's High Society with an insider's perspicuity.' - ***HELLO!***

'This book arrests a reader's attention till the end. There is hardly a dull moment in Awais Khan's *In the Company of Strangers.* Read it. You may want to send a 'thank you' note to the novelist.'
- ***The Free Press Journal***

'I particularly loved Khan's book because he managed to write his female South Asian characters as people who actually exist. Even in their flaws, his characters maintain their relatability—particularly Mona. The book also touches upon some sensitive topics but manages to do so while maintaining its gripping tone and appearance of everyday life in Lahore.' - ***Book Riot***

'Khan explores the double speak of this segment of the society, the stereotypes they hold of others and the ones they live with. It is a fast paced read without any parts where it feels like a drag and this is a big plus for a debut novel.' - ***Mashable***

'The debut novel explores the lives of Lahore's beau monde and the seedy underbelly the glitter of their lives obscure.' - ***Outlook India***

'Emotional' - ***New Lines Magazine***

'Khan's writing does complete justice to a sensitive subject making this must-read novel a likely strong contender at award ceremonies.' - ***Eastern Eye***

'A moving book that centres on the price paid to protect a family's honour. With twists and turns, your heart will go out to the women.' - ***Woman's Weekly***

'Unflinching. Gritty. Important. A powerful story of a young woman who defies convention in rural Pakistan.' - ***Guernsey Press***

'A poignant, powerfully wrought story of love, family and the battle for change, in a society where tradition and the modern world brutally collide.' - ***Living Magazine***

'A biting criticism of patriarchy, power and corruption in a small Pakistani town.' - ***Journal of Commonwealth Literature***

'Khan's novel is fluid and shows a holistic understanding of humanity... powerful writing.' - ***Science Direct***

'From the whirlpool of characters and events, *No Honour* allows the reader an immersive read into an important issue through interesting characters.' - ***The News International***

'Awais Khan, has written an immensely powerful, important and significant book. I recommend everyone read *No Honour*. It will shake you, anger and sadden you, but also one restores hope in the power of love to triumph over evil, even in the face of seemingly insurmountable obstacles.' - ***Daily Times***

'An engrossing novel that takes one into the underbelly of Lahore's high society and lets you in one some of the city's best kept secrets!' - ***Newsline***

'Khan's gripping narrative brings together complex characters who are driven by a hypocritical desire of retaining their elevated status at the cost of moral transgression and pain. Khan's book should be read for its brutal portrayal of people who find themselves caged by fidelity and familial obligations.'
- ***The Daily Telegraph, India***

'A revelation!' - ***Pakistan Today***

'*Someone Like Her* is arguably Khan's best work!' - ***The Pakistan Daily***

"From horrifying opening to powerful end, it holds back no punches in its strong indictment of misogyny, but always with a warmth to its beating heart of the relationship between father and daughter. Very well done!" - ***Harriet Tyce, author of Blood Orange***

'Both tender and powerful, *Someone Like Her* manages to have all the hallmarks of an Awais Khan novel, whilst still marking itself out as his best yet. A compelling novel.' - ***Sonia Velton, author of Blackberry and Wild Rose and The Image of Her***

'Stunning, shocking, compulsive reading... a breathtaking masterpiece.' - ***Hazel Prior, author of Away with the Penguins***

'Beautifully written and immersive... a must-read.' - ***Sarah Pearse, author of The Sanatorium***

'An emotional rollercoaster that exposes the ugliest aspects of Pakistani society while gripping the reader from start to finish. A

terrific book that will disgust, sicken, and reward you.'
- ***Alan Gorevan, author of The Kindness of Psychopaths***

'Awais Khan is well-known for his insightful storytelling especially on thorny issues like violence against women. He gives us sensitive, authentic stories of women in Pakistan who refuse victimhood and embrace life, warts and all, with heroic strength and optimism.' - ***Faiqa Mansab, author of This House of Clay and Water***

'Rarely has a writer affected me so deeply. *Someone Like Her* is an epic story of love, power and extraordinary courage. A fearless and important novel set between Multan and London.'
- ***A.J.West, author of The Spirit Engineer***

'*Someone Like Her* by Awais Khan is a dark and frightening story of corruption, oppression, possession and violence yet is beautifully and sensitively written by a brave, bold author.'
-***Michael Wood, author of the DCI Matilda Darke series***

'In *Someone Like Her*, Khan lifts the veil on the crushing and (physically) threatening realities for women in Pakistan. A gripping and emotive story of ambition, resilience and love.'
-***Heleen Kist, author of Stay Mad, Sweetheart***

'An epic story of love, abuse and revenge *Someone Like Her* is an emotional rollercoaster as Awais Khan confronts societal injustices with unflinching honesty, leading us into a world where women are treated as chattels and money rules supreme. Beautifully written: I loved it.' -***Eve Smith, author of The Waiting Rooms and Off Target***

'*Someone Like Her* is a ground-breaking novel of love, courage and revenge that took me on a rollercoaster of emotions. I was gripped from the first page. Khan has triumphed once again!'
-***A.A. Chaudhuri, author of She's Mine and The Final Party***

'Khan is an excellent storyteller and *Someone Like Her* explores the too often heartbreaking dance between the traditional and the modern serving up an astute mirror to a Pakistan continuing to search for an identity. Explosive.' - ***Soniah Kamal, author of Unmarriageable***

'As intimate as it is galvanizing, *Someone Like Her* is a wake-up call that is both timely and timeless, offering fiction that is often truer than fact. Read this novel, remove your rose-coloured glasses and let Khan take you on a journey to disrupt, in the most potent way possible.' - ***Saba Karim Khan, author of Skyfall***

'Pacy, gripping and fast-moving but also a very nuanced look at the destructive effects of class, misogyny, money, power and the lasting effects of trauma. I literally could not put it down!' - ***Edel Coffey, award-winning author of Breaking Point***

'Compelling, painful and defiant, *Someone Like Her* takes on the oppression of women and the damaging legacy of men's violence through its protagonist's journey. *Someone Like Her* cries out for every Ayesha facing misogyny, discrimination and trauma today.' ***-Elyse John, author of Orphia and Eurydicius***

'Khan lays bare the trauma of women, relegated to second-class citizenship in this compelling tale of brutality and bravery. First class writing. I could not put it down.' ***-Marion Todd, author of the DI Clare Mackay series***

'Khan explores power, family, corruption, misogyny and love. I loved this story of courage and resilience, which shows the best and worst in human nature, while also giving a fascinating insight into slices of contemporary Pakistani society. A gripping novel that kept me turning the pages late into the night.' - ***Aliya Ali-Afzal, author of Would I Lie To You?***

'*Someone Like Her* is a heart-rending and compelling story. Khan treats his characters with love and respect. I couldn't put it down.' ***-Alice Clark-Platts, author of The Flower Girls and The Cove***

'Another stunning novel by the phenomenal talent that is Awais Khan. *Someone Like Her* breaks your heart but then gradually heals it again with every prose-perfect chapter, until you're basking in hope and spirit.' - ***Mira V Shah, author of Her***

'If you're a fan of Khaled Hosseini, or if you like your thrillers fast and powerful, this is for you.' - ***Paul Waters, author of Blackwatertown***

'Khan brings sharply into focus the troubling attitude towards women's rights in parts of the subcontinent Khan presents us with a shocking portrait of lives lived under the shadow of threat and prejudice. A brave book.' - ***Vaseem Khan, author of Midnight at Malabar House***

'A novel that explores misogyny and honour killing, but which is also a compelling and compassionate story.' - ***Anna Mazzola, author of The Clockwork Girl***

'A gripping, horrifying, compulsive read with two rich, compelling lead characters. I love books where you learn without any awareness of being taught.' - ***Jennie Godfrey, author of The List of Suspicious Things***

'In *No Honour,* Awais Khan has crafted a deeply engaging story that keeps you hooked from the first sentence to the end. It is a masterful story of courage in the face of seemingly impossible odds.' - ***Sopan Deb, New York Times writer and author of Missed Translations***

'The book is both shocking, deeply moving & hugely important. Highly recommended.' - ***Carol Lovekin, author of Wild Spinning Girls and Ghostbird***

'An amazing, passionate piece of storytelling. Harrowing and redemptive in equal measure.' - ***Leonora Nattrass, author of Black Drop***

'Addictive, brave and powerful. A page-turning book, it opened my eyes to the horrific practice of honour killings that are still carried out today. Bravo!' - ***Louise Fein, author of People Like Us***

'It's about as comfortable a read as *Shuggie Bain* was. I can definitely see it making the next round of awards lists.'
- *Peter McLean, author of War For the Rose Throne Series*

'An absolute belter of a novel- kept having to put it down and some deep breathing. Hypnotic, atmospheric and by the end, so hopeful. Loved it.' - ***Sarah Sultoon, award-winning CNN journalist and author of The Source***

'A beautifully rendered, moving and insightful novel, *No Honour* takes us deep into lives that many of us in the West probably know little about. Highly recommended.'- ***Neema Shah, author of Kololo Hill***

'A bold, gifted storyteller, dealing with a gritty, thorny issue of female honour. Compulsive reading. I was hooked from the first page.' - ***Qaisra Shahraz, MBE, author of The Holy Woman***

'*No Honour* is a beautiful, striking, eye-opening book... shocking, sensitive, powerful, and very important. Highly recommended.' --***Louise Beech, author of This Is How We Are Human***

'A tense yet gripping story of 16 year old Abida, who desperately wishes to flee her village in rural Pakistan where girls are subjected to honour killings.' - ***Polly Crosby, author of The Illustrated Child***

'Spectacular... a joy from start to finish. Keep an eye out for this guy, folks – he's going to be big, perhaps our generation's foremost chronicler of Lahore.' - ***Charlie Carroll, author of The Lip***

'A truly heart-wrenching tale of the human spirit's quest for love, freedom and survival. One to look out for!' - ***Tim Glister, author of Red Corona***

Someone Like Her

AWAIS KHAN

Simon & Schuster

First published in the United Kingdom in 2023 by Orenda Books
This edtition is published in India by Simon & Schuster, 2023

1 3 5 7 9 10 8 6 4 2

Simon & Schuster India

818, Indraprakash Building,

21, Barakhamba Road,

New Delhi 110001.

Simon & Schuster: Celebrating 100 Years of Publishing in 2024

Simon & Schuster India, New Delhi

www.simonandschuster.co.uk
www.simonandschuster.com.au
www.simonandschuster.co.in

Paperback ISBN: 9788194643012

EBook ISBN: 9788194643074

Printed and bound in India by Replika Press Pvt. Ltd.

MIX
Paper from responsible sources
FSC® C016779

Simon & Schuster India is committed to sourcing paper that is made from wood grown in sustainable forests and support the Forest Stewardship Council, the leading international forest certification organisation. Our books displaying the FSC logo are printed on FSC certified paper.

For my Nani,
Begum Mumtaz Tarin

'People will forget what you said, people will forget what you did, but people will never forget how you made them feel.'
—Maya Angelou

'There will come a time when you believe everything is finished; that will be the beginning.'
—Louis L'Amour

Ayesha

Multan, Pakistan

The mud clung to her sandals as she ran through the rain, the dirty water splashing her cotton shalwar and staining it brown. But Ayesha carried on. Nothing mattered when it came to Insaaniyat – the charity where she worked – and today was supposed to be a big day. Her friend Saira had called her saying a very rich man was coming to the office today, which could translate into a very big cheque.

'If word is to be believed, his cheque could change a lot of things here at Insaaniyat. It could pay our salaries for life, that's for sure.'

The overcrowded city of Multan had done its best to delay her, but Ayesha was persistent. Had been since childhood, when she would force her father to drive her all the way to Lahore for swimming tournaments, to compete with the rich kids from the elite schools. Maybe if she had become a champion, their financial situation would have been better today, but sadly that was not to be.

Her family only had one car left now, so Ayesha either had to brave public transport or dish out money on one of those ride-hailing apps. Today was supposed to be dry outside, but the moment she had boarded the bus, rain began to patter on the windows. She couldn't help but laugh at nature's injustice. Street hawkers had rushed to cover their goods with plastic sheets, particularly the men selling chickpeas roasted in sand and salt – they couldn't afford to let the sand get wet. The rain fell down in icy sheets, turning the concrete buildings a dark-grey colour, making Multan look even duller than usual. Maybe it was her mood, but it was as if the rain had leeched all the cheer from the city. She had endured the entire ride through the traffic-choked city, inhaling the noxious fumes and scolding herself for not taking an Uber. They had managed to retain the family house in Cantt – one of Multan's poshest addresses – but it was quite a trek to get to the less savoury parts of town, and that's exactly where the charity was headquartered.

Her stained shalwar was impossible to salvage at this point, but she adjusted her sopping-wet dupatta over her chest, ran her fingers through her wet hair, patting down any stray strands, and smiled as she entered the gates of her workplace, brushing her shoes against the mats placed on the brick floor. *No matter how you feel inside, there must always be a smile on your face at work.* She'd learned that from her father, who'd tried to do his best throughout his tumultuous career. And so far, his advice had worked. Her fellow workers and her boss loved her, as did the people who visited Insaaniyat.

Saira was popular for her hyperbole, but that didn't mean that she spoke falsehoods. She only embellished the truth a bit. If she said it was a rich man, it was going to be a rich man. Charities in Pakistan were always in dire need of money, not because nobody donated – it was a Muslim's duty to give, after all – but because there was so much to do. And this organisation, committed to eradicating domestic violence, had its plate well and truly full.

'When a country has a population of over two hundred million, is it any surprise that nothing is ever enough?' her boss, Shugufta Raheem, always said. 'All we can do is our best and trust the government to do the rest.'

As if that will ever happen, Ayesha thought, looking at the whitewashed building ahead, some of the paint already peeling. Shugufta kept the place clean, but Ayesha knew that she wouldn't waste any precious money on vanity projects, not when there was so much else to do.

Her father had frowned when he first visited the offices of the charity. 'Girls in our family do not work, *beta*,' he had murmured, surveying the place with distaste. 'What will people say – that Safdar Khan Khakwani is now incapable of looking after his daughter?'

'They will say that our daughter is learning to be financially independent,' her mother had quipped, steering her husband away from the offices and towards the courtyard, where they could sit beneath the shade of a towering shisham tree. So many trees had been chopped down in Multan in recent years, such specimens had become a rarity.

'I can still provide for the family, Begum,' Safdar Khan had said, puffing up his chest, an indignant expression on his face. 'Never let it be said that a Multani man cannot look after his family.'

'Nobody is saying that, Safdar Sahab, but we need to let the girl breathe, don't we? God knows this city is claustrophobic enough.'

'Ah, you're right there.' At that, Safdar Khan had visibly deflated, and thus Ayesha had been the first in the family to be given permission to work, much to the dismay of those family members who, over the years, had uttered scathing remarks about an unmarried Multani girl working in an office – without a head-scarf, no less. Ayesha had ignored them, as had her parents. Multan was changing, and if these people were going to remain stuck in the past, then so be it.

Thankfully, the murky brown water on the roads hadn't permeated the premises of the office yet, and seeing her wiping her feet before entering, Bashir, the security guard, beamed. 'You're one of the only people here who bothers to clean their shoes, Bibi. Thank you for making my work easier. I won't have to mop the floor for the thousandth time.'

She smiled at him, fishing a five-hundred-rupee note from her wallet and handing it to him. 'Here, use this to buy your kids some *jalebis* today.' He had eight children, and a security guard's salary didn't leave much room for treats.

Bashir's grin widened. 'May God bless you, Bibi. May you marry the richest man in Multan.'

His words made her laugh. 'Oh Bashir, pray that I become a rich woman all by myself. I don't need a man for that.'

Her buoyant spirits dipped as soon as she entered the office. It was full of commotion at the best of times, but today it was as if lightning had struck the building. People were scrambling around carrying documents and there was a bunch of police officers standing outside Shugufta's room.

That was never a good sign.

The police officers stared at her, as if she were somehow to blame for whatever had happened. It only occurred to her a moment later that they were probably looking at how the wet clothes clung to her body. Shuddering, she pushed into the room, where she was immediately met with the sound of heart-wrenching moans. She clapped her hand to her mouth. A young woman was lying on a stretcher with her entire face bandaged. Only her eyes were visible and they were filled with tears. Ayesha knew at once what this was. She'd seen it here before. Sadly, more than once. And it never got easier. She couldn't imagine the pain the poor girl was in. Was it acid? A knife?

Shugufta too was in tears, as were the girl's parents, who stood on either side of the stretcher.

'For the last time, I want an immediate FIR to be registered against her husband,' Shugufta cried. 'This is my cousin, for God's sake.'

'Rabia,' Ayesha whispered to herself. Of course. She had seen her in the office a few times in the past. It broke her heart to see her in this state.

'A first information report is a serious step. And why couldn't we have done this at the girl's residence, where this allegedly happened? Or better yet, register the case at the station.' The investigation officer sounded weary, as if he was doing them a massive favour by just being there.

The father stepped forward. 'It's because we married our daughter to her cousin, thinking that if she stayed in the family –

in the same house – she would be safe.' He shook his head, tears vanishing into his white beard. 'But look what happened. Nowhere is safe for our girls in this country. We never dreamed that my nephew would turn out to be a monster. He carved up her face with a knife. I want him behind bars!'

The mother wept into her hands. '*Haye*, what will become of her now? Her entire life is ruined. Nobody in Multan will ever marry her again. Look at her face, Ji.'

'She must have done something,' the police offer remarked, a smirk on his face. 'Men don't just cut their wives' faces like this for no reason. I'd like to hear the other side of the story.'

'You should be ashamed of yourself,' one of the female police officers said, her face a mask of disgust. 'Casting aspersions on people's daughters like that. Remember you answer to God too, just like anyone else.'

The man shrugged. 'I'm just saying that one should look at both sides. As police, that's our role.'

'You have a female boss, don't forget. Would you like me to take this up with her? I'm sure she'd be interested to hear about the contempt you seem to have for women.'

The man blushed. 'No need to tell her anything.'

His colleague strode forward. 'This is a clear-cut case of domestic assault. Her husband deserves to be behind bars. We will take the victim's statement here, and then I will guide you on what to do next.' She flicked a hand in the officer's direction. 'Forget about him. People like him are a dime a dozen. No wonder our country is in this state.'

The male police officer scratched his head. 'But why summon us here? They should register a case at the police station. And apart from that, we'll need to visit the house where the crime actually took place and get the rest of the story.'

'Shut up, Iftikhar. Do you expect them to register the case in front of the attacker and his family? One more word and I will call Amna Habib.' Then turning to the family, she murmured, 'That's the deputy superintendent of police, who we both report to. One of you will need to visit the station, though. That is necessary.'

Ayesha rolled her eyes, marvelling at the man's stupidity. Wasn't it obvious that pressure from the attacker's family had already prevented them from openly registering the case? The police in Pakistan could be so dense sometimes, although money generally helped them understand things better. At least the father hadn't turned against his own daughter. She'd seen many cases where the family abandoned young women to their fate.

Shugufta reached for her purse before calling for everyone to leave the room. Spotting Ayesha, she marched over and pulled her out into the corridor.

'Listen, I am so sorry—' Ayesha began, but Shugufta cut her off.

'Thanks, but as you can see, I will be busy here for a while. She's my cousin, after all. Bloody monsters! Both the husband and that *kanjar* of a policeman.' She flicked a tear from her cheek. 'I will need you to handle the donor coming in today.'

Ayesha stared at her and then at her own drenched clothes. She took a step back. 'Shugufta, I can't. This is your domain. I've never done anything like this before. I work in accounts and only sit in on the meetings. I never take part. And look at my clothes.'

'You can, and you will. Just stand under a ceiling fan and the clothes will dry.' Shugufta took her hand in hers and squeezed once. 'I have full faith in you. His name is Raza Masood, and he will be coming with his lawyer. These rich types like to donate for the optics, so it should be pretty straightforward. Show him the office and the centre, and get that money out of him. We need it.'

'May I at least take Saira along with me?'

Shugufta hesitated. 'You know I love Saira, but she can be a bit flaky. Besides, she's running an errand for me, so it has to be you. You've sat through dozens of meetings, Ayesha. If anyone can do it, it's you.'

Ayesha gulped. Handling the charity's accounts and accompanying Shugufta to meetings was one thing, but doing it all solo was something else entirely.

But then she remembered what her father had told her once: 'You have the Khakwani family genes, Ayesha. We can do whatever we put our minds to.' And then he had kissed her on the forehead. Imagining him doing the same now, Ayesha walked towards her small office at the end of the hall, the one she shared with Saira, mentally preparing herself for the meeting.

She had barely had time to dry herself before someone came in and touched her on the shoulder.

It was one of the junior staff. 'Ayesha Madam, Raza Sahab's cavalcade has arrived.'

A sense of panic engulfed her. The police were still here. That poor girl and her family were in Shugufta's room. What would he think?

'Already?' She glanced at her ruined shalwar with regret before applying a fresh coat of lipstick and running a comb through her hair.

Sure enough, when she stepped outside, there was a gleaming Beemer parked in the courtyard, flanked by pickup trucks with armed guards dressed in black.

It was Raza's lawyer who greeted her first, a short, balding man in a grey suit. If he was surprised when Ayesha shook his hand – something most females in Multan didn't do – he didn't show it. 'A pleasure to meet you here,' he said. 'My name is Naeem Siddiqui and I represent the Masood family, who really need no introduction.'

She tried hard not to laugh, as the man proceeded to do just that, launching into a flowery account of all the Masood family had done for Multan. Midway through his monologue, she craned her neck, saying, 'Has Raza Sahab not come here with you?'

Naeem blinked and turned around to see the empty space behind him, only a few of Raza's guards visible in the trucks. 'Oh, he was right here with me. I have no idea...'

Raza's overpowering cologne announced his presence well before he did. A mixture of musk and sandalwood, it made Ayesha's eyes water. She turned around to see a tall man clad in a black shalwar kameez heading their way. So, that's where the rest of the armed guards had gone, she thought; five of them walked behind Raza, their fingers on the triggers of their guns. She shivered. This was a charity. What were they thinking?

'There he is,' Naeem cried, clapping his hands together. 'The Raza Masood.'

The Raza Masood wasn't at all what she had expected. He was over six feet tall with hair gelled back and a dazzling, thousand-watt smile that seemed genuine, but didn't quite reach his eyes. Those jet-black pupils smouldered as they surveyed Ayesha from head to toe. She didn't know what she'd expected, but certainly not for him to be so handsome.

He came to a stop right in front of her, a bit too close for comfort. Extending a hand in her direction, he said, 'It's a pleasure, Miss...'

'Ayesha,' she stammered, not trusting herself to say anything more for the moment, and she took his hand. It was rough and dry in her own damp palm, and she cursed herself for being so nervous. His smile grew more playful as he realised the effect he was having on her. She shook her head. What was wrong with her? Drawing herself up to her full height, she dropped his hand and said, 'It is an honour to have you here, sir.'

'Call me Raza. Everyone else does.'

'They sure don't. They call you Raza *Sahab*,' Naeem piped up.

One glance in his direction and Naeem said no more.

Trying not to smile, Ayesha gestured at the office behind her. 'Well, Raza, if you would allow me, I'd like to give you a tour of the office and our centre, where we take care of all kinds of victims of domestic abuse.'

'Tsk. I do despise men who raise their hand to a woman,' he said.

Admirable, she thought, smiling to herself, imagining how

incensed her boyfriend, Saqib, would be if he knew the impression Raza was having on her. He wouldn't need to worry, though; she loved him more than she thought possible.

Raza said nothing as she showed him the property, following her with his hands clasped behind his back. *Ever the gentleman*. His lawyer kept babbling about how much the family donated to the poor, but Raza didn't say a word. Whether it was pride or humility, she didn't know.

As they passed the centre building, Ayesha paused. 'I cannot take you inside as we always respect the privacy of the victims, but I would like you to know that every year, our charity helps thousands of women in need of a place to stay after suffering abuse at home. But we don't just provide shelter, we also provide legal support, and we have various people coming in to teach them the skills they need to survive alone.'

'Survive?'

'Get jobs, housing...'

'Impressive,' Raza said, but he wasn't looking at the centre building. His eyes bored into hers. 'Very impressive.'

For the first time since he'd arrived, Ayesha felt a prick of unease, but she dismissed it. Raza Masood was a billionaire. What would he want with someone like her, whose father had ceased being rich many years ago?

'Thank you for this splendid tour, madam. Raza Sahab would very much like to donate a sizable sum to this wonderful charity,' Naeem Siddiqui gushed. 'Of course, we would like this generosity on behalf of the Masood family to be covered in all the leading newspapers.'

Ayesha hoped her cringe wasn't obvious. 'Err, sure. Most people like to keep their donations anonymous, but if you want coverage, then I'm sure we can arrange something.'

'Forget coverage,' Raza said suddenly.

'But, sir, why else are we—' Naeem began, but was silenced by a look.

'I am happy to donate thirty million rupees to this charity.'

Ayesha's mouth dropped open. 'Thirty million? That's a sizable sum. Thank you.'

'However, I would like to learn a little more about everything you do here,' Raza continued. 'After all, I need to know I'm getting my money's worth, don't you think?' His eyes met Ayesha's, making her flinch. 'Would coffee next week in the city be fine?'

She'd never met a donor outside of the office, and was about to say no, but then she pictured Shugufta's face after seeing the much-needed thirty-million-rupee cheque; she saw her father's chest swell with pride at her salary raise, the raise she so desperately needed. Lowering her gaze, she tried her best to smile. 'Of course, sir. Happy to. Coffee sounds good.'

He flashed her another of his dazzling smiles. 'I think I told you to call me Raza.'

A whisper is all it takes to condemn a woman for life.

These were words Ayesha had grown up hearing. Sometimes from her grandmother but more often than not, it was her mother who drilled them into her.

'A woman's life isn't her own, Ayesha. Especially not in Pakistan,' she'd say while lining her eyes with kohl in the mornings. One quick swipe around the eye was all she could manage, with the chores of the day looming over her. They had help, but her father insisted that nothing tasted as good as his wife's cooking. It was touching, but only served to increase her poor mother's workload.

Ishrat was one of those women who didn't dare question their husbands, not in private, and certainly not in public. Sometimes Ayesha was surprised her mother didn't have a permanent hunch from the way her head was always bowed in submission.

'Ayesha!' she called her now, her voice brimming with the

impatience she reserved only for her daughter. 'Why aren't you ready yet? Neelam Khala will be so upset if we're late. It's her only daughter's wedding.'

As if anything could upset Neelam Khala, Ayesha thought. All she did was meddle in other people's affairs and try and trick their daughters into unhappy marriages. Ayesha had seen first-hand just how miserable most of these girls were as they sat in their expensive designer dresses and handmade clutches from Italy, but with faces that were vacant and forlorn. She'd seen them flinch at their husbands' merest touch. Middle-aged aunties like Neelam Khala scouted girls of marriageable age like hawks stalking their prey. These weddings were a battlefield, and the losers were girls who were gullible enough to fall for all that pomp.

She had lost count of the number of times she had been thrust towards 'eligible' men herself, but Ayesha was having none of it. And in a way, she also felt sorry for some of the young men. Everything would be so awkward with them standing in a room full of people, trying to make small talk while everyone watched them. Thinking back to her meeting with Raza Masood the other day, she wondered if he had ever been subjected to this sort of embarrassing matchmaking. For some reason, she doubted it. Raza Masood seemed like a man who knew what he wanted from life, and how to get it.

Shugufta had all but kissed her after hearing how well the meeting had gone, but now Ayesha had to meet the guy for coffee. There was nothing to suggest that it was a date, but that gleam in his eye when he'd asked for the meeting put her on edge. But she only loved one person in her life, and he was the one she was going to marry.

Her stomach flipped as a message from Saqib arrived on her phone at that very moment. It was as if he'd read her mind.

Lovely morning today, my love. How about some coffee in Gulgasht? I miss you.

Ayesha blew a ringlet of hair out of her eyes, and thought of what to say. She'd known Saqib for many years, but it was only last year that she'd realised he was the one. They'd gone to school together, Saqib being a round boy who was relentlessly bullied, and had subsequently continued a platonic friendship. Then, sometime after they both turned twenty-five, things started to change. Saqib asked her out for coffee one day – only her – and sitting in that cosy place in Gulgasht, they'd realised how much they had in common. He was no longer the shy, embarrassed kid she knew from school, but a tall, striking man who'd just started working at a telecom firm. However, even now Saqib had a long way to go before he could match the exacting standards of Ayesha's parents. They certainly weren't rich anymore – hadn't been for a long time – but Ayesha's father, the great Safdar Khan Khakwani, had the same aura of arrogance and pretentiousness around him his forefathers had. And when people whispered about him behind his back, he either didn't notice or pretended not to.

'Oh Saqib,' Ayesha whispered, 'If only you were rich...'

She typed a quick reply:

Off to a wedding today. Can't meet up. Sorry!!! Love you xxx

Her screen lit up with Saqib's face, but Ayesha rejected the call. She had no time to waste. Their ancient Toyota Crown had started already, judging by the smell of gasoline wafting into the house. If she wasn't ready in five minutes, her father would kick up a storm.

When she eventually slid into the car, she was proven right.

'The world doesn't revolve around you, young lady,' her father remarked as the car groaned into action. 'Neelam is your mother's sister, your khala. She's not some stranger whose wedding you can prance into whenever it suits you. We've been waiting for almost an hour.'

'Ji, let the poor girl breathe. We're not that late. I'm sure the event hasn't even started yet. And besides, she's my sister. She'll understand.'

'I don't remember asking for your opinion, Ishrat.'

Her mother's shoulders sagged, and she said no more. Ayesha

had lost count of the times her father had shut her down like this. It infuriated her, but according to her grandmother, Ishrat had it easy.

'At least, he doesn't beat her. Your grandfather beat me to within an inch of my life and expected me to prepare dinner for him the next minute. And I did. Like clockwork. Beatings, dinner, and then some more beatings. Your mother is lucky I raised such a good boy.'

Good boy, indeed.

He ranted on. 'You have spoiled our daughter. With her lofty ideas and devil-may-care attitude, is it any wonder that she is still single at twenty-seven? I told you to get her married as soon as she graduated from high school, but no. When has anyone ever listened to me?'

'Marriage is not the most important thing in this world, Abbu,' Ayesha added, her face breaking into a smile.

'I rest my case. Do you hear your daughter, Ishrat? She says marriage isn't important. Oh, my poor naïve fool.'

Her mother turned back to stare daggers at her.

Her father banged his palm against the aging steering wheel in frustration. 'She'll be thirty soon, and in a city like Multan that is akin to turning sixty. Neelam's daughter is only twenty-two and she's getting married. If I didn't know any better, I'd say you two enjoy seeing me hang my head in shame.'

Her mother sighed. 'Safdar Sahab, if you'd allow me to speak, I'd tell you that I've approached all the *rishta walis* and have spread word about Ayesha far and wide among family and friends. The matchmakers have all come back with the same comments. The issue is not her age, but your expectations. The kind of money you want our daughter to marry into just isn't possible given our own financial situation.'

'What financial situation are you yapping about, woman? I am the son of one of Multan's richest feudal families. We used to piss money.'

'*Used* to is right,' Ishrat whispered. 'They see us as we are now, not as we were.'

'The family name counts for something, Ishrat. How can you be so dense? Besides, as Amma liked to say, our fortunes took a nosedive the day I married you.'

'Yes, Ji, of course it's my fault. Why don't you blame me for giving birth to a daughter as well?'

As Ayesha expected, her father's attitude changed at these words. 'You know that's not true, Ishrat. I'm sorry. It's just that I want what's best for our daughter. I can't help it ... I just worry.'

Her mother patted her husband on the shoulder. 'I know, Safdar Sahab. I'm sorry too. I know how much you love us.'

'So, can I expect your famous chicken biryani for dinner?'

'When have I ever disappointed you? I left the chicken out to defrost before we left the house.'

And just like that, her parents had made a 180-degree turn. This was how all their arguments started – her father too stubborn to accept that he had drained the family of its money, her mother trying and failing to stand up to him, only for them to make up in the end. Ayesha averted her face and leaned back against the headrest. It was too early in the day for her to cry, and besides, her makeup would be ruined. If only she could tell her parents that she had already found the right man by herself, but she knew that it was still too early. She watched Multan go by as her parents whispered to each other. Dust rose from the asphalt as their car whipped through the narrow residential roads, finally turning into one of the main arteries of Multan Cantt.

Ayesha worried because Saqib didn't have a fancy car or a big house in Cantt. He lived in a tiny 'seven marla' house – hardly big enough for two bedrooms and a lounge – somewhere in old Multan and only had a motorbike. His father had saved every rupee to make sure he went to Bahauddin Zakariya University, but he was nowhere near getting the plush job they needed him to. He was stuck in the marketing department of a telecom company that undervalued his skills. Ayesha knew without a shadow of a doubt that her father would sooner die than agree to marry her to Saqib. She was his last chance to become rich again, or at least to be associated with the rich, and he wasn't about to squander that on someone like Saqib.

He'll just have to, won't he, said a small voice in her head. *There really is nothing else for it.*

She sighed as they left the leafy boulevards of Cantt behind and joined the throng of vehicles on Bosan Road, most of them heading into Central Multan. Despite it being February, they had lowered their windows to allow the cool breeze to blow over their faces. The car had been baking in the winter sun for ages and was still rather warm.

It was a good thing they weren't all a sweaty mess by the time they arrived at the wedding, because Neelam Khala immediately found plenty of other things to criticise.

Rushing towards them, all three hundred pounds of her, the first thing she did was tut at Ayesha. 'Baji, I told you to make her wear sleeveless or short sleeves at the very least. Multan isn't as old-fashioned as you think. The cream of the crop is here. So many eligible bachelors, and you've got your daughter covered up like a spinster. There's still time. Before you enter the event, I say we go into the bathroom and I call my tailor. I have him here for precisely such emergencies. He'll remove the sleeves in a second.'

Safdar drew himself to his full height. 'Well, excuse me if I don't want to parade my daughter around naked, Neelam. I don't see your daughter wearing a sleeveless dress.'

Neelam sniffed. 'She's not the one in need of a husband, Bhai Jaan.'

'Neelam!' Ishrat held a hand to her chest. 'What is wrong with you?'

Ayesha watched her father walk on with his head held high, but she knew he was smarting from the impertinence. Twenty years ago, someone like Neelam would have thought twice before taking that tone with him. She saw him sag when he thought nobody was looking, sinking into an unoccupied sofa. Nobody would deign to join him. He was a has-been and he knew it, and she felt sorry for him then.

She blinked the tears away before turning to Neelam. 'Why, Khala, do share the number of Sabeena's dentist. Look at how he's fixed those horse teeth.'

Neelam glared at her. 'With that attitude, my dear, good luck getting a suitable husband.'

'Who said I needed a husband?'

Neelam raised an eyebrow. 'Why, Baji. Have you taught your daughter no manners at all? Didn't you hear what happened to poor Shaila's daughter?'

Ayesha had never known two sisters to be so different. Neelam Khala had hated Ayesha since the day she had accidentally tripped up her daughter, Sabeena, on a mountain path with jagged stones. Sabeena had needed dozens of stitches on her cheek, which had left an ugly scar. Ayesha had only been ten, and she'd tripped up when Sabeena had, but her aunt was one to keep grudges for decades.

Ishrat took a deep breath. 'Rabia? The girl who was married to the professor? What about her?'

Neelam looked back at the guests teeming around the stage, but Ayesha knew that her aunt wouldn't be able to resist telling them the gossip. She adjusted the decorative *tikka* on her forehead before recounting the unfortunate incident. Of course, Ayesha had already seen Rabia at work just the other day, all wrapped up in bandages, her father begging the police to register a case, but she hadn't told her parents about it. What was the point of worrying them? She wasn't surprised when her mother clapped a hand to her mouth.

'He used a knife on her face? Her own husband?'

Neelam nodded. 'Of course! Who else would do it? Apparently, the little slut was having an affair on the side. Can you imagine? The good girls of Multan gone bad ... The West has infiltrated our little city as well. Hardly any of the younger girls cover their heads anymore.'

'Sabeena doesn't wear a chaddar either, Khala.'

'The rules are different for the rich, Ayesha. Keep up with the world, for once in your life.'

'Maybe Rabia was unhappy,' Ayesha offered. 'I wouldn't blame her given how many girls are married to complete strangers with no say in the matter. I actually saw Rabia the other day at work. I'll tell you something, nobody deserves to have their face slashed with a knife. Nobody.'

Her mother turned to her. 'You never told me.'

Before Ayesha could reply, Neelam gripped her arm, hard – enough to leave a bruise. 'Listen to me, *girl*, these statements might look good on social media, but don't forget the city you live in, the country you live in. A few more years and you'll be overage. Nobody wants a girl over thirty here. And people might wonder why you're supporting a girl who has been spreading her legs for God knows how many men.'

'Neelam, don't forget this is your niece.' There was a warning in her mother's voice, which Neelam clocked. She let go of Ayesha's arm.

'I tell you, Baji, we are living in dark times. This is precisely why it has become so important to find good, respectable matches for our daughters. Who knows what might happen. Ayesha isn't getting any younger. You ought to find her a good husband or all she'll be left with are the rotten ones, and we certainly don't want her to fall prey to such an attack. Look at that smooth flawless skin. My dear niece.'

All Ayesha could do was gape at her. The nerve of the woman. She found it hard to believe that they were actually related. She watched in horror as Neelam abandoned her trembling sister and went skipping back to meet the other guests. Like it was all nothing.

Ayesha gripped her mother's elbow and steered her towards where her father sat alone, lost in a world of his own. She looked straight ahead so she wouldn't have to acknowledge their other relatives. 'Don't look at them, Ammi,' she whispered to her mother.

Her mother wrapped her sari's *pallu* around her shoulders. 'They'll all be wondering about our financial situation, and why our daughter is still single.' She pulled herself up and added, 'Of course, *beta*, I don't mean in any way that it's your fault. It's just...'

Ayesha squeezed her mother's hand. 'I know, Ammi. I know.'

Sure enough, as they made their way to her father, the whispers followed them. Her mother nodded politely at the elderly ladies, but they only narrowed their eyes at them, muttering to each other all the while.

'Her mother-in-law bought her that sari decades ago,' one of them said. 'Very expensive, but so outdated now. Of course, these days they call it vintage.'

'It's obvious that money is still hard to come by, poor things.'

'Look at the daughter. Bold as brass. As if being unmarried at her age is something to be proud of. Is that grey hair on her head?'

'*Haye, bechari. Ye toh kunwari reh gayi.*' – She'll be a spinster for life.

Ayesha blinked back the traitorous tears that sprung in her eyes. She had to be strong, not just for her parents, but for herself. For Saqib.

Her mother collapsed on the sofa when they finally reached it. 'I don't think I can do these weddings anymore, Ji. It's become unbearable.'

Safdar sat chewing at a cuticle. 'It's your damned sister who's unbearable. *Kanjari*.'

'It isn't her fault that our society is like this. She wasn't this crass when we were young, I swear. She used to be such a nice girl.'

'If it weren't for her connections, I'd have given her a piece of my mind. Who does she think she is?'

'Her husband is minting money with the provincial government in Lahore.'

'Bullshit! Last I heard, he was polishing shoes on Bosan Road.'

'That was decades ago and he had a shoe polish factory, Ji. Not the same thing.'

'Whatever.'

The fact that they were arguing again was healthy, because Ayesha knew that they would soon be leaning on each other for support, everything forgiven. She left them to it and walked towards the centre of activity. The fragrance of the thousands of flowers decorating the stage was overpowering. Her cousin, Sabeena, sat in a traditional red bridal dress and clunky gold jewellery, and despite how unpleasant her mother, Neelam, had just been to her, Ayesha felt a surge of love. Everyone deserved to be happy in life. She imagined how she would feel when she married Saqib. If there was one thing she knew, it was that she wouldn't be wearing that ghastly red. She hated tradition. No, it would be a peach-coloured dress for her with fake diamond costume jewellery. Even in her wildest fantasies, she knew her parents would never be able to afford real diamonds.

Not in this lifetime.

Sabeena caught her eye and waved her over to the stage. Up close, she looked even more stunning. Ayesha could see that the salon had done a good job. Sabeena's face hadn't been painted white to reflect the society's obsession with white skin; she just looked like herself. A more made-up version, but essentially herself. Even the scar on her cheek had been concealed to a great extent. Ayesha made a mental note to ask which salon had done it, before realising that her parents would never be able to afford that either.

'Ayesha, you came. It's so nice to see you after such a long time.' Sabeena's hand was cold in hers, but Ayesha could see that her cousin was happy, happier than she'd ever seen her. She nodded at Sabeena's husband, who looked handsome enough if it wasn't for the bulbous pimple on his forehead that he'd clumsily tried to hide with some concealer. The overall effect was quite comical.

'Iqbal's father owns the largest chemical factory in the city. We're thinking of moving to Lahore, aren't we, Iqbal? There's enough money to go around and Lahore is ... well, Lahore. The city of dreams.'

Iqbal grinned and threw his arm around Sabeena's shoulders. 'Anything for you, my love. I'll buy you a house in Defence. What do you say to that? You'll live in the best housing society in Lahore.' His gaze slid over Ayesha, drinking her in. 'I have to say, it seems like beauty runs in the family.'

Someone coughed behind her, and Ayesha almost sagged with relief. This was her chance to escape the scrutiny of Iqbal and his male friends who surrounded the stage. Although Multan had made a lot of progress over the decades, with some women finally being able to roam freely without heavy chaddars covering them from head to toe, there was still some way to go, especially in terms of how men looked at women. Even so, for a man to leer at other women on his wedding day...

'Aren't you going to introduce us to your cousin, Sabeena Bhabhi?' a deep male voice asked from behind. It sounded vaguely familiar.

Ayesha looked around and caught a blast of heavy men's cologne. Through the haze, she caught sight of a familiar, bearded face and dark eyes staring at her. His black hair was gelled back, which brought out the black of his eyes even further.

Of course Raza Masood would be here, she thought to herself. She gave him a small smile, which he acknowledged with a playful one of his own.

Sabeena's hand was still clasped in hers. 'This is Raza Masood,' she said when Ayesha was finally able to break free from that steely gaze. 'His family owns half the agricultural lands around Multan. Plus, they're the textile lords of this city.'

Ayesha raised her eyebrows. 'That's basically the story of every person from Multan. Feudal lords, the lot of them. However, some of them can be very kind too.'

Raza smirked. 'Ooo, I like that. Finally, someone who isn't enamoured by my obscene wealth. It's nice to see you again, ma'am.'

'I thought we were on first-name terms.'

That elicited a laugh from him. 'I was hoping you would say that.'

Sabeena's jaw dropped open. 'You two know each other?'

Ayesha nodded. 'Only through work. The Masood family's philanthropy is well known.'

'I see.'

Her cousin seemed to have forgotten that it was her own wedding. Ayesha could see the jealousy clouding her face. It made her want to laugh, it was so misplaced.

Raza extended a hand towards Ayesha. 'May I tempt you with a dance, though? The DJ has chosen a particularly peppy number.'

Ayesha recoiled. Her family would have a fit if they saw her dancing with a stranger. Besides, she was very much in love with Saqib. Raza might be kind, but she had no interest in becoming the subject of gossip. 'No, thank you. I think I'm okay.'

The smile on Raza's face slipped, and Ayesha caught a hint of annoyance cross it before he hitched the smile back up.

'No matter. Plenty of fish in this pond.' It was obvious that he wasn't used to being refused.

She had to think quickly. 'But of course, I look forward to our meeting this week.'

He gave her a curt bow. 'Of course.'

Sabeena gave her a nudge. 'You don't refuse Raza Masood, for crying out loud,' she whispered. 'Are you nuts, Ayesha? He doesn't ask just about anyone for a dance. This is the kind of chance every girl in Multan dreams of. God knows I did,' she added. 'Snag him if you can. Your parents will thank you for it. We will all thank you for it.'

Ayesha knew that her cousin didn't mean to cause offence, but her skin still prickled from her words. Why did everything begin and end with money? So what if Raza had all the money in the world? Her father once had a lot of money. It had done him no good at all, only filling his head with lofty ideas and ultimately preventing him from finding gainful employment. They wouldn't be in the state they were if it hadn't been for all that wealth. She knew she was being uncharitable towards her father, but she couldn't help it.

And what gave Sabeena the right to force her unsolicited advice on her? Her mind wandered to Saqib with his cute little Vespa and those honest grey eyes, and Raza's leering grin looked even worse in comparison. Not that there was anything wrong with being rich, but she couldn't change who she loved.

She pushed through the crowd, heading for the relative safety of her parents, when she felt someone brush their fingers with hers. It was a man's hand.

'A dance might have been too forward, but I would really like for you to meet my mother,' Raza murmured, his cologne overwhelming her, now that he was so close again. 'I've told her a lot about you.'

Before Ayesha even had a chance to think, he'd taken her hand and walked her to the front row of seats, where the richest and most influential people were stationed.

She pulled her hand away from his, looking around to see if anyone had noticed. Who was she fooling? The eyes of every single person in the front row were on her. She wanted nothing more than to turn around and make a run for it, but seeing an elegantly dressed woman get up from her seat and walk towards her, she had no choice but to stay put.

'Mama, this is Ayesha Safdar Khakwani, the girl I was telling you about.' Gesturing in his mother's direction, Raza continued, 'Ayesha, please meet my mother, Begum Rabbiya Masood.'

Rabbiya Masood's eyes took her in, a strange expression on her face, as if she was trying not to laugh. For a moment, Ayesha was conscious of her hand-me-down clothes and local brand shoes, but then she put out her chin and said the customary greeting.

Rabbiya's expression didn't change, but she quietly returned her greeting before turning to her son. 'So this is the girl you met at the charity? Charming.' Moving closer, she ran a finger down the sleeve of Ayesha's dress. 'Is this dress from the famous Karachi-based designer? The attention to detail is incredible.'

Ayesha drew herself up. 'Actually, it's a knock-off my mother got from Anarkali Bazar the last time we visited Lahore.'

Rabbiya raised her eyebrows. 'I see. Well, at least, you're not a liar.'

Oblivious to the hidden connotations of the conversation, Raza said, 'We're meeting for coffee later this week to discuss the particulars of the donation our family will be making.'

Compelled to echo his thoughts, Ayesha added, 'It is a very kind gesture from your family. It will change many lives.'

Rabbiya arched a neatly plucked eyebrow and tilted her head to one side, her enormous diamond earrings dangling. 'Correct me if I'm wrong, but aren't you the daughter of Safdar Khan Khakwani?'

'I am,' Ayesha replied, instantly wary. 'Do you know him?'

Rabbiya's lips twitched. 'No, my dear, I don't know him or your mother, but I've heard of them. Everyone in Multan has.' She reached out and squeezed Ayesha's hand. 'In a good way, I assure you. Nobody brings up your – ah – current circumstances.'

The insult wasn't lost on Ayesha. 'Of course,' she replied, the blood rushing to her face. It was a testament to how much she loved her job and Shugufta that she didn't snap at Rabbiya Masood. 'It was lovely meeting you. Now, if you'll excuse me, I need to return to my parents.'

'Would you like to meet them too, Mama?' Raza asked, to which Rabbiya shook her head.

'Not today. I'm afraid I need to get back to my friends, who I've kept waiting long enough, but have a nice coffee later in the week. I dare say I'll hear all about it from you.'

'Come on, Mama. Don't be a nuisance. Meet them.' His eyes flashed. 'Please?'

'Enough, Raza. I told you not today. Stop this.'

A look passed between mother and son, but Ayesha wasn't going to stand there being insulted. She turned on her heel and walked away without saying goodbye, hurrying back to her parents, but not before she saw an entire contingent of aunties staring in her direction, whispering to each other.

'Looks like someone caused quite a stir at the wedding,' Saqib remarked over the phone later that night after Ayesha had told him almost everything, only leaving out the part about how handsome Raza Masood was. Saqib was insecure at the best of times. She sat in bed, painting her nails, the cell phone balanced precariously between her ear and knee. 'I'm not surprised,' Saqib continued. 'It's simply not possible not to rise to the occasion when you're around.'

'How disgusting, Saqib.' Ayesha pretended to be offended, but deep down she was pleased. The bastard knew exactly what to say. 'You know full well I am not interested in anyone else.'

'So, you are interested in me, then? Sometimes I'm not sure how a simple man like myself scored such a prize.'

'I'm hardly a prize. Maybe thirty years ago when my father was a rich man.'

Saqib snorted. 'You weren't even born then.'

'Trust me to miss the good times. You ought to make it official before someone else does, though, what with the way Raza was eyeing me.' She was only half joking. Raza Masood's attentions had made her uncomfortable.

'I'd bring my father over tomorrow if you allowed it. Just say the word.'

Ayesha hesitated. As much as she would like to make it official, Ayesha knew that her father wouldn't agree. Not yet. Either Saqib had to rise higher in the world or her father had to fall a little lower for there to be any chance. She was ashamed of herself for thinking this, but if Safdar Khan had taught her anything, it was to be pragmatic.

Saqib took a deep breath, usually an indication that he was about to make a declaration of love. Ayesha screwed the lid on the nail polish tight, anticipating those glorious words, but a knock on the door threw her off. Somehow, she knew what this was about. Her mother's head poked inside.

'Are you up?'

Ayesha sighed. 'I am now.' She ended the call without saying good bye. Saqib would understand, and if he didn't she'd make it up to him over WhatsApp. She didn't even need to ask her mother the reason for this midnight visit. The journey home from Sabeena's wedding had been uncharacteristically silent, as if her parents were digesting what had transpired. And Ayesha was sure Neelam Khala had made things worse for her.

Her mother sat down on the foot of the bed, fussing with the sheets. 'Why is it that your room is always messy, Ayesha? What will your in-laws say when you're finally married?'

'You do realise that this is the twenty-first century, don't you? I couldn't care less what my in-laws think of my room. They wouldn't be allowed inside.'

Ordinarily, she would be chastised for uttering such words, but today there was a twinkle in her mother's eyes and the hint of a smile, as if she couldn't quite believe what she was about to say.

Ayesha's stomach fell. 'What is it? Did Neelam Khala say something?'

'How well do you know Raza Masood?'

Ayesha stared at her. 'I don't know him at all. I just met him at work the other day. He's making a very sizeable donation.'

'He was at the wedding too, and word is that you also met his mother, Rabbiya.'

'Oh, for fuck's—'

'Watch your language, Ayesha. One would think you were brought up in a brothel and not a respectable Multani household.'

Ayesha tucked her hands beneath her legs so her mother wouldn't see them shaking. She did not like where this conversation was going. 'I don't know him at all, Ammi,' she whispered, her bravado gone. 'He simply introduced me to his mother. Why do you ask?'

Her mother tucked a stray lock of hair into her lilac dupatta. 'Boys don't just introduce girls to their mothers for no reason. Neelam says that you two were inseparable at the wedding.'

Ayesha exhaled in exasperation. She'd been right. It was the same old nonsense from Neelam Khala. 'It was nothing, Ammi. I barely exchanged two words with him, and his mother was insufferable. She couldn't stop judging me.'

'Sabeena has told Neelam that he couldn't take his eyes off you.'

'Well, that's his problem, isn't it?'

'Your father thinks we should try and take this further.'

All of a sudden, it didn't sound like nonsense anymore. Ayesha could feel her heart rate picking up. 'What for? So he can drive a Mercedes again?'

'Ayesha! He's your father.'

'You know full well who I want to spend my life with,' Ayesha said, tears gathering in her eyes. She tried to blink them away, but instead they slid down her cheeks. She did not want her mother to see her cry.

'Oh, Ayesha. You're not harbouring dreams of marrying that boy from college, are you?' her mother replied, ignoring her tears. 'That was a college romance. Nothing else.' She leaned forward, taking hold of Ayesha's arm, squeezing hard. 'You haven't done anything foolish with the boy, have you? You're still a … a…'

Ayesha lowered her head. She couldn't meet her mother's eye. 'No, Ammi. I am not a virgin anymore.'

Her mother clapped her hands over her mouth. '*Haye*! How could you do this to us, Ayesha!' she said, horror writ plainly on her face. But then straightaway she enveloped her daughter in a giant hug. '*Bas bas*. We must never speak of this again. To all intents and purposes, you're untouched. Do not mention this to your father. Ever.'

'Won't he understand?' Ayesha's voice came out muffled.

'Of course he won't. He's more understanding than most, but he's still a man. You've dishonoured the family name. Never before has any girl from our family done this.'

She wanted to ask her mother if she'd been checking between everyone's legs to see if they were virgins, but she pursed her mouth and pulled away from the hug. 'There's nothing dishonourable about love,' she said instead. 'And why does nobody question boys when they do the same thing?'

Blood rushed to her mother's face. 'Because it's a man's world, Ayesha. Uff, I just don't understand this infatuation with the idea of love girls have today. In our time, husbands were chosen for us, and we had to make do. I just pray your father never finds out about this. Naturally, he'll blame me.'

Ayesha sighed. 'Give him some credit, Ammi. He isn't that bad.'

Her mother seemed to have lapsed into her own world. 'The only thing to be done is for you to sprinkle a few drops of hot sauce or something in bed after the first night. That should do the trick. I'll need to make sure to keep some on hand. That way they might not suspect anything. My God, what a travesty. My daughter is not pure.' She looked up. 'What will I tell Neelam now?'

'What does Neelam have to do with all of this?'

'It's Neelam Khala who's arranging for you to meet with Raza.'

It was just like Neelam Khala to take the credit for everything.

'Not that it matters, but I'm already meeting him for coffee.' Seeing the hope in her mother's eyes, she added, 'But don't get your hopes up, Ammi. It's a work meeting, and you cannot force me to fall in love with a rich guy.'

Kamil

London, United Kingdom

Kamil had come to love the noise in the restaurant. It was familiar, and it helped to drown his more disturbing thoughts. Blinking once to clear his head, he focused on the plate in front of him. The chicken was grilled to perfection, but today it tasted like sandpaper in his mouth.

'The chicken's pretty good,' he remarked, attempting to break the ice, but Madiha was quiet. Kamil's heart skipped a beat. Madiha's silence could only mean that an argument was in the offing. She had been subdued for weeks, taking days to reply to his texts, or in some cases, not replying at all. If he didn't know any better, he'd have thought she was sick of him. 'I am glad I got the rice this time and not the broccoli,' he offered again.

Madiha rolled her eyes, pushing her chips around the plate with a fork. Kamil would have liked to help himself to some of those chips, but he dared not. She'd no doubt explode, and he didn't want to create a scene in his precious Nando's.

'Food is all you care about,' Madiha finally said, lifting her eyes from her plate. 'You have no sense of responsibility, Kamil. We've been going out for three years and all you can say to me is that you're glad you ordered rice and not broccoli? Really? *Really*? Do I look like I give a damn about the rice?'

He knew now why the chicken tasted like sandpaper. He gulped down some Diet Coke and attempted to make his expression friendly. 'It's precisely because we've been going out for three years that we understand each other enough to say such things.' He covered Madiha's small hand with his large paw. 'What's brought this on? Is this why you've been avoiding me?'

She put her cutlery down, abandoning all pretence of eating. 'I feel like I don't know you, Kamil. All these years and you still seem to keep me at arm's length. I don't *know* you.' She spoke the last few words too loudly for comfort.

Kamil looked around, but it was too noisy for anyone to hear, or indeed, care.

'Maybe you have trust issues,' she continued. 'I don't know what's wrong with you. For someone born and raised in London, you are such a Pakistani sometimes.'

'What's that supposed to mean?'

'Exactly what you think it means,' Madiha shot back. 'You're a typical Pakistani man who believes in keeping his feelings to himself and not showing any love to someone he's been seeing for years.'

'That could apply to a lot of guys, Madiha. Not just Pakistanis.'

'That is not the point!' Madiha hissed the last word.

If he wasn't watching his precious relationship of three years disintegrating right in front of his eyes, he'd have been amused by Madiha's over-the-top reaction. What had got into her all of sudden? He rubbed the back of her hand with his thumb. 'Look into my eyes, Madiha.'

She pulled her hand away. 'Oh, please.'

'Please, just look at me.'

It pained him to see the turmoil on her face, the distrust gathering in her eyes. With a jolt, he realised that she was going to break up with him. His heart started thudding in his throat.

'I may not always be very expressive, but I love you very much.'

Madiha tilted her head. 'Love ... you don't say that word enough. You may think you do, but you know what? I'm looking in your eyes, and I see nothing. Just a chasm. I don't even know who you are anymore ... I don't think I ever did.'

He wanted to tell her that she was speaking the truth. There was a chasm behind his eyes, but how could he ever fully open himself up to her? To anyone? It was impossible. He had killed that part of himself a long time ago. But the man he was today was far more stable than the man he'd been a decade ago.

'Don't do this, Madiha,' he whispered, but she didn't hear him.

She used a napkin to wipe the tears away, smudging her mascara. She looked a mess. 'Three years of my life wasted on someone with a heart of stone. It was a mistake to date you in the first place. I should have let my parents find a guy for me, or even better, I should have dated someone who wasn't a bloody Pakistani.'

'You're Pakistani yourself.'

'I'm a British Pakistani, and most of the time, I wish I wasn't. I can't take all this emotional baggage that comes with being one. Three years and not a peep about getting engaged, or married. Do you have any idea how much pressure my parents have been putting on me?'

Kamil had met Madiha's parents on several occasions and wasn't surprised in the least that they were pressuring their daughter. They seemed the kind who would.

'Is it marriage you're worried about? Didn't you say yourself that you wanted to take things slow?'

'Not this slow, Kamil.'

'Well, let's get engaged then. You know my family loves you. They'll embrace you with open arms.'

Madiha dabbed at her wet eyes. 'Bullshit. You're such a liar, Kamil. You're saying this now, but in a few hours' time, you'll get cold feet. Do you think I don't know you?'

'You just said you didn't know me at all.' He winced. He shouldn't have said those words.

Madiha held up her hands. 'Uff, I should have known you'd behave like this. Our whole relationship has been a joke. We should be married with kids by now. I am thirty-three-years old. Where are my kids?'

Kamil didn't know the answer to that, so he just shrugged.

She banged her fist on the table. 'This is what I'm talking about. You simply don't care!' A few people glanced at them.

Kamil smiled at the elderly lady staring at them. He could feel the dampness in his armpits. This was exactly the kind of situation he liked to avoid. 'Keep your voice down, Madiha. Look, I promise I'll improve my behaviour. I'll do whatever you want. Just allow yourself some time to think. We've been together for a long time. It seems foolish to throw it all away.'

'Yesterday was the anniversary of the day we met, at the Embankment. You forgot it, just like you forget everything else. You're not human, Kamil. You're a robot.'

He didn't know how to reply, so he just looked at his plate. Madiha was right, of course. She'd hit the nail on the head. Maybe he was a robot. To his horror, he found himself shrugging again.

'Fuck off, Kamil,' Madiha whispered, getting up. Turning back, she said the only thing she knew would hurt him, 'I hope I've managed to ruin Nando's for you.'

Kamil thought of following her, but he knew she wouldn't listen to him. He knew it was over, like all of his previous relationships. He was surprised this one had lasted so long. He looked at his half-eaten chicken with longing, but rose from the table. He wouldn't be able to stomach it now.

Stepping into the cold night air, he paused for a moment, taking deep breaths as he watched the world go by. Most of the couples walking down the crowded Earl's Court Road were holding hands, something Kamil had struggled to do for many years. He had held hands with Madiha sometimes, but only briefly because his palms started sweating and Madiha would bat him away with a look of mild disgust.

He could be mistaken, but right at that moment, he felt free ... unshackled. The walk back to his flat was bracing, the wind picking up and somehow permeating his very bones. That was London for you. Bearable one moment and frigid the next. By the time he turned onto Warwick Road, the crowds had thinned to a trickle, residents the only people around. While the flats here were good enough, there was an eerie darkness to the place, unlike the bright lights and heaving crowds of Earl's Court Road. As he entered his building, the gloom deepened and a hush descended. Even the sound of his footsteps was absorbed by the thick carpet on the stairs, and it was only after he unlocked the door to his studio flat and turned all the lights on, down to the last lamp, that he felt like he could breathe again.

Everything was as he had left it, the two-seater sofa with the mussed-up blanket, the dining chair standing at an odd angle, the door to the bathroom open wide. Not for the first time, it occurred to him that if he were to die here somehow, it could be many days before he was even discovered. A shudder went through him, and he quickly fixed himself a snack before turning the television on full volume.

As the sound of sirens filled the air, as it did so often in this city, he realised that he was once again completely alone.

Ayesha

Saqib ran his fingers through his brown hair, his eyes crinkling around the edges. Those grey eyes were still enough to steal her breath away.

'So, your parents want you to meet this guy. So what? I meet plenty of girls in my everyday life.'

Ayesha blinked several times to make sure she had heard him right. 'You're not expected to marry those girls.' All of a sudden, Saqib's grey eyes didn't appeal to her as much. He could be so childish sometimes. 'If you haven't noticed, I am almost thirty. A spinster by Multani standards.'

Saqib sipped on the coffee she'd brought him from inside. 'Then Multan probably needs to grow the hell up.'

'Sometimes, Saqib, I wonder how you've made it this far in life.'

Ayesha shook her head. This wasn't going the way she wanted. He had come all the way to her office just to spend some time with her, and here she was, looking for ways to argue with him. Of course, she knew why. Just as the meeting with Raza loomed over her, so did her parents' expectations. And she did not want to break their hearts. A man like Raza could never want to marry a girl whose father's fortunes had taken such a nosedive, but the merest possibility that he might, could change their lives forever.

'Let's not argue anymore,' she said. 'It's a beautiful day, and one of those rare moments when we can forget about work.'

Saqib's frown cleared when she took his hand, his smile telling her that all was forgiven. She led him towards the tall shisham tree so that they could sit in its shade. Her office was a safe place for them to meet. The security guards all loved her and would never say a thing to anyone, and neither would Shugufta and her team.

In many ways, the office was her second home, a place where she could be herself.

'I am so proud of what you're doing,' Saqib said, once they were seated on the wooden bench under the tree. 'Your work changes lives. There really can't be anything more noble than that.'

She beamed at him, and for a moment her heart threatened to break from all the love it bore for Saqib. 'I like to think I'm making a difference in people's lives. The women who arrive here have suffered so much.'

'Of course you are, and that's why I love you. You have a kind heart even if you don't know it sometimes.' He laughed as she shook him off.

'You're impossible sometimes, and that is why I love you,' she said.

He raised an eyebrow. 'Because I'm impossible?'

'Among other things...'

Smirking, he edged closer. 'Like what? Do you like it when I do this?' His finger ran down her face, past her throat and slid lower. 'Or this?' It reached the lace of her bra.

She gasped, nudging his hand away. 'Don't forget that we're in Multan.'

He smiled, but pulled his hand back, giving her a small bow. 'Whatever you say, madam.'

'Promise me that you'll never leave me, Saqib. I don't think I could bear it.'

'Why would I ever leave you?' His face was incredulous.

'Just promise.'

'Okay, my love, I promise. Happy? God, what's got into you today?'

'I don't know,' she whispered, unsure herself.

A breeze stirred his hair, and Ayesha drew her shawl tight across her shoulders. In the shade, it was much cooler than she had anticipated. They were on the tail end of winter, but that didn't mean that Multan couldn't spring a surprise or two on them.

'Ayesha?' Saqib said after a few minutes.

'Mmm?' She'd closed her eyes by then, leaning against the bench, letting the breeze catch her hair.

'It will all be alright in the end. You'll see. Keep your chin up.'

She didn't open her eyes for a few moments, letting his words calm her. Maybe he was right. Maybe everything would be okay. She was an only daughter after all, and she knew just how much her father loved her even if he couldn't express it sometimes. He would never willingly hand her over to a man she didn't approve of, let alone love.

They talked about everything and nothing, Saqib reaching out to brush a tendril of hair from her forehead from time to time. They would have sat there in companionable silence for hours if Saira hadn't brought them fresh cups of coffee.

'Lunch break is nearly over, Ayesha,' she said, but there was a smile on her face. 'Although, you'll probably get a free pass for securing that big funding.'

'He hasn't paid us yet,' Ayesha murmured, the spell between her and Saqib broken. The real world beckoned.

'Oh, he will. According to Shugufta, it's a done deal – his lawyer has been in touch regarding the press release and associated fanfare.' Removing her dupatta from her head to tighten her ponytail, she added, 'God, these rich people are so hungry for good press, I swear. They'd sell their souls...'

'Raza isn't that bad,' Ayesha replied, examining her nails. Ignoring Saqib's hooting, she sat up straight. 'No, I mean seriously. His mother was very condescending, but this guy doesn't seem too bad. He's spoilt, but seems human.' Glancing at Saqib, she added, 'But not someone I'd like to know very well.'

He smiled at her. 'Of course.'

Saira's mouth twitched as she watched them. 'You do know you're the cutest couple in the city, right? I mean look at the two of you. Flawless features, wicked sense of humour and so in love. Honestly, you ought to compete in one of those dating shows abroad. You'd win with flying colours.' Picking at a bit of mascara in her eye, she rubbed it between her fingers and smeared some of it on Ayesha's neck. 'To ward off the evil eye,' she said.

'I don't need a dating show to tell me how much I love Ayesha,' Saqib said, rising from the bench and brushing the dust from his jeans. He extended a hand towards Ayesha. 'Mind if I take you for a spin? The weather is perfect for it, as is my little Vespa.'

'Saqib, I have to work.'

Saira looked around before lowering her voice. 'I won't tell Shugufta if you won't. Go and have some fun. I'll tell her you're in a meeting if she asks.'

'Meeting whom?'

'Oh, just go already. I'll come up with a suitable excuse.'

Ayesha hesitated. 'Well, if you're sure. I don't want to put you in an awkward position.'

'Go!'

Fifteen minutes later, as the wind whipped through her hair, the city of Multan a blur around her as she rested her chin on Saqib's shoulder, her arms encircling his waist, she knew she had made the right decision.

'I love you,' she whispered, but her words were lost in the wind.

Two days later, as she sat waiting for Raza Masood in a coffee shop, she wished she could be on the Vespa again with Saqib. What she'd felt with her arms around him, oblivious to the world, was what they called freedom. People gawked at them, but not with suspicion. Rather, it was with curiosity and in some cases, admiration. To their eyes, Ayesha and Saqib could have been husband and wife on a trip together. It had felt like that too. She could see herself easing into a life with Saqib, and it didn't concern her that he only had a Vespa. But it would concern her parents. Sometimes, she wished that her family didn't come from old money, for it was exquisite torture to have been rich, only to have it all snatched away. She would see her father lost in thought sometimes, gazing unseeing at the television with the remote control in his hand, and she would realise that his yearning would never end.

Banishing these thoughts from her mind, she focused on the task at hand. She'd chosen a table in a far corner outside, so that people wouldn't be able to spy on her. Multan wasn't called the land of gossip for no reason. People in this city had a lot of free time, most of which was spent spying on others, especially women, and since a lot of people preferred to marry within the extended family, everyone seemed to be related.

Although the overwhelming majority of women in Multan wore scarves or chaddars to hide their hair and faces, Ayesha had ditched her chaddar years ago. Her father had made it clear that it was her own choice and had never forced her to cover her head. Her mother covered hers, as did most women her age, but Multan was changing, although not fast enough.

The moment she saw Raza's balding and sweating lawyer in the distance, she knew that he had arrived. Naeem Siddiqui panted all the way to her table, raising his eyebrows in surprise when she once again shook hands with him.

'Good to see you, madam. Raza Sahab is just coming. I'm here a bit early to stake out the place a bit. One can never be too careful, you know.' Giving her a wry smile, he added, 'It always takes me by surprise when a woman in Multan shakes my hand.'

'Honestly, you should accept the fact that women can be professionals too, Naeem Sahab,' she said, then bit her tongue. She had to ensure the charity got this funding, and these smartarse one-liners were not going to help.

Thankfully, Naeem didn't seem to have noticed, as right then, Raza Masood came with an army of armed guards behind him, all of whom, however, paused at a respectable distance, allowing him to approach their table alone. Once again, he was dressed in black, but today he seemed to have chosen a different fragrance, and without realising, Ayesha found herself inhaling it – deeply. She caught herself just in time for them to shake hands.

'It's a pleasure to see you again, Ayesha,' Raza said, inclining his head slightly. 'You look very nice.'

She hadn't paid too much attention to her appearance, having thrown on whatever shalwar kameez she could get her hands on, but she appreciated the compliment all the same. 'You're very kind.'

Raza arched an eyebrow when Naeem slid into a chair as well, scooting it closer before pulling a sheaf of papers from his briefcase. 'Now, since we are here, I wanted to go through everything from the press release to events and interviews.'

It took a while, but Naeem finally caught Raza's eye, and he instantly reddened. 'I shall leave this with you then, sir?'

'That would be very wise,' Raza replied, his tone icy.

It took Naeem another minute to gather all his things, before he finally stammered out a goodbye and left them, waddling away as fast as his legs could carry him.

Raza exhaled as soon as he'd left. 'I swear, that pig will give me an aneurysm someday. He really gets on my nerves.'

'I thought you two got along famously.'

There was a beat before he realised that she was joking. 'Good one. We get along so well, all I want to do is wring his neck. But he's been our family's lawyer for ages. That's the only reason I tolerate him.'

'He seems to know his stuff,' Ayesha replied, glancing at the papers Naeem had left, most of which seemed to be very official-looking with signatures required. 'I'm afraid, Shugufta is the signatory, so I can't help with these at all.'

'You don't need to,' Raza said, reaching into his coat pocket and producing a slip of paper. 'Here's the cheque for thirty million rupees. It is my honour to be able to donate to your charity and help women in need.' Holding it out of her reach for a moment, he added, 'This has only happened because of you. I want you to know that.'

Their fingers touched as she took the cheque from him and gazed at all the zeroes on the piece of paper. 'This will change so many lives, both in Multan and beyond.'

Ayesha looked up from the cheque to see that he had scooted his chair closer to her. Resting his arms on the table, he asked, 'May I be honest with you? Seeing as we're meeting for the third time now, I think we can call each other friends.'

Ayesha would have begged to differ, but she was too careful to say no, so she just nodded.

'Brilliant!' Then rubbing his palms together he said, 'I wanted to apologise for my mother's behaviour the other day. She was way out of line. You see, she wants me to marry someone who is as rich as me, someone who isn't ... middle class. Someone she can be proud to call her daughter-in-law.'

His words went through her like electricity. Now, she appreciated how her father must feel every time someone reminded him of how far he had fallen. 'Why are you telling me this?' she said, unable to hide the anger in her voice. 'If someone is middle class, that doesn't mean they shouldn't be allowed to exist. They're human too, you know.'

He shrugged. 'Of course. I didn't mean it like that. It's just that my mother is from a generation that puts a lot of stock in money. I guess she has to since I'm the only son. Very important, you know.'

'I'm an only child too,' Ayesha murmured, as their coffees arrived.

She looked at her white chocolate mocha with distaste, wanting nothing more than to run away from here. Raza belonged to a social circle she wanted nothing to do with. And everything he said now grated on her nerves.

He ran his fingers through his gelled hair, and then wiped them on a paper napkin. 'I didn't mean I was an only child. I've got sisters, but I'm the only son, and that's what really matters, doesn't it? In a society like ours?'

Ayesha had lifted the mug to her lips, but she put it down. 'I beg your pardon?'

'You're an intelligent woman, Ayesha. You should know that men rule our world, like they always have, and always will. I love my sisters, but they're not as important as me. You only need to ask my parents that. Hell, even the law says so.'

'Goodness me,' she whispered to herself, the coffee forgotten. 'And I thought your remarks on middle-class people were bad enough.'

Giving her a wink, he added, 'I've dated a few girls from middle-class backgrounds, and let me tell you, they look the same ... that is as long as they don't open their mouths to speak English.'

She felt as if she had gone mute for a moment. All she could do was stare at him.

'You seem like someone who has never heard the word "no"', she said finally.

The sarcasm was lost on him. He threw his head back and laughed. 'You've got that right.' Leaning forward, his breath smelling of coffee and mint, he whispered, 'I knew you were a smart young woman the moment I saw you. You are absolutely correct. I have never been refused, and I never will be.'

'That's not how the world works, Raza.'

'That is exactly how my world works, Ayesha. What I want, I get.'

Quietly, she slid the cheque in her bag and closed her mouth. She knew that this would be the last time she would be meeting Raza Masood.

'I am so proud of you!' her father announced at the dinner table later that day, holding the cheque to the light.

'It's authentic, Abbu, I can assure you,' Ayesha said, laughing into her fist as she watched her father admiring it. 'Now, hand it back before you smear oil on it.'

Safdar Khan's eyes were wide. 'Can you imagine what an amount like this could do for us?'

'Safdar Sahab,' her mother cried. 'Please return the cheque to Ayesha. If it is God's will, we will also get this kind of money from somewhere.'

They were having her father's favourite for dinner: fried fish with naan and tamarind chutney. Ayesha hated having to pull all the bones from the fish – in fact she hated this kind of fish, period – but she indulged her father and tried to forget how she had once almost choked to death on a bone that had lodged itself in her windpipe.

Her father had already cleaned his plate once, and before reaching for another piece of fish, he returned the cheque to Ayesha. Most people ordered this kind of fish from restaurants, but these days, they couldn't afford that kind of luxury, so her mother made it herself.

'Do you think Shugufta will give you a raise?' he asked.

Ayesha shrugged. 'Saira thinks she will, and I hope she does. I am saving for a solo trip to the UK.'

'That would be nice,' her mother said slowly. 'But the UK isn't the same as it was in the nineties when we visited. The pound is through the roof. Maybe you should spend your money on getting the ancient sofas in the lounge reupholstered.'

Her father paused while desiccating his fish. 'Ishrat, that is not her responsibility.'

Her mother sniffed. 'I was just saying…'

'So, how was it, meeting Raza Masood?' her father continued, stuffing some of the white flesh into his mouth. 'Is he as stuck up as his mother?'

'Safdar Sahab, please!'

Ayesha pushed away her half-eaten plate of food and pulled out a wet wipe to clean her sticky fingers. 'I thought he was a nice man, but today when we talked, he came off as very spoilt and entitled. Scary, even.'

Her mother tutted. 'He belongs to one of the richest families in Multan. I would be surprised if he's not entitled.'

'But the way he spoke about women, about possessions. I don't know ... it sort of rubbed me up the wrong way.'

'Unfortunately, that's the sad reality of life in Pakistan.' Her mother sighed. 'Still, I think it's good that you're friends with him. Neelam Khala speaks very highly of him.'

'He is not my friend, Ammi,' she said, her tone brokering no argument. 'I do not like the man. At all.'

Her mother held up her hands. 'Uff, fine. Forgive me for thinking about your future, Ayesha. It's not like you have to listen to your father's rants about how I've failed as a mother.'

'Begum...' Safdar Khan began.

'Don't begum me, Safdar Sahab. You and your daughter always gang up on me. Earlier, it used to be you and your mother, and now, my very own daughter has taken up the mantle. Like father, like daughter. Oh, how I suffer.'

Without warning, Ayesha and her father broke into laughter, and after a while, her mother joined in too.

'You know we love you very much, Begum. What would we ever do without you?'

Ayesha was so caught up in the moment that she didn't realise until she was in her room that she had missed a call from Raza Masood.

There was a text message too. The sense of well-being she had felt after dinner evaporated as she read the message:

Please call me back. I don't want to scare you, but I have to be honest – I can't stop thinking about you. Can we meet again? Please?

She switched off her phone and collapsed into bed, her heart pounding.

Kamil

The wind bit into his skin as soon as he stepped off the District Line train at Southfields Station. Being outside of Central London, the platforms here weren't underground, and thus were exposed to the elements. A dark, grey sky bore down on him, as stormy as his mood, but he took a deep breath and climbed the steps towards the station exit.

Over the years, this station had become a kind of home for him, given how often he came here to meet Madiha. Even in the icy drizzle, the scene outside the station looked homely, some people winding down in the coffee shops after a long day at work, others grabbing groceries from the various stores dotted around the area. Being outside the hubbub of Central London, Kamil felt that he was able to breathe here, and the slightly hilly landscape was good for his health, forcing his lungs to work harder as he walked up the steep incline leading to a row of squat but beautiful buildings, most of which contained flats. He had lost count of the times he and Madiha had simply kept walking down the road, ending up somewhere in Wimbledon, which was almost like being back in Central London. Like everything in the world, London was changing too. As the central part of the city got busier, people kept migrating to the suburbs, which sent the people in the suburbs even further outside of London. And so, the cycle continued.

The bouquet of roses he had brought with him felt wet, but he thought that the droplets shining on the flowers added a nice touch. Madiha had never been able to resist flowers, and he knew that they were the way back into her heart. Despite initially thinking that he could do without her, he had been struggling recently, dragging his feet to work and not really caring much about his appearance. He had even stopped visiting his parents in North London, an unforgivable offence in Pakistani culture, as his mother liked to remind him.

'Marriage solves everything,' she would tell him whenever he felt down. 'All you need is a wife and a bunch of kids to look after, and you won't even have time to eat, let alone any to waste on being depressed.' Marriage was her answer to every ailment in the world.

He *had* been married, and look how that had gone for him. He would remind his mother as much, but she'd wiped that time period from her memory. She refused to believe he had ever been married and treated him like a child who knew nothing about relationships.

Perhaps she was right. What did he know, after all?

Shaking his head and pulling up the hood of his jacket, he forced himself not to think about the past, and instead focused on the task at hand, which was to mend ties with Madiha. Her absence had left a gaping chasm in his heart. Maybe that was what they called love – what else could that vacancy be?

His heart lifted at the sight of Jamie, one of Madiha's white neighbours, who was bringing out the trash. Kamil had bumped into him on several occasions, and the good man had always held the door open for him, as he did today. How was Jamie supposed to know that Madiha had broken up with him?

'Thanks, mate,' he said, as he stepped inside the heated lobby, his fingers instantly starting to thaw. Before the roses could look any less fresh, he raised a hand in goodbye to the neighbour, and hurried up the staircase, taking the stairs two at a time. Now, he could properly surprise her.

By the time he reached the door of Madiha's flat, his heart was pounding. Raising his hand to knock, he paused, suddenly feeling out of sorts. What was he doing here? Did he even want to get back with someone who had broken up with him?

Madiha's face swam in his mind, along with the countless good times they had spent together. With a little bit of work, this relationship could become something good. He could feel it.

The sound of Bollywood songs filtered out of the flat, making him smile. Quintessential Madiha. He knocked and closed his eyes for a moment, swaying to the tune of one of Shahrukh Khan's romantic numbers, the song taking him back to the early 2000s, when he had seen the film with his family in the fancy cinema in Leicester Square.

'Kamil? What are you doing here?'

He opened his eyes to see Madiha's head peeking out of the door. She seemed to have just got in from work as her face was all made up, but then it occurred to him.

Today was Valentine's Day.

He hadn't even realised it. Behind her, he could see red balloons touching the ceiling. Did Madiha know he would be coming? All of a sudden, the roses seemed like a fantastic idea.

'Kamil!' Madiha's voice brought him out of his reverie. 'I asked you what you're doing here?'

'I came to see you, Mads,' he said, holding out the bouquet. 'Happy Valentine's Day.'

Her face reddened. 'You didn't have to. I told you that we're done.'

He stepped forward, hoping she would open the door and let him in. 'I can explain. I wasn't thinking the other day, and for some reason, I didn't stop you. But I am here now.' Pointing at the balloons inside, he added, 'It seems you were expecting me, anyway, so why not let me in?'

'Kamil, I...'

'Who is it, Madiha?'

Kamil froze. He knew that voice. It was Dilshad, Madiha's cousin from Lahore. 'What's Dilshad doing here?'

The door opened wider, and there he stood in all his bulky glory, muscles threatening to burst out of his black gym T-shirt. 'Ah Kamil, how do you do?'

He held out a hand, but Kamil didn't shake it. He hid the bouquet behind his back. A sickening sensation hitting him as he put two and two together.

'Are you two dating?' he blurted out finally.

Madiha looked like she wanted the earth to swallow her whole.

It was Dilshad who came to her rescue. 'Of course, mate. It's been going on for some time now. As a matter of fact, we're about to—'

'That's enough, Dilshad.' Madiha seemed to have found her voice. She looked at Kamil, her eyes pleading with him to not cause a scene. 'Kamil, please,' she whispered.

Kamil had always known a lost cause when he saw one. With a nod, he backed away from the door, the bouquet still hidden behind his back.

Dilshad began to protest, but Madiha pulled him inside and closed the door. Kamil was grateful for that; he didn't want anyone to see his tears. It didn't occur to him until he was on the train back to Earl's Court that Madiha had been dating Dilshad while they had still been in a relationship.

Ayesha

The mood at the office party to celebrate Raza Masood's big donation had soured. The giant chocolate cake Shugufta had brought in from a famous bakery in Cantt lay uneaten as they digested the latest news from the courts.

'I can't believe that the bastard will get off scot-free,' Shugufta cried, pulling the dupatta from her head and bunching it in her hands. 'For every step forward, we take two steps back. When will this country be safe for women?'

Ayesha looked at her female colleagues as they gazed at the TV screen, horror on their faces. Sitting beside her, Saira reached for her hand. It was cold and clammy, exactly how Ayesha felt inside.

Despite a case being registered against Rabia's husband by the Multan police, her parents had ultimately caved under the pressure from her husband's family and retracted the allegations. Rabia had even been forced to give a statement claiming that her injuries were self-inflicted and that her husband had nothing to do with it.

'As if anyone would ever take a knife to their own face,' Shugufta shouted, brandishing a fist in the direction of the television. 'Do they take us for fools? After all we did to get that woman justice, her parents are just going to pretend like nothing's happened? Their daughter is blind in one eye, for God's sake. Blind!'

Sohail, one of their marketing people, held up his hands. 'Now, don't shoot the messenger, but a lot of people are saying that Rabia was having an affair with someone, which is why the husband was so angry.'

Ayesha gasped, along with a few other women in the room. Shugufta looked like she was ready to breathe fire. 'What?'

Sohail shrugged, evidently unaware of the danger in Shugufta's tone. 'The woman wasn't a proper wife. She'd been sleeping with another man, which prompted the husband to go wild with rage. A lot of people are actually supporting him, you know.'

Looking at Sohail, Ayesha was reminded just how deep male entitlement ran in this country, where a man could voice such thoughts in a room full of women – one of them his employer – and expect no backlash.

'Out,' Shugufta whispered.

Sohail frowned. 'Madam, I am just telling you what the word on the street is.'

'If you don't leave now, Sohail, so help me God, I will have you dragged out screaming. You mark my words. Out!'

Applause followed Sohail's exit from the office, but Ayesha wasn't able to join in as just then, her mobile pinged. She was filled with unease.

As she'd expected, it was another message from Raza Masood.

Did you know we live close to each other? I just found out today.

Was he stalking her now? Her vision began to blur, a sweat breaking out on her forehead and her throat tightening. She couldn't breathe.

'I need to get some air,' she said, rushing out of the office.

It was a panic attack, and she knew it would pass, but that didn't make it any less terrifying. She staggered towards the old shisham tree, her fingers clutching her throat as she struggled to breathe.

Saqib's sweet face swam into her mind as she collapsed on the bench, trying to take long, steadying breaths. Raza's message was anything but innocent. Over the past few weeks, his text messages had become more frequent, as had his calls. She had avoided everything, but in a city like Multan, where even the smallest secrets couldn't stay hidden for long, how could she conceal the fact that someone like Raza Masood was interested in her?

As her breathing steadied, her phone rang.

The name Raza Masood glared at her. This time, she took his call.

'Yes?' she said, packing as much brusqueness in her voice as possible.

'You just made me lose one hundred thousand rupees. I'd bet with a friend that you wouldn't pick up the phone, like always.'

A friend. So, he was telling people that he phoned her now. She pushed down the bile that rose up her throat. 'What do you want, Raza? I thought our work was over once you'd so kindly given us that cheque.'

There was a moment of silence, before he said, 'Is that all I am to you? A cheque?'

She regretted taking his call. 'I'm at work. Can you please stop calling me? I would really appreciate it. It's very unprofessional.'

'I could, but I don't want to. If I stop calling you, what will become of me? Who is going to nurse my broken little heart back to health? You can't just flirt with a guy and then hang him out to dry.'

Her hand gripped the bench. 'I never flirted with you. I was completely professional.'

'You don't meet donors for coffee randomly, at least not in Multan. A girl has to be interested in a guy if she risks her reputation for him. Sitting there with your boobs thrown out, what did you think was going to happen? Of course I fell for you. It would be hard not to, and you should be happy. My family is one of the richest in Multan.'

'I wasn't aware we were still living in the stone age.'

'Worse,' Raza whispered, his voice light, but there was menace in it too. 'Multan is worse than the Stone Age, I assure you. Here, reputations are as flimsy as kites in the wind.'

Ayesha gasped, the phone slipping from her hand and landing in her lap. She picked it up again and quickly ended the call, then threw the phone in her bag and rushed out through the gates, not caring that it wasn't yet five.

In her confusion, rather than wait around for a taxi, she climbed into the nearest rickshaw she could find. It had to be a very old one, because it emitted clouds of toxic black smoke, forcing her to cover her nose with her dupatta. The seat she sat on had seen better days, the orange leather cracked and torn in several places, revealing grey, moth-eaten foam underneath. And despite the smell of smoke, a burst of body odour from the driver reached her nose from time to time, making her want to gag.

She looked outside to pass the time, but she'd seen everything so many times that nothing stood out. In the city centre, there was little greenery, the skyline dominated by squat, grey concrete buildings and equally grey and dull flyovers, one after another.

Things were getting a bit out of hand now, and that scared her. If Raza was an ordinary guy, she would've simply blocked his number and got on with her life – precisely what she had done with the previous men who had tried to woo her – but this was different. Not only was he powerful, he was connected to all the people Ayesha knew. She still couldn't figure out his plans, whether he needed her for a night or for life, but she knew that she couldn't stomach the thought of his touch. Over the course of their various meetings, he had revealed his ugly mindset, his obsession with getting what he wanted, and now Ayesha didn't want anything to do with him.

She was meant for Saqib, and Saqib alone. They were soul mates, and Raza would have to understand that.

As they entered the marginally cleaner and greener roads of Cantt, Ayesha's mood lifted. She would tell her parents that Raza had been harassing her – and confide in them about her fears. They would take her side, she was sure. Her father would never willingly allow her to marry a misogynistic, controlling pig like Raza.

However, the moment she spotted two Mercedes Benz parked in front of her house, she knew Neelam Khala had somehow beaten her to it. Her aunt never visited them unless it was to her benefit, and the fact that there were two cars didn't bode well. Ayesha had a fair idea of what had brought her here this afternoon. She should never have taken Raza's call. When nothing else worked, men involved their families to negotiate on their behalf. Although it was sad, it didn't come as a surprise that Neelam Khala would side with them, and not her.

The rickshaw driver overcharged her, but she didn't care. There was still time; she knew she could still convince her parents, and they would listen. Her legs shook as she made her way up the marble-floored porch and towards the main door.

Sending up a silent prayer for strength, she turned the handle.

Neelam Khala's smug smile was all she needed to see to know that she'd done her damage. '*Mashallah*, look at my beautiful niece,' she cried, rising to meet Ayesha, planting firm kisses on each cheek. Turning to her sister, she asked, 'I didn't know Ayesha had stopped wearing a dupatta. Very progressive of you, I must say.'

'I forgot it in the rickshaw,' Ayesha mumbled, realising only now that Neelam Khala wasn't alone. Raza Masood's mother, Rabbiya, was seated with Ayesha's parents, her eyebrows raised, the same expression on her face as at the wedding, as if she was trying not to laugh. Ayesha looked down at her crumpled dupatta-less attire and hoped it would be enough to send Rabbiya on her way.

'Why don't you freshen up, and then we can talk?' her mother said, her disapproval at Ayesha's sleeveless outfit obvious. 'I have been trying to call you for hours.'

Ayesha was still rooted to the spot. 'My phone was switched off.'

'Why?'

'Give the poor girl a moment, Ishrat, what is wrong with you?' Her father indicated the seat next to his. 'Come and sit here, *beta*. Forget about the bloody dupatta for a minute.' Turning to Rabbiya, he continued, 'We are firm believers in culture and tradition, but I have always made it a point to let my daughter make her own choices. She is an educated young woman who deserves the chance to make her own way in the world.'

As Ayesha sank into the seat next to her father's, she felt him squeeze her hand. He was on her side. She could have wept with relief.

Having returned to her seat, Neelam Khala adjusted her dupatta over her expansive frame and scooted closer to Rabbiya. 'Well, here is our beautiful Ayesha. I promise you she looks better in makeup. She's just a bit windswept from the rickshaw aren't you, *beta*? She just arrived in one. I saw from the window.'

Ayesha turned her face away, refusing to dignify such a humiliating statement with a reply.

'Well, I don't blame her for looking like this,' Rabbiya began. 'I've never really travelled in a rickshaw before, but I assume I'd look the same if I did.'

'You should try it sometime,' Ayesha said, before she could stop herself. 'It is liberating.'

Rabbiya laughed, unfazed by the taunt. 'You must jest, girl. Multan is no place for such things. The only thing that would unleash for me is gossip.'

'Quite right,' Neelam Khala agreed. 'I would rather die than be seen in a rickshaw.'

As if a rickshaw could hold you, Ayesha thought.

'She usually takes a car,' her mother said in a small voice. 'I don't know why you took a rickshaw today, Ayesha. I've warned you about how dangerous they can be.'

'And so what if she did?' Safdar Khan said. 'Taking a ride in a rickshaw will not erase the fact that my daughter comes from one of Multan's oldest and most respectable families.' Turning to Neelam, he added, 'I would thank you not to bring up the rickshaw again. There really is nothing wrong with travelling in a rickshaw.'

Neelam Khala put a hand on her chest. '*Haye* Bhai, I was only trying to make conversation. You talk as if I have something against my dear niece. All I did was accompany Rabbiya because she wanted a familiar face with her.'

Clearing her throat, Rabbiya began, 'I came here only on the behest of my son, who seems to have been spending time with Ayesha and would like to know her more.' She spread out her hands. 'Things have changed in this country. Gone are the days when we could force our children to bend to our will. Today, we must listen to them, even if we don't like what they're suggesting.'

'And what is your son suggesting that is so unsavoury to you, Rabbiya Sahiba?' Safdar Khan boomed, edging forward in his seat. 'What is wrong with my daughter? What exactly are you insinuating here?'

A smile crept up the edges of Rabbiya's mouth. 'I can see where Ayesha gets her flair for theatrics from. I am merely suggesting that our children ought to spend more time together and see where that takes them.' She looked around their humble living room. 'I wouldn't be here if my son wasn't absolutely adamant. He can be quite wretched when he chooses to.'

'And was your husband too grand to come here?'

'Excuse me?'

'He didn't mean it, did you, Safdar Sahab?' Ishrat's eyebrows knotted together and she stared daggers at her husband. 'Maybe you should leave us women to talk.'

Rabbiya still wore her taunting smile. 'My husband is a busy man. He's in Germany right now, on urgent textile-related business. He travels a lot.'

Her father slumped in his seat for a moment. 'You're right, Begum. Perhaps I should leave you ladies to your talk.'

Rabbiya had hit him where it hurt, and as he stood up and walked away, Ayesha knew he was taking with him the only hope she had of deterring Rabbiya.

Raza Masood was not going to leave her so easily.

Sitting in a café two weeks later, Ayesha was convinced that Neelam Khala had spent the days after the visit from Rabbiya brainwashing her mother. Ishrat Safdar wasn't one for drama, but last week, she had done something she'd never tried before. Her mother had put Ayesha's hand on her head and made her swear that she wouldn't tell anyone about her affair with Saqib.

'You don't know this place, Ayesha. Society will kill us.' Tears had streamed down her mother's prematurely lined face, but her eyes still shone with a silent determination. 'It takes decades to build a reputation and a second for it to come crashing down. Don't do this to your father, I implore you. He will not survive it.'

Ayesha had tried to pull her hand away, but her mother was persistent. 'Swear on my life, Ayesha. You must swear that you will give Raza Masood a chance. He is our way out of this predicament. He will be your father's salvation.'

'If Abbu were to see you right now, demanding oaths in his name, he would be ashamed of you, Ammi.'

Her mother had slapped a palm over her forehead. 'Don't you have any sense at all? Look at all the money he has. You will want for nothing. You will live like a queen!'

Ayesha didn't swear the oath. 'Ammi,' she said instead. 'I cannot stand the thought of him touching me. I only love Saqib.'

Her mother had collapsed in a chair. 'Oh my poor, naïve daughter. What do you know of men? All you have to do is endure his touch for a couple of years. Men tire easily. He will move on to greener pastures, and you can then live your life, hopefully with a child to keep you company.'

'And what kind of existence is that? Are you so blinded by money that you are willing to see your only daughter live in pain with someone who is bound to abuse her?'

Her mother hadn't replied for a moment, hitching the dupatta back on her head. 'You don't know that. Men change after marriage.'

'Yes, for the worse.'

'Silence! You will meet Raza and get to know him. You will not disappoint us, Ayesha, or so help me God, I will never forgive you.'

Ayesha had always thought that a mother's heart melted easily, that nobody could understand you the way your mother did, but now, sitting in the café where she was supposed to meet Raza Masood again, she wondered about her own mother. Did she really love her? Did anyone?

'Doesn't look like you're in the mood for a chat,' Saqib said, pulling her out of her reverie.

Not even his beautiful face could improve her mood today. Dread had settled like a rock in her stomach, refusing to budge. She looked at Saqib, and saw the easy life she could have with him disappear right in front of her eyes. The white pillars of Raza's mansion loomed over her, the barbed wire that lined the boundary walls threatening to envelop her. She saw one petty argument, and her untimely death. Domestic abuse was common enough in Pakistan, but when it came to the filthy rich, it was almost guaranteed, especially when the woman came from a humble background.

She shivered, raising the mug of white chocolate mocha to her lips. The sweetness tasted bitter on her tongue. 'The reason you're here today is because I want Raza to see we're together.' She held a hand against her chest to steady her heart. 'I'd rather die than marry someone else. I don't care how much money he has.'

Saqib's lips curved up into a smile. 'Touching, ma'am.'

'Don't call me that. It makes me think of that bastard.'

Even though they were sitting in an upscale café in Gulgasht, one of the more progressive parts of Multan, it was still rare for a couple to hold hands, so Ayesha hesitated when Saqib reached for hers. His grip was firm, his palms dry, unlike hers. His gaze was steady.

'Raza can have all the money and resources in the world, but what he can't have is a love like ours. And that is going to be our salvation in the end. Believe in it, Ayesha. Believe in us. Our time will come.'

'I hope so, because my mother reminded me the other day that I'm damaged goods.'

Saqib's grin widened. 'Well in that case, a little more damage won't hurt. Just say the word.'

Ayesha pulled her hands away, but she was laughing. 'You're such a cheap bastard.'

This was what she wanted – to be able to breeze through life with someone she trusted, someone who made her laugh, someone it wasn't a chore to be around. How many people could boast of having partners like that? Very few in Pakistan, she was sure. Most people were stuck in loveless marriages, sometimes finding joy elsewhere, behind closed doors. She sometimes suspected her father of the same, but he didn't have the money to do that anymore. Still, her parents' marriage wasn't one she envied. She'd lived through those nights of countless tears, the petty skirmishes that would inflate into full-blown arguments. It was proof of how low the bar was for a good Pakistani marriage that she commended her father for never raising his hand against her mother. She wanted – no, needed – to be with Saqib.

It was him or nobody else.

Before they could say anything more, there was a screech of tyres then doors opening in rapid succession. She turned around. A black Beemer surrounded by a melee of vans containing armed guards had appeared, and out of the car emerged Raza Masood – in black as usual. It was March, with Multan really starting to warm up, so wearing all black in this dreadful heat only proved the swaggering arrogance of Raza Masood and his cronies.

'Wow,' Saqib said. 'The man sure knows how to make an entrance.'

Ayesha's heart sank. Saqib was trying to be nonchalant, but deep down, she knew he felt threatened. She could hear it in the stammer of his voice and the way droplets of sweat beaded his forehead. He'd never looked like this when proposals had arrived for her in the past. Some of them were so ludicrous that she and

Saqib would laugh about them afterwards. There was one from a feudal family in Larkana who wanted Ayesha as a trophy wife. The fact that they expected her to live in interior Sindh was a joke in itself. That place was lawless.

Raza Masood entered the café like he owned it, which he could have, given the way the staff treated him. He drew glances from everyone seated in the courtyard, but he had eyes only for her. Ayesha met his gaze head on. She refused to be intimidated by him. After all, she had managed to convince her mother that she'd meet Raza on her own terms, which were here, in this coffee shop, at this hour. That, in itself, was a triumph.

When he finally arrived at their table, he looked completely at ease, as if Saqib wasn't sitting there, gawking at him. Ayesha wished Saqib would close his mouth.

Raza had to wait while a waiter scurried to get him a seat, which Ayesha counted as another triumph. Sinking into the creaking bamboo chair that the café was famous for, he gave her an indulgent smile that didn't quite reach his eyes – they told a different story. He jerked his head in Saqib's direction. 'A friend?'

Ayesha jutted out her chin. 'Boyfriend.'

Raza's eyebrows almost disappeared into his hair. 'I see. And how long has this been going on?'

'None of your business. My family insisted that I meet you, although I don't know why.'

Raza blinked. 'What do you mean, you don't know? The moment I met you, something in us clicked. You stole my breath away. It's as simple as that. I'd like to get to know you and possibly marry you in the fullness of time. Is that really such a bad thing?'

'What's bad is you forcing me to return your feelings. You're a handsome man, Raza, but unfortunately, I am not interested in you like that. How hard is that to understand?'

The smirk was gone, and without it, Raza's face looked dead. Those jet-black pupils almost pierced into her soul. 'And I told you that nobody refuses Raza Masood. How hard is *that* to understand?'

Saqib rose from his seat. 'Listen, brother.'

'You sit down right now, *brother*.' Raza's voice could have frozen oceans.

Saqib sank back into the chair. This time, the bamboo didn't creak.

Ayesha felt like she would be sick. Maybe this was a bad idea after all. What had she been thinking, pitting two men against each other like that? She took a deep breath. 'Listen, Raza. I appreciate your honesty. You're a fine man, but as you can see, I'm already in love with someone.'

Raza shrugged. 'Then you'll just have to fall out of love with him, sweetie. Nobody says no to Raza Masood.' His tone brokered no argument. 'I haven't wasted all this time and money on you only for you to leave me hanging. It doesn't work like that. Even if I may not yet have your love, I will have your respect, Ayesha.'

Ayesha could feel the sweat trickling down her back. She couldn't believe how quickly the situation had got out of her control. 'I'm afraid my answer will always be no, Raza. As much as it pains me.'

The merest flicker of a scowl crossed his face. 'I doubt your father will be happy with that answer. Imagine all I can do for him. Poor Safdar Khan with his tired old car and his long-dead dreams of getting rich again. I could make him rich again. Just saying.'

Ayesha looked away, but her heart was pounding. How dare he? 'If I were you, I'd save my breath. Every word you utter makes me more convinced than ever that I would never want to be close to someone like you.'

'We'll be married before you know it,' Saqib piped up, but it sounded flat. It was obvious he was afraid of Raza.

'I hope you didn't think I'd be intimidated by this little mouse, Ayesha. If that was your plan, then I'm afraid you've failed. You belong with me, not this useless tosser.'

Ayesha shook her head. 'What do you have to gain from this,

Raza? Aren't there enough loveless marriages in this city already that you want to add us to the ranks? Can't we part as friends?'

But looking at him, it was obvious that her request was falling on deaf ears. She had grossly misjudged him; she realised that now. That first meeting had been a mistake. She should never have agreed to secure that funding. That's where it had all started. She'd forgotten that she lived in Multan, where the merest hint of a smile could be misconstrued as flirting.

Raza laid both his palms flat on the table and stood up. At that moment, leaning towards her, he looked scary. She could imagine why nobody had ever dared to refuse him.

'This meeting has gone quite well, I think,' he said with a smirk. 'I shall inform Neelam Aunty that we should take things further. I'll see you soon, Ayesha.'

And with a wink, he was gone.

After that, things progressed quickly. Looking back Ayesha would remember her grandmother's words: 'Before marriage, a girl bends to the will of her family. After marriage, she bends to the will of her husband. There is no in-between. Not for us women.'

After their meeting with Raza Masood, she detected a change in Saqib's behaviour. Gone was the carefree young man with his rolled-up sleeves and twinkling eyes. He'd been replaced by a man hell-bent on trying to earn as much money as possible in the least amount of time. It had been a few weeks since she had last seen him, he'd been working so much, and she knew he was busy selling whatever meagre land he had so that he could move to a decent house before he proposed to her.

Ayesha called him for the tenth time that day. To her surprise, he picked up.

'What is it? I'm just off to the *patwarkhana* for another

meeting. I need to get this land sorted and sold before you get betrothed to that bastard.'

Ayesha scoffed, parting the net curtains of her room to look outside. 'I'm not getting married to anyone else, Saqib. I told you.' She inhaled deeply, preparing herself to say what she'd been wanting to say for weeks. 'I shouldn't have asked you to that meeting. I didn't mean to alarm you. Raza is a like a spoilt brat. There is no such thing as love at first sight.'

'He looked pretty serious to me.'

'Actually, I recently refused another meeting with him. He's like a lovesick rat. I don't know what's got into him. Men these days...' She laughed, but it sounded hollow to her, and she knew it sounded the same to Saqib.

'Listen, I need to go. I need money.'

'What you need is a good shag. Oops, please excuse my language.'

Ordinarily, something like this would have him on his knees, begging her to see him, but this time, he just sniffed. 'No time for that at the moment, I'm afraid.'

'Uff, why did I ever agree to meet that guy? Listen, you've got nothing to worry about.' She hesitated before adding, 'I love you.'

Saqib hung up without replying.

Ayesha swore, throwing her cell phone on the bed. She was burning up, and despite her mother's warnings about hefty electricity bills, she turned on the air conditioner. The blast of cool air settled her nerves a bit. She could see that it was going to be another hot day. The heat seemed to be rising from the ground. Cantt was shaded by thousands of old trees, but they did little to help make the heat tolerable. Even at night, the wind did nothing to cool the sweltering city, the hot gusts only serving to add a layer of dust to the parched trees and roads.

She ought to be on a Zoom call with her colleagues, but right now, the bed looked very inviting, and she was about to curl up under the covers when a loud clang downstairs rattled her.

Hurrying down, she found the living room in a state of disarray. All the crystal ornaments her grandmother had hoarded over the decades lay strewn on the floor in bits. As she watched, her father smashed another one of the Lalique pieces on the floor.

'We've been ruined. What little we had has been snatched away from us. We are ruined, Ishrat.'

Ayesha had never seen her father like this. The sight chilled her to the bone. Her kind, sometimes pretentious, but compassionate father, who had always been her rock, who had always protected her from Multan's heartless society, had been reduced to a weeping mess. It was because of her ... all because of her. She was sure of it. Only a fool wouldn't connect the dots. Raza Masood was punishing her for rejecting him. The paratha she had eaten for lunch earlier threatened to rise back up. The bitter taste of it filled her mouth.

Before she could confirm her suspicions, her mother's gaze found her. She was standing in the far corner of the living room with her hands over her mouth, away from the debris; but seeing Ayesha, she marched over, and before Ayesha could even process what was happening, she was struck across the face. 'This is all because of you, *haramzadi.* Look what he's done to your father. To us.'

It was the embarrassment more than the pain that brought tears in Ayesha's eyes. She hadn't been struck since she was a child. 'What do you mean? Who has done what?' Her eyes slid towards her father. 'Why is Abbu behaving like this?'

'Raza Masood has taken over our agricultural land.' Her father sat on the sofa now with his head in his hands. 'He's sent vans full of goons to drive our people off our property outside of Multan. They're saying he's going to burn the crops. That's our bread and butter he will be setting fire to. And on top of that, I've just received notice from the bank as well. I'm afraid we had defaulted on the loan payments against the house, but given our family's track record, they'd given us a grace period. Now all of a sudden, they're initiating litigation against us.'

Ayesha cursed Raza under her breath. 'I can't believe he would do that. How do you know it's him?'

'Give me some credit, girl. I am fifty-eight years old. I'm not a child. I know it was him, and I also know why he's doing it. He left a message with the *muzairay* who look after the farms. He told them that a simple yes from my daughter could solve all my problems.' He used the back of his hand to wipe the sweat from his face. 'Can you imagine my shame? A man I barely know leaving a message like that about my daughter with people who have worked for me for decades?'

Ayesha felt the sweat break across her own face. The prospect of a nap felt like centuries ago. She looked at her mother, and whispered, 'You can't be serious. Please don't tell me you're considering this. I've only met him a couple of times. He's a monster, Ammi. I won't even think about being with him.'

'I told you that your sister was trouble, Ishrat. I told you that the day we married. Do you remember? Neelam is the one who encouraged all of this. She knew Ayesha didn't like the man, and yet she pushed it. She's always hated how beautiful our daughter is.'

'Of course, everything that happens in the house is my fault in the end,' her mother cried.

'Ammi, please!' Ayesha said. 'This is not the time for one of your pity parties. You can't expect me to go off with Raza Masood. You can see how demented he is. I'll be like a goat for slaughter.'

'He's got money, though,' her father grunted. 'And plenty of it. And he wants to propose properly. He wants your hand in marriage. Nothing unsavoury.'

'Nothing unsavoury?' Ayesha was lost for words. 'Getting married to someone I don't even know let alone like is nothing unsavoury?'

'I married your father without even seeing his face,' her mother said, hitching her dupatta over her head. 'Our parents decided everything.'

'You saw his money, though.'

She got another slap across the face from her mother. This one was expected.

'*Badtameez*. God knows how I raised such an impertinent and disrespectful daughter.'

Before Ayesha could reply, her father rose from the sofa. For the first time that evening, he met her eyes, and what she saw in them made her eat the clever retort she had planned. His eyes were sunken, defeated. He seemed like someone on the precipice of collapse.

'You're right, Ayesha,' he said. 'Of course you are. I can't believe I am putting you in this position. Let's just forget this, and look for a way forward.'

'Be quiet, Ji,' said her mother. 'You are doing nothing wrong here. It is our daughter who needs to shoulder some responsibility at last. She needs to forget about fairy tales and face real life head on.'

'She is our only child, Ishrat. It's not her fault that I lost the family money.' Her father's voice was small and he held on to the back of the sofa for support. He looked far older than his fifty-eight years. 'As long as I draw breath, I will not let my daughter suffer.'

Her mother was openly weeping now. 'Look at the state of him, Ayesha. You father is finished. Won't you take pity on him – on me? Were you not raised with love? Didn't we try to do our best by you?'

Ayesha's vision blurred with the tears gathering in her eyes. 'Ammi, I—'

'Don't force her, Ishrat. When Ayesha was born, I made a promise to myself, that I would never let our society dictate how she lives. Our daughter will be her own person, and we must let her.'

But her mother continued as if she hadn't heard her husband at all. 'We gave you whatever you desired in life, Ayesha. Even when your father couldn't afford it. Today, he needs you. Are you so selfish? Have you forgotten your duty as a daughter? I beg you to think of your aging parents.'

Before Ayesha could think of what to do, she found herself nodding her assent. 'If marrying him will solve all your problems, I'll do it.'

Her father raised a finger in warning. 'Stop this. Ishrat, you listen to me...' But before he could continue, he staggered forward and fell to his knees, his hands clutching his chest.

Her father suffering an angina attack in front of her was something she had never expected. Seeing him stagger and fall to the floor had undone her. Saqib's beautiful eyes and soulful smile had disappeared, and her all-encompassing love for him had flown out of the window at the sight of her father in such a state. He had raised her and protected her for twenty-seven years. Surely she had a duty to him, to both her parents. She couldn't push them into destitution, by refusing Raza.

According to the doctor, her father would survive, but there were tests that needed to be done and medicines prescribed to ensure that it didn't happen again. These justifications swirled in her head all the time, pacifying her mind, but they did nothing for the ache that had settled in her heart. As she arrived at her destination in Raza's chauffeur-driven car, she massaged her aching jaw, a result of grinding her teeth all night. It had taken over an hour to get to the Masoods' mango farm outside of Multan, and although it was a beautiful sight, seeing thousands of mango trees, most of them bearing fruit, Ayesha was on edge.

As she climbed out of the car in the warm evening air, the scent of fresh mangoes and barbecue meat assailed her. A short distance away, Raza stood holding a Kalashnikov, probably aiming it at some poor animal, she thought. There was a loud bang followed by clapping.

'Bravo, Sahab,' one of his servants cried out. 'Your father is going to be so proud of you. A perfect shot.'

'Shut up, fool. He is already proud of me.' Raza thrust the Kalashnikov at him. 'I pay you for your service, not your stupid opinions.'

The servant's head was bowed. 'Ji, Sahab.'

As Raza turned around, his scowl transformed into a grin. 'Well, well, look who has finally managed to arrive.' It took everything in her to not shudder as he looked her over from head to toe. 'You're looking radiant today. Must be a result of finally seeing sense. Could I be so bold as to call you sexy?'

In the distance, a couple of men were dragging a dead deer by its feet.

'Poor animal,' Ayesha said. 'What was the point of killing it? For sport?'

Raza's eyes gleamed. 'I love how you don't hesitate to speak your mind. But you eat meat too, don't you? So please spare me the lecture.'

Ayesha took a deep breath. It was going to be a long evening. 'So, did you ask me here just to witness the death of that animal?'

Brushing his hands on his jeans, Raza threw one arm around her shoulders and pulled her close. Even in the fresh air, the smell of his cologne was powerful. 'I wanted to show you a glimpse of what my family owns. The land you see all around you is ours ... as far as the eye can see. And this is only a small fraction of our lands. The mangoes alone will be exported for millions.'

'Your point is?'

He pulled her close enough that she could count the droplets of sweat on his hairy chest. 'My point is that you made a wise decision saying yes to our marriage.'

She tried to pull back, but his grip was strong. 'You didn't give me much choice.'

His chest rumbled with silent laughter. 'There's always a choice, my love. You may fool your parents into thinking that you're a martyr, but I know you. Deep down, you can't wait to ditch your silly job and live like a queen.'

This time, Ayesha was able to break free. 'Excuse me? Who told you that I'll quit my job?'

Raza laughed again. 'Women in our family don't work, Ayesha. They never have. And no wife of mine will be working in a crappy charity for a pittance, that's for sure. Your pocket money alone will be ten times what you earn at the charity.'

Ayesha folded her arms against her chest. 'I don't think I will be quitting my job. I enjoy working there.'

'You'll be so busy travelling the world that you'll forget all about your job. You'll see...'

'I don't think so.' She wanted nothing more than to leave this place. 'Plenty of women work today, and I am not leaving my job just because you've said so. It doesn't work like that.'

With one swift movement, Raza snatched the gun from the servant, loaded it and pointed it at him. 'Tell me, Hameed, what do I do to people who defy me?'

'You beat them, Sahab,' Hameed answered at once.

'And if they still don't listen?'

'You torture them, Sahab.'

'Show her!' he ordered.

Ayesha's breath caught as the nuzzle dug into the side of the servant's neck. It occurred to her that Raza could kill him right now and nobody would care.

Looking terrified now, the servant lifted his kameez to reveal a multitude of bruises, most of them old, but some of them new.

Ayesha could feel her heart rate picking up. 'Raza, what is this?'

Lowering the gun, he glanced at her. 'I just wanted to show you what happens to people who defy or displease me. Maybe I won't hurt your pretty skin, but who knows what might happen to poor Safdar Uncle when he finds out that he's going to be poor again. Think about that and revise your attitude. You no longer call the shots.'

Before Ayesha could say anything else, the men dragging the deer arrived, panting. They deposited the dead animal at her feet with such force that large droplets of blood splashed on her white kameez. She drew back and gagged as the smell of fresh blood hit her.

Raza wasn't smiling now as he looked at her. 'And now, we will cook and eat this deer.'

'It's over, Saqib,' Ayesha told him over the phone later that night.

She'd seen a truly diabolical side to Raza today. She'd run straight up to her room when she got home, without seeing her mother. Her hands were still shaking and the unpleasant taste of the half-cooked venison still clung to her tongue.

'Forget about us,' she told Saqib. 'We can't get married.'

Saqib exhaled. 'Ayesha, I told you I'm busy trying to buy a bigger house for us. What's happened now? Why the sudden change of heart?'

'Raza Masood is not a man to be trifled with. I realise that now. He will go to any lengths to claim me.'

'You are not a thing to be claimed. You are your own person, and in this day and age, nobody can force you to marry someone you don't want to.'

Ayesha peeked through the net curtains, half expecting Raza to be outside. She shuddered. 'You don't understand, Saqib. That man ... he's unlike anyone I've ever met.'

'Don't you love me anymore?' There was a hint of desperation in Saqib's voice. 'Has his money enamoured you that much? Why don't you say exactly what you want to say?'

Ayesha looked away from the window, the phone in her palm slippery with sweat. 'How could you think that? I will love you till the day I die.'

'Then, what's stopping us?'

'He has connections. I'm afraid he might harm you.'

Saqib laughed. 'I don't care about that. Let him try.'

Ayesha sank onto her bed. 'Don't take this lightly, Saqib. As much as I love you, I can't play with the lives of people I care for. Besides, my parents will never agree to our marriage now.'

'Let me be the judge of that. I can convince them, Ayesha. Even they cannot stand in the face of true love. Them or Raza Masood. Love trumps all.' His breath caught. 'You know that...'

He didn't understand at all, and Ayesha didn't know how to make him. Maybe a part of her wanted him to take the reins of their relationship. Perhaps this was why she didn't stop him when he said his next words:

'I'm coming to ask for your hand in marriage this week, Ayesha. My father will accompany me. I will win your parents over, and then Raza Masood can go to hell.'

As was customary, she wasn't allowed to be present when a proposal was made, so she waited on the first-floor landing, looking through the gap in the bannisters to see what was happening downstairs. She closed her eyes as she heard the squeal of a scooter outside. Saqib had arrived in his Vespa. She had told him to rent a car.

The living room looked strangely empty without the crystal ornaments, but Safdar Khan still held his head high, rising to greet Saqib and his father when they arrived in the living room even though the effort cost him. Her heart pounding, she hoped that her father might be swayed if he saw Saqib's sweet, earnest face or the obvious love he had for her – so unlike Raza's lust – but as much as her father loved her, she knew he would also see that Saqib was in no position to support her now or in the near future.

When Saqib said, '*Assalam alaikum*,' and extended a hand in her father's direction, Safdar Khan pretended not to have heard, spending that time examining his nails. He nodded in Saqib's father direction when he said his greetings, and only then replied, '*Walaikum Salam*.'

She was seeing a new side to her father, his public face that he kept hidden from his daughter – the pragmatic face.

This was a bad idea.

'What brings you here?' was the first thing her mother asked. Not a greeting. Just these terse words. Ayesha realised then that this was a charade. Her parents had only agreed to meet Saqib as a formality.

Their part-time maid had left for the day, so it was down to her mother to serve refreshments. She brought in two glasses of lukewarm Rooh Afza and slammed the tray on the table, not even bothering to ask the guests if they wanted anything. Saqib downed the sweet rose-water drink in a single gulp. Ayesha watched that Adam's apple bob up and down and remembered how many times she'd kissed him right there.

Saqib's father cleared his throat. 'My name is Ghulam Mustafa. I am Saqib's father. Safdar Bhai, as you know—'

'He's not your *brother*,' her mother retorted, interrupting the poor man. 'Call him Safdar Sahab.'

It broke Ayesha's heart that her father didn't say anything. She knew her mother could sometimes be cold, but not her father.

Ghulam gulped, running his fingers through his neatly coiffed white hair, disturbing it so that it stood out at an awkward angle. Clearing his throat, he continued, 'Safdar Sahab, as you know, Ayesha Beti and Saqib here have been meeting for several years and have expressed a wish to make things, ah, more official.'

'Official, is it?' her father replied, stroking his moustache. At that moment, Ayesha just wanted to cry out. It was unbearable. 'I am sorry, Ghulam Sahab, but our daughter is already engaged to Raza Masood.'

Lies! There had been no engagement yet.

'Won't you call Ayesha Beti downstairs to meet us?'

'She is not in the business of meeting strange men,' her mother added. 'Especially since you haven't deigned to bring your wife. Why is that?'

Ghulam bowed his head. 'My wife has been dead for ten years.'

'Oh.' Even her mother had the sense to look ashamed.

Ayesha felt like her heart would break into a million pieces. That's when she decided to end the suffering of those two poor souls. She walked down and quite simply asked them to leave, not meeting Saqib's eyes, because if she did, she wouldn't be able to stop herself from crying.

'Ayesha, I've got us a new place. It is a bigger ten-marla house with three bedrooms.' The hope in Saqib's voice almost killed her.

She shook her head. 'No, Saqib. This can't go on. I'm sorry. You shouldn't have come.'

Ghulam Mustafa rose from his seat, the disgusting lukewarm drink still clutched in his hand. 'Beti, we have come to ask for your hand in marriage.'

Her mother snorted. 'A ten-marla house? I think not.'

'Begum, please behave.' Her father was still weak from his angina attack, and his feeble plea fell on deaf ears.

Her mother, however, was in her element. 'Leave it, Ji. The entire city will laugh at us.' Turning to Saqib's father, she continued, 'While we appreciate the sentiment, Ghulam Sahab, as a Multani, I am shocked you believe in lofty ideas like love. There is no such thing.' She rubbed her thumb and forefinger together. 'Money. That's what makes the world go round. Always has. Always will.'

Ayesha didn't stay to watch them leave. She didn't think she could have survived that. Naturally, Saqib refused her calls afterwards, and she couldn't say that she blamed him. All she knew was that her parents ought to have treated them better. It didn't take anything to be kind. No matter how many times her father told her that their behaviour had been deliberate, that a clean break from Saqib was just what she needed, she just couldn't reconcile her parents in the two people who acted with such callousness towards two perfectly polite and respectful men. She'd never seen them like that.

Her mother was unrepentant when she found Ayesha upstairs crying a few weeks later. 'When you have children, Ayesha, you will understand the sacrifices one must make for them. One day, you will realise why I did what I did. Now, get ready. We're getting late.'

Ayesha dabbed at her eyes with a tissue, careful not to ruin her mascara. She was supposed to be going to Raza's house today to discuss her upcoming engagement. She'd only met him a handful of times since going to the mango farm, and her opinion of him hadn't improved. The man was arrogant and cruel, a lethal combination. Still, in these few weeks, he'd managed to make a remarkable impact in her house. Her father was selling his crop for triple the price he usually did and he had mysteriously received a huge donation of money to help him back to his feet. Ayesha knew full well who his mysterious benefactor was.

Was killing her one chance at true love worth the smiles on her parents' faces?

She wasn't sure.

Kamil

Kamil was at work when Angela, one of his colleagues, sent him a news article.

'Psst!' she whispered, her head poking out of her cubicle. 'Aren't you originally from Multan?'

Kamil wanted to reply that he was originally from Britain, just like her, but he bit back the retort. There really was no point. Instead, he sighed and said yes.

'You might want to check out the article I just sent you.'

Kamil tried not to roll his eyes. 'How very considerate of you. I'll read it when I get home.' He really had very little patience for Angela today. He was still smarting from his recent encounter with Madiha. The impression he'd left on her couldn't have been lasting if she'd moved on already.

Before he could return to his keyboard, Angela called out to him again. 'Read it now. You'll thank me later.'

'Our boss certainly won't,' he replied, but he was laughing now. Angela could sometimes be tactless to the point of foolishness. 'I've got a million things to do.' People often underestimated digital marketing, thinking it was just throwing money into a social-media post and hitting a boost button. It was actually a lot more complicated than that. As the digital marketing assistant for the various high-end clothing brands he managed for the agency, it was Kamil's responsibility to ensure that the clothes reached the eyes of people with money who would then proceed to place their orders through the website. Standing out in a flooded market was an art in itself, and in order to retain his job, Kamil had to do just that. Along with a few more people, he reported to Amelia Scott who headed everything.

Angela shrugged, pushing her spectacles up her nose. It was easy for her to find time to browse the news as all she did was report to Amelia about trends and media campaigns.

Looking at her screen, she murmured, 'Amelia will probably be on the phone with her husband, discussing where they should go for their next holiday. Maldives or Mauritius? Hard work isn't meant for posh women like her. She was born for greater things, apparently. But suit yourself. Just don't come crying to me later.'

Why would I cry? he thought, but chose not to say it aloud. It was probably best not to antagonise her, especially not when she was trying to be nice to him. At thirty-five, Kamil had already had several jobs and somehow always seemed to be on the bottom rung of whatever organisation he joined. He tried not to dwell too much on this. His bank balance gave him enough nightmares.

Bloody Angela, he thought, because now he felt he had to open the WhatsApp message she'd sent him. He rued the day he ever gave his number to her. The link directed him to an article about an attack in Multan. That made him sit up straighter.

HUSBAND SLASHES THE FACE OF HIS WIFE
OF EIGHT YEARS. NO CHARGES FILED.
MULTAN IN TURMOIL.

The southern Punjab city of Multan is no stranger to human-rights violations, especially when it comes to women. It has borne witness to plenty of atrocities over the decades, but even in this day and age, men are still getting away with repulsive crimes against women, and this latest incident has only added to the image of a city steeped in violence.

Rabia Shahbaz, thirty-one, a resident of Shalimar Colony Multan, married to Shan Shahbaz, a professor, was found horribly mutilated with knife wounds to her face outside her residence after the couple's son, aged six, called emergency services. Rabia survived the attack, but it has left her with lasting injuries, blindness in one eye, and a permanently disfigured face. Possibly fearing for her life, she has decided not to press charges, calling the attack 'an accident'.

It remains to be seen what will become of Shan Shahbaz, but given the outcomes of previous cases of this nature in Pakistan, it is very much possible that he might get off scot-free.

Rabia remains under the care of doctors in a local hospital in Multan. They have described her condition as 'very delicate' and have warned her that a long road to recovery lies ahead, not to mention coming to terms with her new appearance. A local charity, Insaaniyat, headed by renowned philanthropist Shugufta Raheem, has stepped up to foot her medical bills, and her family has also set up a GoFundMe to raise funds for her treatment abroad.

Kamil winced as he closed the tab on his phone. It was an insensitive article that had laid bare the name and address of the poor victim. In a city like Multan, where everyone knew one another, that was like giving her a death sentence.

He didn't want to give Angela the satisfaction of seeing how much the article had disturbed him, so he feigned needing another coffee and left his desk. In the small kitchen, he took deep breaths, trying to steady his racing heart. The names Rabia and Shan sounded oddly familiar, but it could be his mind playing tricks on him. He made a mental note to visit his mother later that day to see if she might confirm his suspicions.

As always, it was hot and claustrophobic on the tube. With the gusts of warm wind blowing through the tunnels, it was impossible to imagine that the last remnants of winter still clung to the city above. London – ever the city of contrasts. It was a long ride to Totteridge and Whetstone, a picturesque suburb in North London. The carriages filled and emptied as the train shot its way through the tunnels and finally into open space. He was certain he'd known a Rabia when he'd visited Multan as a kid. That Rabia had married someone called Shan. Could they possibly be the same person? If it was, then it was even more heart-breaking. *Damn you, Angela*, he thought. The photo in the article showed the face of a woman who was mutilated beyond belief. It could be her, but there was no way to be sure. It was common enough for the media to take photos without permission in Pakistan, but in this case, he had hoped for some compassion.

One of his mates from childhood, Tahir Bashir, texted him about having a pint, but he declined. After the day he'd had, the last thing on his mind was drinking beer. Besides, things with Tahir had become awkward after Kamil had moved out of North London. Kamil wanted to be more sociable, but the ghosts of the past meant he struggled to build friendships, and relied more on his family. His mother would be mortified if she were to smell alcohol on his breath. As far as she was concerned, he'd never touched the stuff.

'*Haye*, this is poor Shaila's daughter, Rabia,' his mother exclaimed, beating a fist against her chest when he showed her the article. She resorted to speaking in Saraiki when impassioned. 'I'd heard the gossip, but didn't believe it until now. Oh, the poor girl. What kind of monster would do that to a woman? I thought she had married a professor.'

Kamil stowed the phone back in his pocket. 'Even if she is married to a professor, Ammi, it doesn't mean anything. Professors can be monsters too.'

His mother fixed him with a beady stare. 'What *bakwaas*. Next you'll say that doctors and engineers are monsters too.'

'Of course they are, Ammi!' Sharmeela, his sister, spoke up now. 'There are plenty of psychopaths who have degrees. I'm sure you must know a few. A lot of Pakistanis could fit the profile.'

Their mother slapped a palm against her forehead. '*Koi een chuair kun samjhaway'* – *Someone please help this girl.* 'You know nothing of the world, Sharmeela. There is no such thing as a psychopath. There are just good people and bad people, and I wish you associated with the good ones. Is your friend, that Mexican boy, feeding you these stupid ideas?'

'His name is Juan, Ammi.' Sharmeela's voice was icy, but of course their mother ignored it.

She batted a hand in Sharmeela's direction. 'Yes, yes, whatever. I don't know why you can't have decent Pakistani friends. I wouldn't mind Indians and Arabs either. What is this fascination with the West?'

Sharmeela was sitting at the dining table, plaiting her hair, but upon hearing this, she paused and looked up. 'Umm, because we live in the West?'

'Pah, since when has that mattered? If I lived in Antarctica, would I be friends with the penguins?'

'I wouldn't mind being friends with a few penguins, to be honest. Also, you're being very racist.'

'Sharmeela!'

Sharmeela caught Kamil's eye and winked. She loved tormenting their mother. At twenty-eight, Sharmeela, or Shar as she was known among friends, was on her way to becoming a successful banker with a job in the City, but according to their mother, she was a massive failure. Being unmarried at twenty-eight was the worst thing that could happen to her, apparently. Kamil didn't have it in him to tell their mother that Shar was actually dating that 'Mexican boy'. That would likely finish her off for good. To all intents and purposes, Juan was a friend. A bit too close for comfort, sometimes, but still a friend.

'Mrs Bashir next door asks me all the time about when my children will get married. I just hang my head in shame. What else can I do? It seems my children are simply incapable of giving me happiness.'

'Mrs Bashir can mind her own bloody business.' Shar tied the rest of her hair with a hairband. 'Didn't her son go to the same school as you, Kamil?'

'We don't really talk anymore,' Kamil murmured.

'Anyway,' Shar continued. 'Even if we don't get married, would it be that bad? I mean, there are plenty of people out there now who simply choose not to get married.'

Their mother nodded, her chin wobbling. 'It would be very bad. It would mean death for me. I'd rather be dead and six feet under than see my children with their hair greying in front of my eyes, unmarried and childless. *Haye!*'

Kamil couldn't help but laugh. 'Come on, Ammi. You don't really believe that...'

'Oh, I do. I certainly do. It's a travesty of epic proportions. My sisters in Pakistan have grandchildren. Plural! And here I am sitting with two unmarried children, destined for God knows what fate. I don't even want to start with you, Kamil. You had—'

'Ammi – stop.'

The dupatta had slid off her head, but she had clocked the warning in his tone. She fixed the dupatta back with force. 'Fine!'

Despite having been in the UK for several decades, Jamila Akbar refused to adapt to the country's culture. In a way, Kamil admired her for it. He didn't know where she got the henna from – probably an Asian store – but she point-blank refused to dye her hair with anything else. 'Never forget you're Pakistanis,' she'd always told them. 'No matter how tempting it is to become white, always remember your roots.'

'Then why did you move to the UK?' Kamil would sometimes ask, just to tease her. He'd always get a slap across the face for it. At least, he used to.

'We didn't bring you to the UK just so you could talk back. I'm telling you now, don't mistake me for a *gori* mother who won't beat her children. I firmly believe that there is nothing a good slap can't fix. God knows my mother did the same. Beat us to within an inch of our lives. See how well we turned out.'

'That's abuse, Ammi,' Shar would always tell her, but Jamila Akbar ignored her.

'You're just a stupid little girl, Sharmeela. You don't live in the real world.'

Looking at his mother now, Kamil could see that age had mellowed her a little, but that spark was still alive in her eyes. He needed to be careful around her, because that infamous slap could always make a comeback.

She sighed, reclining a little on the sofa in the living room. 'As much as I want my daughter married, I really don't understand what has happened to men these days. Your father, bless him, has never dared raise his hand against me. No matter what happened.'

Sharmeela snorted. 'I'd like to see him try that with you.'

Jamila looked back at her daughter. 'I had to be feisty or else my in-laws would have eaten me alive. That's a lesson for you for when you get married.'

'Oh, Ammi!'

Jamila reached for her mobile phone on the coffee table, an ancient relic that could barely manage WhatsApp. 'I'll call Shaila and ask about poor Rabia. She must be devastated. Have you told Madiha yet, Kamil?'

Kamil didn't have it in him to look his mother in the eye. 'Uh – about that. The thing is, Ammi, that Madiha and I, well we're—'

'Getting married?' To his horror, his mother leapt up from the sofa, rushing to embrace him, but Shar had seen the expression on his face.

'Oh, Kamil,' she said, shaking her head. 'I'm so sorry.' Shar had got on with Madiha famously.

Jamila stopped midway, her eyes swivelling between Kamil to Shar. 'Oh,' she said. 'Oh. It's the other way around, isn't it? There will be no wedding. No kids. Has she left you?'

Kamil nodded, looking anywhere but in his mother's eyes.

'*Haye.*'

Ayesha

Raza Masood's house was a sprawling property in Cantt, just a stone's throw from their own house. Their wheezing but loyal Toyota Crown had been abandoned for a new Honda Civic. It smelled so good inside that it was sometimes hard to leave the car. This was a meeting 'between the ladies' as Rabbiya Masood called it, with her father back home, probably grinning from ear to ear as he went over his finances. The news of Ayesha's upcoming engagement with Raza Masood had taken Multan by storm. It had only been a few weeks since Ayesha had agreed, but the news had already spread. People they hadn't heard from in decades had come calling to their house. Fully utilising the money that was now coming in, her parents had redecorated the house. The sofas in the living room had been reupholstered after over ten years. The marble floor shone to perfection and her mother had gone to a market in Gulgasht to get a few Lalique knock-offs to adorn the coffee table. They were building an empire on the demise of her relationship with Saqib and it sickened her.

She took a deep breath as they entered the large foyer of Raza's house. It was all tall white arches and gleaming marble floors with vases full of fresh flowers strewn about. Looking closely, Ayesha noticed that most of these flowers were nowhere to be found in Multan's flower markets. They must have come from the fancy flower shops in Lahore.

As if by magic, two maids appeared in front of them.

'Bibi will see you in the small living room,' one of them said, fixing her hijab. 'If you would like to follow us, please.'

'Is there a big living room as well?' her mother asked.

'Yes, and a drawing room and a study. The house is very big and the family has been living here for generations.'

Ayesha winced when she heard her mother's sharp intake of breath.

The small living room wasn't very small at all. It was perhaps double the size of theirs. Lined with wooden panels and luxurious velvet drapes, it looked like something out of an English home. In a hot and dusty city like Multan, it looked out of place. She could only imagine the amount of dust those thick drapes had gathered. She took deep breaths, inhaling the cool air blasting from the air conditioners.

'Ah, Ishrat. There you are. And little Ayesha too.' Rabbiya Masood rose from where she was seated in a plush armchair, pretending to look surprised although it was evident that she had been expecting them. Decked out in her finest diamonds, she gestured to the sofa opposite.

Ayesha and her mother silently took their seats. Despite herself, Ayesha found herself gaping at Rabbiya. It was obvious she'd had a lot of work done on her face, but she still looked beautiful. She'd dyed her hair ash blonde and her eyes were done up with heavy liner, kind of like the yesteryear actresses of Bollywood.

'You look beautiful in your lawn outfits, ladies,' she observed. 'Personally, lawn is not for me. It's cheap cotton and starts to smell if you so much as step outside in this weather.'

'This is designer lawn, Rabbiya,' Ishrat said.

Ayesha almost felt sorry for her mother.

Rabbiya sniffed. 'It's still lawn, though, isn't it? If I started wearing it too, what would be the difference between the maids and myself? So, no thank you. They're involved enough in our lives in any case. I don't need to look like them too. I'm fine with my silk kaftans.'

If her mother was shocked, she didn't show it. Ayesha thought Neelam Khala would be right at home with this woman. She only hoped that her mother would see it too – how ill-suited Raza Masood's family was for her.

'Do you have many maids?' she asked, instead.

Rabbiya laughed, a savage bark. 'An army. They come for free, anyway. Their parents deliver them to us when they're mere kids, and they simply work for free until it's time for us to marry them off. We're just supposed to feed and clothe them in the meantime, if that!'

'But that makes them no better than slaves!' Ayesha spoke before she could stop herself.

'Ayesha,' her mother whispered. 'Quiet.'

Rabbiya laughed again, but this time it sounded more like a taunt. 'Slaves, she says. Are you not familiar with how things are done in Multan, my dear? This is how it has always been, and will always be. Why should we pay these people salaries if their parents so willingly leave them at our door?'

'Because there's something called humanity,' replied Ayesha. 'And you can afford to.'

Rabbiya's lips twitched. 'You talk as if I'm a brute. The maids will tell you that I pay them all a small allowance from my own pocket. I am not obligated to, but I still do it, because everyone deserves a bit of money.' Shaking her head, she added, 'This is what happens when you allow your daughters to sit at home for too long, isn't it, Ishrat? They get ridiculous ideas in their pretty but ageing little heads.' She sighed. 'Not that I have anything against age. I married late myself because I wanted to finish my degree, and good thing I waited, because Masood Sahab's proposal arrived well after my early twenties. Anyway, who am I to say anything? You're my son's choice, so automatically mine. He's my only son, you see, and he's always got whatever he's wanted. He's never really known any other life.'

'Isn't that wrong? Letting him have whatever he wants?' said Ayesha.

Rabbiya shrugged. 'With the kind of money we have, why not? Why should my son suffer?'

Ishrat bulged her eyes at Ayesha.

Changing tack, Ayesha asked, 'You've got daughters, though, so it's not like he's an only child.'

Rabbiya wasn't going to rise to the bait. 'I have daughters, yes. Lovely daughters who have found kind, loving homes.'

'Raza's a lovely young man,' Ishrat said, dabbing her lips with a tissue even though Rabbiya hadn't so much as offered them tea.

Rabbiya sighed again. 'Yes, he is. He has quite a temper if crossed, but otherwise, he's a kind and loving young man. Anyway, I'll be sending over some clothes for you and Ayesha to wear at the engagement party two weeks from now. The cream of the city will be at the event and we need to maintain our reputation. I've ordered dresses from that famous designer in Karachi.'

'Two weeks?' Ayesha and her mother said in unison, looking at each other. Things were happening way too fast for Ayesha to even think. What was she going to do, and how long before these people set a date for the wedding as well? She wasn't ready.

'It's hardly May yet,' Ayesha said.

Her mother hesitated. 'We were thinking of having it in a few months, just so we can get things ready.'

Rabbiya's face was devoid of expression. 'The engagement will be held in mid-May. Do you want to bake in the heat by having it in high summer? I told you already that if it's the clothes you're worried about, I'm organising them.'

'I've got plenty of those,' Ishrat whispered.

Kindness flickered across Rabbiya's face, making her look human for the first time that day. 'I'm a mother too, Ishrat, so I understand you wanting to take care of everything regarding your daughter's wedding, but please rest assured that things are in hand. I've ordered brand new clothes for you, and there's an end to it. One of my tailors will come in to take some measurements, and I'll text them to the designer. Your outfits are almost ready. It's just a matter of stitching them now. Just make sure you show up at the hall at the appointed hour. We'll be sending directions.'

'But isn't it the responsibility of the bride's parents to organise that too?' her mother pressed.

Just as quickly, Rabbiya's face hardened. 'Ordinarily yes, but these are exceptional circumstances. Sorry, Ishrat, but our reputation is at stake. We'll arrange everything.'

Ayesha wanted to smash Rabbiya over the head with the ugly crystal vase that sat nearby. She looked away, not trusting herself to speak anymore. It was sick, having to continue this charade. She closed her eyes tightly, before opening them again, so that Rabbiya wouldn't see them burning with tears.

Rabbiya cleared her throat. 'While we wait for tea, why don't you go upstairs and have a chat with Raza, my dear?'

Ayesha's head whipped back in Rabbiya's direction. 'Excuse me?'

'Don't play coy, dear. You don't seem like the naïve and ignorant type.' She raised a hand, stopping Ishrat from saying anything. 'I'm not judging your daughter, Ishrat. God knows we women should be allowed to have a few desires of our own. I'm only saying that since she's an educated young woman, she shouldn't feel shy about spending some time with her prospective partner. It's only fair that they get to know each other.'

'It's not like that at all, Rabbiya,' her mother said, looking at her shoes. 'Ayesha has never really had any male friends.'

'Spare me. I was young once too. I know exactly what desire is like. I told you already that I don't believe in being so conservative.' She turned to Ayesha. 'Will you go upstairs or not?'

'I thought he'd be at work,' Ayesha observed, and it pleased her to see the shock on Rabbiya's face. 'Doesn't he work from nine to five like most people?'

'When you're rich, my dear, you'll realise that you don't have to follow the nine-to-five routine. That's for the rabble. Watch and learn.' She pressed the bell, which brought a maid running into the room. 'Take her to Raza Sahab,' Rabbiya instructed her. Ayesha saw her mother fidget, desperate to raise an objection but unable to pluck up the courage. Ayesha stood up. She wasn't a coward like her parents. If she was to spend her entire life with Raza, she might as well start getting to know him, or even better, control him in some way.

The rest of the house was not as decadent as the small living room. Ayesha hated to admit it, but the Masoods oozed class. Everywhere she looked, she saw tastefully decorated spaces, minimalistic mirrors that gave the already large house a more open feel, the smell of the hundreds of fresh flowers they seemed to have all over their home.

'Raza Sahab likes to meet his guests in his living room upstairs, but he's asked us to lead you to his bedroom,' the maid said, her head down. Ayesha could see that the poor girl was terrified out of her mind.

'Maybe he wants to show me my future lodgings.'

'Just be careful, Bibi,' the maid whispered.

'Why?'

She glanced up, a series of lines breaking across her forehead. 'Raza Sahab, he ... he's not a kind man. He has certain habits that are not right.' She knocked on the door once before hurrying away.

What habits?

Before Ayesha could compose herself, the door opened and Raza stood there, leaning against the doorframe, dressed in just a pair of jeans. This was the first time she'd seen him wearing something that wasn't black. She looked away, which made him laugh.

'You don't need to act like a saint on my account, Ayesha.' He gestured to his bare chest. 'You'll be seeing a lot more of this in the near future, so you'd better get used to it.'

She felt like doing something to wipe that smirk right off his face. 'Why don't we take a walk outside? I'll wait downstairs until you're presentable.'

'In this weather? You must be kidding me.' His smirk widened. 'Fine, I'll put a shirt on. God, you're such a difficult girl. No wonder I want you.'

Ayesha watched the muscles in his back contract as he pulled the shirt on, and for a moment she felt like driving a dagger right into his spine. This man was going to ruin her life. She looked around his bedroom in an attempt to distract herself. Like the rest of the house, it was well decorated, with dark wood-panelled walls and genuine leather sofas. She wanted to scream.

'Why did you ask for me?' she asked instead.

Raza put on a serene expression as he took her hand and guided her towards the leather sofa. It took everything she had not to bat it away. 'Your hand is clammy. Relax, will you? I'm not going to kill you or anything. I am marrying you. You should be overjoyed.'

She snorted. She couldn't help it. 'Sure. If you say so.'

The irony was lost on Raza. He smiled, sitting next to her on the sofa. 'That's my girl.' His long black hair was still wet from the shower. To anyone else, he would have seemed irresistible, but Ayesha had seen his true face, and it was very ugly. Edging closer, he added, 'I don't know what's come over me. All I can think of is you. It's like you've taken over my life. Sometimes, I rue the day I came to your blasted charity.'

As do I, Ayesha thought. She was desperate to distance herself from him, but she couldn't see how. She felt his hands move up her forearms, pausing near the elbow, where he massaged her skin with his thumbs. 'When exactly is the engagement?' she asked, watching with mounting horror as his hands climbed further. 'What day?'

'If you picked up my calls, you'd know,' Raza whispered, his eyes half closed, his face impossibly close to hers. She could smell his mint toothpaste. 'You are such a tease. We're going to be married soon and we still don't know anything about each other. About each other's bodies.'

His hands were on her shoulders now, his fingers venturing inside her kameez, touching her bra strap. Ayesha stopped breathing. She couldn't face it. 'I think we ought to go downstairs.'

'Mmm?' Raza's eyes were closed. 'What was that?'

'I … I wanted to say…' She was never lost for words, but here she was, trembling like a leaf.

The moment his lips brushed hers, she sprang away as if she was scalded. She adjusted her dupatta back over her chest. 'After marriage,' she said, panting. 'This stuff is for after we're married.'

Raza's eyes crinkled as his face broke into a smile. 'Are you telling me that you haven't done this before? Not even with that jackass of a boyfriend you had? Do you think I'm a fool? Shall I do the two-finger test on you?' His smile widened as he held up two fingers.

'That's disgusting and misogynistic. You should be ashamed of yourself.'

The smile vanished. 'I'd advise you to save that crap for social media. It won't fly in Multan.'

'That's what your mother implied, that a woman's place is lower than a man's.'

'I am my mother's son.'

'Of that I have no doubt.'

'So, better not cross me. I'm serious, Ayesha.'

She pretended to do a curtsy. 'My Lord.'

Before she could turn to leave, Raza crossed the distance between them and grabbed her by the arms. This time, there was no softness in his touch. He wanted to inflict pain. He grinned when she yelped in alarm.

'Listen, you little bitch. I am indulging you because right now, I want you. Badly enough that I want to do it properly, otherwise I'd have kidnapped you and had my fun. But girls like you are worth the wait. You're not one-night-stand material. Not yet, anyway.' His eyes flashed. 'Don't you dare make fun of me again. I am warning you. I am not someone to be crossed.' Releasing her from his grip, he pushed her away so that her back hit the door. She winced. 'Now get the fuck out of here. You've ruined my mood.'

Ayesha rushed out of the door and would have burst into tears in the passage if at that moment, she hadn't received a text message from Saqib.

I can't stop thinking about you. Please come back to me.

She burst into tears, anyway.

Kamil

Tinder. Bumble. eHarmony. Kamil's phone was littered with dating sites. After his breakup with Madiha, something in him had snapped. His mind threatened to retreat to that very dark place, the one he'd been in all those years ago, and almost lost his sanity to. To stave off the worst of the depression, he plunged headfirst into dating, not caring about the fact that he hadn't done this for years. It felt weird, but to his utter surprise, he was matching with several people every day, and had been on a couple of dates over the past few weeks.

This was perhaps one of the reasons he'd moved out of the family home in Whetstone years ago. There was no chance of bringing back a girl for the night. His father would disapprove, but his mother would literally have a heart attack, especially if the girl turned out to be anything but Pakistani. And even if she was it would be a problem. He could see his mother giving that poor girl a solemn lecture on how a Pakistani girl ought to carry herself in the big bad world.

He shuddered, thanking his lucky stars that he earned enough money at the agency to be able to rent the studio in Earl's Court. It suited him fine. It was compact but with plenty of windows, which allowed for a generous view of Warwick Road and plenty of air when it got hot. He felt like he could stay there forever.

Even his colleagues had noticed the change in the way he dressed. Angela had given him a thumbs-up as he'd approached his cubicle today, which had pleasantly surprised him. He didn't tell her that he had another date planned for after work. Maybe all this dating was just a way of coping with the loss of Madiha. She certainly had wasted no time in getting together with her cousin, despite telling him once that she despised relationships between cousins. He was tempted to talk to her, and even went ahead and phoned her, but she didn't reply to the countless messages he left her. Perhaps that was how things were supposed to be. So he'd left it at that.

This was how his days usually went: thinking about how he'd screwed things up with Madiha and then looking forward to his new date at the same time. Who knew? He might find someone better this time. Holding that thought in mind, he immersed himself in work.

As it turned out, his date didn't go exactly as he'd planned. When Safiya arrived at the café, he couldn't help but stare at her. She was the kind of woman whose very presence commanded respect. An investment banker with more than fifteen years working in the City, she looked like the type of person who took no nonsense. As Kamil watched her take off her scarf and hang it over the chair, he couldn't help but wonder why on earth she'd matched with someone like him, and had agreed to a date. They'd decided to meet in Temple as it was closer to where she worked, but for Kamil it had meant a trek on the crowded District Line. Still, it seemed to him that Safiya was worth it.

'Just to let you know, I've been divorced three times. I need to put it out there, because you Pakistani men can be a bit weird about full disclosure.'

Kamil couldn't help but smile. 'It doesn't matter to me.'

Safiya's eyes almost popped out of their sockets. 'Well, that's refreshing. Finally, a Pakistani guy who can look beyond beauty and divorces. At forty, I'd kind of given up hope.' Her eyes glittered. 'How about full disclosure from you as well. You're good-looking, fairly successful, I imagine' – that earned a guffaw from Kamil – 'and you seem pretty progressive. There must be a catch.'

'This date has got off to an awkward start.'

'Ah, a lopsided grin too. You really are the complete package, aren't you? Come on, spill your secrets. Surprise me!'

Kamil just shrugged.

'Any relationships in the past?' Safiya tried again.

This time, he met her gaze. 'A few ... just like everyone.'

She laughed, taking a sip of her coffee. 'I meant if you had been married before.' She grimaced. 'Gosh, this coffee is too sweet.'

Kamil wasn't listening anymore. His gaze travelled to the barista in the distance as he poured milk into a mug. His heart was hammering in his chest. If he wasn't careful, he would start hyperventilating.

Marriage ... the word alone sent a shiver down his spine.

Safiya clicked her fingers at him. 'Lost you for a moment there. Are you okay?'

He nodded, unsure of what to say. His forehead was breaking out in a sweat. What was it about this woman that had him on edge?

'I take it from your reaction that you *have* been married before.'

'Yes,' he said finally. 'But I don't want to talk about it.'

'I take it that it wasn't pleasant.'

He hoped there was a finality in his tone when he said, 'Please, I really don't want to talk about it. Why don't we talk about something else?'

She didn't push him, but thirty minutes into their meeting, Kamil knew that there wouldn't be a second date. Meeting Safiya was refreshing, but he was letting his guard down. There was something about her that was causing him to lose his inhibitions.

'Is this just first-date jitters or have you been through some pretty serious stuff in life? You're wound up pretty tight, even for a first date.' Her silky black hair fell over the side of her face as she sipped her skinny latte again. 'Relax, Kamil. I'm not going to judge you. That's not what we're here for.'

Kamil found himself nodding. 'I was actually accused of being a robot by my ex.'

Safiya threw her head back and laughed. 'I can see why. You're a bit of a tragic hero, Kamil. I feel sorry for you.'

Kamil began to shrug before catching himself. 'Everyone has been through stuff in life. There's nothing to be sorry about.'

Safiya blew away a strand of hair. 'Right. Fine, don't tell me. I doubt we'll be seeing each other again in any case, so here's a bit of friendly advice, Pakistani to Pakistani.' She leaned forward, close enough for him to see the strands of mascara on her eyelashes. 'Get help, Kamil. You need it.'

He shook his head, folding his arms across his chest. 'That's pretty bold for a first date. I thought we were here to get to know one another, not discuss our respective mental health and judge each other.'

'That's me. I'm bold. And besides, what's wrong with talking about mental health? It's been taboo for way too long.' Her expression softened. 'Listen, at forty and after dating dozens of guys, you learn a thing or two about assessing people. Call it my superpower.' She pulled out a card from her wallet. 'Matt Ross. He's not a psychiatrist as such, but he runs a local support group up in Euston. He's brilliant. He might be able to help.'

'What kind of support group?' Kamil was intrigued enough to indulge her.

'It's a group for domestic-abuse survivors.'

The blood ran cold in his veins. 'How did you—?'

'Told you... it's a superpower.'

It was disconcerting how quickly Safiya had figured him out. When his marriage ended, he had promised himself that he would never speak about it again – never think about *her* again. He had no idea that he was so easy to read.

He looked around for a way out. 'I have no idea what you're talking about, and besides, I need to head off. Late for a meeting.'

Safiya raised an eyebrow. 'Another date?' She pulled another card from her wallet. 'Here's my card as well in case you delete my number out of sheer rage.'

Kamil threw both the cards in the bin outside after they'd said their goodbyes.

Ayesha

Over the next couple of weeks, there was a remarkable shift in her mood. Gone was the doleful and temperamental Ayesha, and in her place, there was someone who was happy and hopeful about the future. It was only after she'd parted from Saqib that she'd realised how important he was in her life, how much he mattered to her. They were like two parts of a whole. They fit each other perfectly. It was the kind of love people yearned to find someday, and Ayesha had it. She couldn't understand why her parents couldn't see it.

She had given up trying to make them understand. She was done prioritising other people before her. Life was way too short to spend it in a perpetual state of sorrow. As she arrived for her engagement ceremony with Raza at Multan's international hotel, it was obvious now that things were over between them. There had never been anything to begin with.

She'd just patched things up with Saqib and wanted to drop everything and run back to him. If only she could break things off with Raza right here and now, she wouldn't have to carry on with this charade. However, one look at her parents and she knew that there was no way she could do that to them. Not here. No, she would have to endure this for now.

She was wrenched from her thoughts by a sharp pain in her side. Raza's hand gripped her waist hard, his fingers digging into her flesh as he steered her around the hall.

'Behave,' he whispered in her ear. 'You are in my world now, in front of my people. If you so much as put a toe out of line, my love, you'll have me to answer to, not to mention my parents.' At this, he dug his fingers harder into her waist. She knew the bruise would take days to fade.

However, before she could object, she came face to face with the elusive Masood Khan, Raza's father. She'd expected him to be arrogant and pompous like his wife and son, but given the way he was talking to his friend, he didn't look too bad. A bit aloof, maybe, but not unkind. It just went to show that exceptions to the norm did exist.

As soon as he glanced at her, his face broke into a smile and he announced, 'Ah, the famous Ayesha. Welcome to the family, *beta*. Welcome.' With arms outstretched, he proceeded to embrace her, planting a small kiss on her forehead. 'I am so happy that my son is settling down with someone of substance and class.' With a conspiratorial smile, he added, 'My father spoke very highly of your grandfather.'

Her father wasn't in earshot or he would have passed out from happiness.

'The wedding is yet to take place, Masood Sahab,' Rabbiya pointed out, swanning in in her best designer outfit and diamond jewellery, Ayesha's parents following her. 'Let's not be so quick to make announcements.'

Leaning towards Ayesha, Masood Khan murmured, 'Ignore her. She's just a bit unhappy that Raza rejected her Harvard-educated niece and chose you instead.'

Under her heavy makeup, Rabbiya turned red. 'Maybe it's for the best. Nobody wants a wife that's too pretty, as then you'd be spending all your time keeping watch. Ayesha is perfect that way.' Everyone except for her parents joined Rabbiya as she bared her teeth and broke into laughter.

Her mother covered her mouth with one hand, but said nothing. It pained Ayesha that her father said nothing as well. Sickened her, in fact.

Rabbiya had gifted her an outlandish dress that was so heavy with beads and stones, she could barely walk. Her mother was equally uncomfortable in a dowdy sari. Ayesha relished the fact that she hadn't even taken a shower after spending the afternoon with Saqib. She hoped Raza would smell him on her, but his own cologne overpowered everything. The entire city was here, but Ayesha didn't notice anyone. She hardly even noticed her cousin, Sabeena, who hugged her as if they were long lost siblings.

'My dear sister! It's such an honour to be invited to your engagement. I always knew you'd land the best guy in the world.'

At this, Raza's grip on Ayesha's waist tightened. 'She's very lucky.'

The only person Ayesha was glad to see was Neelam Khala. Her beady gaze surveyed her from top to bottom several times, taking in the diamonds and outfit, before her face broke into a big fake smile. 'My lovely niece. Engaged, at last. You had us all worried.'

Ayesha took pleasure in holding out her hand in front of her aunt, if only to show her the large diamond ring. Neelam Khala's eyes became as round as dinner plates. '*Ya Khuda*, what a beauty that ring is. If I weren't your aunt, I'd say it's wasted on the likes of you.'

'But of course you wouldn't say it, since you're my dear khala who loves me very much.'

Neelam Khala's face remained impassive. The sarcasm wasn't lost on her.

Everywhere she went, compliments were lavished on her and Raza.

'Best couple!'

'Look at the two of you. Lucky girl to have bagged Multan's most eligible bachelor.'

'The talk of the town.'

She could see that Raza took immense pleasure in it all. The sycophantic behaviour was something he had grown up with, so he knew exactly what to say, but it left Ayesha a bit tongue-tied.

'Enjoy this moment, my love,' Raza whispered in her ear. 'This marks your entry into Pakistan's high society.'

Ayesha tried to ignore the pain in her waist from the way he held her, but after a while it became impossible. 'You're hurting me.'

Raza looked into her eyes then, his gaze fierce. 'But you must remember to never hurt me, Ayesha. Never.'

Raza's warning ought to have frightened her, but Ayesha wasn't really paying attention. Her mind was elsewhere. This engagement was probably something every girl dreamed of, but the smile on her face wasn't because of the lavish event and gifts. It was because she couldn't stop thinking of Saqib and their rekindled romance.

She reasoned that her parents had accumulated enough to be quite comfortable even if she broke things off with Raza. Since agreeing to marry him, the agricultural lands had been returned to her father and the mysterious donation had made things easier. If Raza created trouble for them again, she could just appeal to Masood Khan. A semblance of humanity still lurked inside him, quite unlike his wife and son.

And she *had* to break things off, because there was no way she could marry Raza, not when she was in love with someone else. As horrible as he was, Raza didn't deserve that either. Nobody deserved to be in a loveless marriage.

It was this thought that comforted her enough to bear the rest of the event.

'What are you thinking?' Saqib asked her, several weeks after the engagement, his arm tucked behind his head. She smiled into his chest, which made him laugh too. 'You're tickling me. Stop!'

Shifting away from him so that they faced each other, Ayesha closed her eyes. 'Right now, I am just content.'

They were tangled together in a mess of sheets and limbs in the bedroom of one of their friends, who worked in Lahore, so his house was often empty. Saqib tipped the security guard to keep his mouth shut, but Ayesha always felt embarrassment radiating from her as she passed the guard on her way into the house. He might keep his mouth shut, but his eyes wandered, and although she kept herself wrapped from head to foot in a long chaddar, she felt naked under his gaze. Still, there really was no other way for them to meet. The hotels were too risky in a city like Multan, because if she were spotted coming out of a hotel room, she'd be dead meat. No, this was the only way, a nondescript second-floor bedroom where they could forget the outside world for a couple of hours and just be themselves. Given how long Saqib's friend stayed away from Multan, it was a miracle the sheets smelled so fresh.

'Let's get married,' Saqib said, kissing her on the forehead. 'Enough of this sneaking about. We're not teenagers. We're adults, and we are fully entitled to get married and live an honest life. Nobody can stop us.'

Ayesha smiled, leaning into him. 'An honest life? That does sound like a good idea. Because all this sneaking about is getting a bit much. And if it's uncomfortable for you, just imagine how humiliating it must be for me to pass that rotund security guard each time we want to have sex.'

'Ayesha – you don't have to say the word.'

She sat up in bed, holding the sheet up to her chest. 'So you have no problem having sex, but calling it by its name makes you uneasy?'

'I only meant that I'd like to marry you, Ayesha! You seem to be on edge. What's up?'

She tried to steady herself. It was obvious why she was on edge. 'I'm sorry. It's that bastard Raza. I feel like I won't be able to be myself until I'm out of his shadow.'

Saqib sat up too. 'That's why I keep saying that we ought to get married. I earn enough money to keep a roof over our heads and with the sale of our land, we'll be able to move to that nice house I told you about. Hell, I say we move to Dubai or something. Let's say goodbye to this shithole.'

Ayesha looked around the barely furnished room and nodded. 'You're right. Enough of this. We should just get married. And I won't tell my parents first – they'll only try to stop us. We'll get married and then tell them it's done. I'm their only daughter. Surely, they won't disown me.'

'When two people are in love, all they need to worry about is each other. To hell with the rest of the world. Being in love is not a crime.'

They decided to make arrangements and tie the knot the following week, a good few months before her wedding with Raza Masood was scheduled. When they left the house, Ayesha held her head high, not caring that the chaddar fell from her head and shoulders. She didn't care that the security guard stared at her, scratching his round stomach as if he couldn't believe the audacity of a girl sneaking around for sex. Throwing caution to the wind, she took Saqib's hand and led him back to the house for a second round, not breaking eye contact with the security guard. She was going to show him that women didn't just exist for the pleasure of men, that they had desires of their own, and that right now, she was done listening to orders.

'Again?' Saqib asked, to which she just nodded.

If he was surprised by the urgency of her desire, he didn't show it. On the contrary, he lapped it up.

With Saqib, everything felt right. Their movements were so practised, everything so familiar, that it was hard not to envisage a life with him. She was irrevocably in love.

She felt a pang when they said goodbye outside the gate, as if her heart was so full it might burst from the pressure. Never before had she felt such love, such tenderness for Saqib. 'Do take care getting home,' she said, eyeing his light-blue Vespa. 'Multan's traffic is so bad. It's a wonder you manage with this blue devil.'

Saqib grinned at her. 'Soon I'll be upgrading to a car. Then there will be nothing to fear. Come now, give me a kiss.'

Ayesha pushed him away, laughing. 'You're in Multan, not Madrid. Now get lost.'

Behind them, the security guard's eyes widened. Ayesha waved at him.

Despite the claustrophobic heat of Multan, she breathed in deeply before climbing into her taxi. In fact, she was feeling upbeat enough to check the gazillion messages and missed calls she'd received from Raza while she'd been with Saqib. Scrolling through them, all she could do was frown. He wanted to see her at his friend's place on Sher Shah Road.

—Where are you?

—Where the hell are you, woman? Hussain has thrown a party for us and your presence is needed urgently.

—Don't panic, his wife is also here ;). Just get here asap.

—For God's sake, where are you? Get here now!

She couldn't go back home now even though all she wanted to do was take a shower and collapse into bed. She also knew that if she didn't go to the party, Raza would come to her home and drag her there. And her mother would let him.

'A slight change of plans,' she told the taxi driver. 'We need to go to Sher Shah Road.'

She pretended not to see the driver scowling at her. Right now, she had bigger fish to fry. Perhaps this would be her last meeting with Raza before she finally eloped with Saqib. Holding on to that thought, she rested her head against the window. This hope was the only thing sustaining her right now. Since the engagement, she had rarely met with Raza alone, preferring to see him only where there were plenty of other people around and physical contact between them was limited. He'd still managed to grope her numerous times and the very thought of his hands over her body again made her want to throw up. Someone like Raza Masood was not going to take her betrayal lying down. His revenge would be swift, but somehow she didn't care. She worked at a well-reputed charity organisation. She could access the press if she wanted to. The rich in this country may have plenty of influence, but everyone had their limits. Besides, Raza's father would never allow him to sully the family's name.

But, what about her family? Such a big step would have disastrous ramifications for her parents, and she'd be a fool to ignore that. She banged her head repeatedly against the headrest, thinking of a way to do this in which her parents didn't get hurt. Did her love for Saqib really trump everything?

It was more than that, though. What she didn't want was to be raped for the rest of her days, and that's what life would be like with Raza Masood.

It was early July, but the weather wasn't too oppressive. There was a hint of the monsoon rains in the air, the thick black clouds obscuring Multan's punishing sun. By the time they reached Sher Shah Road, there was a gentle breeze stirring the trees, and for a moment she wondered if this was what the Western world looked like. She'd heard stories of it always being overcast and windy in London, and right now, nothing sounded better to her. Her grandfather used to have an apartment in Mayfair back when there was money in the family, but like everything else, it had been taken away from them. Now all she was left with were photos of her parents vacationing in London as a young couple and her father's nostalgic tales of shopping on Sloane Street and in Harrods. She shook her head at the sight of Multan's sad-looking trees. They had layers of dust on their leaves from the months of drought that the city usually faced. The Western world probably looked nothing like this. Maybe she and Saqib could relocate to London after their marriage. It was a fool's hope since Saqib didn't even have a visa, and no prospect of acquiring one, but there was no harm in dreaming. She lowered the window and closed her eyes, allowing the sudden cool breeze to blow over her face as she imagined herself to be somewhere – anywhere – other than Multan.

The sun was setting in the sky by the time she arrived at

Hussain's place. Ignoring her mother's missed calls, she sent her a quick text explaining where she was and threw the phone inside her handbag without waiting for a reply. Her mother would probably be pleased that for once she was meeting Raza of her own volition. If only she knew where her daughter had been all afternoon. Ayesha thought back to all the places Saqib's hands had been and a warmth spread across her lower belly. She hadn't been able to take a shower afterwards, and Saqib's scent was still on her. Just as well. She breathed in deeply, relishing the musky scent on her skin.

The driver sped away as soon as he'd dropped her off, and in the absence of the car's headlights, the street seemed very eerie. Although large, Hussain's house was in a narrow street off Sher Shah Road and, with night falling, the darkness seemed to penetrate her very being. Not only was the house not illuminated, but the gate was shut and there were no cars parked outside.

How strange, she thought to herself, pushing the gate open. The iron creaked, but the gate slid open easily enough. Now she could see some lights inside, which helped steady her nerves. She exhaled the breath she didn't even know she was holding. Maybe it was a candle-lit dinner or something. She wouldn't put anything past Multanis. Like the rest of Pakistan, Western ideas were fast infiltrating Multan with people throwing baby showers and dance parties, which were unheard of twenty years ago.

There was Raza's Beemer parked in the driveway with a couple of other cars. *Not exactly a party*, she thought. The wind was picking up now, and Ayesha could feel the first droplets of rain on her face. Stretching her mouth into a fake smile, she knocked on the door.

No response.

Inside, she could hear the thump of music. Were they at it already? She knocked again, but when nobody came to open the door, she pulled on the door handle. It opened.

Inside, it was dark with shadows dancing on the ceiling. It was a kind of reception area with a staircase leading to the upper floors and doors dotted around. She got a whiff of something familiar, and her heart sank. Before she could turn around, Raza had wrapped one giant arm around her, deliberately pressing it against her breasts.

'My love,' he whispered. 'Late as usual.'

His breath stank of alcohol, his manner immediately unsettling her.

'You're drunk,' she told him.

'On you, babe.'

She struggled to free herself, but his grip was too strong.

'Raza, what is this? Have you called me here to bully me? Have you forgotten that I'm your fiancée? Get your hands off me at once.'

Raza was kissing the nape of her neck. 'Mmm, my gorgeous fiancée. I love you so much.' He turned her around, so that she was facing him. His drunken eyes were steeped in desire, but there was something else as well, something that looked like anger. She recoiled, but Raza's grip on her arm was firm. 'You know what you smell like, Ayesha?' He pulled her closer and buried his face in her chest. 'You smell like ... like sex. You reek of it.'

Ayesha could feel the blood rushing in her ears. 'What nonsense, Raza. How dare you! I came here straight from home.'

Raza tilted his head. 'Really? Because I called your mother and she said you weren't home and were out to meet friends. So which one is it?'

Ayesha tried again to break free from his grip. 'I am under no obligation to explain myself to you, but if you'll let me go, I will. I promise.' He was beginning to infuriate her. 'Is this how you treat your fiancée? With such contempt? If you do not let me go, I promise you that you'll regret it.'

Raza shook his head slowly. 'No, no, no, if I were to let you go, who's to say you won't go running off in the rain to God knows where? No, ma'am, you tell me now where you came from. As your fiancé, it is my right to know.' He pulled his mouth into a smile, but his eyes were hard. 'Have you been fooling around?'

Ayesha stopped breathing. Was he bluffing? Could he know where she'd just been? She shrugged, exhaling slowly. 'Well, I had to run an errand so I stopped over at a friend's place for a few minutes.'

'Minutes or hours? And what friend is this?'

Again, she wondered if he knew something. 'I'm not sure. I didn't count. Also, I don't think I need to tell you about each and every one of my friends.'

Again Raza's lips spread into something that resembled a smile, but it looked more like a grimace. 'You know, what? I could fuck you right here, right now, and nobody would blink an eye ... but where's the fun in that? No, girls like you are not meant to be ravaged. Because you know how to make passionate love. I can see it written all over your pretty face. You're a girl who knows how to keep a man happy. Girls like you ought to be savoured.' And he licked his lips.

'Thanks for reminding me what a misogynist you are.' Her tone was nonchalant, but inside she was scared out of her mind. Her stomach lurched, threatening to bring up the contents of her lunch. She feared that Raza would hear the way her heart was barrelling around in her chest. She steadied her breathing. 'Now, if you don't mind, I would like to leave. These threats of rape don't scare me, and this party is ridiculous.'

Raza's narrowed his eyes. 'Quite. Even if I were to rape you, what's to stop you running off to Saqib again and spreading your legs for him for the umpteenth time?' His face broke into a wicked grin. 'Wasn't that where you were all afternoon? All of last month? Banging Saqib into oblivion?'

Ayesha winced. 'I don't know what you're talking about.' *How could he have known?*

It was as if she'd asked the question aloud. His eyes gleamed in the semi-darkness as he laughed. 'That security guard you tip to keep your secrets gets much bigger tips from me. Did you think I wouldn't find out? Multan is a very small place, my love.' He exhaled. 'I waited and I waited, hoping that you would see the error of your ways, but nope. It's like you were born a whore.'

The nausea was building up. This bastard seemed to know everything. What had she gotten herself into? She'd have clapped her palm against her forehead if she could move it freely. It was beyond foolish of her to come here tonight. She looked around, but there didn't seem to be anyone else in the house.

'Raza, please let me go. Let's take some time to think things through, and then we can meet again.'

Far from releasing her, Raza's grip intensified. But his eyes had a faraway look to them. 'I can't bear to see you opening your legs for that bastard, but how can I prevent it? *Gushtis* like you will let nothing stand in their way. I mean, there is a way to put a stop to this, but...'

Ayesha watched him in horror, her heart threatening to pound out of her throat. 'Can you even hear yourself? You're barking mad. Let me go or I'll call the police.'

'And tell them what? That you fucked a guy twice this afternoon? I'd like to see who the police believe. Do you think they'll use the two-finger method on you?' His smirk widened into something alien, something inhuman. 'Oops, my bad. That's for virgins, not seasoned sluts like you.'

'Raza, please,' she whispered, trying to tug free. 'I'll do anything you want. Just don't harm me. I am your future wife.'

'Damn, you're so calculating,' he breathed. 'I can't believe I didn't see it before. You deserve a punishment worse than death for throwing my love away like that.'

Held so tight, and out of ideas of how to convince Raza to let her go, Ayesha did the only other thing she could think of: she screamed. As loud as she could.

It made no difference. She was sure there was no one to hear her. But then a couple of Raza's cronies came sprinting out of the room in the far corner, throwing the door wide open with a bang. Bright white light flooded into the room, illuminating Raza's features, making them look more crazed than ever.

One of the men – Hussain – inched closer, his arms spread out in front of him. 'Listen, man,' he murmured. 'This is my house. Let's not have any drama here. We've got neighbours.'

Ayesha nodded. 'Please listen to him, Raza. Let's talk about this later, shall we? I promise to make it up to you.' She was going to do no such thing. Her plan was to escape to Lahore with Saqib right this moment, everything else be damned. Raza was deranged.

'*Oye hoye*, a couple drama, is it? I do love it when these rich people argue.' A woman clad in a silk shalwar kameez with garish makeup hurried over to them. She was holding hands with a man Ayesha didn't recognise. Nudging a younger woman who stood next to her, she added, '*Haye* Chandni, would you look at that glowing skin? That's what you get when you're rich.'

Chandni didn't seem to be enjoying herself. Her eyes were lowered and she was fussing with the hem of her own kameez. 'I want to go home, Rasheeda Baji.'

'Go home?' Rasheeda echoed. 'And miss this drama? I think not. Besides, what home are you talking about? Do you want to go back to that *gushti* Mehreen who sells our bodies to strangers? Aren't you happy in this rich man's home?' She leaned into the man she was holding hands with, kissing his neck. '*Kyun* hero, how about you show me some action again? You know you want to.'

Ayesha watched everything around her in horror. These women were nobody's wives. She turned her head to Raza, who was still holding her. 'You should be ashamed of yourself for calling me here. How dare you!'

'Oye, how dare *you*?' In a split second, Rasheeda had slapped her across the face. 'We are women same as you. Just like you, we spread our legs for men. The only difference is that you spread them willingly, while we consider it work.' Turning back, she winked at her man. 'Of course, Sami, I don't mean you. For you, I'd never close these legs. Open house forever.' Rasheeda laughed savagely. 'Chandni here is learning. In many ways, she's still a green little girl from Vehari, but I daresay she's got a lot of juice in her.'

'She sure does,' Raza said. 'Look at those jugs.'

Rasheeda shrieked with laughter. 'Hear that, Chandni? Rich boy likes your jugs. That's an additional ten thousand rupees to touch them though, Sahab.'

Ayesha wanted to disappear. She tried once more to pull herself free. 'Raza, let me go. You're welcome to enjoy yourself with these ... these women.'

'But, I want you, Ayesha.'

'Raza, please me go,' she replied, her mouth set in a firm line. 'Be the bigger man for once.'

Despair flashed across Raza's features, his eyes brimming with tears for the first time. 'In my own way, I did love you, you know. I loved you so much that it hurts.' He touched his chest. 'Right here.'

'Of course. As do I.' Her gaze flitted to the entrance, and to her horror, Raza noticed.

Hi expression hardened. 'Thinking of running away, are we?' Far from loosening his hold on her, he intensified it, causing Ayesha to yelp in pain. 'Come with me.'

He dragged her towards a sitting room, where the light from the TV cast a blue halo on everything. Ayesha tried to resist, putting all her strength into breaking free, but it seemed like she would sooner dislocate her shoulder than be able to extricate herself from Raza's grip.

Hussain followed them, his arms still held up like a referee's. 'I know what you're thinking of doing, Raza. Please don't. Not in my home.'

Ayesha craned her neck to look at Hussain. 'What do you mean? What is he trying to do?'

'I'm out of here,' said Sami, backing away.

'Don't be a spoilsport, *Jaanu*,' Rasheeda said. 'Let Raza Sahab have some fun with his girl. Let's see him wipe that smirk off her face. She deserves it, doesn't she, Chandni?'

Chandni looked like she might burst into tears. 'Nobody deserves that. Stop this, please.'

'Deserve what?' Ayesha squawked. 'What is he planning to do with me? Hussain, tell me now!'

When he didn't answer, she followed his gaze, which was focused on the table and a half-empty bottle of wine. What was Raza going to do? Get her drunk? She almost laughed, but the sound died in her throat as another, more terrifying thought entered her mind. Unless he was planning to...

'You wouldn't!' she cried, desperately trying to free herself. She beat Raza's chest with her fist. 'Let me go. Hussain, stop him.'

'Raza, you can't! Not in my house.'

Chandni whimpered. 'Rasheeda Baji, we must stop him. This is wicked.'

Raza's fingers curled around the bottle. He lifted it and held it up to the light. 'Don't you see?' he whispered. 'If I don't do this, then you'll continue to be the way you are. If you cannot be mine, then I want to make sure that you'll be no one else's.'

The room swayed around her, her legs threatening to give way. 'Raza, please don't. I'll do anything. Just don't do this.'

'I have to. What would people think if I let my fiancée continue cheating on me? What kind of man would that make me?' He raised the bottle higher. 'Such a beautiful face. It's almost a pity ... almost.'

Ayesha's eyes widened. 'Raza, don't you dare—'

'Raza, don't,' Hussain began. 'Do it outside.'

Indecision flickered on Raza's face. Ayesha saw it, latched on to it. 'If you do this today, Raza, you will regret it for the rest of your life. There is no coming back from this. I promise I'll be good to you...'

'Is that what you tell your disgusting boyfriend too? That you'll be a good girl?'

'Don't ruin the girl's life,' Chandni cried. 'Have a heart, Sahab.'

The veins in Raza's neck stood out, his forehead dripping sweat as the bottle trembled in his hand. 'I ... I don't know...'

'Raza, if you do this, so help me...'

The rest of the words died in her throat as the liquid splashed from the bottle just as Hussain's hands reached towards her face – to protect her or put her in harm's way, she didn't know. She jerked away from the contents of the bottle, as far as she could crane her neck...

Acid.

She knew before it hit her skin that her life was damaged beyond repair, that she might not even survive. The acid splashed all over the right side of her face and neck, searing and melting her skin, the rivulets sinking deep into her flesh, right down to her chest. For a moment, she felt nothing, but then, every nerve in her body came alive, and the pain she felt was beyond anything she had ever experienced.

Blinded by it, she screamed. It was an inhuman sound, like the roar of an animal dying. Beside her, Hussain shouted too as some of the acid landed on his fingers. She saw Raza's eyes pop as he realised what he'd done, and in the confusion, he released her.

'You *gu-ushti*,' he stammered. 'You deserve it. Now, no one will ever touch you, you bloody freak. Serves you right. Look at your face.'

'You have lost your bloody mind,' Hussain shrieked, rubbing his hands across the sofa to remove the acid. His skin and flesh peeled away instead. He screamed again. 'You bastard!'

Raza backed away. His face was ashen, but there was also a gleam of victory in his eyes.

Ayesha felt like something was eating her alive, but in a strange way, she also felt nothing at all, as if it was all just a bad dream, and the numbing pain on the side of her face was just an illusion.

She knew better than that. She had read the horror stories of women mutilated beyond belief, and she knew that the same thing was now happening to her. She couldn't breathe. The acid was probably melting her nerves right now, which was why the pain had dulled.

In a moment of respite, she leaped up from the sofa. She raised her hand to touch her wounded face, but stopped herself. Instead, she made a run for the main door. Pulling it open, she felt the spray of the monsoon rain on her face.

She'd never been more grateful for rain.

Staggering out in the garden, she let the rain fall on her face.

She let the rain fall on her face until her knees buckled and she fell onto the cool earth.

She let the rain fall on her face until she didn't know where her tears ended and where the rain began.

And then, nothing. Just darkness.

Kamil

It was Madiha's Instagram photo that did it. He had been meaning to delete the blasted app for weeks, but something would always stop him. Now, he wished he had. It caused him more pain than he ever could have imagined to see Madiha sporting an engagement ring given to her by someone who wasn't him. She'd posted a photo of the two of them in Hyde Park, Madiha dressed in a traditional golden outfit with a net dupatta on her head as she gazed in wonder at the diamond rock on her finger.

Rab ne bana di jodi ... with the love of my life, Dilshad.

Kamil scoffed at the caption. So much for not dating Pakistani men anymore. With bulging muscles and a trim waist, Dilshad seemed more suited to a photo shoot in a gym rather than a park. He stood next to her, seemingly admiring the stupid ring as well. What was it with Pakistanis and their unshakeable love for diamonds? Both men and women.

He swore, reported the photo out of sheer spite, and then proceeded to unfollow Madiha and delete the app – for real this time. It felt good to have done something productive, even if it was to falsely report Madiha's photo. He doubted it would be taken down, but he wouldn't be hanging around to find out.

'Is it that older woman again?' his mother asked from across the room. She'd been rolling the beads of her *tasbee* constantly since she learned of Kamil's breakup with Madiha. He had no idea his mother had been so attached to that '*ajeeb larki*' – that strange girl. But he imagined Madiha to be far better than Safiya in his mother's eyes.

'It's not Safiya, Ammi. And she's not old. She's only forty.'

'Might as well be fifty-eight for all the children she will give you. Why couldn't you find someone your own age, Kamil? Someone you could actually have kids with?'

'Ammi, I am thirty-five. And, you can't say stuff like this. You're being ageist.' He was trying hard not to laugh. 'Also, can you stop prying into my private life? I don't remember telling you about her.'

'Uff, I meant someone in her late twenties or something. That Safiya is probably fifty years old. They all lie about their age on the internet.' She flicked her hand at him. 'What is a mother's job if not to pry?'

Kamil ignored her. It was true that he had been back in touch with Safiya. He wouldn't go as far as to call it dating, but it was something close. In a strange way, Safiya settled him – grounded him. She listened to him when nobody else would. He'd only met her a few times after that first date and nothing had happened between them yet as far as sex went. He hadn't even told her about his past yet, and she hadn't brought up the domestic support group again. Not yet, anyway.

'Making out is overrated,' Safiya had told him, yawning. 'I'd rather get to know you before you slobber all over me.' When Kamil protested at the rude term, Safiya had given him a middle finger. 'I'm not a virgin, Kamil. I've been around. I know exactly what men want, so spare me the lecture.'

That is what he loved about Safiya. She was so nonchalant about everything. Nothing affected her, not even when he talked to her about Madiha.

'I don't know her, but sounds like it was all your fault. You men are all the same.'

Kamil hadn't protested to that in case he got another middle finger.

He looked up to see his mother staring daggers at him. 'What now?' he asked, laughing.

'If it wasn't for Sharmeela, I wouldn't have known you were seeing this woman. I want grandkids, Kamil. I am not dying without seeing my grandchild's face.'

Bloody Shar, Kamil thought. He ought to reveal *her* secret, that would teach her a lesson.

'Maybe Sharmeela will be the one to give you a grandchild, Ammi.'

His mother slapped her palm against her forehead. 'I'd be surprised if that girl knew how babies are made. She's always so busy counting money at the bank.'

Kamil narrowed his eyes at his mother in mock concentration. 'How *are* babies made? Do tell, Ammi.'

Jamila took the chappal off her foot and aimed it at him. '*Haramzada!*'

Kamil ducked as the chappal hit the wall behind him. 'Oh Ammi, you do make me laugh. And working in a bank doesn't just mean counting notes.'

Jamila's eyebrows knit together in a frown. 'Make fun of me all you want, but when you are old and frail with no children to support you, you will remember my words. Of course, that *aurat* will be dead long before you. You will be all alone, Kamil. I despair. Sometimes, I wish I could get a nice girl from Pakistan to come over and be your wife. And maybe a nice man for Sharmeela too while I'm at it.'

'Don't let Shar hear you say that,' said Kamil. 'And besides, women live much longer than men.'

He was relieved when he heard the familiar tread of his father descending the stairs. He was going to save him from this onslaught.

'Sometimes I wish you hadn't retired, Ji,' her mother immediately announced as her husband entered the living room and took the armchair. 'The children listened to you more when you were working.'

Akbar Khan may have been in his seventies, but he was still robust and agile, and hadn't let age mellow him. He'd been an accomplished police officer, stern and unforgiving, except when it came to his wife. He indulged her in a way he hadn't his own children. Kamil had lost count of the times his father had been cross with him, but it was as if his anger melted the moment he set eyes on his wife.

Leaning back in the armchair, he said, 'Don't you like having me around, Begum? We get a chance to spend so much time together, something we couldn't do with my job and the kids.' Nodding at her, he added, 'Tell me, don't you enjoy it when we sit together, knee to knee, watching movies and whatnot.'

'Watching late-night movies together, are we?' Kamil asked, turning to his mother.

She reddened, but couldn't stop the smile from erupting across her face. 'At least have some shame, Ji. Saying such things in front of your grown son. What would he think?'

'He would think that his parents are in love, and he'll love them for it,' Kamil replied.

'There's no such thing as love. Just companionship. That's the bedrock of every marriage.'

Akbar Khan shook his head. 'Pigs will fly before your mother acknowledges love, Kamil. She can't help herself, can you Jamila Begum?'

Kamil could see his mother chewing her tongue, trying to stop herself from talking back. She said plenty to her husband when she thought her children weren't listening, but in their presence, she tried her best to respect her husband. As if Kamil and Shar cared about such obsolete customs.

'I better go,' Kamil announced, rising from his seat. 'Plenty to do today.'

His mother turned to him, her previous anger forgotten. 'Would you like me to come back to your flat with you? I could cook a week's worth of meals. I don't like you living there all alone. It keeps me up at night.'

His father looked up from his newspaper, the skin around his eyes creased. 'He's thirty-five, Begum, not three. You don't need to spoon-feed him.'

His mother had a hand on her chest. 'I just worry for him, that's all. Single at this age. Sometimes, I wish what happened to you hadn't happened. Things would be so much simpler. Don't you think so, Kamil?'

Kamil waited for his father to intervene, but even he didn't have anything to say this time; his eyes stayed on his newspaper, even though he clearly wasn't reading anything.

Kamil looked out of the window. He wasn't going to answer his mother's question, because it was a question he'd been asking himself for years.

Safiya laughed when he recounted the incident to her, making sure to exclude his mother's more savage remarks about her.

'Your mother sounds like so much fun,' she said. 'I'd love to meet her someday. Both your parents.'

'My father isn't very sociable,' Kamil muttered. 'You'll be bored to death. All he does is read the newspaper. And my mother ... She's very feisty, I'm afraid.'

'I'll be the judge of that.'

They were walking from Euston Station towards Gower Street. True to its reputation, the British summer had disappeared without warning, leaving cold gusts of wind in its wake. It took ages for the crossing light to turn green, and even then, they had to pause to let crowds of impatient people pass first. Kamil buttoned up his denim jacket. As they crossed the road, Safiya took his hand.

He stiffened, but then allowed himself to relax. For a moment, he wanted to shake her off and run back to Madiha, but then he remembered her Instagram post and his mood soured.

'You mother is right, by the way,' Safiya said, her head brushing against his shoulder as they paused in front of a white-washed hotel. Was she resting her head on his shoulder? It turned out that she was. Kamil held his breath, counting to ten before releasing it. It was going to be okay. 'I will be forty-one next month. Time is marching on. I may be only five years older than you, but in the eyes of society I might as well be as old as your mother. And while the idea of having kids isn't that important to me, I have to acknowledge that I only have a few years left to have them.'

'Mmm,' Kamil replied, his mind still on Safiya's body language. They hadn't even had sex yet, and here she was pretending to be his wife and talking about kids. 'I don't understand society's obsession with age, and I find it frustrating that we haven't outgrown these ideas, even here in London. I'm not too bothered about our age difference.'

Safiya lifted her head from his shoulder. 'You don't need to do me any favours, you know,' she scoffed. Then before he could respond, she pressed his hand. 'Sorry, I didn't mean to snap. It's not your fault, and you don't need to say anything. It's still early days. Let's try and get to know each other first. Besides, Pakistani people are the same everywhere. Some things will never change.'

They walked on in silence. Safiya was beginning to make him nervous. Almost on cue, it started to drizzle, not a deluge, but enough to make him uncomfortable as the pitter patter landed on his head, ruining the hair he'd painstakingly arranged.

'Good God, does it ever stop raining on this damp island?' he exclaimed. 'Perhaps we'd be better off in Pakistan, after all.'

'I can feel your palm sweating, you know. What are you really mad at?'

Damn her.

'You know Matt's support group is on Gower Street? We could drop by after lunch. I think they're meeting today.'

Was that why she'd brought him this way?

'No, thank you.' Kamil had to force the words out. Why did Safiya think he needed a domestic-abuse support group? There was nothing wrong with him.

'You don't need to have anything wrong with you to want to

join a support group,' Safiya added, seeming to read his thoughts. Before he could respond, she released his hand and turned to him. 'Look at me.'

They stood facing each other in the middle of the pavement. He could feel himself sweating. 'This feels weird.'

Safiya stared at him. 'You need help, Kamil. I don't know what kind of burden you're carrying, but it was obvious to me the first time I met you that you needed help in letting go. Your nonchalance doesn't fool me. And if you're wondering why we haven't had sex yet, this is the reason. I don't *know* you.'

That is exactly what Madiha had said to him. Why did people say that about him?

Her gaze softened. 'You can tell me, you know.'

'What makes you think I need help? For someone who has only known me a few weeks, you seem to be awfully familiar with my life.'

It was Safiya's turn to sweat. He could see a bead of it running down her forehead. It could have been a raindrop, but he swore, he saw some droplets gathering on her upper lip. 'I may have looked you up,' she murmured.

He flinched as if someone had punched him. 'What? Looked me up where?'

Safiya couldn't meet his eye. 'Your Facebook profile isn't as private as you think. I saw some of your tagged photos from years ago, and once I saw the name of what looked like your ... umm ... ex-wife. It wasn't that difficult to put two and two together. We all...'

His heart thudding in his throat, Kamil tried to look away, but it was as if he had nowhere else to look. 'You're probably mistaking me for someone else,' he sputtered.

'I know what it's like to suffer in a relationship. I've been through it all, and that's why I gave you the details for the support group. If you refuse to do anything about the pain inside you, it will fester and eventually overwhelm you.'

Her confession took him by surprise. 'You never told me, Safiya. I don't know what to say. I'm ... sorry.'

She blinked back tears. 'I conquered my pain, Kamil. You can too. Get help. You're lonely. Don't you see that? Don't you want someone you can spend your life with?'

How could he tell her that the moment he entered his flat, he could feel the walls closing in. As a compact studio flat in the heart of Earl's Court, the hustle and bustle should be enough to keep anyone company, but he felt so alone, as if life had truly lost its meaning for him. He'd watch television, but his mind would often be vacant. How could he admit that he was desperately lonely, and as much as he would like to be with someone, the reason why he couldn't commit was his traumatic past. He didn't know where to start unravelling that particular thread, so he didn't even bother. He let his past haunt him rather than facing it head on.

He was a coward, and Safiya had figured it out.

Summoning all the brightness he could muster in his voice, he said, 'Nice day for a coffee, don't you think?'

Safiya's face fell, and he could feel her drawing away from him. 'I don't have time for a coffee. I'll see you around, I guess.' She turned away from him without another word.

As she walked away, Kamil couldn't help but notice how much she looked like Arooj, his ex-wife. The very thought sent a shudder through him.

Ayesha

Beep. Beep. Beep.

Ayesha tried to block out the sound, but it was insistent. It was trying to wake her, but she didn't want to leave the comforting embrace of sleep. The world was an ugly place, and she wanted nothing to do with it.

'Ayesha, *beta*, open your eyes.'

That was her father, but he sounded so unlike himself. His usual authoritative tone was gone, replaced by a sort of pleading. She heard him sob, and her heart threatened to break. Why was he crying? Her father never cried.

'Look at the tears sliding out of her eyes,' someone whispered. Her mother, perhaps. 'She can hear us, Ji. I am sure she can. The doctors have said that she's been stable for days. She's just sleeping. Take heart in that and wipe away your tears. I'll call the doctor.'

Doctor? Why would she need a doctor? Her mind galloped from thought to thought, never staying in one place. It was as if she didn't want to remember what had happened to her, but of course she remembered. Before she knew it, it all came crashing back with such force that she opened her eyes.

'Abbu,' she whispered, her eyes finding her father's tear-stained face.

'*Meri bachi*,' her father wept. 'Look at what they've done to you. The monsters.'

Her face was numb, her body in shock, but she could remember what had happened to her clear as day. What monsters was her father talking about? There was only one.

His name was Raza.

'Check the airways and her breathing,' the doctor had shouted when she'd been brought into Nishtar Hospital. She had no recollection of the journey there, whether she'd arrived in an ambulance or in someone's car. All she knew was pain. It was as if her face and neck were on fire. The rain had washed away much of the acid, but the nursing staff still spent a lot of time washing her face with water and saline.

The pain was such that she went in and out of consciousness, barely aware of what the doctors were doing to her. The only thing she remembered clearly was the pity on one doctor's face when he said, 'Bastards, the people who do this to girls. She'll wear these scars for life.'

She looked around the room, only now registering how much it must have cost her parents to book a private room. Holding up her arms, she noticed how pale they looked. 'How long have I been in the hospital?'

'Several days. You were in shock when you were brought in. They had to sedate you and then treat the affected area as best they could.' He broke down again, just as her mother returned. 'Maybe you're still in shock. They wouldn't let us near you earlier in case you caught an infection. You're still very vulnerable.' Her father wiped his face with a tissue. 'I need to step outside ... I need a moment.'

'Don't touch your wounds,' her mother said as soon as the door closed. 'The skin grafts are still pretty new. They've given you a lot of antibiotics and painkillers, so you'll be feeling woozy.'

One look at her mother and Ayesha saw she knew. It was written all over her face. Her mother knew exactly who had done this to her. The dam of emotions inside her threatened to break. 'Ammi,' she sobbed, holding out her arms, yearning for some human contact after days of being in isolation.

To her credit, her mother didn't cry. She enveloped her in her arms, careful not to touch the affected area. Ayesha couldn't feel the wounds – and guessed she must have been given a lot of pain-killers. Still, there was an odd comfort to be had in her mother's embrace. Something in her calmed.

'Don't say a word about who attacked you,' her mother whispered in her ear. 'If you value your life, our lives, you will not say a word, Ayesha. You accuse Raza now, and you might as well be digging all our graves.'

'What?' She couldn't keep her voice down. 'Ammi, what are you talking about? How could you say such a thing?'

'Do not underestimate them. He's too powerful. Very well protected. Pointing fingers will only damage you and your reputation.' Her voice threatened to break, but she composed herself. 'They are already spreading nasty rumours about you. You must lie when the doctor and police arrive. Lie to your father, lie to everyone. You must do this. Stick to the story I have told them: you were attacked by some rogue boys on the street. If Raza can ruin your face, he can also take your life. As I said, do not underestimate him.'

Her eyes were still raw from the acid vapours, so she was surprised when tears slid down her cheeks. She could have wrapped her head around being betrayed by other people, but her own mother?

'It's our lot, us women,' her mother continued. 'We have always made sacrifices, and to survive in this country, that tradition must continue. You must do this for yourself, Ayesha. For us.'

'Can't you see what he's done to me?' she cried, pushing her mother away. 'How can you be so selfish?'

'If you ruin them, don't for one minute think they'll let you settle down with Saqib. They'll chase the two of you to the ends of the earth. Stay silent and we may yet get out of this alive.' Her mother backed away, her eyes pleading. 'Ayesha, please!'

'What is she talking about?' her father asked, coming back into the room, his face still pink from the tears. 'How are you being selfish? And what's this about Saqib?'

'She's gravely injured, Ji. She doesn't know what she's saying. I say we talk to the police ourselves. There is no need to involve her. Our daughter is so fragile. Always has been.'

'Our daughter is the strongest woman I know. She has worked with abuse victims for years. She can speak for herself. I believe in her.'

'Let's be serious, Ji. Our daughter is sitting here with acid thrown on her face, and you're discussing her work?'

'Why must you underestimate your own daughter?'

'Why must you overestimate her?'

Before her father could answer, there was a sharp knock on the door.

'What now? Don't tell me it's the police already.' Ishrat sighed. 'Yes, come in.'

The door opened to reveal Rabbiya Masood.

And behind her, to Ayesha's horror, her son.

'Is it okay to come in?' Rabbiya asked, her face a mask of worry.

A large bouquet obscured Raza's face, but Ayesha would have recognised those hands anywhere. Those were the hands that had doused her with acid.

An involuntary gasp escaped her.

'Rabbiya Ji, what a pleasant surprise,' her father said. It seemed to her as if he was speaking from a great distance. 'I'm surprised they let you in. Ayesha is not ready for visitors yet.'

Almost immediately, her heart rate began to climb, her ears ringing. She could feel a burning sensation creep down the right side of her face all the way to her neck. She remembered her skin coming apart, melting away. It made her feel light-headed.

'What is he doing here?' Her breathing was shallow, her voice coming out as a rasp. 'Tell him to leave.'

Her mother bulged her eyes at her in warning, before plastering a smile on her face. 'He's your fiancé, *beta*. Of course, he would want to check up on you.' She turned to Rabbiya. 'Even in this state, my daughter worries about you inconveniencing yourselves.'

Rabbiya's mouth thinned. 'I see. We were most distraught to hear about her ... injuries. Our Raza has been absolutely beside himself with worry, so naturally I had to come and see for myself.'

She assumed an expression of concern. 'Don't worry, I am not carrying any infection, if that's what you're worried about. My husband is out of the country on important business, but he sends his regards. As you know, he has a soft spot for Ayesha. He was most distressed when he heard.'

'Of course,' Safdar Khan replied, his head bowed. 'We understand, *behen*. Masood Sahab has been most kind to us.'

Rabbiya inched towards Ayesha. 'Perhaps I could take a closer look?' With a forefinger she turned Ayesha's face first left and then right, clucking her tongue as she did so. 'Poor girl. Her face will be quite a sight. All these bandages and God only knows the number of surgeries she'll require later on.'

'Her face is largely unaffected,' her mother said. 'The injuries are mostly on her neck.'

'You need new prescription glasses, Ishrat,' Rabbiya whispered, pink tongue between her teeth as she leaned to observe Ayesha more closely. 'Her face is ruined. Look at the shape of her nose. Look at where the droplets have spattered near her chest. These marks will turn black with time. Try explaining them away at her wedding.'

'The damage is quite extensive, isn't it, Mama?' Raza spoke up, but there was a tremor in his voice. 'Look at the state of her.'

Ayesha sucked in a breath. Even his voice was like an assault. 'Get him out of here,' she said.

Rabbiya sniffed. 'Looks like her tongue is intact, at least. What a shame. I know you've never really liked me, Ayesha, but I really am heartbroken. No one deserves to suffer like this.' Ayesha thought she saw a flicker of pity pass across her face, but it was gone in an instant, and her expression once again suited the designer outfit and glittering diamonds. Rabbiya Masood had come to make a statement. Standing away from Ayesha's bedside, she put a hand on Ishrat's shoulder. 'It cannot be easy for you to see Ayesha like this, and it really pains me to break this to you during this time, but this *rishta* cannot go on. I am here to break things off. My husband forbade me to tell you this given how much you are suffering, but I don't believe in giving people false hope. I never have. You can't expect us to put up with someone so ... damaged. I'm sorry.'

Ayesha's head sank back into the pillows. She had never felt more relieved in her life. She wouldn't have to marry the bastard.

Ishrat gasped. 'My daughter is lying here, fighting for her life, and you come to us with this news? You cannot be serious.'

'I've never been more serious in my life.'

'You know full well why she is damaged. How could you?'

'Please don't make it more difficult than it is already, I beg you. Don't make me open my mouth.'

'To say what?' shouted her mother. Ayesha looked at her in wonder. Her eyes was bloodshot, but her face was blazing with anger. 'Spit it out, Rabbiya.'

Rabbiya's mouth pinched. 'Then so be it. You see, the damage runs deeper than her skin, Ishrat. There is other, more alarming news that has come to light.'

'The damage isn't that extensive, though, Mama—' Raza began, but Rabbiya cut him off.

'Be quiet, Raza. You've said and done enough, don't you think? Now let your mother speak.'

'But Mama, we should postpone our decision until the bandages are off. Surely—'

'I said *shut up*!'

It took some effort, but Ayesha lifted her head again to see what was happening. While her father's head was still bowed, her mother was visibly shaking.

'I have been keeping this a secret, Rabbiya,' Ishrat said, 'and this is how you repay me? You cannot do this to us. Breaking things off at this point will send the wrong message to everyone in Multan. You will be ruining my daughter's life. You've already ruined her face. Don't test me.'

Even from a distance, Ayesha could see Rabbiya's grip on her mother's shoulder tighten.

'You are the one who shouldn't test me, Ishrat. All the luxuries you've recently come to enjoy can easily be taken away. Be grateful we are not withdrawing our support. I didn't want to say these words in front of your husband, but you've forced me.' She drew herself to her full height. 'Not only is Ayesha damaged beyond repair, she's not even a virgin.'

Her father's head shot up. 'Excuse me? What did you just say?'

'Just go away,' Ayesha whispered, but nobody heard her.

Rabbiya's face gleamed with triumph. 'Rumours are swirling all over the city that your daughter has been seeing some ragamuffin from God knows where in a secret house. We are absolutely disgusted. Sleeping around isn't something we approve of. If we weren't in polite company, I'd say more.'

Ishrat laughed. 'This ceased being polite company some time ago. Don't hold back on our account.'

'I would suggest you take yourself, your son and your ugly tongue out of this room,' her father said. 'Make yourself scarce before I throw you out. Nobody gets to malign my daughter.'

'Your daughter is a little *gushti*, Safdar. And do you know what they call men who enable harlots?' Rabbiya bared her teeth. 'They're called *dallay*. Are you a pimp? Your daughter opens her legs for men and you count the notes?'

'Given the kind of language you use, I'm not surprised your son turned out the way he did,' Ishrat said, matching Rabbiya's tone and removing her hand from her shoulder.

Her father had turned scarlet. 'Get the hell out of this room! I regret the day I agreed to this *rishta*. I should have listened to my daughter.' He turned to Raza. 'Take your mother out now before I come to regret my actions.'

Rabbiya lifted a shaking finger. 'Let's see how loud you shout when we withdraw our support. I'll see how this tongue wags when you're starving.'

'You will do no such thing,' Ishrat replied. 'You put one toe out of line, and you know what I can do, and believe me, you don't want to test people who have nothing left to lose. I will expose you.'

Rabbiya screeched with laughter. 'You have no proof, dimwit.'

'Are you willing to take that risk?'

'You're just as calculating as your daughter, aren't you?'

Ayesha looked at her mother with renewed wonder. There wasn't an ounce of fear left on her face, only a wild determination to protect her daughter.

They had been backed into a corner, her and her parents. And Ayesha knew only one way to get them out. 'I will testify against him.' She met Raza's eyes. 'You know I will, and so will Hussain. He can't be happy with what you've done to him.'

Rabbiya laughed, adjusting the dupatta back on her shoulder. 'Be my guest. I'd like to see you being paraded around in the courts. You'd be a laughing stock, that is if someone even deigns to glance at you. As for Hussain, it was an unfortunate accident. He shouldn't have been playing around with dangerous substances. The boy's been foolish, but we've made sure he's learned his lesson. If anyone is guilty, it's him.'

Ishrat lifted a finger in Rabbiya's direction. 'Rabbiya, I am warning you. You cannot—'

Rabbiya took her son's hand. 'Consider this *rishta* over.'

'*Gushti*,' her father muttered as soon as they left.

To Ayesha's surprise, her usually stoic mother burst into tears. 'Our daughter is ruined. Everything is ruined.'

Her grandmother had always said, 'In Pakistan, a woman's appearance is her most valuable asset. It is also her honour. She must guard it with her life.'

She had heard many variations of this statement all her life, but she'd always dismissed the idea. Surely, no society could be so shallow as to judge a woman solely on her appearance, but now she realised just how true it all was. It was as if her world had imploded overnight. She'd gone from being a beautiful woman to a creature to be pitied and gawked at, like an animal in the zoo.

She'd only been to the hospital a few times in her life, to see various sick relatives, but her principal memory was of the time she spent there with her *dadi*. Her grandmother had pneumonia, and after a time, it had become obvious that she wasn't going to survive. Ayesha remembered how they'd brought her to the hospital walking, but within days, it became a struggle for her to even take a few steps before getting out of breath. After that, it was a wheelchair for her until she died.

In a way, she too would leave the hospital a shadow of her former self.

Many people came to visit her – none of them Saqib. In the early days, the pain was so intense and her vision was so blurred from the fumes of the acid that had reached her eyes, that she wasn't able to think straight. Seeing Raza's face hadn't helped matters, neither did the knowledge that he had got away scot-free. Long after her parents had gone to sleep, she would lie awake, staring at the ceiling, her lips pressed together against the pain, helpless tears sliding into her hair as the reality of her situation hit her.

Life as she knew it had changed. From now on, she would only be viewed through a prism of either pity or disgust. Nobody would see the real her, the Ayesha that used to be, and that cut deeper than her physical pain.

She did have a few visits from the police. Initially, she wasn't in any fit state to talk, and she saw little point in engaging with them knowing their reputation, but then the deputy superintendent of police, Amna Habib, arrived to see her. Dressed in olive-green trousers with the shirt tucked in, the badges on her shoulders catching the light, DSP Amna Habib cut an impressive figure. Perceptive as ever, DSP Amna took one look at Ayesha's mother, and sent her to the canteen to have some tea.

Her mother resisted, but Amna was firm. 'Mrs Safdar, you need the distraction. You've been cooped up in here for too long. Go and have some tea in the hospital gardens. Get some fresh air. I would like to speak with Ayesha alone, if that's okay.'

Her mother twisted the edge of her dupatta in her hands, and with one final, pleading look at Ayesha, she left.

As soon as the door closed, DSP Amna stepped closer, her face betraying not even a hint of emotion. She seemed to be in her early forties, her hair tied in a tight bun, a neutral expression on her face. Ayesha thought she must have seen things far worse than an acid attack.

'Ayesha,' she said, her voice gentle. 'I am very sorry that this happened to you, and I wanted to assure you that we are doing everything we can to bring the perpetrator to justice.' She paused for a moment, looking in the distance before exhaling. 'That is the speech I am trained to give victims, and we both know it's rubbish.' Her eyes found Ayesha's. 'In order to help you, I need to know who did this to you?'

Tears welled in Ayesha's eyes and she looked away.

'You needn't protect him, Ayesha. Just tell me who did this to you. We have been hearing rumours, but I want confirmation from you. You know that you can fight this, don't you? The majority of the police in this country may be corrupt, but I am not one of them. I want to help you. Men who do this to women need to be brought to justice or this will never end.'

He has damaged your face for now, but how long until he kills you? You expose him, and you might as well be signing all our death warrants. The Masood family does not forgive.

Her mother's words swirled in Ayesha's mind, preventing her from saying anything. Besides, what could Amna do? She had said herself that the police were corrupt. There was a limit to the protection she could give Ayesha, and what would happen if she was transferred to another city? Very few abuse victims ever got justice. Ayesha wasn't a fool. She'd worked in the charity business long enough to know that for most justice was merely an illusion.

'Over one thousand women have suffered such attacks in recent years in Pakistan alone. Won't you be their voice, Ayesha?'

'I didn't see his face, madam. It was too dark.'

'But what were you doing in an unknown place in the dead of night?'

She had no response for that. Telling her anything would be implicating Raza Masood, and where would that leave her? Masood Khan seemed like a good person, but who could say what he might do if she accused his only son, and who was to say that their lawyers wouldn't decimate her in court?

'I am fine,' Ayesha lied, her voice tight with emotion. 'At least I will be. I just need time. I'm sorry I cannot help you.'

Amna placed her hand over Ayesha's and squeezed. 'While this is not the answer I was looking for, I understand your hesitation. I have seen my fair share of horrors, but I want you to know that things are changing, Ayesha. I promise you they are.' She pulled a card from her pocket, and placed it next to Ayesha's hand. 'Whenever you're ready to talk, you call me. I will come. Nobody can evade justice forever.'

Welcome to Pakistan, Ayesha thought, her eyes burning again, *where men* can *evade justice forever.*

It wasn't long afterwards that her mother returned, and the mood changed. Her eyes narrowed as she watched DSP Amna, but she didn't say anything. There was nothing to say.

You needn't worry, Ammi.

As she watched DSP Amna leave the room, closing the door with a click, Ayesha knew that she had lost the one chance she had of bringing Raza Masood to justice. She turned away from her mother, and watched the empty space between the sofa and stool for hours.

Ayesha made a point of staying away from the mirror in the bathroom, but deep down, she knew that she couldn't avoid looking at herself forever. It wasn't denial that prevented her, rather a sense of self-preservation. She just wasn't ready.

However, one day, as they returned from the canteen hand in hand, her mother took a wrong turn and they ended up near the labour room and nurseries. Generally, Ayesha didn't even lift her gaze from the ground, afraid of what she might see in the eyes of people who saw her, but maybe something about the cries of newborn babies made her look up. In the nursery, there were a dozen babies, some asleep, others mewling and crying, and for a moment she was transported. Here was new life, a new chance. She didn't notice the people stopping to stare at her, some of them covering their mouth with their hands.

Her mother pulled at her. 'Ayesha, *chalo*. People are starting to stare.' She bristled at a few of the most curious ones. 'Nothing to see here. She's human, just like you.'

But Ayesha was transfixed. She kept looking at the babies in the window, wondering if she would ever have a chance to hold one of her own. She had never considered herself the maternal sort before, but at that moment, she wanted it.

She wanted it all.

A new life with Saqib and children – plenty of them.

Her dream shattered when she caught her reflection in the window. Her face was still partially bandaged, and it seemed like she was looking at someone else entirely. She'd never known that human skin could take on so many shades. She was a walking rainbow. The doctors had said that the burns would heal with the grafts, but the scars wouldn't be pretty. There would be more surgeries in the future, and even then, there was no guarantee that she'd get her old face back.

Her throat burned with emotion, just as the rest of her face and neck burned from Raza's assault – an assault he'd got away with.

'The fact that you can feel the burning is good,' Dr Ikram said.

'It means the nerves in your face are still working and that there is minimal muscle damage. Running out in the rain and letting it wash away the acid was a very good idea. It has saved you from the more heinous long-term effects.'

What do you know of the effects of this attack, she wanted to say, but she pursed what was left of her lips. It wasn't the doctor's fault. Ayesha had tried not look at her reflection again.

Her heart yearned for Saqib, but still there had been nothing from him. It was as if he had vanished into thin air. She'd called him several times, left hundreds of messages, but he hadn't called her back. Something truly horrible must have befallen him. There was no way that her love of several years could abandon her like that. She could only hope that the Masoods hadn't reached him before her.

Over the next few weeks, Ayesha was in the care of Dr Ikram, a well-known plastic surgeon in Multan. He tended to her raw wounds and also made the grafts using skin taken from her thighs. When he visited her for the final time before discharging her, his eyes betrayed how emotional he felt.

'As plastic surgeons, we usually see patients who want to change something about their appearance, and we know what we're dealing with. But incidents like this' – he gestured to Ayesha – 'really hurt and anger us. As doctors, we are taught not to feel anything, but sometimes I can't help it.' Turning to her parents, he said, 'It will be some time before Ayesha can come to terms with what's happened to her. You must be patient with her. There will be more surgeries, but let's take it one step at a time. Right now, it's time to rest and recuperate.' Smiling at Ayesha, he added, 'Maybe a change of scene would be good for you. Go and see a new place. Be free, child.'

Ayesha knew he meant well, but all she could think about was how she was trading one hospital for another, as her treatment would have to continue at home as well. She would never be the same again. She would always see pity in people's eyes, she would always know they would like to fix what was broken. But Raza Masood had not only ruined her appearance, he'd wounded her soul too. When she looked in the mirror, she saw a stranger.

How was she to come to terms with that?

Back home, the only welcome party for her was Naseeba, their house help. '*Haye* Bibi, may that *kanjar* who did this to you burn in hell. How could anyone even think of doing this?' She wrapped her arms around Ayesha, her chest heaving, but Ayesha couldn't return her hug.

She felt dead inside.

'Ayesha?' her mother began, rubbing her back in circular motions. 'You're home, *beta*. There's no reason to be scared anymore.'

She looked at her mother as if she was mad. 'There is every reason to be scared, Ammi.'

Her mother looked stricken. She turned to Ayesha's father. 'Maybe a break from Multan is what she needs, Ji. I don't like seeing my daughter terrified out of her mind.'

Without waiting for his reply, Ayesha began climbing the stairs to her room, one at a time, her hand gripping the rail so hard that her knuckles turned white.

'Do you need help with the stairs?' her father called.

'No,' she said with more force than was necessary.

Raza had taken everything from her, but she wouldn't let him take her self-respect too.

In the following days, she had visits from several relatives, along with friends and colleagues, like Saira and Shugufta. And then, Neelam Khala arrived.

'Hospitals are not for me, Baji,' she said to her sister as soon as she stepped in their house. 'The negative energy gets to me and you know how frail I am at the best of times.'

They looked at her enormous form in silence.

'*Haye, meri bachi.*' Not caring about Ayesha's injuries, Neelam went in for a hug. Ayesha winced. 'Look at you. What an absolute fright. I tell you Multan is no longer a safe city for women. Look what they've done to my beautiful niece. Now who will marry you?'

'We are more concerned about her health at this point,' her father pointed out.

'That's correct,' her mother added. 'We might actually send Ayesha abroad for a break, just so she can gather herself.'

With a small smile, Neelam asked, 'Where exactly are you planning to send her?'

Safdar Khan exhaled. 'We will see ... whatever Ayesha wants. That much I know.'

Neelam simply shook her head. 'Oh, you know nothing, Safdar bhai. There is only one thing worse than a daughter sitting unwed at home, and that's a daughter who is damaged goods in every sense of the word. Do you know how much Rabbiya has maligned your daughter's reputation?'

'Enough, Neelam,' her mother interrupted. 'You're disturbing Ayesha. Come, let's sit in the living room and have tea.'

'Let her speak, Ammi,' Ayesha murmured. She wanted to see just how much her aunt could fall.

She didn't disappoint.

Sitting close to Ayesha on the bed, she fanned herself with a hand. 'God, it is stuffy in this room.' Her voice wobbled, but Ayesha was sure she was acting. 'Sabeena is already pregnant and expecting twins, and to see my darling Ayesha, years older than her, sitting here unmarried and unwanted. *Haye.*'

Ayesha noticed her father shaking his head and withdrawing from the room. She thought she heard him mutter 'bitch', but she couldn't be sure.

It didn't seem like Neelam had heard. She inched even closer to Ayesha, her flesh pushing her against the bed's headboard. 'I tell you what, Baji. I know a matchmaker who has been known to get even the ugliest girls married. I tell you, she works wonders.'

'My daughter is not ugly, Neelam.'

Neelam's cheeks reddened. 'Of course, Baji. She is my niece too, and I am just looking out for her. My manner may not always be kind, but that doesn't mean I don't love her. If I didn't love her, I wouldn't be here. And besides, won't you indulge your little sister, your *titli*? Please let's meet that matchmaker. Who knows, she might give us some ideas.'

'But we're not looking to get her married yet.'

'That's the only way you'll get rid of that horrible man. That much I know.' Her gaze levelling with Ishrat's, she continued, 'Of course the entire city knows who did this to Ayesha. But will anyone come to your aid? No, they won't. They're just sitting in their homes, watching the drama unfold. The only person here to help you is your little sister. I want you to remember that.'

Her mother protested, but nobody stood a chance when Neelam had decided something.

'Leave it to me. As soon as Ayesha is up and about, I'll bring the matchmaker to your house.' She patted Ayesha on the shoulder. 'Don't you worry, *beta*. Neelam Khala is still here to take care of you.'

Ayesha sat in front of her dressing table, debating whether to put on concealer. It was probably unwise, so she didn't. Although it had been several weeks since the doctors had performed surgery to salvage the right side of her face, all the way to the neck, makeup was probably not recommended. They had put in several skin grafts, in a kind of patchwork, but she still didn't look anything like before. The acid had destroyed her face, and she knew that no amount of surgeries would ever fix it. Her mother thought that if Ayesha watched enough survival stories on television, she'd learn to accept her new appearance, but she just couldn't. The survival stories made her feel worse. They reminded her just how widespread acid attacks were and how many lives they destroyed. It boiled her blood. It made her want to kill all those men. 'Almost one thousand cases have been reported over the last couple of years,' Saira had told her over the phone, echoing DSP Amna's words. 'This problem is more widespread than we thought. Please don't feel like you're alone in this, Ayesha.'

Saira meant well, but she had no idea what Ayesha was dealing with. Maybe her parents were right, and she really did need to go abroad to gather herself. But, where would that leave her and Saqib?

She still hadn't spoken to him. He wasn't as strong as her. Despite his nonchalant behaviour, he was a bit of a coward. She hated to admit it, but it was true.

She put the concealer away, and stared at her face in the mirror. Neelam and the matchmaker had just arrived. She could hear them downstairs with her mother. All Ayesha wanted at this moment was to disappear. Did she really have the strength to go through such scrutiny? And for what? It wasn't like she was going to marry any of the men the matchmaker was going to suggest. With a jolt, she realised that many of them would not want to marry her when they saw her face. The new reality of her life always took her by surprise. She looked nothing like she had before the surgery, and never would. Once she got over feeling sorry for herself, she took a good look at herself in the mirror. The damaged skin had become shiny in places, and in others the scar tissue seemed to have made the skin so taut that if it wasn't for the grafts, she feared her face would tear open. A little bit of her nose had melted away in the attack, and Dr Ikram hadn't reconstructed it yet, wanting to restore her basic appearance first. It was like her face was a blank canvas for Dr Ikram to work his magic on, except that there had been little magic, and a lot of pain. Sometimes it felt like someone was branding her with a red-hot poker. Whether it was phantom pain or the real deal, it kept her awake at night.

'I commend your cleverness in turning your face away when you were attacked,' her doctor had said. 'You are very lucky that much of your face is still intact, especially your eyes. Very lucky.'

Very lucky, she thought as she rubbed at the affected skin. She would never sweat again from this area as the acid had destroyed her sweat glands. If she covered a part of her face with a scarf and wrapped the rest of it around her neck, her injuries were still noticeable, but not as much. However, she knew full well that it wasn't just these visible injuries that Raza had given her. Her self-confidence was shattered.

Her eye caught a pair of tweezers on the dressing table, and she wondered if they'd be sharp enough to plunge into her neck, severing an artery. A quick death, but not painless. Picking them up, she touched the sharp edge of the metal with her thumb. If she pressed it hard enough, she knew it would draw blood. Just a few minutes of pain and then it would be over.

She'd be free.

She held them to the unblemished part of her neck and closed her eyes.

Do it, a voice inside her said. *Don't think about your parents. It's not them who are suffering. It's you.*

Opening her eyes, she put the tweezers down. That was selfish, even for her. She couldn't do that to her parents, to herself. She couldn't let Raza win. Her destiny was with Saqib, and she'd be damned if she didn't find out what had happened to him. Saqib wouldn't just disappear like that. She did the breathing exercises she'd been taught until some of the despair blew out of her, leaving her calm and in control. Feeling more confident, she thought she might be able to leave the house now. Maybe after she'd met the matchmaker she'd head over to Saqib's office later. Find out if they knew anything about his whereabouts.

Looking at her reflection, she put bright red lipstick on her now permanently cracked lips and made her way downstairs. When had anyone ever succeeded in talking Neelam out of anything?

she thought. Never. So she would have to endure whatever she had planned for her.

Ayesha's feet felt constrained in the heels she was wearing, but she still held her head high and strode into the living room, where Neelam Khala and her mother were already seated with a curly-haired woman who appeared to be wearing sunglasses indoors.

'It's not easy, Aapi,' the woman was saying. 'Reputations are so delicate, and from what I've heard, things are not looking good for your niece.' Her face was heavily made up and she wore a garish lawn suit quite similar to Neelam's. All three women sat up when they noticed Ayesha approach.

Immediately, Ayesha felt self-conscious. They were staring at her like she was a goat in the market. She half expected the woman to poke a finger into her mouth to check her teeth.

'Ayesha, *beta*,' said Neelam. 'This is Saima Aunty, one of Multan's leading matchmakers. She is very busy, so we are very grateful to her for taking out the time to see us today. Come and sit.' When Ayesha didn't move, Neelam Khala added, 'Please.'

When her mother reiterated the request, Ayesha had no choice but to acquiesce.

Saima sat stirring her tea, tapping the spoon against the porcelain cup several times before putting it down. Ayesha winced at the sound as she sank into one of the armchairs.

Saima peered at her, the sunglasses still on. 'With the scarf she looks somewhat unblemished. Beautiful, even. She was engaged to Raza Masood, wasn't she?'

'Yes, she was,' her mother spoke up. 'She isn't any longer, as everyone in Multan knows.'

'We don't have high expectations,' Neelam piped in. 'Even a middle-class boy would do.'

'Man,' Saima corrected Neelam. 'The girl is no spring chicken, Aapi.'

'That she is not,' Neelam replied. 'All of twenty-eight soon.'

'You want to get her married to a man in his mid-thirties, then.'

At that moment, Ayesha wanted to kill her aunt. Did she have no heart at all?

Saima adjusted her dupatta and took a noisy sip of her tea. 'Perhaps someone from one of the smaller cities of Punjab might do the trick? The girl is fair enough, and I'm sure they'll overlook her – ah – other faults. Is there any money in the family?'

Before Ayesha or her mother could reply, Neelam spoke, 'Hardly. They used to be rich a hundred years ago, but now they barely have enough to keep a roof over their heads. No, there will be no money to entice suitors, unless mine counts.'

'Your name is generally enough in Multan, Aapi. This world bows to the rich.'

Neelam tucked into a chicken pakora, the oil dribbling down her chin. 'Of course, you're right, Saima. No wonder you're so successful in what you do. You understand our society.'

Ayesha noticed her mother's cheeks turn pink. 'We have some money tucked away. Neelam doesn't know everything. We have more than enough to ensure she has a good wedding and an equally good dowry.'

A dowry? In this day and age, Ayesha couldn't believe these women were talking about things like complexion and dowry.

She had had enough. Sitting up straighter, Ayesha uncrossed her legs, letting them spread a little. 'Why the sunglasses, Aunty? Why inside? They look a bit – umm – comical.'

Saima's eyes flashed. She put her tea down. 'None of your business, girl. And sit with your legs closed. What is this, Aapi? If you want a match for your daughter, you'd better teach her to behave like a girl. I'm one of Multan's top matchmakers. People beg for a moment of my time.'

'Sure,' Ayesha replied. 'I suspect they break your door down knocking?'

'Exactly,' Saima replied, oblivious to the sarcasm.

'Shouldn't you see the full package before you make any promises?' Ayesha caught Neelam's eye and smiled. She was going to enjoy making her squirm. Removing the pin holding the scarf in place, she let it cascade around her shoulders and into her lap.

Saima gasped. 'Uff! Neelam Aapi, look at the state of her. Who is going to want to kiss that neck?' She shuddered.

It was Neelam's turn to blush. 'Outrageous behaviour from your daughter, Ishrat Baji, especially when I've been trying to help her. She needs to keep those scars covered. Nobody wants to see that.'

Although Ayesha thought she'd steeled herself, the words were like knives. Her aunt never ceased to amaze her with her tactlessness. 'If this is you trying to help, Neelam Khala, then we don't need it. Where were you when my parents were being ostracised from society due to their lack of money? Couldn't you have taken a stand like they did for you back when your husband polished shoes on Bosan Road?'

'He never polished shoes on the roadside, Ayesha,' her mother whispered. 'For God's sake, stop listening to your father.'

Neelam clutched her chest, her eyes wide.

Beside her, Saima was drinking in all the gossip. 'Your husband used to polish shoes on Bosan Road? Well, well. That is certainly news to me. Pretentious Akhtar Sahab who rules the provincial government of Punjab came from such a humble background.'

Neelam gritted her teeth. 'He did not. Don't be ridiculous, you stupid cow. Focus on the task at hand, or are you so useless that you cannot give us a single *rishta* for my fool of a niece who doesn't know what's best for her?'

Saima gasped. 'Uff, your language, Aapi! You're showing your class, you know.'

'And what about your class, you four-eyed *kuti*?'

Good, Ayesha thought. Let Saima tell the entire city what her aunt was like.

Ayesha flicked a hand in her mother's direction. 'The fact is, Ammi, that your sister is an incredibly selfish and self-centred woman who takes joy in our misery. She only brought this ... this woman here to poke fun at us – at me. She's always been jealous of me even though her own daughter had so much more than me in every sense of the word.'

Neelam was panting and for once in her life seemed close to breaking down. 'Do you think I haven't heard the stories about you and that awful boy, Saqib? Where is he now? Probably left you the moment he saw what you've become.' She laughed, packing as much venom into her voice as she could. 'A freak of nature.'

Saima pushed herself onto her feet. 'Aapi, you didn't tell me there was another boy in the picture. My clients are conservative and respectable people, and they want girls that are like them. Besides, the damage on the face and neck is quite extensive. I think I should leave. This is not a girl I could find a partner for.'

'I'll come with you,' Neelam added, rising from the sofa. The seat bounced back as soon as her enormous weight shifted from it. 'I want nothing more to do with this family. No matter how hard I try to improve my niece's life, she just doesn't seem interested. I'm out of here.'

'Make sure the door doesn't hit you on the ass on your way out, Neelam, and never show your face here again.' Ishrat turned her face away from the women, busying herself with her handbag. Her hands were shaking. 'My daughter means everything to me, you hear. She means to me more than you ever did.'

'Like mother, like daughter,' Neelam muttered.

As soon as Neelam slammed the door, Ayesha threw her arms around her mother. 'Thank you, Ammi. Thank you for standing up for me.'

Her mother was sobbing. 'I should never have allowed Neelam to invite the matchmaker. She's my sister, but her opinions have become so misguided that I don't really recognise her anymore. This city, this country is not for you anymore, *beta*. I am sorry I put you through so much. You need some time away from this place.'

Without Saqib? Ayesha couldn't go anywhere until she knew where things stood with him, Besides, as much as she had thought about going away, she had no idea where she could go. Everywhere was expensive these days. She couldn't afford to live in a hotel for weeks.

'You talk about sending me away, Ammi,' she began, 'but, where will I go?'

Kamil

Kamil was in Euston again. Although it was still high summer, there was a hint of autumn in the late-August air, a turning of the weather. In a month it would be cold. Usually, he enjoyed London's breezy, unpredictable weather, but today he was on edge. He pulled the piece of paper from his pocket and read the address. It was only a few minutes' walk away.

His heart skipped a beat.

Apart from his immediate family, nobody knew what he'd suffered. He'd promised himself years ago that he would expunge the incident from his memory. If he didn't think about it, it would lose its power over him. At least that is what he believed and had lived by. It had taken him years, but somehow he had tried to piece himself together, and become once again the kind of man he used to be. It was a lie – he knew that – but at least it didn't hurt anymore. There were days – weeks even – when he wouldn't even think about it.

'Avoiding something isn't going to make it go away,' Safiya had told him during their last meeting. 'You need to face your demons head on, Kamil. Whatever they are. If you've survived them, they can't be that bad.'

You have no idea, Kamil had thought. Still, he'd indulged her. Their relationship had become more platonic than anything, and they were still struggling to have any romantic feelings for each other. But he'd come to rely on her for advice and support – and that made him uncomfortable. He couldn't allow himself to rely on anyone; he'd vowed long ago not to. That was the reason he'd kept Madiha at arm's length. He'd never wanted to regurgitate all that he'd been through in front of her. So why would he do it with

Safiya or with this strange support group for victims of domestic violence?

He'd looked up Matthew Ross online, but he'd found very little except for the fact that his face looked open and honest and that he had a degree in psychology.

Figures, he thought as he pressed the button to be buzzed in. The support group met in an ancient building that had been converted into an open space for meetings. Matt's profile said the support group was free, although they only took on people who were recommended by one of the core members.

Good old Safiya, ever so helpful. The black polished door opened and Kamil finally ventured inside. The grey carpet absorbed the sound of his footsteps as he climbed the stairs, and before he knew it, he'd reached the third-floor landing. On a set of pale-wood double doors, there was a sign that said *Meeting in Progress*.

Here goes nothing, he thought, pushing his way in.

It wasn't at all like the support groups he'd seen in movies. People weren't sitting in a circle with an open space in the middle. This was like a conference room with people seated around a U-shaped table. His entry made them fall into a pin-drop silence. The person seated at the far end of the table glanced up and smiled, making the skin around his eyes crinkle. It was a genuine smile.

He strode across the room and shook Kamil's hand, his palm dry and grip firm. 'I'm Matthew Ross. Matt for short. Safiya has told me all about you. She's one of our core members, even though we don't see much of her these days. Thank you so much for coming, Kamil. We are absolutely delighted to have you here.'

'Are you?'

Kamil looked at the curious faces staring back at him. Some wore inviting smiles, but others had expressions that reminded him of closed doors. What was he doing here? For a moment, he wanted to turn around and make a run for it, but before he could act on the impulse, Matt grabbed his elbow and steered him towards the table, seating Kamil right next to him.

Great, now he was in the spotlight.

'Friends, if you remember, I mentioned that a special new member might be joining us. It wasn't certain he would, but well, here he is now. Kamil, isn't it?'

'Yes, that's right.'

Kamil sat with his hands folded on the table. He was at a loss. The fluorescent lighting made everything look sharp and unforgiving. He looked back at the door; it might have been as far away as the moon at this point.

Matt cleared his throat. 'Okay, so I think we're all here. Let's start off with the introductions. Sandra, would you like to start by telling Kamil who you are and why you're here.'

A middle-aged blonde woman smiled at him. Then she turned to the group. 'I'm Sandra and I'm an alcoholic. I drink to lessen the pain of my husband's affair and our daily arguments. I drink to forget him. I drink to forget life.' Her smile faded. 'I have tried drinking myself to death.'

'But not anymore, right, Sandra?'

Sandra's smile was back. 'That's right, Matt. Never again. I should probably call myself a recovering alcoholic.'

'Domestic abuse is not easy,' Matt said. 'Don't be too hard on yourself.'

'I'm Shabbir,' a South Asian man sitting at the other end of the table said. 'I'm thirty-three years old. I came to the United Kingdom three years ago after marrying a British-Pakistani. I have been miserable ever since. They make me work like a dog at home and refuse to let me get a proper job. I miss my country, and wish I had never bought into the promise of a good life in the UK. I was suicidal until I joined this group.'

'I'm Mary. My husband is dead, but I still have marks on my body from where he beat me.'

'I'm Stephanie. My husband has a very bad problem with alcoholism. And I've been diagnosed with chronic depression.'

'I'm Rob.'

'I'm Tina.'

One by one, everyone introduced themselves until Kamil felt the knot in his stomach loosen. He looked around at all the faces, noticing that even the most serious ones were starting to give him encouraging smiles.

Sandra nodded at him, her smile still in place. 'This is a safe space. Whatever you say here, stays here. Nothing has ever gotten out, and nothing ever will.'

He decided that he liked her very much. In fact, he liked how they had all taken the time to introduce themselves, even when they didn't have to. They'd done it for him. He unclasped his sweaty palms and wiped them on his trousers. Taking a deep breath, he said, 'I am Kamil...'

Ayesha

Even with the scarf on, she noticed the taxi driver glance at her in the rear-view mirror for a beat too long. His gaze kept travelling to the right side of her face and neck. She ignored him, hitching up her sunglasses. She tried to focus on the view outside, but the heat in the car was stifling.

'Turn on the AC, will you?'

The driver smirked at her. 'Do you have any idea how expensive petrol is these days? Who will pay for that? Your father?'

'*Kanjar*,' Ayesha muttered under her breath and lowered the windowpane. The little makeup she had put on the undamaged part of her face was going to get ruined in Multan's muggy heat. There was no way she'd still look presentable by the time she reached her destination.

Perhaps it was a good thing it was so hot in the car. The heat took her mind off other, more pressing matters. She hadn't told her mother where she was going, but from the look on her face, she knew exactly where her daughter was headed. It was only after the acid attack that her mother had started acknowledging Saqib. Now her parents were probably secretly praying that he would marry her. The thought made her want to cry. So much of a woman's prospects in Pakistan depended on her beauty, her ability to bear beautiful sons who would keep the family's legacy alive and take its name forward. Daughters ... well, they were expendable burdens that had to be unloaded on the first unsuspecting family that could be found. She had female cousins who'd been married off to unknown families in small cities like Vehari, never to be heard from again. All Ayesha ever heard about them was how many sons they'd pushed out of their wombs, and how many more were still to come.

'Once you go to your husband's home, only your funeral should emerge from those gates. Don't come back to us alive.'

These were the words she'd grown up hearing in the family, uttered mostly by men, but also by lots of women. Ayesha knew her parents were different, more progressive, but not enough to allow her to choose how to lead her life. It took her almost dying in the hospital for them to accept that she loved Saqib.

Saqib's workplace was somewhere in Gulgasht Colony, and it wasn't long before they arrived outside his office building – one of the more modern buildings that were sprouting up all over Multan. 'Not exactly a small, regional city anymore,' her father had taken to saying. 'Soon, these feudal bastards will be booted out of the city for good.'

The irony wasn't lost on anyone – her father had been a feudal lord himself; still was in a manner of speaking, since he owned plenty of agricultural land outside of Multan, and earned income from it. But, of course, Ayesha knew that his words were aimed at the filthy rich of the city. The ones that made fun of their downfall.

She didn't realise that she'd arrived at her destination until the driver said, 'Are you going to get out or not?'

His rudeness made Ayesha want to give him a piece of her mind, but she thought better of it. Before she got out, she heard him mutter, 'Bloody freak.'

His words felt like a slap, and she stopped breathing for a moment. Was this going to be her life from here on?

It was a cloudy day, but the air was still and oppressive. She thought of waiting in the lobby until Saqib came out, but that would only attract attention to her new appearance, and she didn't need that. So she stood underneath a towering mango tree in the parking lot and waited, trying to prevent other, more disturbing thoughts enter her mind. What if he didn't come out? What if Raza had done something to him? She shook her head and focused on the scenery around her, striving to look for the familiar, but after the attack, everything looked different to her.

Earlier, she would go wherever she wanted, stand wherever she wanted, not caring that there were men around her. She'd go into Multan's old bazaars with her mother to buy spices and other household essentials, picking her way through throngs of people and trying not to slip into the stinking open drains that had black sludge oozing out of them and spilling into the streets, and even though men in the older and more conservative part of town gawked at her uncovered head and arms, she didn't give them a second glance. She was so confident in her skin that her mother would often accuse her husband of raising Ayesha like a son.

There was no breeze today, so soon the sweat ran down her back, soaking into the elastic of her shalwar, but she kept her arms folded against her chest and waited. She'd come all this way, and she wasn't about to let the weather ruin her plans. She passed the time by giving the driver a one-star rating, looking up only when a steady stream of people started exiting the building.

So many men, she thought, hoping to see some colour in the sea of white and blue, but only catching a couple of females, who were also dressed in drab outfits that didn't make them stand out. Not for the first time, she wondered how a progressive girl like her could have been born in a place like Multan. If she had to be a Pakistani, she would much rather have come from Karachi, or even Lahore, despite its many shortcomings. But Multan ... it suffocated her.

She took a deep breath and focused on the people who had now entered the parking lot and were heading towards their respective vehicles. As the motorcycles and cars started clearing, she caught sight of Saqib's Vespa sandwiched between two Honda motorbikes. And there he was, walking towards it with his head down. She could see the tension in his shoulders from where she stood. But at that moment, the sight of him filled her with such unadulterated joy that she forgot the months of silence and rushed towards him. It was Saqib – her Saqib. Surely he still loved her, and if he didn't, she would make him.

She was out of breath by the time she reached him, the attack having robbed her of all her stamina. 'Saqib,' she wheezed. 'Saqib, it's me.'

He was putting his key into ignition, but his face whipped up upon hearing her voice. 'Ayesha.' Their eyes met. 'Wh–what are you doing here?'

Her heart threatened to melt at his voice. She blinked back tears. *Get a hold of yourself.* It took her a moment to realise that her scarf had slid from her face completely and that Saqib's gaze had shifted from her eyes to her scars.

'Is that where he…?' He looked away, fiddling with his keys.

She nodded, not trusting herself to speak. Up close, she could see there was dirt underneath his fingernails. She was shocked – Saqib was always obsessive about cleanliness. His hair was also unwashed and his face had an oily sheen to it, as if he hadn't showered for days. He had let himself go.

'Why didn't you come to see me?' she finally said in a small voice. 'I left you hundreds of messages. Did you not think of me even once?'

'This isn't the place, Ayesha.'

'I asked you a question, Saqib. I've travelled all this way just to see you. I deserve some answers.'

He was looking anywhere but at her. 'I've thought about you every waking minute of my life, Ayesha. I visited you several times when nobody was around. You didn't realise. You were unconscious or asleep ... But…'

'But?' She hated the hope in her voice, and then, 'You visited me? I – I didn't know.'

He sighed. 'Ayesha, it's complicated.'

Her heart, which had been pounding in her throat all this time, dropped. 'How is it complicated?' She touched her face. 'Is it my injuries? Do you hate the way I look?'

Saqib still wouldn't look at her. 'It's not that. It can never be that.'

'Then what is it? Because the last thing I remember before I was attacked is that you simply couldn't get enough of me. But now that I'm disfigured, you seem to want nothing more to do with me. If it's not that, Saqib, then what is it?'

'Let's not do this here. This is where I work.'

Ayesha slapped a palm against the seat of his Vespa. 'No, let's do this here, because this is the only place I can find you.'

Finally, he met her gaze again. 'After you were attacked, I had a visit from some people.'

'What kind of people?'

'The kind you'd never wish to find on your doorstep. They took my father away right in front of my eyes, Ayesha. I don't know where. For three days, they kept him somewhere, deprived of everything except food and water. I couldn't tell the police, because they're a joke, and besides, they wouldn't have listened to me without a hefty bribe.' The keys jingled in his trembling hand. 'For three days, I didn't hear anything from them, and just when I was about to lose my mind, I had a visit from Raza Masood.'

Ayesha felt suddenly light-headed. She gripped the seat of the Vespa and closed her eyes. 'Raza Masood?'

'He forbade me from ever seeing you again. He told me that if I did, not only would he torture my father, but would also harm you again, and that this time, he would bathe your entire body in acid.'

'Forbade you?' Ayesha could feel her blood pressure rising, a rushing in her ears. This was worse than she could possibly have imagined. She could see it in Saqib's eyes now. The fear and uncertainty. She could see him leaving her forever, and the thought chilled her to the bone. 'You shouldn't have listened to him, Saqib. He can't hurt me now even if he wanted to. The entire city is watching him, and besides, what more damage could he do to me?'

'Did you not hear a thing I just said? He only returned my father to me after I agreed never to see you again. My father isn't as young as he used to be. Those three days took a toll on his health.' His voice broke. 'I can't lose another parent. I am sorry, but nothing is more important to me than my father. Not even you. I'm just not strong enough for this.'

'But you were strong enough to fuck me, weren't you?'

'Don't be vulgar, Ayesha.'

Ayesha's heart was breaking and there was nothing she could do to stop it. She looked at the man she had given all these years of her life to, and saw only fear in his grey eyes, and an instinct to protect himself and his family. And in that moment, she was so distraught, she thought she saw a coward. And an opportunist.

'He must have compensated you well, though. Don't tell me he didn't pay you. Raza Masood always pays.'

Saqib's cheeks reddened. 'What do you take me for? I'm not that person.'

Her nails scratched the leather. 'Tell me now, Saqib, because I will find out anyway. How much did he pay you to keep your distance? How much did you sell our life for? I want to know.'

'Ten million rupees,' he whispered. 'But that was only because he felt bad about treating my father like that.'

She whistled. 'Ten million, and you're still on a Vespa? Put the money in a savings account, have we? I honestly don't know what to say.'

Saqib frowned before shoving her hand away from the Vespa. 'You don't get to take the moral high ground. Your parents basically sold you to Raza.'

She slapped him across the face. The sound of it rang out in the now-empty parking lot. '*Haramzaday*! I hope you rot in hell.'

'If you can't see beyond your own self, then I don't know what to say to you.' He exhaled as he covered his cheek with a hand, hiding the angry red mark that already bloomed there. 'I hope you find someone, Ayesha. I really do. But, I just can't be with you. I guess our journey ends here.'

Our journey ends here.

Her scars burned, the pain bringing tears to her eyes. Without a backward glance, she walked away from him.

She walked and walked the streets, until her heels broke and some kindly lady took pity on her and gave her a ride. Before the attack, she'd be wary about getting in a stranger's car, but what did she care now? She'd lost the one person that mattered the most to her.

She'd lost Saqib.

She promised herself that she wouldn't shed another tear for him, and she didn't. Her eyes remained bone dry throughout the journey home, but as the car turned into her street, something else took her attention. There was a black Beemer idling at the opposite end of the street. The blood in her veins froze. The sun reflected from the windscreen, making it impossible to see who was inside, but she knew.

What more do you want from me? She wanted to scream. As she hurried out of the car and into the relative safety of her home, all she knew was that she needed to get out of Pakistan.

'I knew he was a *haramzada* from the start. Didn't I tell you, Ayesha?' Her mother was pacing the living room, her hands folded behind her back. 'I knew he'd use you to his heart's content and then ditch you.'

'Thanks, Ammi. I *really* needed to hear that.'

Her mother continued pacing. 'Of course, your father has no idea you've been seeing the boy in *that* way. He'd have another heart attack if he knew.'

'It's okay. You can say the word "sex". You must have done it. You gave birth to me, after all.' She didn't enjoy angering her mother, but sometimes she forced her hand. 'You're all so prudish around it, which is exactly why men get away with so much. Everything has to be done in secret.'

She picked up her phone. She hated herself for checking her notifications so often, half-hoping for a message from Saqib telling her it was all a huge misunderstanding.

Her mother stopped pacing and stood in front of her. She half raised her hand, but then her face sagged. 'I can't even raise my hand against you anymore. I ... I just feel so sorry for you. I wish things were different, *beta*. I wish he had married you.'

Ayesha steeled herself. 'I don't need anyone to marry me. I am perfectly capable of looking after myself.' She saw tears slide down her mother's face. 'And I don't need your pity. I'd rather suffer those slaps.'

'London,' her mother said, collapsing on the seat next to Ayesha with a sigh. 'That's the only way. You have to go to London. As horrible as the Masood family was, their financial assistance helped your father sort out a lot of his affairs. We have enough money to send you away for a few months.'

'Money I gave up my face and life for.' She regretted the words as soon as they were out of her mouth. Her mother's face paled, and her bottom lip quivered. 'Sorry, Ammi. I didn't mean it like that.'

Her mother's face crumbled. 'No, you're right. They haven't demanded that we return their money, and if they did, we might not be able to. So they feel they've bought our silence.' Shaking her head, she added, 'However, my point stands: you need to get away from this madness. This family will not let you breathe if you stay in Multan. You need to take time off work and just go. I'm sure Shugufta won't object.'

'Of course she won't.'

'Your father and I have been discussing this for quite some time. You need to be out of this country for now, and when you return, we can re-examine the situation with Saqib.'

'Ammi—'

Her mother threw up her hands. 'Will you let me finish? What I mean is that you need a fresh start, something to take your mind off things here. By the time you return, things will have cooled down and you can think about what you want to do with a calm mind. Our priority right now is to get you away from the Masood family.'

Thinking of Raza waiting for her outside her house yesterday, Ayesha had to agree. If he'd started doing this, how long until he cornered her, or even kidnapped her? She needed to get out of Pakistan. Things were going from bad to worse. 'Why not somewhere closer? Dubai, perhaps?'

'We don't know anyone there.'

She'd never been to London. She knew her father kept their visas up to date in case things went belly up in Pakistan, but travelling was something the very rich did, who could actually afford to go abroad if things really did get out of control in Pakistan. She never thought she'd actually go herself. London was always supposed to be an unrealisable dream. 'Well, I don't know anybody in London,' she croaked. 'And, as lovely as your idea is, I can't stand to see all that money wasted on me.'

'Don't be silly. There's Jamila Aunty there. She's a family friend, and let me tell you, she's a much better person than my own sister. Jamila will take care of you. She'll let you stay in her house, I'm sure. I'll speak to her.' And to Ayesha's utter surprise, her mother hugged her. 'You're our only child, Ayesha. If we don't spend our money on you, then what on earth is it all for?'

They cried together for a long time, and even though Ayesha knew that going to London was a big risk, she also knew, deep down, that it was the only option open to her right now.

She had to get out of Pakistan.

Kamil

Apart from Shar, he hadn't told anyone in his family about attending the support group. His mother would have a fit. He knew exactly what she'd say.

'*Haye*! My mentally ill son. Will you need the hospital next? Do you already?' All while beating her chest.

No, he would avoid telling his mother for as long as he could. His father generally didn't interfere in his life – he hadn't for a long time – but Kamil knew that something like this would elicit a raised eyebrow even from him. He found it strange that despite having lived in the United Kingdom for so long, they'd been unable to live freely. No matter how much he believed that he was independent, there was always that niggling doubt in his mind, that fear of *log kya kaheinge* – what will people say? As much as he didn't want to care, he did. He shuddered to think what his extended family would say if they found out. At one point, he was worried about Shabbir from the support group snitching on him, but thankfully, they weren't related in any way. In fact, Shabbir came from Gujranwala, which was far away from Multan.

Whatever the case, he was surprised at how well he'd responded to the group. He'd only been twice, but the people already felt like friends – friends who knew him. He'd bonded well with Sandra and Shabbir, both of whom were a bit shy, but he liked everyone and couldn't wait to go back. He kind of wished they could meet twice a week, but sadly, it was just twice a month. He knew he ought to tell Safiya how much he was enjoying it, but he just couldn't. Things were fizzling out between them. It could be the absence of sex, but Kamil suspected it was predominantly down to their personalities. Safiya was too outspoken, too confident, and just too damn good for the likes of him.

'And too old,' his mother liked to remind him.

He rolled his eyes as he watched his mother sitting on the sofa with her feet up on the table, knitting a sweater. The ball of beige wool bobbed around the floor.

'Are we expecting a baby in the house?' he asked after the silence became stifling. His mother had resorted to giving him the silent treatment in protest at his relationship with Safiya, but he could see the frown between her eyebrows. Whatever it was, she was dying to tell him. 'Spit it out already, Ammi. What's up?'

His father sat on the sofa opposite, his face obscured by a newspaper. 'Your mother does have some news,' his father remarked from behind the pages.

'My dear Khan Sahab, will you ever get out of your world of newspapers and books?' his mother said.

'Books are life, Jamila.' Putting the newspaper down, Akbar Khan tapped his forehead, a network of wrinkles breaking across his face as he smiled. 'They keep the mind sharp.'

'Uff, as if.'

'My dear, have you forgotten the Mills & Boon books you loved reading? And all those romantic notions you had.'

Kamil laughed as his mother blushed.

'Your son is sitting here with us, Khan Sahab. Such vulgar talk in front of him about his own mother?'

'Jamila Begum, I hardly think Mills & Boon classifies as vulgar. Do you remember wanting to try –'

'*Bas*!' Jamila put her palm up to stave off more humiliating recollections. 'Stop right there. I need to share the big news with Kamil.'

'What big news?' Kamil's ears perked up. He knew there was something she wanted to tell him, but he didn't know it was big. 'Is Shar finally getting married?'

'*Haye*, I wish. Don't torment me. And it's Sharmeela. No, for once, it isn't about you lot. You remember my family friends, Ishrat and Neelam?'

A distant memory tugged at him. 'Is Neelam the one whose husband polished shoes on the roadside?'

His father snorted. 'That's right, my boy.'

Jamila fixed Kamil with a beady stare. 'He had a shoe-polish factory. Honestly, I have no idea where that rumour even started. Anyway, there's nothing wrong with polishing shoes on the roadside. It is a perfectly respectable profession. But this is not about Neelam. It's about Ishrat and her daughter.'

Kamil held up his hands. 'Ammi, if this is about some stupid matchmaking—'

His mother threw a cushion at him. 'Don't be ridiculous. It's nothing to do with a *rishta*. It is actually something much worse. Ishrat's daughter, Ayesha, has suffered a major acid attack.'

Kamil leaned back on the sofa, the funny retort he was planning dead on his lips. 'Oh. That's terrible.' His own past loomed up at him as he recalled the time he was scalded by water from a boiling kettle. He couldn't help the involuntary shudder that passed through him.

His mother nodded. 'The poor girl was engaged to marry one of the richest scions of Multan, but apparently she was in love with someone else, and the rich boy took revenge on her. Raza Masood, son of that horrible Rabbiya. That woman is pure evil, I tell you. I used to know her back when we were girls in Multan, and even then, there was something wrong with her. She's like rotten fruit, and from what I hear, she's only got worse over the years. I don't understand how my poor friend got tangled up with these people.' She sighed, massaging her arm. 'But then, poor Ayesha is twenty-seven, and by Multani standards, that's quite old.'

'Shar is twenty-eight.'

'Must you rub it in? I am fully aware of the fact that my daughter is an old maid.'

'Ammi, how could you live in a place like London and say such stuff?'

'Don't patronise me, Kamil, or so help me God, I will beat you with this slipper right here, right now. I don't care how old you are.'

'Kamil...' There was a warning in his father's voice.

Changing his mother's antiquated beliefs was an ongoing war for Kamil, but he decided to put it aside for another day. Instead, he asked if the authorities had arrested the man.

'If you have to ask this question, Kamil, then you're an even bigger fool than your mother thinks you are,' his father replied. 'The rich in Pakistan answer to no one. They adhere to no laws. The boy is free.'

Kamil's heart sank. He looked around their cosy living room, the house he had grown up in, and not for the first time, realised how easy life had been for him. For a moment, the group therapy seemed like a joke. What the hell was he even doing, picking at past wounds, when such mindless cruelty was inflicted on people in Pakistan every day? And to people they knew. 'How is she? Ayesha, I mean.'

His mother sniffed. 'All I know is that the girl was admitted to the hospital and underwent surgery to fix her damaged skin. But Ishrat didn't just call me to share this news. She called to ask something else.' His mother's eyes were twinkling now. Then she clapped her hands together, the knitting needles thrust aside. 'They're sending Ayesha to London. To stay with us.'

Kamil raised his eyebrows. 'And you said yes?'

'Of course I said yes. Anything we can do to help the poor girl, we will. I've already readied your old room for her. Despite popular opinion, I am not a bad person. *Bechari*. I feel awful for her. May that dog rot in hell.'

As he put an arm around his mother and let her rest her head on his shoulder, Kamil realised why he loved her to bits. Beneath the traditional beliefs and all that judgement lay a very kind heart.

All thoughts of his own troubles left his mind as he thought of that unfortunate girl, grievously injured and trapped in that country. Even though he barely knew her, he was delighted that she was coming to London.

Ayesha

As the doors of the plane sealed shut, Ayesha felt the claustrophobia pressing against her chest, her heart beginning to gallop a million miles a minute. *Deep breaths*, she told herself, looking around to see if anyone had noticed her hyperventilating.

After a few minutes, her breathing returned to normal. She focused on the screen in front of her, watching the white arrow pointing from Lahore to London. It was okay. It was all going to be okay.

Right up till the last minute, Ayesha had contemplated telling Saqib about her trip, to somehow find a way back to him. She hated herself for it, but she couldn't deny the fact that despite everything, she was still in love with him. There was no way she could fall out of love with him so quickly, she realised. It wasn't like she could wave a magic wand and suddenly stop feeling. No, love – true love – didn't work like that. Love was pain – the most exquisite pain – and right now, she was hurting.

She had hardly travelled anywhere in her adult life, and never alone. Her last trip had been to Dubai, but that had been with her parents and Neelam Khala. There weren't any good memories associated with that trip, as Neelam Khala had spent most of the time lording her money over them. She and her husband would take them to fancy restaurants and then spend the rest of the day reminding them of how expensive the food was, ever hungry for compliments and gratitude.

Ayesha shook her head and smiled at the air hostess walking by. There was a beat and alarm crossed her features, but she quickly covered it with a friendly expression and smiled back. Shocked, Ayesha held her head high and her scarf close, but no matter how much she covered herself, there was no hiding her scars. The right side of her face had recovered well after the skin grafts, but on her last visit to Dr Ikram, she had been warned to expect more surgeries. The mere thought of another surgery made her nauseous, just like she'd felt after the anaesthesia had worn off.

It seemed to her that there was no hard-and-fast rule to recovering from an acid attack. Everyone's skin seemed to respond differently, depending on the extent of the damage. Dr Ikram kept telling her that she was one of the lucky ones, to have escaped severe nerve damage and death, but at this moment, she didn't feel it.

She hated her life.

Her finger hovered over Saqib's name, but instead, she dialled her mother.

She picked up on the second ring. 'All okay? Have you boarded the plane?'

Ayesha's heart ached at the anxiety in her mother's voice. 'I have,' she whispered. 'It feels odd to be travelling alone.'

Her mother sucked in a breath. 'Oh, *beta*. If we could spare the money, I would have travelled with you, but you know how things are. The pound is through the roof, and even though you have a place to stay in London, you need to have some cash about you. I can't ask Jamila to give you spending money. That would look so cheap. Use the money you have carefully.'

Ayesha had heard this speech a thousand times since they'd first decided on the UK trip. 'I know, Ammi. I just meant that I miss you. I'll be fine.'

'We miss you too, Ayesha. Imagine how empty the house will be. But you mustn't let it affect you. London is a beautiful city, a joy to be in. You'll see. Just you wait.' Her voice wobbled then. 'Just take care of yourself. Remember, I will be praying for you every night, and I am just a call away if you need me. I love you. And, if you need more money—'

'I work, so I have some of my own savings too, Ammi.'

'Those savings are not to be touched. They're for emergencies. You must tell us if you need any more money. We will provide.'

'I'll be fine!'

Ayesha ended the call before she burst into tears. It was strange that even though she'd always gotten along better with her father, it was her mother that she felt more connected to now, especially after the attack. Her mother, usually so aloof and preoccupied, had finally admitted to her love for Ayesha. Not that it was ever in any doubt, but still, it felt good to hear her say it. Her parents had driven her to Lahore for the flight. The atmosphere during the journey was so strained that you could cut the tension with a knife. Ayesha knew how badly her father had taken the news of the matchmaker coming to their house.

'Do you like making a fool out of your daughter, Ishrat?' he'd roared when he'd discovered that Neelam Khala was behind the little visit from the matchmaker. 'That sister of yours is always interfering in our lives, and you just let her? What was the point of asking a matchmaker to come to the house? She's still recovering!'

'I don't know what I was thinking, Ji. Neelam is just so persistent that it's hard to say no to her. She really believes she has Ayesha's best interests at heart.'

'God knows what kind of stories you people told that woman. She'll go ruining our daughter's reputation everywhere, calling her names. I know her kind. I refuse to let anyone use my daughter for entertainment. I won't have it.' At this, he'd covered his face and sobbed into his palm, turning his back to them.

That was when they'd decided that it was best for Ayesha to leave as soon as possible. Calls were made to Jamila Aunty again, and once everything was settled and the ticket booked, they'd asked Ayesha to pack a few clothes and get ready for London. The entire journey to Lahore, where she'd be boarding a plane for London, had passed in silence, her mother regularly giving her meaningful glances. Ayesha knew what she wanted. She wanted to know if Saqib had reached out.

How the mighty had fallen. A few months ago, her mother would not have even entertained the notion of her daughter marrying someone as lowly as Saqib, and here she was now, desperate to marry her off to the same man. It infuriated Ayesha. She was not a pity case.

It was afternoon by the time they reached Lahore, the perfect time to admire the beauty of the city. They passed the mighty Canal Road that ran across the length of the city, ending somewhere along the border with India. Usually grey and polluted, Lahore seemed like a new city during the monsoon season. Everything seemed to shine in the embrace of sunny blue skies, with dark clouds gathering in the distance, a reminder that rainfall was never far away. Flawless, paved roads with lane markings were a bit of a rarity in Multan, but in Lahore, proper attention seemed to have been given to such things. While there were plenty of unsavoury places in the city, on the whole, Lahore was impressive with its lush greenery and friendly people. Even the stray dogs running around the streets seemed much happier than the ones in Multan. Wherever she looked, there was life. People rushing to their destinations, their faces focused. There was no dawdling like she saw in Multan, people stopping to gossip about everything, casting furtive glances at whoever passed by, narrowing their eyes at young couples. She could see herself settling down in Lahore someday. Unlike Multan, this city spoke to her.

'Packed with people, of course,' her father had muttered. 'Best place to lay low, if I'm being honest. We could get Ayesha to settle somewhere here when she comes back from London.'

Her mother shook her head, once. 'The risk is too great, Ji. The Masoods are well-connected people. They would weed her out of this city in no time. They have means.'

'And I don't?' That familiar anger again, one that had attached itself to Safdar Khan like a second skin.

'Of course you do, Ji, but I simply meant that London is safer for her. Let's just get her to the airport and on her flight. Then we can both breathe easy and plan ahead.'

Just as the anger had spiked, it died down. Her father sighed. 'You're right. Besides, I don't have that kind of influence anymore. I'm a nobody.'

That more than anything else broke Ayesha's heart, and watching her mother brush a tear from her eye, she suspected the same of her.

Before she could voice any of her thoughts to her parents, they'd reached the airport – a large red brick building that somehow didn't seem very large for a city like Lahore. Like everything in Pakistan, the airport was supposed to be much bigger, but had suffered from budget cuts and ended up being a quarter of its original size.

'*Kamlay log*,' her father had muttered, pulling into the parking lot. 'Not an ounce of intelligence in these people. Look at the hordes that have arrived to see off a single person.' He wasn't wrong. Ayesha had to wade through throngs of people who had showed up to see off relatives, only to be met by even larger crowds inside. It was so bad that she didn't even manage to hug her mother properly. Her father stayed back in the parking area, but her mother had braved the muggy weather and walked all the way to the departures area with her, only to be jostled around by people.

Her mother never failed to surprise her. One moment hot, the other cold. Maybe she was a bit like her, Ayesha thought. It had taken some effort to get through check-in, with Ayesha freezing for a moment when she was asked to remove her scarf by a female official. She hated herself for checking if the curtains to the little cubicle were closed before she took off her scarf. To her credit, the airport official hadn't given her face a second glance, but Ayesha had noticed her expression softening. The pity of others ... She still didn't know how it made her feel.

If she was being honest with herself, right now, she was so

anxious, she hated everything and everyone. London ... the word sent a shiver down her spine. She'd heard all sorts of stories of women being mugged and kidnapped in that city, not to mention being doused with acid. But then, what more damage could they do to her? And it wasn't like Multan was any safer. If anything, it was more dangerous, with actual relatives causing damage with their out-of-date attitudes.

She shuddered and looked out of the window as the pilot announced take-off. The plane soon began moving and gaining speed. Before she knew it, they were climbing out of Lahore. She'd once heard a rumour that there was always a huge explosion from the plane's rear during take-off and landing, and it never failed to crack her up. Whoever had made this bold claim had either never flown or had been on a very decrepit aircraft. She tuned out the pilot's monologue and saw the city of Mughals becoming smaller, the lights growing dimmer until there was nothing to see except clouds.

There was no going back now.

It had been a while since she had seen people who weren't Pakistani. Everywhere she looked, she saw someone of a different nationality rushing towards immigration. A lot of her fellow Pakistanis who had been jumping queues and shouting expletives at Lahore airport were now walking down the corridors in single file, speaking to each other in subdued voices. Fixing her scarf in place, she followed, not wanting to get left behind, or worse, lost. It was still supposed to be summer, but the airport was chilly with its long, draughty corridors and fluorescent lighting. Buttoning up the cardigan she wore over her shalwar kameez, she hurried past the signs leading to the immigration hall. Her mother had suggested she wear Western clothes for the journey, just to blend, but Ayesha had resisted. She'd found that she had been resisting a lot of things lately.

Good on you, she thought to herself.

She needn't have panicked so much. To her utter relief, the immigration officer didn't interrogate her, in fact she barely glanced at her as she stamped her passport, and before Ayesha knew it, she was picking up her bag and taking the green channel out of baggage reclaim. Her mother had said that Jamila Aunty would be there to meet her. Ayesha had spoken with her on the phone, but now she realised that it might have been better to have made a video call as Jamila Aunty had initially suggested. She'd thought Jamila was being nosy, but looking back now, it probably made sense to see each other's face rather than rely on photos taken years ago. The arrivals hall had people from everywhere in the world, something never seen in Pakistan, and in the melee, she felt panic set in, the walls closing in on her from all sides. She blinked furiously to keep the tears at bay. Her father would have known what to do. She missed her parents. *Where are you, Jamila Aunty?*

People must have noticed her looking lost, because a kindly woman who had been on the same flight smiled at Ayesha. '*Beta*, you look a bit lost. This airport has free internet, so if you want you can easily call the person you're meeting on Whatsapp.'

Of course. How could she have been so dense? She thanked the woman, but she just shook her head.

'Happens to the best of us. I am a seasoned traveller now, but if you'd seen me ten years ago, you'd have laughed. I once got my shalwar stuck in the baggage reclaim belt. Don't ask me how on earth I managed that, but I did.'

They laughed, and some of the weight on Ayesha's heart shifted. Maybe this city wouldn't be so bad. Already the walls seemed to be retreating, the light seeming brighter than before. Before she could reply to the woman, however, she heard someone say, 'Ayesha?'

It was a man's voice.

She turned around, only realising now that the woman hadn't commented on her face at all. She hadn't even glanced at her injuries.

Kamil

She turned around and Kamil was struck by how much she had changed. He could barely remember his childhood visits to Multan, but he did remember her to be a tall, gangly girl, always coming first in swimming competitions and giving all the other kids a hard time. His father used to say that Ayesha would be an athlete, and that might have happened if she'd been brought up in a more liberal family.

He also couldn't help but notice how beautiful she was. It broke his heart a little to see how careful she was to cover the right side of her face. She kept tugging her scarf over her cheek, but even then, it was obvious that there was a great deal of skin damage. For a moment, all he could feel was rage. How dare that bastard do this to a woman, to Ayesha? He might be rich and influential in Multan, but he was no one outside Pakistan.

Ayesha tilted her head as if she was trying – and failing – to place him, so he held up his phone, showing her a photo of his mother.

'I'm Jamila Akbar's son. Kamil Akbar.'

Relief flooded her features. 'Oh, Kamil! *Assalam alaikum*. How are you?' But then she immediately grew suspicious. 'How can I be sure that you're actually Kamil?' she said.

'WhatsApp calls are your friend,' the woman next to Ayesha spoke up, eyeing Kamil with distaste. 'Call your aunty. You don't want to get mixed up with the wrong sort.'

'Well, excuse me—' Kamil began, but his retort was cut short by his phone ringing. He held it up to Ayesha. 'Here, you can speak to my mother yourself. And you can watch, lady,' he added to the woman.

Even in the throng of noisy travellers in Heathrow, his mother's voice rang out like a siren. 'Ayesha, *beta*! *Haye, meri bachi*. Have you reached London already? Where is Kamil? Has he left you alone, the *haramzada*. You just wait. I'll fix him.'

It took several attempts before his mother finally agreed to put the phone down, but not before she got the contact details of the woman who stood with Ayesha.

'Never hurts to know a fellow Pakistani in this lawless land, dear Najma. Thank you for taking care of our Ayesha.'

Lawless, Kamil thought, trying not to laugh.

Najma, having satisfied herself that Ayesha was in safe hands, bid them farewell with promises to see Ayesha soon. 'As your aunty said, it really is useful to have fellow Pakistanis around in this *lawless* land.' She winked at Kamil.

The cheek of her. Nobody made fun of his mother except for him and Shar. As he watched the older woman glide out of the terminal building, her kaftan floating behind her, Ayesha touched him on the shoulder.

'Shall we head out too?'

He looked back to see her smiling at him. Half of her mouth was still hidden behind the scarf, and sensing his gaze on her, she stopped smiling and tugged at it. Kamil wanted to tell her to not worry, but he didn't know how. He'd probably end up embarrassing the poor girl.

'Sorry, I was late,' he told her, not meeting her eyes this time. Pointing towards the exit, he took hold of the luggage trolley, ignoring Ayesha's protests that she could wheel it herself, and started walking. 'Just follow me. The car isn't very far. I parked in the nearest space I could find.'

'You didn't have to go through so much trouble for me. I could have taken public transport.'

This time, he glanced at her. 'Have you ever been on the public transport here?'

Ayesha shook her head.

'Well, then you ought to be relieved I came to meet you at the airport. The trains here can be confusing for a new person.'

'It really is very kind of you.'

Kamil laughed. 'You used to be a very loud kid. I hardly recognise you anymore.'

Ayesha smiled again, but it was sad smile. 'Sometimes, life gets in the way, Kamil.' Perhaps realising how doleful she sounded, she perked up. 'It feels nice to be here. I can't wait to get some fresh air. I've been breathing stale air for far too long.'

'London isn't exactly known for its fresh air.'

'Well then, all I can say is that you've forgotten smog-infested Multan.'

It was a beautiful September afternoon outside with a strong breeze blowing and he heard Ayesha sigh. 'We don't get this sort of weather in Multan in the summer. I just came from excruciating humidity that would curl the silkiest hair in the world. An absolute disaster.'

'Do you get out of Multan a lot?' he asked. 'For holidays?'

Ayesha paused for a moment as if she couldn't decide what to say, but then straightened her shoulders. 'Not for quite a while now, actually. We're not that wealthy anymore.'

Fool, he thought, almost kicking himself. Of course, he had to embarrass her.

Ayesha didn't seem to have noticed. She continued: 'It took some doing to get me here and thanks to your mother's hospitality, I won't even have to pay rent.'

'You're like family, Ayesha. You can stay with us for as long as you like. And family members don't pay rent.'

Ayesha shook her head, but she was smiling. 'We're hardly family. Our mothers are friends. But then, in Multan that is enough to make people family, I guess.'

Kamil shrugged. He felt a bit tongue-tied in front of her, which he put down to his anxiety that he might say the wrong thing. It didn't take much for him to infuriate people, especially women, so he was grateful when they finally reached the car, his father's ancient Beemer. He didn't have a car himself, and if he really needed to use one, he just borrowed it from his parents. And his mother had absolutely insisted that he bring Ayesha back in a car.

They passed through Hounslow and made their way north. It was going to be a long drive. He glanced sideways at Ayesha, wondering if she was bored of him already, but she was taking in the city, her eyes darting in every direction.

'It is so clean!' she exclaimed. 'Everything is so neatly laid out. It must be a treat to live in a place like this. Each day the same. No need to worry about anything, especially not the bloody heat and power outages.'

Kamil snorted. 'Don't be deceived by this tranquillity. It's just a slow day in London. You should see the city during the morning commute. Do you take your car to work?'

As soon as words left his mouth, he knew he'd make a mistake.

Ayesha's expression darkened, and she lowered her head. 'I am an accountant at a charity organisation, but I don't have a car. It doesn't pay that well for me to be able to afford it. I ... I wanted to be able to afford a lot of things, but somehow I've ended up being a burden on my parents. A burden they can ill afford. And now, I've made them spend a fortune on a trip that is as inconsequential as my life.'

Damn. He could have hit the steering wheel in frustration. His mother had told him that Ayesha was still recovering from the attack, and yet he'd still asked her a foolish question. 'I'm sorry. I didn't mean to pry.'

Ayesha's face had assumed an expression of serenity. 'It's a fact. There's no shame in talking about one's way of life. I've made my choice, and I am living with it. As is everyone.'

Way to go, Kamil, he thought. *Way to go*. A silence ensued. He focused on the gathering traffic, wishing he could be anywhere but in the car. Why did he always have to ruin things? As if the poor girl hadn't suffered enough already.

Before he could think of something to salvage the situation, Ayesha spoke again, 'You mustn't think I'm some sort of a yogi or something, with smartarse one-liners.' She gestured towards her face. 'As you may have gathered, I've been through some things, so I'm feeling a bit disillusioned.' Kamil stole a glance at her and saw she was red in the face. She shook her head again. 'I have no idea why I am telling you this. I guess it takes a change of scenery and a new person for me to spill my guts like this.'

Without warning, they both started laughing, and Kamil felt some of the tension dissipate.

'You'll like London,' he assured her. 'Just wait and see. This break will be worth it.'

'Not really. Everywhere I go, people judge me. They look at me and see a freak.'

'You're no freak, Ayesha. You're a perfectly normal human being. Don't let the world get to you.'

'Kind of rich coming from someone who has had it easy in life, living in the UK and all. You don't know Pakistan, but thanks for your sage advice. I shall consider it.'

Easy in life? He bristled, feeling the familiar anger rising in him. What did this girl know about his life, what he had suffered? He thought back to the meeting he'd just had with his therapy group and took a deep breath.

As if on cue, Ayesha immediately apologised. 'I'm sorry, Kamil. You must excuse my unacceptable behaviour.'

'And I'm sorry too. I shouldn't have asked personal questions in the first place.' Pausing for a moment, he added, 'I hope you will enjoy your stay here.'

She turned her head away and gazed out of the window again. For a moment, she didn't say anything, but then he heard her whisper, 'I hope so too.'

Ayesha

She was furious with herself. What was wrong with her? Here was a nice guy with impeccable manners trying to make her feel better and she was snapping at him? She wasn't surprised, though. Ever since the attack, her first reaction to everything was distrust. Raza had made it impossible for her to ever trust anyone. But she knew the problem hadn't really started with him. Her family's financial situation, the people who had swindled her father, and Neelam Khala with her fake affection – all of these had contributed to making her the person she was today.

Without even realising it, she reached for the scarf and fixed it so that it covered her affected side. The action frustrated her. This was going to be her lot in life, always adjusting her scarf, hiding herself from the world one day at a time. Without the scarf, she was a pariah, an object for people to gawk at. Even Saqib had made her feel unwanted. The thought made her want to shudder, but she didn't. There had been enough drama with Kamil already. He was the first man around Saqib's age she had spoken to since he'd rejected her, and she had the urge to unleash all the pent-up rage she felt towards Saqib on him. She realised she'd already done that to an extent and that wasn't fair on the poor guy.

Life isn't fair, she thought. So what if she had given Kamil a piece of her mind? She noticed how he kept glancing at her. He probably had a girlfriend – the name 'Safiya' kept blinking on his cell phone. He finally picked it up and stowed in his pocket. *Well, good for you,* she thought. Everyone deserved to have someone they cared for in their life. It was a bonus if that person cared back. She couldn't help but wonder whether Saqib had ever really cared for her. Perhaps he had only been in it for the sex, because she didn't have any money to speak of. She'd likened her relationship with him to true love, but now she knew that true love didn't exist. It was a lie touted by Bollywood films, corrupting the minds of impressionable young people who either got their hearts broken or simply became pregnant.

What a waste.

Thankfully, she was rescued from having to engage in more small talk by their arrival at Kamil's parents' house. They were in a residential neighbourhood with medium-sized brick houses of a similar design lining the street. In Pakistan, these were called town houses. Ayesha knew exactly what someone like Neelam Khala would say about town houses.

She felt even worse about snapping at Kamil when he opened the car door for her. He was Pakistani, but much better behaved than the men she knew back home. Even her father, for all his qualities, was not always kind to his mother. In fact, he took her for granted most of the time, and that was after thirty years of marriage. She couldn't imagine how bad things must have been in the early years. In those days, a woman was lucky to have any rights at all in her husband's home.

'Thank you,' she said, without meeting Kamil's eye. She wanted to apologise again, but something told her it would only make things worse.

Kamil's mouth was set in a straight line. 'Before we head inside, I want you to know that my mother can be a bit over the top with her opinions, but her heart is pure. She is a good woman, so if she ends up saying something odd, you must not mind.'

She couldn't help but smile. 'You don't have to worry. I am sure she's lovely.'

'That's not the word I'd use to describe my mother.'

Now she laughed. 'I am looking forward to meeting her.'

She didn't know what exactly she was expecting, but it wasn't the *Welcome to London* banner and balloons that greeted her. As soon as they stepped inside, there was a collective cheer, and Ayesha was suddenly buried in someone's warm, soft embrace.

'*Haye*, my dear girl. I am so glad you have finally arrived. I almost thought Kamil would end up getting lost or worse. We've been waiting for ages. What took you so long?'

It was another minute before Ayesha was released and could take a look at the person who had hugged her. Jamila Aunty looked exactly like her photos, an open and friendly face with eyes that brimmed with warmth. Her own head was covered with a dupatta, but she eyed Ayesha's scarf with distaste.

'What is this, *beta*? You are so young and you've covered yourself up like this. When I was your age, I used to wear sleeveless. In Multan, yes! Those were the days. How else do you think your uncle fell for my charms.'

Behind her, Kamil groaned. 'Ugh. Give her some space, Ammi. And covering one's head is a personal choice. You must learn to have a filter when you speak.'

Jamila Aunty's eyes gleamed. 'Oh Kamil, you're such a spoilsport. Of course, I'm lying. Back in our day, we were lucky to be allowed to remove the dupatta from our heads, much less wear sleeveless. I just said it so Ayesha doesn't feel like she has to stay fully covered here.'

Ayesha considered removing her scarf, but she didn't want to see that inevitable look of pity pass across Jamila's features. 'I'll consider it, Jamila Aunty,' she said instead. 'It's lovely to finally meet you.'

'Look how skinny you are. We must feed you.' Jamila Aunty took her hand and steered her to the living room. She pointed at a black-haired girl who seemed to be about the same age as Ayesha. 'This is my daughter, Sharmeela. She works in a bank in London. Unfortunately, she is still unmarried, but I can assure you I am looking for a good boy for her. If you have any suggestions or know of anyone in Multan...'

'Enough, Ammi,' Sharmeela said firmly, leaning in to air kiss

Ayesha. 'It's Shar, if you don't mind, and I honestly don't care that I am' – she used her fingers as quotation marks – '"unmarried". Much to the sorrow of my mother.' Her eyes lit up in a genuine smile, which Ayesha found herself returning. 'Great to have you here, Ayesha. I can't wait to show you around.'

'She has a nice Mexican friend called Juan. Not that kind of friend, I assure you. *InshAllah* she will marry a Pakistani, but Juan is a nice boy. He is good at showing people around. You must meet him.'

Sharmeela exhaled. 'Imagine if he was my boyfriend, Ammi.'

Jamila Aunty clutched her chest. '*Haye*! Don't even joke about these things, Sharmeela. Do you want to give your mother a heart attack? Your boyfriend – no, husband – will be a well-to-do Pakistani man.' She nodded. 'That is how it has always been in our family and how it will always be.'

Sharmeela looked like she had more to say on the matter, but one look from Kamil put an end to that. 'You're so boring, Kamil,' she protested. 'You don't even let me torment Ammi.'

Jamila Aunty's husband, Akbar Khan, was also unlike the elderly men of Pakistan. Clearly he'd spent a lot of time in the UK because before dinner, he insisted on helping his wife lay the table.

Sharmeela shrugged when Ayesha asked if they ought to help. 'She doesn't let anyone except Abba help when it comes to food, so we've basically given up. Besides, we enjoy it. One less thing for us to do. Work is so busy, and just because Ammi insists on cooking for us doesn't mean she cleans after us as well. That's my job.' She glanced at Kamil. 'My brother is free from all this in his swanky flat in Earl's Court.'

'Swanky, you say?' Kamil replied. 'I just have a studio. Still, I am glad that I'm independent.'

'He'll only move back home when one of us breaks a hip,' Jamila Aunty said, plonking a pot of bubbling chicken karahi on the table. 'It's so humiliating that the son of this house lives somewhere else – not a thought for his elderly parents.'

'I thought you said you were only in your late forties.' Kamil winked at his mother.

'That is beside the point.'

'You need to let go of your kids, Jamila Begum,' Akbar Khan said as he brought in fresh rotis. 'They're in their thirties.'

'Sharmeela is twenty-eight, Khan Sahab. Don't give me a heart attack for no reason. There are still a couple of years to go before she's on the shelf.'

They all broke into laughter, but Jamila Aunty didn't seem to mind. 'Ah, my beautiful children.' She turned towards Ayesha. 'And you too, *beta*. You're just like my own child as well.'

What a lovely family, Ayesha thought. They had no need to put on airs like families in Pakistan did. The families she knew in Pakistan could learn from them. She thought of her relatives back home, even her own parents, and realised what a vicious circle they were stuck in. In their desperate need to prove themselves as rich, they lived in perpetual misery. The constant battle to throw the best parties, buy the most expensive designer handbags and associate with the richest people had consumed them, depriving them of even the most basic pleasures that life had to offer.

Like this family dinner.

Unlike Pakistan, there were no power outages or honking cars to awaken her. If it wasn't for the alarm, she wouldn't have woken up at all. After many weeks of nightmares and light dozing, she'd sunk into a 'sleep of the dead'. Even though it was still September, it had cooled significantly during the night, enough for her to wrap the thick quilt around her. Back in Multan, she slept with just a thin sheet covering her. It was too hot for anything else.

She opened her window and there it was again: a peculiar scent that was foreign to her. She'd noticed it the day before while getting out of the car. Breathing in the early-afternoon air, she finally realised what it was. She couldn't smell the smoke and pollution. What she was smelling was pure, unadulterated fresh air. If London, which was supposed to have the worst air quality in the United Kingdom, smelled like this, she could only wonder what the English countryside smelled like. Certainly nothing like Multan or Lahore, where your nostrils choked on the pernicious fumes.

They'd given her Kamil's old room, which was of a decent size, and while he'd cleared lots of his things out, the room still held mementos of him. All it took was opening a drawer for her to find everything from Bollywood posters to football souvenirs. She regretted intruding on his privacy, but looking at posters of Sushmita Sen and Tom Cruise cracked her up. She'd probably laughed more this past day than she had over the last several months. It occurred to her that she ought to check her phone for messages from Saqib, but then she realised that at the moment, she didn't care.

She was in a new country, and for the first time in a long time, it was actually easy to breathe.

Just breathe.

By the time Ayesha had taken a shower, put on some clothes and makeup and made her way downstairs, it was almost lunchtime. Initially thinking there was a loud film playing, she was surprised to see an entire flock of women crowding the living room. The coffee table was laden with tea things, and Jamila Aunty bustled around bringing in more. As Ayesha arrived at the foot of the stairs, a hush descended. Every single face in the room was turned in her direction. Her heart fell. This was going to be Pakistan all over again. What were all these women doing here?

She stood rooted to the spot, one hand on the bannister, her nails grinding against the wood. Her other hand reached for her face to make sure the scarf was in place. To her utter horror, her fingers grazed her ridged scars. She'd forgotten to put on her scarf. Her face was on display and there was nothing she could do to hide it. No wonder the room had gone silent, all the women watching her like a bunch of hawks. What a fool she'd been to have worn western clothes. If she had a dupatta, at least she could have used it to cover her face.

But why should you, a small voice inside her asked. *Are you not human? Do you not live and breathe like the rest of them?*

She knew the answer to that, of course. Appearances mattered, and if one didn't conform to the universal idea of beauty, then one might as well not be human. It was too late, anyway. They'd all seen her.

'Oh, there you are, *beti*,' Jamila Aunty called, coming in from the kitchen carrying a roast chicken. Even in the haze of embarrassment she was feeling, she saw that Jamila Aunty was wearing a smart outfit, her hair pulled up into a bun so that the dupatta sat on it well. She looked like a different person. She smiled at Ayesha. 'You're just in time to join us for our monthly kitty party. Did I not tell you about it last night? God, I must be getting old.' Depositing the chicken on the coffee table, she moved closer to Ayesha. If she'd seen the burnt part of her face (of course, she had!), she didn't show it. Her eyes didn't even venture there, not even a fraction. Jamila Aunty met her gaze and held it. 'Are you okay?' she whispered, leaning forward. 'I'm sorry, I should have given you better warning, but I thought you might like to see some new faces.'

Well, you thought wrong. Then Ayesha immediately stamped on her uncharitable sentiment. The poor woman was only trying to be nice. She took a deep breath and put the biggest smile on her face that she could manage. 'I've never been better.'

'Do you want me to get your scarf for you?'

Ayesha considered that for a moment. 'They've already seen me. I don't think it matters now.'

Jamila Aunty beamed, but Ayesha's stomach clenched. What had she just said? She was not ready for this kind of scrutiny, but it was too late to grab her scarf now. Or was it? She almost turned back to run upstairs, but Jamila was already announcing her:

'This is Ayesha Safdar from my home city, Multan. She's my darling Ishrat's daughter, and you can consider her my own daughter. She will be staying with us for a while.'

'*Haye*,' an elderly woman spoke up in Saraiki. 'Have you brought any of that Multani clay with you, *beta*? There's nothing quite like that for one's face.'

'My dear Saeeda, if she had some of that clay, don't you think she'd be using it on herself?' another middle-aged woman piped in. 'From what I can see, she could use some of that. What happened to you, dear?'

Ayesha stood there like a deer caught in the headlights. As much as she wanted to disappear, her legs betrayed her. They would not move.

'Looks like a kitchen accident,' one of them said.

'Be quiet, it is rude to ask,' another said.

The woman's lips twitched as she watched Ayesha. 'Mute, are you?'

Saeeda drew herself up. 'Enough, Moeeza. You're being mean.' She turned to Ayesha, a smile on her face. 'Don't mind Moeeza, *beta*. She was born rude. Her heart is in the right place, though. I think.' She patted the seat next to her. 'Come, sit with us. Let us get a good look at you.'

Her legs, the old traitors, obeyed, and before she knew it, she was sitting with Saeeda, the rest of the women gawking at her. There were about ten of them, most of them in their fifties and sixties. A couple of them had their teacups poised to their lips, but seemed to have forgotten that they were supposed to sip from them.

They were watching her like she was an animal in the zoo. She craned her neck to see where Jamila Aunty was, but she seemed busy in the kitchen. Her forehead broke out in a sweat.

'We meet every month,' Saeeda told her. 'It's called a kitty party, similar to what you have in Pakistan. We call them committee parties too. We all pool money together, the same amount every month, and one person gets the entire lot. That way, we can afford to buy things that are usually out of our budget.'

Ayesha tried not to roll her eyes. She didn't need anyone to explain what a committee party was. They were the bread and butter of Multani society. Her mother was too poor to get involved in them now, but Neelam Khala had her hand in plenty of them. Since there was little concept of savings in Pakistan, a lot of people relied on the money from the kitty to buy things they wouldn't ordinarily be able to afford. Back in the day when her mother used to be part of a kitty, she had bought a huge flat-screen television with the money when her turn arrived. They still used the same set.

One of the women seated directly in front of Ayesha leaned forward. 'Hello Ayesha, my name is Muneeba. Correct me if I'm wrong, but weren't you engaged to Raza Masood? I saw your photos on Instagram.' She touched her neck. 'It's sad what happened to you. You'd have made a beautiful bride otherwise.'

'If she covers those scars, she might yet make a decent bride,' Moeeza observed. 'These days, anything is possible. Just look at all the celebrities.'

'I wonder how you got the scars,' Muneeba continued. 'I'd love to hear your side of the story. What are kitty parties for if not gossip?'

Ayesha's mouth opened and closed as laughter rang out in the room. What on earth did they expect her to say? Judging by the silence that now ensued, they were expecting her to say *something*. She thought back to the girl she used to be before this attack, the kind who had been able to silence even the likes of Neelam Khala. She stared back at the woman, a tsunami of emotions gathering inside her.

'Rabbiya's son did this to me. He lured me to his friend's place and in the presence of several witnesses, he doused me with acid. That is the kind of person he is, the kind of family they are.' Several gasps from the ladies greeted this revelation. 'And if that wasn't enough, he visited me in the hospital while I was battling the injuries he had left on me, only to break off the engagement and level petty threats my way.' She was breathing hard, but it was like a dam had broken in her.

Muneeba's face paled, her cheeks thinning. 'I ... That sounds awful.'

Ayesha took a deep breath. The woman looked obviously contrite about probing. 'It was.' She exhaled. 'And I'm sorry. I've just arrived in London, so bear with me while I get accustomed to this city.'

One of the women who had thus far not said a word leaned forward. 'You are still a very pretty girl, Ayesha. Don't let anyone tell you otherwise.' She glanced at Moeeza. 'She probably had an argument with her husband before coming here, which explains her mood.'

Moeeza scowled. 'Hina, please! You don't know anything about my life.'

Hina grinned. 'Except I do.'

'So, what are we discussing?' Jamila Aunty said, bustling back in, wiping her hands on a dish cloth. 'The food will take a little while yet, ladies, so be patient.'

Hina smiled. 'I was just telling Ayesha how beautiful she is.'

Jamila Aunty beamed. 'That, she is. A rare gem.'

Ayesha looked up at the ceiling so her tears wouldn't slide out of her eyes.

'What a rotten family that did this to her, though,' Saeeda boomed. 'That's why I left Pakistan in the first place. Women's rights don't exist there. I brought my children here the first chance I got.'

Ayesha could tell that this was an unpopular opinion by the looks that passed between the women.

'*Pakistan zindabad*,' one of them murmured – *Long live Pakistan.*

'I love my Pakistan. We live here, but our hearts are in our home country. That's where we come from.'

Saeeda laughed, a deep throaty sound that rang around the room. 'Then why don't you go back and live in your precious Pakistan? What's stopping you?'

Silence greeted her question.

'I thought so,' Saeeda said. 'It's very easy to love Pakistan with your first-world privilege, my dears. But you wouldn't last a day in that country. The society vultures alone would finish you off.'

Jamila Aunty nodded. 'Saeeda does have a point. As much as we love our country, we cannot deny all the atrocities that happen there.'

'And, don't they happen here?' Muneeba asked. 'Are you telling me that Britain is free of crime.'

'What I am saying is that Ayesha didn't deserve what happened to her. And yet, here she is sitting with her head held high. We ought to celebrate that, and her, don't you think?'

Saeeda held up a hand. 'Settle down, ladies. Why don't you check on the food, Jamila?'

'Ayesha, would you like to come with me?' Jamila Aunty asked, turning towards the kitchen.

Ayesha shook her head. She wanted to hear what these ladies would say next.

As soon as Jamila Aunty was out of earshot, Moeeza tutted. 'Forgive me if I take this sob story with a pinch of salt. Do you expect us to believe that a grown woman was *lured* into some house?' She gave Ayesha a look. 'What are you, twelve? The stories you girls come up with these days. You give our country a bad name. Is it any wonder the *goras* here think of Pakistan as some sort of shantytown?' She shook her head, adjusting the embroidered shawl on her shoulder so that it was more prominent. 'And before Saeeda starts, I'd like to clarify that unlike most of you, I spent a good chunk of my life in Pakistan. And I don't come from a big city either. I hail from Bahawalpur. Back in my day, girls were taught obedience, and if someone rebelled, she got beaten. No wonder we didn't see any acid attacks or God knows what in those days. Life was more elegant then.'

Muneeba nodded slowly. 'For once, I kind of agree with you.'

'Who knew someone as small as you could harbour so much poison, Moeeza,' Saeeda remarked. 'What kind of heartless people do we have in this kitty?'

'I'd like to ask you the same question, Saeeda,' Moeeza replied, blowing at her nails.

'What is going on here now?' Jamila Aunty marched in from the kitchen, holding a large tray. A dozen seekh kebabs were laid out among parsley. It didn't take long for her to clock the mood in the room. 'Sorry, it took a little time to get the kebabs ready, but I hope you've been treating my Ayesha well in the meantime?' She offered her a winning smile, which Ayesha tried to return, but couldn't. Her heart was pounding in her throat. She realised that she wasn't ready to face so many people. Not for the first time, she wondered why exactly she'd come here. What had she expected? People didn't change ... not in Pakistan and not in London either. It was foolish of her to even entertain the idea of coming to this city.

Saeeda grimaced. 'Why don't you let Moeeza tell you?'

'I've nothing to say,' Moeeza replied drily. 'I actually need to get moving soon. I need to be back home to take over from Julie. She'll be done for the day. And then it's the kids and dinner.'

'Coward!' Saeeda shot back. 'You're probably off to High Street Kensington.'

'I haven't been there in ages.'

'I saw you at The Ivy last week. What a liar. No wonder wealthy women like you need to join kitty parties. You're terrible at saving money.'

Moeeza blew at her nails again. 'Kitty parties are just for gossip, Saeeda. They're not really about saving money. Haven't you learned anything in all your years?'

Saeeda's expression was stony. Turning to Jamila Aunty, she said, 'I am sorry to say, but these women haven't treated Ayesha well. And they call themselves hospitable Pakistanis. We should all be ashamed of ourselves.'

Jamila Aunty was no fool. The smile was gone from her face. She placed the tray of kebabs on the coffee table as quietly as she could and wiped her hands on her dupatta. 'Why don't we all call it a day? We can transfer the kitty money to Saeeda's account through PayPal later. She's the winner this month, after all.'

'What about the food?' Muneeba asked. 'I'm starving and these kebabs look marvellous.'

'You can take some for yourself, Muneeba. Now out. All of you. I'm very disappointed with you.' She pointed at Ayesha. 'Look at her. She looks miserable. She came from Pakistan to escape this invasive scrutiny, and instead of welcoming her, you make her feel uncomfortable? You make her cry? Shame on you all.'

'Careful, Jamila.' There was warning in Moeeza's tone.

'Uff *dafa ho*, Moeeza. Get out of my house.'

'Yes, get lost, Moeeza,' Saeeda chimed in, pushing herself off the sofa. 'Thanks for ruining a perfectly nice afternoon. And you too, Muneeba. Get lost, all of you. I'll wait for the money to be transferred by no later than tonight.' She turned to Ayesha. 'You've got a spine, girl. And a tongue. Learn to use them more. This world goes easy on no one.'

That may be the best advice anyone has ever given to me, she thought, as the ladies filed out, some with barely concealed fury, others laughing the unpleasantness away.

She hadn't asked for one, but Jamila Aunty gave her a hug anyway. 'I'm so sorry, Ayesha. I should have rescheduled the kitty. I should have known. Please don't tell my kids. They will murder me.'

As if on cue, Kamil arrived, ready to take her out for an afternoon of sightseeing.

Jamila Aunty groaned. 'Trust him to arrive at the worst possible time.'

Ayesha closed her eyes. He had seen her face.

Kamil

As soon as he saw his mother's kitty friends leaving, he knew there had been drama. It was like mini-Pakistan in there. Not all of them were bad, but the gossip was sometimes too much for him to stand. Moeeza, in particular, drove him insane. Her barbed remarks about his personal life and his inability to keep a girl rattled him, but he endured them for his mother. But Jamila Akbar's kitty was her life blood. That was how she managed to buy expensive things every year, with one woman getting the whole lot every month when everyone congregated for a celebratory lunch, but more than that, these horrible women were his mother's only friends, her only contact with the outside world. Although they spent most of the time gossiping about their kids and grandkids, which inevitably depressed his mother, he was still glad for her to have some company. There were a few good ones in the kitty too, especially Saeeda who had always taken his side.

'Allow the boy to live his life, Jamila,' she'd said once. 'The world has moved on. Nobody *needs* to be married today. You can simply live without. These are hard-won freedoms – don't take them away from your son. And if someone objects, you can tell them where to shove their opinions.' To drive her point home, she gave Akbar Khan a meaningful glance, and added, 'Where the sun doesn't shine.'

His father had dissolved into fits of laughter as his mother blushed and muttered, '*Astagfirullah!*'

He'd have liked to meet Saeeda, but meeting her meant coming face to face with the other lot, and he knew better than that. He turned away and busied himself with his phone as the women left in their respective cars, while others walked to the nearest train station.

He'd got off work early today, on his mother's behest. She

wanted him to show Ayesha around London, and although she had taken some convincing, his boss, Amelia, had been in a good mood after the success of his latest Facebook marketing campaign for one of the fashion brands they managed, and had eventually relented.

It was late afternoon now and poor Ayesha looked done in, rushing upstairs when she saw him arrive. This was the first time he'd seen her without her scarf, and his first thought was how beautiful her hair was – a lustrous brown that shone when it caught the sunlight. Looking at the scars on her face and how the acid had eaten away some of her nose, he could understand her need to hide herself, but as far as he was concerned, she needn't have bothered. She was a beautiful woman.

'Never disregard other people's problems just because you can't understand them,' Matt had said during their most recent session. 'Empathy is a very strong emotion, and sometimes that's all you need to make the other person feel better.'

'That's something my wife could learn more of,' Shabbir had said, lifting his shirt up to show them the bruise she had given him, just because he'd spoken kindly to another Pakistani girl in their neighbourhood.

Kamil blinked away the memory, focusing on his mother, who seemed completely beside herself. 'Oh, Kamil *beta*, I shouldn't have had the kitty today. Ayesha looks absolutely miserable. I think that Moeeza said some horrible stuff to her.'

'Where were you?'

His mother looked at him as if she couldn't quite believe his stupidity. 'In the kitchen, of course. Where else? Do you honestly think I'd host a kitty party and not have food? I missed most of what transpired.'

'Ammi...'

'The thing is that I don't know what exactly they said to her although I got the gist of it. I'll ask Saeeda later, but right now, I need you to take Ayesha and show her around. I know it will be evening soon, but just go. I can't believe I let her out of my sight, and that too on her second day in London. *Haye!* Your father is no help, and you know Sharmeela. She wouldn't leave work early even if her mother was dying. The only person I can rely on is you, *beta*. You are my only hope.'

These theatrics were reserved for when his mother was truly desperate. He hoped the kitty ladies hadn't given Ayesha a hard time. She'd already been through enough. However, before he could say anything, his phone rang.

It was Safiya again. She was becoming more of a burden than a friend. What did she want with him now? She clearly didn't want to have sex, so what on earth did she want? It was an uncharitable thought, but what was he supposed to think?

His mother raised her eyebrows. 'Is it that woman? I told you to stay away from her. She won't be giving you any children.'

'For the last time, Ammi—'

'I want grandchildren! And preferably before I die.'

'Right now, the priority is to look after Ayesha, remember?'

That worked like a charm on her. She immediately changed tack. 'Yes, of course. You take her out now. Forget about everything else.'

Thank God for you, Ayesha, he thought.

They were supposed to meet Shar and Juan for drinks, but he wasn't sure if Ayesha drank, or indeed, would want to after what had happened this afternoon. Her scarf was back in place, and she seemed even quieter than she had been yesterday. This time, they hadn't taken his parents' car. Instead, he'd taken Ayesha on the tube. He thought she might enjoy the experience, but it was after they entered the tunnels and the train started filling up that he felt it was getting a bit hot. Too hot, actually, and it took forever for the Northern Line to get into Central London. Still, it was better than taking a car into the city – nobody did that except for the millionaires. As the train rattled into King's Cross, he risked another look at her. Her eyes kept darting at the people sitting in their carriage, as if she was worried they'd be staring at her. Nobody was. For all its faults, that was one of the good things about London – nobody cared enough to give anyone a second glance.

'I was thinking I could show you around Soho, and then we could make our way to Foyles and check out some books.' Ayesha didn't look at him, but he hoped she was listening. One could never know for sure since the train made so much noise as it whizzed through the tunnels. 'If you'd rather we hang out in a café, we can do that too although we will be meeting Shar later anyway. She's also bringing Juan.'

She tilted her face in his direction. 'Her Mexican friend, Juan? Jamila Aunty told me about him.'

So, she *was* listening. 'He's a nice guy.' He took a deep breath. 'Look, I am sorry if my mother did something to offend you. She's really not a bad person, and she was angry with her friends for swarming around you. Her kitty friends are all she's got though. That's her entire social life. We don't have any relatives here, so Ammi has built her world around her kitty.'

'Jamila Aunty has been nothing but kind,' Ayesha murmured. Kamil had to crane his neck in her direction to make out the words. 'Please do tell her that she's done nothing wrong. As a matter of fact, she locked horns with her friends over me.'

Kamil smiled. 'That sounds like her.'

'I just don't want to be a nuisance. Wherever I go, whatever I do, people look at me like I'm different. Like I am somehow ... inferior. That has become my life now, thinking I'm inferior and inadequate all the time. Can you imagine how that feels?'

He could, because that is how he felt most of the time himself. 'Ayesha, I—'

'I either get treated like a legit freak or like delicate china that could break at any moment. I hate it, you know.' She was still looking away from him, but he could sense the anger in her voice. 'I want to smash things. I want to do damage. I want to make this world as damaged as I am. I hate it. I hate myself.' With that, she buried her face in her hands.

'Listen—'

'No! You listen to me.' She whipped her head in his direction and he saw that her face was streaked with tears. 'Nobody listens to me. Not really. I want to be treated like a normal human being. Is that too much to ask? Is it too much to ask of Moeeza to treat me like a human and not an animal she's spotted in the zoo?'

'Moeeza has always been a bitch.'

'That doesn't excuse her behaviour.'

Kamil cleared his throat, rising from his seat. 'This is our stop.' He extended a hand.

When they emerged out of Leicester Square Station he checked his phone: several missed calls from Safiya and a couple from his mother. Bloody Safiya! Just as he was dialling his mother, Safiya's name sprang on his screen. He picked up.

'Playing hard to get doesn't suit you, Kamil. Do you have any idea how many times I've called you? And I'm not the kind of person to call people. They call me.'

'Welcome to the real world, Safiya.'

'Oh wow, I like that. I am this close to breaking my vow of abstinence, you know? I've been thinking of little else for days. Days you've spent ignoring me.'

Kamil relented. 'I'm not ignoring you.' He glanced at Ayesha, who took the hint and walked over to a souvenir stall. Holding the phone closer to his mouth, he added, 'Maybe I would like to be there when you break your vow of abstinence from sex.'

'Would you now?'

He could picture her smiling. 'It would have to wait, though. I've got a family friend visiting from Pakistan and I am showing her around the city.'

'Her? I see.'

There was silence from Safiya as she waited for him to elaborate. It was ridiculous that he was standing here, justifying himself to someone who even after months of friendship had only now felt close enough to have sex with him. And yet, she was the one who felt entitled to be jealous. He could hear her breathing over the phone, and Ayesha was starting to cast glances at him from where she stood examining faux scarves. He sighed. 'We're having drinks with my sister Sharmeela and her friend, Juan, later tonight. How about you join us?'

There was a moment's hesitation before she said, 'I'm actually going out for drinks with my girlfriends in the early evening, but I guess I can just have one with them. I'm not giving up this chance to see you ... and experience what comes after.' She laughed before adding, 'I can't wait to see you.'

'Girlfriend?' Ayesha asked him as he joined her, and they began walking along Charing Cross Road.

'It's complicated,' he muttered, and she didn't press him further on the subject.

It was strange how quickly time passed with Ayesha. It was only when he checked his watch that he saw that they'd spent hours in Foyles, browsing through books, a load of which he ended up buying. With Ayesha, he looked at London with fresh eyes. The city he had been born and bred in seemed more vibrant, alive, and he found himself watching with wonder the thronging crowds, the cafés bursting at the seams and the overall hopeful vibe of the city. It really was as they said: London was the city of dreams. They were walking towards Tottenham Court Road, Kamil doing his best to ignore the Waterstones bookshop beckoning him, when Ayesha told him that she'd had a boyfriend too.

'I didn't know girls were allowed to do that in Pakistan,' he said.

Ayesha laughed. 'Of course we dabble in that stuff. Do you think Pakistani girls don't have a sex drive? Aren't we human?'

There it was again, his woeful incapability to make small talk. 'I'm sorry,' he mumbled. 'I didn't mean that at all.'

Ayesha pretended not to have heard. 'And do you think a girl from Pakistan can't talk about her sex drive?'

Kamil felt his face warm up. 'It's just that my mother presents a very different image of Pakistan to us.'

'Jamila Aunty is very sweet, but she doesn't know how far we've progressed. I had a boyfriend – and in a city like Multan, too. And believe it or not, we regularly had sex. Sure, it's frowned upon, but doesn't mean it doesn't happen.' She laughed when she saw his face. 'You look so funny right now, but please don't think badly of me. There's something in the air here that's making me open up.'

As soon as she'd uttered the words, he felt her deflate. Her shoulders slumped and she said, 'What does it matter? I'm a monster now. Even the women here say so.' Before he could answer, she snapped, 'Now don't you go consoling me. I don't need it. It is what it is.' She tugged at her scarf. 'God, I hate this scarf. As a young girl, I'd promised myself that I'd be a modern woman, the kind who would wear a scarf if she wanted to, but *only* if she wanted too. Who knew it would be forced on me?'

He hardly knew her, but hearing her speak her heart out like this pained him. What was clear, though, was that she hated being pitied, so he held his tongue. But at the same time, he thought she was in need of support – she just didn't know how to ask for it.

After a few moments' silence, he said, 'You know, if you ever needed to talk—'

'About what?' she asked, interrupting him. 'What is it that I need to be talking about? Why do people always think that I need to talk about something?'

Kamil held up his hands. 'I just meant that if you wanted to talk about stuff you're going through in a safe space, I could introduce you to my therapy group.'

Ayesha blinked at him for a moment before breaking into laughter. 'A Pakistani man in therapy? Now, I've seen everything.' She pushed her palm to her mouth to stop herself laughing. 'Damn!'

He was stung. God knew why he had even mentioned it. What was he thinking?

It must have shown on his face, because Ayesha looked contrite. 'I didn't mean it like that, Kamil. You must believe me. I was just trying to lighten the mood. For some reason, whenever we talk, things get a bit serious.' She put her hand on his forearm and squeezed it. 'As for your therapy group, I can think of nothing better. Damaged goods like me, I'd probably relish it.'

'You're not—'

'Damaged. I know,' she finished for him. 'Now, where are we meeting Sharmeela and Juan?'

'It's still some time before we meet them. Do you want to see the place beforehand? It's pretty Pakistani.'

Finally, a smile broke across her face. 'I can't believe I am saying this since I've just arrived from Pakistan, but yes, I think I would.'

Kamil led her from Tottenham Court Road, north to Euston Station, and ignoring the construction work going on, took her around the back of the station, where they turned onto a street that was always packed with people who looked like him.

'May I present Drummond Street? A little slice of South Asia in the heart of Central London.'

Ayesha's face bloomed like a flower when she saw the place. From *pakoras* to *mithai*, everything was sold in Drummond Street.

'Look at those *gulab jamun*!' she exclaimed, pointing at the popular Pakistani dessert that consisted of balls of thickened cream and milk, fried in oil before being soaked in water and sugar.

They ended up eating four of the delicious *gulab jamun* before taking a stroll down the street.

'The cleanliness is the only thing that gives this street away,' Ayesha said, smacking her mouth as she sucked the last of the sugar from her fingers. 'In Multan, you would find everything from plastic bags to random paper and garbage flying around, along with plenty of dust.' When she looked at him, her eyes danced with mischief. 'The best thing about this place is that nobody is staring at me here. I feel like running around to my heart's content. It's a lovely place.'

Kamil cleared his throat. 'About that ... Safiya, my girlfriend, will be joining us too.'

Ayesha didn't miss a beat. 'Perfect. Can't wait to meet her. She sounds amazing.'

Unfortunately, Safiya didn't seem to think the same. By the time she arrived, Kamil was already seated with Ayesha in one of the open-air restaurants on the street. It was a warm evening, even for September, and they'd taken off their jackets. Although Safiya wore a sleeveless top herself, pairing it with a denim miniskirt, she joked about Ayesha's outfit. 'Girls come here from Pakistan and the first thing they do is wear sleeveless tops. It must be claustrophobic in that country. Good for you, Ayesha.'

She laughed at her own joke as Ayesha raised her eyebrows at Kamil.

Safiya planted a wet kiss on Kamil's lips before plonking down on the wooden chair next to him. She reeked of alcohol.

'How much have you had?' Kamil whispered.

'Just a few drinks. It's no big deal.'

'Seems like more than a few. You said you'd only have one. You shouldn't have come like this.'

She ignored him, turning instead to Ayesha. 'It is lovely to meet you, Ayesha. I've heard lots about you from Kamil ... about what you survived. It can't have been easy.' She sighed. 'But what else can you expect from men in Pakistan?'

Ayesha cleared her throat. 'I daresay crime has no borders. Bad people are everywhere. It doesn't make the entire country bad.'

'But still, it can't be easy, living with this...'

'With what?'

Kamil nudged Safiya. 'Nothing. She doesn't mean anything, do you, Safiya?'

Safiya was still staring at Ayesha. 'You've had my boyfriend all to yourself since you got here, Ayesha. What do you think of him? Quite a catch, isn't he?'

Kamil gave her a look, but she just shrugged. 'Come on, I'm just teasing.' She turned to Ayesha again. 'Girl to girl, isn't it the truth, Ayesha? Look at that sexy smile.'

Safiya seemed to be brimming with repressed frustration. What was she so angry about – that he'd spent some time with Ayesha? Surely, someone as sensible as Safiya wouldn't think that, but it seemed that was exactly what was going on. Made worse by the fact she was wasted.

A smile was playing on Ayesha's face. 'If you're trying to scandalise me with these words, Safiya, then I'm sorry to disappoint you. I've heard plenty worse. Secondly, your *boyfriend* has simply played the role of a gallant friend and showed me around London for a bit. You are welcome to take him home with you. I know the way back to Whetstone.' Running a finger over her arm, she added, 'And, if you must know, I wear sleeveless all the time in Pakistan, and in Multan, of all places.'

'I doubt it. From what I've heard, Multan is pretty conservative. Still, that's a nice scarf you've got there.'

'My scarf is my choice.'

'Clearly. Like pairing it with a sleeveless top is your choice.' Safiya began scanning the menu. 'I want a drink, Kamil. A G&T might do the trick. Maybe I'll get two.'

'You've had enough, Safiya—' Kamil began, but she cut him off with a wave of her hand.

Lifting her eyes, she smiled at Ayesha. 'You do know what that is, don't you?'

He could tell Ayesha was trying not to smile. 'Let me guess. A gin and tonic?'

'Bravo! A girl from Multan with some punch. I like it. So you drink, then?'

'I'd rather not say.'

'And why is that?'

'Will you stop?' Kamil exploded finally. 'What's got into you, Safiya?'

Safiya simply blinked at him. 'I have no idea what you're talking about. I'm just trying to make small talk with her.' Glancing at Ayesha, she added, 'You have something on the right side of your face. What's that? Makeup disaster?'

Ayesha's face fell. She pretended to busy herself with the menu. 'I'll probably get an orange juice.'

Safiya must have realised her mistake because her face reddened. 'I'm sorry,' she murmured. 'I probably shouldn't have another drink.'

Kamil felt the heat rising in his head, making his scalp sweat. He was seeing red. However, before he could say another word, Shar and Juan arrived.

His sister was like a breath of fresh air. She lit up the room wherever she went, and on top of everything, she knew Kamil better than anyone. All she had to do was take one look at him, and then at the women, and she understood.

'What a cute little skirt, Safiya!' she exclaimed as she air-kissed her on each cheek. 'Zara, or have you been naughty enough to shop at Selfridges?'

'Harrods,' Safiya replied, her cheeks still pink. 'It is a cute skirt, I agree.'

Within minutes the situation de-escalated, but the damage was done. Drunk or not, he could never have dreamed that someone like Safiya could be so careless and rude. Sitting there, he couldn't bring himself to look at her, even though she nudged him in the ribs several times. All he could see was Ayesha, whose face looked like someone had sapped all the happiness out of it. Even Shar couldn't seem to lift her spirits.

'You do know Juan is my boyfriend right, Ayesha?' she said in Urdu. 'But you can't tell my mother. I wouldn't have cared, but Kamil here says she might actually have a heart attack.'

Juan remained tight-lipped, probably sensing the tension.

Kamil could see that he'd made an effort to dress up for the occasion. He was wearing an expensive-looking button-down shirt with the sleeves rolled up. He tried to engage Ayesha into conversation, asking if she'd ever been to Mexico City, but she didn't look up. She just adjusted her scarf and pulled a shawl from her handbag, throwing it over her shoulders. 'A bit chilly tonight,' she murmured.

'Now you look like a proper Multani girl,' Safiya remarked.

It took everything in Kamil not to slam his glass on the table.

'You don't have to be from Pakistan to wear a shawl,' Juan remarked, laughing.

Safiya snapped at him. 'Sure, but you do need to be Pakistani to talk about Pakistan.'

Shar's eyebrows almost disappeared in her fringe.

This is how you kill someone's confidence, Kamil thought, as he watched Ayesha hold the shawl tight against her chest. Although Shar suggested they have dinner, he found that he'd lost his appetite. He just picked at his food, while Safiya went on about the state Pakistan was in and how lucky they all were to have escaped the country. After a point, it started to sound jarring, and it seemed that Ayesha was of a similar opinion.

'Like I said, Pakistan isn't that bad,' she finally said. 'I am a woman, but I have a good job and a reasonable social life. Sure, some people have antiquated beliefs, but you can't call the entire country bad just because of a section of people.'

Kamil wished he could have disappeared rather than hearing what Safiya said next.

'For someone who seems to have suffered first hand the abuse of violent men, you have a remarkably kind view of that country. Colour me surprised.' The moment she said the words, it was obvious that she regretted them. Her eyes widened to the point that it looked like they would pop out of their sockets. 'Oh my God, Ayesha. I am so sorry. I don't know why I said that.'

Shar put an arm around Ayesha's shoulders. Her bottom lip

trembled as she looked up, willing the tears not to fall down her cheeks. His heart broke for her, and there was nothing he could do.

'You are way out of line,' he whispered to Safiya. 'You ought to be ashamed of yourself.'

Safiya finally seemed to have sobered up. 'I feel terrible. I am so sorry, Kamil. God, why did I drink so much?'

After that, there was nothing more to be done except to return home. Shar and Juan took Ayesha with them, and he excused himself from going anywhere with Safiya, citing a busy day at work. He let her leave in a taxi.

Once he was back home, he realised that he'd hadn't asked Ayesha for her number, and thus, had no way of checking up on her. Calling his mother to ask about her would be a bad idea. Already upset about the events of the afternoon, she might lose it entirely if she heard about this evening. Before he put his phone down for the night, it beeped. A message from Safiya:

I'm so sorry for the way I behaved. It was inexcusable and I am very ashamed, but I also saw how you looked at her. That tenderness is something I've yearned for and never received from you. I think we need a break. I don't like the person I'm becoming. No hard feelings, of course xx

He slammed the phone on his bedside table and lay flat on his back. No hard feelings? Was she actually for real? This was perhaps the weirdest breakup message he'd ever received. What tenderness was she talking about? God, people could be so jealous sometimes. All he'd done was try and show a little kindness to someone who had suffered a lot in life. Was that such a bad thing? He wondered what she meant about the way he looked at Ayesha. How did he look at her? All he'd noticed was how nice her profile looked as she'd gazed in the distance. With these thoughts percolating in his mind, he drifted off.

Ayesha

Her alarm went off at six a.m., ringing incessantly until she swiped at her phone. She was used to staying in bed until eight, not waking up at the crack of dawn. For a moment her mind drew a blank over why she'd woken up so early, and then it all came back to her. Today was her first day of volunteering at Saeeda's charity centre. She groaned. What had she gotten herself into? Considering how she'd behaved over the past week, though, it was no surprise that Jamila Aunty had come up with this idea.

'I want you to be busy, *beta*,' she'd said. 'You're too young to wallow in misery like this. You should be running around the streets of London, busy as a bee, not wasting your time drinking dishwater coffee in cafés twenty-four seven. Besides, you have experience in working with charities, so why not use some of it?'

Although those comments had pinched her at the time, she knew Jamila Aunty had her best interests at heart. And she was right. Ayesha had allowed the attack to take over her life. Ever since that evening with Safiya, she had completely retreated into herself. It was probably unfair on her hosts, but she'd downloaded the Google Maps app and taken to leaving the house at midday and not returning until after dinner when she was sure the family would be busy wrapping things up for the night. She had taken to discovering places that tourists didn't generally visit so that nobody would look at her twice, and as Jamila Aunty so aptly put it, drink dishwater coffee in the hundreds of cafés that lined the streets of London. She longed for the sweet, milky coffee her mother made for her at home, but it was not to be found here.

She sat up in bed, and had the sudden urge to scratch at her face – to make the smooth parts resemble her scars. She clenched her hands together. She felt she was a mere shadow of the person she used to be. She opened her hands and looked at her palms, examining them closely. Who was she?

'Things aren't great here,' her mother had told her on the phone a couple of days ago. 'We're getting visits from Raza Masood's people. They keep asking where you are. For some reason, they want to get in touch with you.'

'To burn me more?' Ayesha had laughed, but deep down, an ice-cold fear had sliced through her. Why did Raza Masood want to reach her? Did he want to finish her off so that she wouldn't be able to tell anyone what he'd done?

'Don't be silly,' her mother told her. 'He can do nothing of the sort. We're not some riffraff he can throw around like that. Your father's name still commands a lot of respect. No, I think he has a twisted idea in his mind that he's in love with you.'

'I hate him.'

Her mother had sighed. 'So do I. But, for now, we've decided that you ought to stay in London until this dies down. I hope Jamila is taking good care of you. She can be a bit over the top, but she's a good woman. Please behave and treat her well.'

'I've got work, Ammi. I can't just leave Shugufta hanging forever.'

'You can if your life depends on it, Ayesha. Please don't come back to Multan yet. And try and have a bit of fun.'

It was as if her mother knew what she was up to in London, how she was avoiding everyone. She wondered if Jamila Aunty had been talking to her. If she was, she was totally entitled to do so. Ayesha had been distant with everyone of late.

Poor Kamil had tried to initiate conversation with her several times, but he'd met a wall each time. She didn't want to look at him, let alone talk to him. Although Kamil had tried to stop Safiya several times, Ayesha still didn't like how everyone else had sat quietly while Safiya said all those things to her – and being drunk was no excuse.

I don't need anyone's protection, she thought, throwing the covers aside and tiptoeing to the bathroom to get ready. On the landing, she bumped into Shar, who was already dressed for work and heading downstairs. She only gave Ayesha a thin smile. Ever since the meeting with Safiya, Ayesha had avoided all of Shar's attempts at conversation, so maybe she'd given up trying.

Her heart fell when she saw Jamila Aunty bustling around the living room, laying out her breakfast.

'Well, well, look who is all set for volunteer work,' she said, wiping her hands on a dishcloth. 'I've made a cheese omelette for you along with some *tale huye aloo*. I've laid out some bread too, but if you want a paratha, I can make a quick one.'

Ayesha almost burst into tears. She declined the paratha, but dug into the omelette and potatoes. Both were divine. Jamila Aunty beamed when she told her so.

'Kamil is coming to drop you off at Saeeda's charity centre.'

Ayesha almost choked on her orange juice. 'What? Why?'

Jamila Aunty flapped a hand at her. 'Oh, he doesn't start work until nine-thirty. He can drop you off, and then head to work.'

'But his office is in Central London.'

'Oh, who cares? You just enjoy the mangoes. Don't count the cores.'

Ayesha couldn't help but smile at that old Urdu proverb.

Kamil … this was going to be awkward. Saeeda's charity centre was somewhere in Muswell Hill, so she knew they'd be in the car for a while, especially with the morning traffic.

She only had to wait outside for a few moments before he arrived. It was a warm morning, so he had the windows down. Having avoided him for the past week, barely speaking, she mumbled a brief greeting and slid in next to him. Apart from returning her greeting, Kamil didn't say anything either. He was dressed for work in a white shirt and black trousers, but owing to the unseasonal heat, he had undone the first two buttons of his shirt. Ayesha averted her gaze. Why on earth was she even noticing such stuff?

'I'm sorry I haven't been myself these past few days,' she said, finally. 'It's just that the circumstances of my departure from Pakistan have been overwhelming me.'

Stopping at a red light, Kamil turned to her. 'Listen, I wanted to apologise for the way Safiya treated you that night. She was inexcusably rude to you, and all I can do is say sorry for her behaviour. I'm not sure we're even together anymore.'

'Oh.' Ayesha kept looking straight ahead, watching a young woman push a pram across the street. She didn't know how to respond to that, but she did know that Safiya was a bitch and someone as kind as Kamil was better off without her. Of course, she couldn't say that to his face, but something in her broke, those invisible defences she had put up to protect herself. Here was someone telling her about his personal life, so who was she to hold grudges, or indeed, hold back? She glanced at him as the car started moving again. 'Like I said, I had a boyfriend too before I came here, so I understand relationships. However, my own relationship – it didn't survive after I was attacked with acid. I thought he loved me, but maybe he didn't love me enough to look past my new appearance.'

'There's nothing wrong with it, Ayesha.'

'You haven't seen me properly without my scarf, so how can you make such claims?'

'Because it doesn't matter!' Kamil was gripping the steering wheel hard. 'If someone's idea of love is outer beauty, then that's probably not a healthy relationship to have in the first place. Besides, I saw you on the day of the kitty party without your scarf. You must stop thinking of yourself as different.'

'He broke my heart.' Her voice shook and she hated herself for it. 'I have gone through a great deal of trauma. I am still not over it. I don't know if I ever will be, so while I agree with what you're saying, please understand that you aren't the one who has to live with this changed appearance for the rest of your life. I used to be known as one of the prettiest girls in Multan, and now...'

Kamil sighed. 'I don't know what to say to you Ayesha, except that the offer to join my therapy group is still on the table. All the people there have had a history of suffering domestic abuse. As a Pakistani man, I never thought that would be something for me, but I was wrong.'

'You were a victim of domestic abuse? I ... I didn't know.'

Unease clouded Kamil's face. 'I was married once, see? I don't like talking about it, but yes, there was a great deal of abuse involved. Both physical and emotional.' Shaking his head, he drummed his fingers on the steering wheel. 'It was a difficult time. So, when I tell you that, to some extent, I understand what you went through, I actually do.'

She was stunned. 'I didn't know,' she whispered again. 'You put on such a brave face.'

'It was many years ago, and while I may look very chirpy, I won't deny I have long periods of sadness and frustration. The sort of abuse I went through never really leaves you, but you can learn to compartmentalise it.' He shrugged, then pulled a slip of paper from his pocket and passed it to her. 'My number, in case you need it.'

'Kamil, you could have simply told me, and I'd have saved it in my phone.'

Kamil flushed. 'I wasn't sure you'd want to save it. Besides, I can be a bit old-fashioned sometimes.'

Ayesha pocketed it and was grateful that they'd finally arrived at the centre. It was curious how conversation with him quickly turned serious. It was probably best that she didn't spend too much time with him.

'I'm so sorry,' she whispered as she climbed out of the car, but her words were lost in the wind.

Saeeda's charity centre was set in a sprawling space with tables and chairs to seat dozens of people. It was still early morning, but there was already a long line of people waiting to get some food. It must have been a recreational building in the past, given the wooden flooring and standard cream-coloured walls. Unsure of where to go in the din, Ayesha leaned against a wall and waited. She watched people from all walks of life approach the counter where food was being doled out on large paper plates. While there were a few white people, it was mostly South Asians who were here, and just as well, because it smelled of *halwa puri* and *aloo cholay*, and all of it was making her mouth water. Before she could decide where to announce herself, a harried-looking woman in an apron spotted her and grabbed her arm.

'Ayesha Safdar? What are you doing standing here? You've got work to do. Saeeda madam told us you would be joining today as a volunteer.' She made a show of checking her watch. 'Already ten minutes late. Pakistani people, I tell you. I'm Naheed and I manage this centre.' Pulling her by the arm, she led her behind the counter and pointed to a corner. 'Get yourself an apron, cap and gloves, and get to work. These people won't feed themselves. Look at the type of portions being given. Don't put too much or the plates will disintegrate. I don't have the time to be dealing with mess on the floor as well.'

'I thought I was supposed to check the accounts.'

Naheed huffed. 'Well, you're needed here more at the moment. We're short-staffed. The accounts aren't going anywhere. Now get to work. Chop, chop.'

For a moment, Ayesha just stood in front of the food counter, looking at the breakfast items. She had never cooked or served food in her life. Her mother had always handled that, and had always fed her the belief that she'd get married to a rich man and that would be that. It wasn't until she fell in love with Saqib that she'd entertained the idea of cooking food, but even then, it had seemed like a distant reality, something she'd only do when desperate. As she stood with her heart pounding, looking at the people watching her, waiting to be fed, she realised what a deadweight she had become. And after what Raza had done to her, even more so.

She frowned, then pulled up her sleeves and put on a fresh pair of gloves. She'd be damned if she was going to let Raza Masood influence her life in any way. He may have permanently scarred her face, but he wasn't going to scar her personality. She watched how the girl next to her ladled food onto the plates and followed her lead. Her portions weren't as pretty and she thought she was putting in more *halwa* than the *cholay*, but the grateful looks she got when she handed people their plates more than made up for it. Some of the people went ahead to pay for the food, but it seemed like there wasn't any obligation. The food was free for all.

She worked for two hours straight without taking a break, until the long line shortened to a few people milling about, after which there was nobody to serve at all. The last person she served – a young girl – looked up at her shyly and said, 'You're very pretty.' And Ayesha was relieved she didn't break into big, ugly sobs right there. She'd spent all her life looking down on people who served food in restaurants in Multan, but now, she had to admit that she'd got a dizzying high from it. She made a note to tell Shugufta to start a kitchen like this at Insaaniyat.

Naheed had her hands on her hips. 'Not bad for a first-timer,' she told her. 'Generally Pakistanis are too grand to do this sort of work, but you've been a pleasant surprise. It gives me hope for our girls in Pakistan.'

Saeeda said the same when she visited her office in the back. It was a small room with most of the space taken up by a big desk and a few chairs. Saeeda was seated in a large black office chair that seemed sturdy enough to hold her enormous weight. 'Naheed tells me you're a pro. I am glad you agreed to volunteer here, Ayesha. It's not that I want free labour, it's just that Jamila and I thought it might do you some good.'

'I've never felt this good about anything in my life,' Ayesha said, and it was the truth. She couldn't wait to go back and prepare for lunch.

As if reading her thoughts, Saeeda smiled. 'You've done enough for one day.' She gestured to the chair in front of her. 'This is not a full-time job, you know. You're a visitor in this country, so you can't take on proper work. Volunteering for a few hours every week should be okay. Besides, we don't want to work you to death. What will your mother say when she hears that you've been working in our kitchens?' She laughed. 'Well, you'll be doing some boring office work too, so don't get too excited. Having said that, we do organise local events here as well, so maybe you'd have fun doing that.'

'I would like that. I love my work in Multan, and doing this today reminded me of that. I'm so glad Jamila Aunty recommended this.'

Saeeda's shifted in her chair. 'Jamila is a good egg,' she said. 'She may not always have the correct opinions, but her heart is in the right place. Did you know that you are all she talks about these days? She used to be consumed by the idea of getting her children married, but now, all she wants is a better life for you. The woman loves you, bless her heart. She's the only reason I'm part of that blasted kitty, anyway. No way in hell that I would ever associate with a bitch like Moeeza. The nerve of her.'

Ayesha didn't want Saeeda to see the emotion on her face, so she looked down, hoping the tears wouldn't trickle out of her eyes.

'Are you getting on well with Shar? I expect you've met her lovely boyfriend too?'

Ayesha's eyes widened. 'How did you—?'

Saeeda laughed. 'At this point, Jamila is the only person in London who doesn't know.' Tapping her fingers on the notebook on her desk, she continued. 'I presume you've met Kamil too, although he doesn't live at home anymore. He's a good lad. Be kind to him. He's not had it easy in life, not after what happened to him all those years ago.'

Ayesha couldn't help but look up, her tears forgotten. 'What happened to him?'

Saeeda frowned. 'We don't speak about it. I don't think the

other women in the kitty even know. The kitty is only a few years old, you see, but Jamila and I go way back. So I know what happened.'

'Was it bad?'

Saeeda nodded – once. And Ayesha knew that she was not going to say another word on the subject.

'I hear that you've been withdrawn lately,' Saeeda said, seeming to focus on Ayesha instead. 'I understand your predicament, you know, but don't take it out on people who care for you.'

Ayesha felt a stab of anger. This woman didn't know anything about her life at all. 'Excuse me, but I'm afraid you know nothing of what I've been through.'

Saeeda glanced at the door to see that it was closed, before pushing up her sleeves.

Ayesha gasped.

The skin on her arms was scarred – large silvery burn marks, along with some angry dots that had blackened with age.

'Not many people know about this, but I am a domestic-abuse survivor too,' Saeeda told her. Her face assumed a faraway look for a few moments as if she was reliving it all. Then her attention returned to Ayesha. 'Of course, this was many years ago and what you see here are only a few of the wounds he inflicted on me in our ten years of marriage. I gave him three children in the hopes that his heart would thaw, but the abuse mounted with each child, each extra responsibility he felt saddled with.' Her voice shook as she pulled the sleeves back down and folded her arms against her chest. 'As if he wasn't the one putting the babies in me.'

'Saeeda Aunty, I had no idea...' Ayesha began.

Saeeda chortled. 'How could you, *beta*? Like I said, not many people know. The funny thing is that in my case, the only part of my body he didn't touch was my face. Just so he wouldn't be found out. Wretched bastard ruined so many years of my life...'

In that moment, sitting in her chair, Saeeda looked vulnerable, and Ayesha saw the same fear in her eyes that she'd seen in Rabia's back at the charity all those months ago. 'See, my husband was not right in the head. A psychopath through and through. And the most vicious kind too.' She laughed to mask the wobble in her voice, reaching forward to shuffle some papers on her desk, her hands trembling slightly. 'I left him eventually. In those days, it wasn't impossible to move to the UK for Pakistanis, so when an opportunity finally presented itself, I leapt at it.' A solitary tear slid down her cheek. She quickly wiped it away. 'I was a fool to have stayed in such a toxic marriage for so long, but at least I got three beautiful children out of it.'

The tears that had been threatening to spill from Ayesha's eyes all this time finally did. 'I'm so sorry,' Ayesha said. 'You look like nothing affects you.'

Saeeda gave her a watery smile. 'I'm sixty-six years old. At this age, even if something does affect you, you learn to compartmentalise it. Hide it. You don't want people to see you as weak.'

'You never remarried?'

Saeeda shook her head. 'Never had the need to. My three children kept me busy enough. No time for love.'

'I'm sorry,' Ayesha said again, not sure what she was apologising for now.

And just like that, the fire was back in Saeeda's eyes. 'Don't pity me, girl. I am not telling you all of this so you can sob for me. I am telling you that I wear my scars with pride. I look at them every morning and smile when I realise that I didn't let them take over my life. Don't let your wounds define you, Ayesha. Don't throw your life away because of what that bastard did to you. If anything, show him how little you care.'

'Too late for that,' Ayesha whispered, rolling the damp tissue into a ball in her hand. 'I try not to think about it, but the realisation hits me whenever I'm least expecting it: I will never be the same again.'

Saeeda gulped down a glass of water, and burped. 'Listen to me, you're a pretty little thing, and don't let anyone ever tell you otherwise. I'm sorry to say, but in Pakistan people love to pity themselves. You must rise above it. Learn to give people who bother you the middle finger. I sound like a motivational speaker, but there you are.' She reached into her bra and pulled out two twenty-pound notes. Holding a finger to her lips she said, 'Don't tell anyone I paid you, but you deserve it. Everyone deserves to be paid. Even for volunteer work.' Winking at her, she added, 'Buy something nice with it. You've certainly earned this money.'

Later, as Ayesha sat on the kerb outside, waiting for Saeeda to give her a ride back home, she unfolded the piece of paper Kamil had given her. Punching his number in her phone, she sent him a text.

I'd love to meet your therapy group.

Kamil

'Strangely, this reminds me of Multan,' Ayesha said, as they trekked up the hilly road towards one of the large local pubs. 'The gates and tall hedges ... it's all the same.'

Kamil gulped down some water, wiping the sheen of sweat from his forehead with the back of his hand. The day had warmed up nicely, but now it was a bit too hot for such a trek. He had decided to spend Saturday showing her the stately homes of Totteridge, a stark contrast from the houses up in Whetstone where his parents lived, or anywhere in Central London, where every inch was taken up by hotels, flats or businesses. Although North London was predominantly white, his parents had somehow found a street where every other house was occupied by Pakistanis.

'This is one of the areas where the very rich live,' he told Ayesha, pointing at a red stone house set back from the road, fronted by a sprawling lawn and with a high-end security system.

'Reminds me a bit of prison, to be honest,' Ayesha replied, but there was a smile on her face. She nudged him. 'I'm just joking. It's a beautiful house. Thank you for bringing me here.'

'I just wish it wasn't so unseasonably hot. It's October, for God's sake, and somehow warmer than it was when you arrived last month.'

She loosened the scarf, so that it fell off from her head. Kamil could see that her smile was lopsided, the scars standing out in the harsh glare of the sun, but all he wanted to do right now was kiss that face, those lips.

He shook his head, hoping Ayesha would think his blush was due to the heat. What was wrong with him?

It was fortunate that they arrived at the pub, because Kamil was finding it difficult to look anywhere but at her.

'The regular, Kamil?' the bartender asked him, but he shook his head.

'Just two Diet Cokes.'

Ayesha jutted out her chin. 'Don't feel shy on my account. Have your beer or whatever you like to drink.'

But he just shook his head again, and carried their drinks to the window seat, trying not to laugh at the bartender's expression.

Ayesha nudged him. 'You didn't have to do that. Now that bartender will think we're prudes.'

'And why should we care?'

She beamed. 'True.'

One of the best things about being with Ayesha was that they didn't need to talk all the time. There were moments when they could lapse into companionable silence, broken only if something important needed to be discussed.

Perhaps it was because the pub was pretty empty, but Ayesha had thrown the scarf in her bag, leaving her face uncovered,. He still couldn't risk looking at her. He was afraid she would read his feelings.

'That kid is watching me,' she said after a while, nodding at the window. Outside a toddler sat in a pram. He was, indeed, watching her, curiosity written on his face. 'He's probably trying to work out why I look so different.' Ayesha was trying to joke, but he noticed how her voice shook. Before he could say anything, the toddler gave her a winning smile.

'Oh!' Ayesha grabbed his forearm. 'Look at him smiling at me, Kamil. Oh, bless him.' Tears shone in her eyes as she met Kamil's gaze. 'Maybe he thinks I'm beautiful.'

'Ayesha, you are beautiful.'

As they watched, the child began to wave and babble, which caught the attention of his mother, sitting on a bench next to him. When she glanced at them, she didn't even miss a beat. She smiled too, giving them a small wave.

'See?' he said to Ayesha as she dabbed at her eyes, one hand still on his forearm. 'What did I tell you?'

It was a while before she removed her hand, and when she did, her hand left an imprint in the hair of his forearm.

'I wonder if we would ever have met, Kamil, if it had not been for the attack. I wonder if I would have had the opportunity to spend all this time with Jamila Aunty, with everyone.' She glanced around. 'And experience this city like this. In a way, this attack has changed everything.'

His heart broke as he saw the turmoil on her face. It was with great restraint that he prevented himself hugging her there and then. Instead, he cleared his throat, and said, 'While I wish that the attack had never happened, I am glad that you came to London. I am glad that we got to know each other and could become ... friends.' This time, it was his voice that shook. 'I was in a very dark place for a very long time. Today, sitting here with you, I feel that I am finally in the light.'

She didn't need to say anything. Her smile said it all.

Little by little, their friendship bloomed. Before he knew it, he was meeting Ayesha every other day. They'd meet over coffee in the evenings or when he visited home to see his parents. It was strange, but in these few weeks, he felt happy to just have a companion – a friend. Someone he could talk to. There were no strings attached. Even though London was slowly preparing for the long winter ahead, the nip in the air more pronounced in the mornings, Kamil felt more alive than ever. He hadn't thought about Safiya, Madiha or any one of his past relationships even once. He felt terrible about the way things had ended with Safiya, but it was all for the best, as they would never have gotten along in the long run. A part of him wished they could have stayed friends, but one couldn't have everything.

At least they hadn't had sex. That would have made things unnecessarily complicated.

For the first time in months, he found himself checking his appearance in the mirror before heading out. He watched what he ate, keeping an eye on his temperamental waistline, which seemed to have a mind of its own. There wasn't anything sexual between him and Ayesha; he didn't know if there ever would be, and he was fine with that ... Or maybe not ... But at least he had a friend, someone who understood him. As an introvert, he struggled to make friends, and even when he did, they didn't last very long. But with Ayesha, it was different. He hated crowds, and he'd only had to tell Ayesha about it once. The next time they encountered a large, heaving crowd, Ayesha quietly skirted it, leading them into a side alley and out of the melee. All of this done without either of them exchanging a single word. If this wasn't understanding, then he didn't know what was.

For the first time in years, he actually yearned to hold someone's hand, something he thought had died in him after what had happened. He tried not to think about the time when Ayesha would finally leave London – she was here on a visit visa after all – but the thought kept him awake at night.

To his utter surprise, she took no time at all to fit in with the therapy group. Of course, there had been that initial hesitation, but he knew that before the acid attack, Ayesha had been an extrovert, and it showed once the shackles holding her back fell away. Uncertainty had assailed him, initially, about introducing her to the group, not knowing if the others would accept her, or if he even had the authority to introduce new people, considering that he was probably on thin ice himself after what had happened with Safiya. But to her credit, she never badmouthed him in the group. As a matter of fact, she'd simply left the group without warning and nobody had heard from her.

'It's not surprising,' Sandra told him once, when they were out of earshot of the others. 'Safiya has always been her own person.

I wouldn't worry if I was you. She will come back when she wants to.'

Like him, Ayesha had become friends with Sandra, Shabbir and Matt as well. During her first meeting, she'd sat with her back erect, her eyes wide as she gulped in the mood of the group. He'd wondered if she had it in her to reveal what had happened, but it turned out that she didn't need to. Not in that first meeting. It was during the second meeting that Matt encouraged her to speak out.

Ayesha had looked around at the twelve people watching her, Sandra giving her an encouraging smile, Shabbir sitting beside her, stoic but also interested. A few of the others leaned forward with their arms folded on the table. Deep down, they all had their secrets. He knew he was still holding on to his all these months into therapy.

Before she began speaking, Ayesha unwrapped the scarf from around her head and folded it on the table. Her brown hair shone, and the mixture of pride and vulnerability in her stance made him respect her even more. Her skin was mottled with light and dark patches and scars, and the perpetual sheen made it look very unlike any human skin he'd ever seen. He'd seen burn victims, but this was different. This was acid. At that moment, he'd felt a rage he never knew he possessed. He wanted to kill the man who had done this to her.

Ayesha's mouth was set in a firm line, but there was fear in her eyes. When she spoke, her voice trembled. 'In order for me to open up about my experience, I felt it was necessary for you to see what I'm really like.'

No one, not even Shabbir, gave the slightest indication that they'd seen anything out of the ordinary. That was something that Kamil would marvel at for days afterwards, the fact that with their apparent indifference to Ayesha's appearance, the group had silently welcomed her as one of their own. During that moment, they truly bonded. Even now when he pictured her sitting there with that scarf on the table, the one she took great pains to wear every single day of her life, looking more vulnerable than he'd ever seen her, he felt goose bumps rise on his skin.

'My story starts on the day I had acid poured on my face. My life before that doesn't matter. Nothing else matters in Pakistan except for your appearance...'

Kamil had never seen his friends look so rapt. They drank in every word of Ayesha's story, and as it continued, he could see some of the insecurity leaving her, as if the silence of the group was giving her strength. She seemed transformed, and he hoped that she had finally begun her recovery.

Her eyes were dry when she finished her story. There wasn't a single moment when she had faltered, and for that he was proud of her.

Leaning forward, her eyes shining from unshed tears, Sandra said, 'I don't know if this is inappropriate – it might be – but I wanted to ask you how it feels. In this group, we always ask each other this question. How do you feel about all this now?'

Kamil froze as a hush descended on the room. All eyes turned once again to Ayesha, whose mouth was slightly open. She seemed to be gazing unseeing at Sandra. 'You know, nobody has ever asked me this before.'

'Ayesha,' Matt began. 'It is okay if you don't want to—'

'I feel angry,' Ayesha blurted out. 'The rage I feel for my attacker is all-consuming. Even after all these months, I look at myself in the mirror and I don't recognise the person I see. I am a stranger to myself.' At that, she did break down, covering her face as she cried. 'What you see are just my external wounds. There is a lot more hurt I carry inside. Every second of every day.'

'Not all wounds are visible,' Matt remarked, looking around the group. 'And that is why we must try to talk about them. All of us.'

His eyes had met Kamil's as he said that, but he just hung his head, hating himself for being so weak. If he didn't talk about it, maybe it hadn't happened.

Around two weeks after Ayesha told her story to the group, they were back in Gower Street together, sitting in another meeting, Ayesha a solid part of the group, when something clicked inside him, and he knew the time had come to allow himself to look at the past.

'Would you like to share anything with us today?' Matt asked him.

All eyes turned on Kamil, and he immediately thought of bolting. He could run off down Gower Street towards the relative safety of Euston Station and take a train home to his parents. His mother would be getting the ingredients ready for today's dinner. But before he could give it further thought, he felt Ayesha touch his hand – gently at first, and when he didn't resist, she held it tightly in her own. 'Go on, Kamil,' she said. 'Be free.'

Matt's blue eyes were intent as they gazed at him. 'Be free, Kamil.'

The way his heart was racing, he could be having a panic attack. He took deep gulps of air. 'I don't think I want to.'

Ayesha increased the pressure on his hand. 'It's worse keeping it bottled up. Take it from me.'

He looked up, trying to find comfort in the warmth of her gaze. 'Arooj,' he whispered. His entire body was shaking. It had been a long time since he'd said her name. 'It all began with Arooj.'

Ayesha frowned. 'Arooj?'

He exhaled. 'She was my wife.'

Arooj ... even now, her name brought up past trauma for him, smashing through the defences he'd set in place. Saying the name aloud brought everything crashing down. It made him remember that day sixteen years ago. They'd both been students at the School of Oriental and African Studies, and although they were in the same year, and the university wasn't exactly sprawling, they didn't get a chance to meet each other until their second year. Kamil still remembered it as if it was yesterday. The Pakistani students on campus were celebrating Eid and everyone was decked out in their traditional best. Growing up in London, he'd only ever worn a shalwar kameez at wedding events, and his father had never enforced the unspoken rule of wearing one on Fridays, so he never did. So it was strange for him to be wearing it at SOAS. Arooj wore a vivid-yellow shalwar kameez with a red chiffon dupatta that kept swirling in the breeze. Here was the most perfect girl he'd ever seen in his life, and all he could do was stand with his mouth open. Almost like in a Bollywood movie, her dupatta would sway over the faces of people as she walked by. When it fell on his face too, Kamil thought, she wouldn't even deign to look at him, but to his surprise, she turned and laughed. 'I swear I wasn't trying to pull a *Main Hoon Naa* on you. London just isn't the right place to wear a dupatta. It won't hold still.' She took it off and put it in her bag. 'There. Now I won't go fooling half the boys in this city into thinking that I'm in love with them.'

Kamil was all of nineteen, and being a nerd who kept his head buried in books, he'd never had a girl look at him twice, let alone talk to him. All he could do was gape at her.

Arooj smiled. 'Are you mute?'

When Kamil shook his head, she laughed again. 'I won't believe it until you speak.'

'Thank you,' he said, immediately clamping a hand on his mouth. *What the hell?*

This time, Arooj almost lost her balance from laughing so much and had to hold on to his shoulder for support. 'What are you thanking me for? Good God, I didn't know they still made boys like you. You're a wonder.' Her eyes brimmed with tears as she continued laughing. 'And look at that blush. What's your name? Don't tell me it's "Thank You".'

'Kamil Akbar,' he mumbled.

He had to repeat it twice before she understood. Extending a hand towards him, she declared, 'Well, Kamil Akbar, my name is Arooj Shahid. Pleased to meet you.' When he nodded eagerly, she burst out laughing again. 'You are so sweet, my heart is melting. I feel like I want to protect you from the big, bad world.'

To say it was love at first sight would be an understatement. After that chance meeting, they met over coffee in a nearby Starbucks, and that's when Kamil knew.

He had fallen in love with her.

Something drew him to Arooj, whether it was the nonchalance with which she leaned over to wipe froth from his lips, her fingers lingering, or simply the way she spoke her mind. He didn't know if Arooj liked him or not, but she seemed to be pretty comfortable in his presence, the way she chatted without pause, telling him about her family back in Lahore and how excited they were that she was making new friends. 'Of course, they live in perpetual fear that I'll end up making friends with the wrong sort. You know, drunkards and that, plus they think that I'll end up with a *gora*, but then, I'm, like, why would you send me abroad to study if you're afraid of me befriending white people? I tell you, brown parents are a law unto themselves. They should get awards for being the dumbest parents alive. Dipshits.'

Even the abusive language sounded like music to his ears.

'You hardly seem the type to have been brought up in London,' she observed. 'You're so shy and retiring.'

'Is that a bad thing?' he asked her, his heart thudding in his chest.

'Not necessarily ... I kind of like it. I think boys shouldn't be afraid of having a soft side. It's cute.'

Cute ... she'd called him cute. He spent the entire night with the word on his lips, trying to say it like Arooj did. His friend, Tahir, from the across the street, saw the change in him before his own mother did.

'You don't seem interested in the PlayStation anymore,' he said when Kamil had spent the last thirty minutes gazing into space, a smile on his lips. 'Have you met someone?'

When Kamil told him, a frown appeared between Tahir's eyebrows. 'My Ammi calls girls like that "fast". You should stay away from her.'

Arooj was very unimpressed when he told her. 'Your friend is such a bastard. He sounds like an insufferable mama's boy. I didn't know you had friends like him.' Looking at his stricken expression, she added, 'I'm *surprised* you have friends like him. Someone sweet and impressionable like you shouldn't be spending time with people like him.'

'Then who should I be spending time with?'

Arooj had smiled at that, her brown eyes glittering with mischief. 'How much pocket money do you have? Want to go meet some real friends at a real party?'

And that's how it began ... Kamil's journey to his own destruction.

The first party she took him to was in Hackney, in a house packed to the rafters with college students, the air thick with cigarette smoke, and something else that he couldn't quite put a finger on. Booze flowed freely, but what really alarmed him were the pills and drugs.

Clad in a black sequinned dress with her hair in a tight ponytail, Arooj looked ready to conquer the world. Flicking a hand at the people doing drugs, she led him to the kitchen. 'Look at those poor people – they're slaves to drugs. One should rule the drugs, not the other way round.' Seeing his startled face, she changed tack. 'We shouldn't touch the drugs, but there's no reason why we can't try some of the booze.' Pausing at the table that had various bottles of different-coloured liquor, she said, 'I wonder if you have a few hundred quid on you?'

Kamil looked around. 'Why do you ask?'

Arooj hesitated before saying, 'I actually owe someone five hundred pounds. He's here at the party, and if he sees me, he might embarrass me if I don't have it for him. I promise that I'll return it all to you.'

Kamil pulled out his wallet and counted the notes inside. 'I've got three hundred right now, which I got from Ammi for my birthday. I don't have five hundred, I'm sorry.'

'But I need five hundred.'

'Why did you borrow the money in the first place?'

A shadow crossed her face then, which put a stop to anything else he had to say. 'Three hundred is fine, then.'

Like an idiot, he handed over all his money to Arooj, never questioning her again. For him, hers was the last word.

There were several times after that when Arooj would ask him for any spare cash he had. She always seemed to come up with a good reason. A friend in need. Some household emergency bill. Her parents being short that month. When his own pocket money ran out, he stole from his mother's secret stash.

It was many months later that he found out that the money he gave her was used to buy drugs, but by then, it was too late.

Arooj had taken over his life.

He was so caught up in her magic that he went from an A+ student to an average one, so much so that even his professors complained. Kamil, however, was in another world.

Whenever he saw her, his stomach would knot up, his heart hammering in his throat. His jaw would ache because he just couldn't stop smiling. In her presence, his whole world lit up. When she wanted to, she could lavish all her attention on him, and it was like the sun was shining on his face. Nothing mattered except for Arooj in that moment. But she could just as easily take it all away. There were days when she wouldn't even glance at him, let alone answer his texts or calls, not until he asked her if she was okay for money. If she needed any. That usually got her interested. It was a dangerous love, the kind that could destroy a person, but he was so far in that there was no going back. There was no point to life if Arooj wasn't in it.

It was as simple as that.

It wasn't until their final year that she allowed him to kiss her. It was a rushed kiss outside Russell Square Station, Arooj letting him graze her lips briefly before pulling away. 'Get lost, you. I'm a respectable Pakistani girl. I don't do this stuff before marriage.'

However, afterwards, she'd pulled him into the public toilets and properly kissed him, her tongue a hot surprise, her lips tasting of strawberry lip gloss.

'Now, that is how you kiss a girl,' she told him.

Marriage. That was the first time she'd ever mentioned that word to him, and it made his heart sing. Every neuron in his body came alive at the idea of sharing his life with her. He could think of nothing better.

'I hope she isn't after your British passport,' his mother told him once he'd finally confessed his love for her to his parents. 'You're only twenty-two years old, *pagal larkay*. This is no age to get married for a man. You don't even have a job. How will you support her?'

'She'll work too,' Kamil replied. 'And besides, she's a British citizen herself. Her parents just choose to live in Pakistan. We're about to graduate. We'll find jobs in no time. We won't be a burden on you.'

'*Dafa ho!* Now, he talks of being a burden. Of course, you two will live with us here. I'm not letting my baby out in the world on his own.'

His father, generally very quiet, murmured, 'Allow me to run a background check on the girl, Kamil. This is all very fast. I can use my police contacts here – and in Pakistan.'

'*Haye*, I hope you haven't done the unthinkable with her, and she's with child?'

'She is not like that, Ammi,' Kamil had replied coldly, and something in his tone must have scared his mother, because she didn't say another word.

'*Beta*, at least date for a few more months,' his father said gently. 'Bring her here to spend some time with us. Get to know her better. Marriage can wait.'

Heady with love, Kamil wouldn't hear of it. He begged his mother to give him one of her diamond rings and presented it to Arooj before he could lose his nerve.

To his utter shock, she said yes. They were married as soon as they graduated. Arooj's parents came for the graduation and stayed over for the wedding. In a crowded event, where they seemed to have invited every single Pakistani they knew in London, there was hardly a chance for them to get to know Kamil or his parents. Afterwards, his mother invited them over for lunch, but from what she told Kamil, it was an awkward affair.

'Zareena kept complaining about my food being too oily for her,' his mother told him over the phone, her voice tight with repressed anger. 'She said that she couldn't see her daughter living so far up in North London. *How will she visit the shops in Sloane Street?*' His mother's mimicry was excellent, and at the time, Kamil laughed it away. Who cared if they didn't get along? He and Arooj were in love. Nothing else mattered.

He found a job in a bank fairly quickly, but somehow Arooj didn't seem to have any luck. She left home every morning with a briefcase in her hand, ostensibly for a day of interviews, but none of the interviews ever materialised into a job offer. As her mother had hinted, she also refused to live with his parents, forcing him to rent a studio in Central London because 'obviously' she didn't want to live outside of zone one on the tube map.

'Unless you have a sprawling mansion, you don't get out of zone one, where all the fun is, and let's face it, Kamil, your parents live in a hovel. That house is so tiny that it's hard to breathe there. My parents almost had a heart attack when they went over for lunch. I come from Lahore where our bathrooms are bigger than your entire flats, so forgive me if I can't live with your parents.'

Kamil pointed out that it was his parents who paid the rent for the flat, but of course, his statement fell on deaf ears. As blissful as those early months of marriage were, cracks had started to appear. It took him some time, but he began noticing more and more money going missing from their joint bank account, small amounts at first, which Arooj dismissed as household expenses, but being just two people in a studio, and with his mother sending them home-cooked food all the time, there was only so much money they could spend on groceries, so it just didn't add up.

Even his mother noticed that something was wrong. 'The way she looks at me, Kamil, I wouldn't at all be surprised if she were to slit my throat. That girl hates me. She hates me even though I try to help out in the flat with food and everything. I've got your father and Sharmeela to look after at home too. It's not easy for me, you know.'

Their sex life became erratic, with Arooj often rejecting even the gentlest of advances. One evening, while getting ready for bed, he put his hand on her thigh only for her to yank it away. 'I'm tired. I've had a busy day. Go to sleep.'

On the rare occasions when he felt brave enough, he asked her what exactly she was busy with because it certainly wasn't work.

'Job interviews, friends, stuff. I don't need to give you a minute-by-minute update on where I've been, Kamil. It's a free country.'

'And yet you don't seem to land a job. Isn't it curious?'

'I did not move here from Pakistan just so you could watch my every step. I will not be stalked.'

Kamil held up his hands. 'Nobody is stalking you, Arooj, but you have a husband and a home to think of. You can't just get up and leave her for hours on end. Do you know how hard it is for me to manage everything? And you keep withdrawing cash from our account. What are you doing with all this money? If I lose my job, we won't have a penny in savings. Are you using?'

'Kamil, I am way too tired to get into this right now. Please leave me alone.'

'If it wasn't for my mother, I don't know how I'd have managed,' Kamil murmured.

Arooj scooted away until she was at the far end of the bed. 'Your precious mother. Of course, that's what all of this is about. Nobody cares about me. Why don't you move back with your parents? I know you're dying to.'

'This isn't about me or my parents. This is about you shirking your responsibility. If you're looking for jobs all day, why do you always look stoned, and why does your breath always reek of alcohol?'

Lying in bed beside him, Arooj stopped breathing for a moment, her body still and rigid. After what seemed like ages, she exhaled. 'I don't expect a loser like you to understand anything. Now, go to sleep.'

The same pattern continued, and may have done so forever if Kamil hadn't discovered cocaine in her bag. It was quite by accident, really, as he needed to pay cash for a food delivery. When he riffled through Arooj's bag to find some, his fingers brushed a plastic pouch at the very bottom. Just the fact that the drugs were in his house alarmed him.

It was hours before she arrived home, and by that time, Kamil was ready to go mad with frustration. She was smiling as she entered the flat, her usually glossy hair tied up in a messy bun, remnants of her favourite red lipstick on her lips. She brought the smell of cigarette smoke and alcohol with her.

He held up the pouch.

Her smile slipped. 'What's this, Kamil?'

He had never felt angrier with her as he did at that moment. 'You tell me. I found it in your bag.'

That gave her the excuse she needed. 'Are you going through my stuff now?'

Kamil rose to confront her. 'Arooj, this is cocaine. These are hard drugs. You could go to prison for this. We both could.'

'It's not mine,' she said quickly. 'I'm so sorry. I was keeping it for a friend. I don't use anymore, Kamil. You have to believe me.'

Kamil balled the pouch in his fist. 'I am going to call your parents first thing tomorrow so that they know what their daughter is doing. I know you're using, Arooj. I can see it in your eyes. You're stoned.'

Her eyes flashed then. 'You wouldn't dare, Kamil.'

'Try me.'

Before he could react, he felt his head whip sideways as a slap landed on his cheek. 'I told you they're not mine,' Arooj snarled.

At that moment, all he wanted was to wrap his fingers around her neck, but instead he closed his eyes and took a long breath.

Her parents didn't believe a word he told them, and he knew exactly how badly his own parents would react to the news, so he did the only thing he could. He threatened to call the police on her if she didn't stop.

Arooj was sitting on the sofa, bleary-eyed with a glass of juice in her hand, when he made the announcement. He dodged the glass she aimed at him, but the juice splattered all over his shirt. 'You bastard,' she whispered, but almost immediately afterwards, she started crying. 'I'm sorry, Kamil. I will stop using. But not because I'm scared of the police. I'll stop because I am pregnant.' Their eyes met. 'Two months gone.'

For the first time in months, they embraced each other with love and not momentary lust, and shed tears of happiness. Wiping the tears from his eyes with her palms, Arooj said, 'I promise to give up every bad habit. I am not just living for myself anymore.'

To ensure that she was true to her word, Kamil took some time off work, and held Arooj's hand through the withdrawal, more often than not enduring her slaps and kicks as well when the pain in her body got too bad. He knelt on the floor next to the bed, holding a damp cloth to her hot forehead, and a small trash can for the frequent vomiting.

'Just my luck,' Arooj said, hiccupping. 'Vomiting due to the baby and this horrendous withdrawal. It's a wonder I haven't had a miscarriage.'

That night, Kamil woke up to a coppery smell in the air and Arooj writhing in bed next to him, the sheets soaked crimson.

'It's gone,' she croaked.

He didn't even have time to mourn because it wasn't long before Arooj started using again. By that time, they had grown distant again. And it seemed to him that she blamed him for the miscarriage, because he kept finding his best shirts cut to shreds, and his laptop smashed to pieces when he made the mistake of leaving it at home. It wasn't uncommon for her to slap him across the face or kick him in the shins. Once she even kicked him in the balls, ignoring his yelp as she said, 'This is just a fraction of the pain I went through during that miscarriage that you induced. If you hadn't stopped me using, the baby would still be inside me, alive and kicking.'

All he ever saw in her eyes was pain and hatred.

Hatred for him.

Arooj began to spiral, and in a way, Kamil spiralled with her.

A few months after the miscarriage, he was about to leave for work when he saw her sitting on the sofa, wrapped up in a blanket as she gazed unseeing at the television. A shadow of his former love for her bloomed in his heart, and he took her in his arms. To his surprise, she let him, even returning the hug.

'Let's try again,' he told her. 'We are both young, Arooj. There is no reason that you won't conceive again. We will do it properly this time. Doctor visits and everything.'

He didn't mention that they hadn't had sex since the miscarriage, but the fact that she was hugging him back made him optimistic.

'Kamil, I can't go cold turkey. I don't have it in me, but I do want to stop using.' Breaking the embrace, she looked in his eyes. 'I want to get better, but for that to happen I need to wean myself off the drugs. That's the only way.'

'Arooj, I—'

'I need the drugs, Kamil. I promise you this will be the last stash. I swear on our unborn child that I will only use it to get better. You can monitor me.'

Kamil hesitated, but the desperation in her eyes told him that she was right. There was no way Arooj could stop using all of a sudden. 'Do you need money?' he asked her.

'There's a place near the Camden Lock where my dealer sells. His name is Eric. I don't have the strength to go all that way today. You'll need to get them for me.'

Kamil shook his head. 'You've gone mad. There's no way I'm getting involved in this.'

'Nobody will see you. It won't be a large amount in any case. Please, Kamil. Do this for me.'

It was the look on her face that convinced him. If he satiated this hunger of hers, he thought, maybe he would get his wife back. Before he could change his mind, he called in sick at work.

'When I return this evening, we will have a discussion,' he told her. 'Don't tell anyone where I've gone.'

Even though he covered his head with a hoodie and wore baggy jeans, he still feared that he looked out of place in Camden. When he finally arrived at the location, underneath a bridge in a quieter area near Camden Lock, he was met by two burly white men with tattoos all over their muscular arms. One look at them, and he knew that they could tear him limb from limb.

'You Kamil? Arooj's man?' The man's English was heavily accented.

He gulped and nodded. 'Eric?'

He grunted. 'Show me the money.'

His heart hammering in his chest, Kamil pulled out a wad of fifty-pound notes.

Eric, his eyes an electric blue, bared his teeth. 'She owes us three thousand quid and you're giving me a tuppence?' His muscles bulged. 'Is this a joke? Where's the rest of it?'

Kamil's hands started to shake. 'I–I didn't know. I thought Arooj just wanted a small amount. I'm here to buy it for her...'

Eric laughed, a harsh and unpleasant sound. 'Your Arooj is a pro. She sent you here to do her dirty work, so she wouldn't have to show her face to me. She knows exactly how much money she owes.' He spat. 'Conniving little bitch. What cash have you got on you?'

Kamil opened his wallet with trembling hands, and gave Eric all the cash he had, which was very little.

'Right, well we'll have to go to a cashpoint,' said Eric, gripping Kamil's shoulder.

this illegal shit for you? What happened to all the gratitude you felt this morning?'

Biting her lip, she smiled. 'Of course, you're right, my gallant husband. I can't thank you enough for what you've done for me.' She took his hand and led him to bed, as if that was supposed to make everything better. And he was in such despair, somehow it did make things slightly better.

The next morning, it was as if he had the old Arooj back. She made a large Pakistani breakfast for him, complete with *shami* kebabs and a spicy omelette, and kissed him on the mouth when he complimented her cooking. 'You see, I know how to keep my husband happy.'

'You're not using yet, are you?' he asked, nervous. 'You look very happy.'

She laughed. 'Not yet, but thanks to you, I know that I won't have to go cold turkey.' Padding over to the sofa, she added, 'And don't worry about the money. I've saved some up and will pay them. It's nothing.'

The pain in his gut said otherwise, but he didn't push the point. 'Promise you won't use until I'm back from work? I need to monitor what you take.'

The frown lines between her eyebrows settled as she wrapped a shawl around her shoulders. 'I promise I won't use until then. I'm only going to use this to wean myself off, nothing more. I'm done with this shit, Kamil.'

He rose from the dining chair and picked up his briefcase. 'Arooj, I am serious.'

'So am I.'

Opening the door to the flat, he looked back at her and smiled. 'See you this evening, then?'

Her smile was fainter now, but it was there. 'See you, Kamil.'

At that moment, if someone had told him that this was the last time he would be seeing his wife, he wouldn't have believed them. She looked happy ... at peace, even. But when he returned home

'I ... I haven't been paid yet this month, and anyway, it'
ible to withdraw more than a thousand pounds anyway–

And before Kamil could say anymore, Eric's colleague
him in the gut, while Eric held him still.

Eric let him go, and Kamil stood, bent over, massaging his st
waiting for the next blow. So he was surprised when Eric said:

'We're not complete villains here, mate.' He threw a pou
him, which Kamil caught. 'We know you'll be good for the m
so let her have fun with this.' His eyes bored into Kamil's. 'Bu
don't see the money in a week, we'll be coming to get it.' He tap
leaned over and tapped Kamil on the head. 'You understand?'

Kamil didn't know what else to do, so he just nodded.

'Say the magic words, mate.'

'I understand.'

'There's a good lad.'

All through the journey home, Kamil kept looking over his shoulder, expecting someone to stop him, the pouch burning a hole in his pocket. Catching his reflection in the window of the tube, it occurred to him how far he had fallen for Arooj. And he didn't even know how much more he still had to fall in order to keep her happy.

By the time he reached the studio, his clothes were soaked with sweat. Far from greeting him, Arooj didn't even look at him or listen to his complaints. Her attention was completely focused on the pouch, which she snatched from him.

'You owe them thousands of pounds, Arooj,' he said. 'You sent me there like a pig to slaughter.'

'Don't worry about it,' she snapped. 'Eric's harmless. I'll take care of it.'

He groaned. 'How? And he didn't seem harmless to me. His mate punched me.'

'I said, don't worry about it.' Glancing up at him, she added, 'Be a man for once, Kamil.'

It was as if he'd been punched in the gut again. Kamil spread his hands in front of her. 'Is this how you're going to thank me for doing from work, having bought some flowers for her, he detected an odd hush from the flat, just the static from the television buzzing in his ears.

The key turned in the lock, but there seemed to be something obstructing the door – something heavy. He put his entire weight against the door, finally flinging it open, knocking aside the chair that had been placed against it. And saw his wife on the same sofa, wrapped in the same blanket, but with a used syringe on the coffee table in front of her, and her eyes wide open, gazing into nothingness.

That had been Arooj's final assault on him, taking her own life and leaving him ridden with guilt and pain forever.

Emerging from his reverie, Kamil opened his eyes and realised that he had his head in his hands, his face damp. 'That was the last time I ever saw her,' he said, looking up at his therapy group. 'I realise now that she was probably high already that morning. Despite the depths to which I had fallen for her, I still wish I had done something before I left home that day. Maybe her smile was a cry for help. Despite those months and months of abuse, she was still my wife, and there were times when we were happy.'

Sandra was openly weeping, and to his utter surprise, he saw tears rolling down Shabbir's cheeks as well. 'Bhai, this is so messed up. Even more messed up than my life, which is the very definition of messed up. But it's not your fault. Drugs ... they change people.'

'And that's not all. It turned out that she owed more than fifteen thousand pounds to various dealers. All my savings went into paying them off. I was left with nothing. Arooj ruined me in every sense of the word.'

Beside him, Ayesha was silent. She'd let go of his hand. Kamil glanced at her and noticed that she had a faraway look in her eyes. 'I didn't know you'd suffered so much, Kamil,' she said softly. 'I'm sorry I've been harping on about my own issues, my disfiguration. Everything pales in comparison.'

'Nobody's issues are insignificant,' Matt said, putting his hands on the table. 'That's the whole point of therapy. I am proud of you two for making so much progress. I'm proud of all of you.'

Later, as they all drank coffee and nibbled on some shortbread, Kamil felt as if a weight had been lifted from his shoulders. It was almost as if he could stand up straight again. The secret of Arooj's ultimate betrayal had been festering inside him for far too long. On his insistence, his parents had sworn never to mention her name again, and to this day, they had stayed true to their promise. Nobody should have to endure such a marriage. There had been a complete police investigation afterwards, because of which he lost his job, but the information that had come to light about Arooj and her habits had made him wonder if he had ever known her at all.

Across the room, Ayesha seemed to be chatting with Rob, a dashing young man who had recently joined the group. Kamil hadn't paid a lot of attention, but he seemed to be battling with depression after splitting up with his abusive wife. Today, however, he seemed to be laughing, his eyes gleaming as he spoke with Ayesha.

Kamil was surprised to feel a stab of jealousy. What reason did he have to be jealous? It wasn't like there could ever be something between him and Ayesha. Or could there? What a monster he'd be if he were to suggest any such thing when she was so vulnerable, but he also couldn't deny that with Ayesha he forgot about all his troubles. They smoothed out as if someone had run an iron over them. Had he felt the same with Safiya? Definitely not. With Madiha? He'd enjoyed her company, and eventually, he might have learned to love her, but she didn't quite light up his life as Ayesha did, which was peculiar as there hadn't been anything remotely romantic between them ... so far. But he couldn't deny that, with Ayesha by his side, he had finally managed to start letting go of his past.

Before he could rein in his jealousy, he was striding across the room to join Ayesha.

'...love it on you,' he caught Rob saying.

Kamil plastered a big smile on his face. 'Love what?'

Ayesha's eyes were dancing with mirth as if she could tell exactly what was going on in his head. 'I'll let Rob tell you.'

Tell me what? His mind was spinning. Had they been meeting outside of the therapy sessions, because there was no way they could have become such close friends so quickly.

Rob turned and smiled at Kamil, the skin around his eyes crinkling. 'We were talking about Ayesha's lovely scarves. My new girlfriend, Lauren, loves silk scarves from South Asia, so I was just asking Ayesha where I could buy them.'

'And I told him that the only way he's getting these glorious scarves is if he lets me send them over from Pakistan. It would be an honour, Rob.'

'At least let me pay you.'

'Over my dead body. I wouldn't be a Pakistani if I were to accept payment for something so trivial.'

'Oh.' Kamil sagged with relief. They weren't seeing each other. He still had a chance, but what on earth would he even say to her? *Ayesha, I think I have feelings for you?* She'd run straight for the hills with such a cheesy line. On the other hand, she'd been here for a while now, and could go back to Pakistan at any time, and where would that leave him? In just a few weeks, she'd become integral to his life. He couldn't imagine not meeting up with her after work or going sightseeing around London. Even his complicated relationship with the city became less complex when Ayesha was around him.

God, he had hoped this wasn't love, but what else could it be? As they walked back towards Euston Station from the meeting that evening, Kamil felt as if even the weather was telling him something. Nights had become very cold, but today, it was pleasant. It was mild enough to walk without a jacket.

Ayesha's heels clicked on the pavement as they walked past the fancy hotels dotting the area. 'You honestly don't have to walk me to the station. I'm a big girl. I know Russell Square is your station, and yet you insist on this long walk.'

Kamil shrugged. 'What else are gentlemen for?'

'A true gentleman, indeed,' she added, but she was laughing. 'Very gallant of you, sir, to walk this innocent, helpless girl to the station.'

'This doesn't suit you.'

They broke out laughing. Her hand was right there. All he had to do was grab it. Taking a deep breath, he brushed the back of his hand against hers. A jolt of static electricity ran through him. She didn't withdraw her hand.

'Kamil?' she said, looking straight ahead, but there was a smile still playing on her face. 'I made a decision today.'

'A decision?' His attention was still on her hand and how much he wanted to hold it. 'What do you mean?'

'I have decided that from now on, I will no longer hide my face.' She removed the scarf and bunched it in her hand. 'This stops now. From now on, I will embrace all of myself, the good and the bad. All of it.'

That was all the encouragement he needed. He reached out and took her hand. It was warm in his own. 'I am so proud of you.'

'And, I am proud of you, Kamil,' Ayesha said, not pulling away. Her grip tightened. 'For what you did at the meeting. I am glad that you have begun your true healing.' Glancing at him, she added, 'It took coming to London for me to realise how much trauma I was carrying, not just from the attack, but also from the unreasonable expectations of others. At the end of the day, we are only human. Is it really so wrong for us to want to enjoy our lives?'

Kamil gestured around the area. 'And, are you enjoying all of this?'

'I am enjoying this moment. Being with you makes me happy.'

The station was growing impossibly close. Soon, they would have to part, and Kamil wasn't sure he could bear it. He had to say something. It was now or never.

'Ayesha, I...'

'Yes, Kamil?' She snuck a look at him, the lopsided smile still in place. Was she flirting with him?

His throat had gone dry. Running his tongue over his chapped lips, he tried again. 'Ayesha, I think I...'

'You think what?' Her smile grew wider. 'Go on, don't be shy.'

Before he could finish his sentence, Ayesha's face completely changed. The smile vanished, her face draining of all colour. Her eyes widened, panic and terror in them. She looked like she'd seen a ghost. 'Oh my God,' she whispered. 'It's him.'

He turned around to see the throngs of people exiting Euston Station. 'Ayesha, what happened?'

Releasing his hand, she proceeded to grip his arm instead, squeezing it hard enough to cause pain. 'Kamil, I ... I think I just saw...' But then, her expression cleared. She tilted her head, reducing the pressure on his arm, but not letting go of it entirely. 'I thought I saw someone I knew, but looking back, it seems that it was just someone who looked like him. My mind must be playing tricks on me.'

Kamil's mind drew a blank. 'But who did you think you saw?'

But Ayesha wasn't listening. She was still craning her neck, biting her lip as she tried to look for whoever it was who'd spooked her so much, and for a moment, it seemed to him as if she might go after the person, but then she shuddered, releasing his arm, and shoving both hands in her pockets. 'Gosh, it's turned pretty cold. I should head back. I'll see you...'

Kamil couldn't bear it. 'When?' he asked. 'When shall we meet again?'

Either she didn't hear him or she pretended not to, because she turned away and was walking towards the escalators that would lead her underground.

Kamil looked at the lights illuminating Euston Station. For some reason, he thought he'd just missed the chance of his life.

Ayesha

'Ayesha, are you listening to me?' her mother said.

Ayesha shook her head, pressing the phone closer to her ear. She was still fixated on what she'd seen at the station – who she had seen. No, it had to be her mind playing tricks on her, because for a moment, she thought she had seen Raza Masood's cold eyes boring into her, but when she looked back, it was just a guy with black hair who looked like him. It couldn't have been him, and besides, it was next to impossible for people to bump into each other in a city like London.

Unless...

'You were saying, Ammi?'

'Jamila said that you've struck up quite a friendship with her son, Kamil. Is he a nice boy?'

'He's thirty-five years old, Ammi. Not exactly a boy, but to answer your question, yes, he is wonderful. A very caring human being. I am very good friends with him.'

'So, he's just a friend?' Her mother sounded disappointed.

'What else did you think he was? My lover?' Saying it aloud sent a jittery feeling through her.

Ishrat tutted. 'Don't be ridiculous, Ayesha. I'm merely asking because it won't ever be safe for you in Pakistan until you're married to someone else.'

A familiar fear rose inside her. 'What's happened now? Is Raza still making your life miserable?'

'Don't be silly. It's nothing your father and I can't handle.'

Ayesha was alone in her room, and Jamila Aunty was not the kind to eavesdrop, but she still lowered her voice. 'So, he's still in Multan then?'

She could hear the suspicion in her mother's tone when she said, 'Where else would he be? Why do you ask?'

'No reason.' Ayesha quickly changed the topic. 'Why don't you come to London too, just until everything calms down?'

Her mother laughed. 'Spoken like a true *farungi*. Has London gone to your head, my dear? Where will we get the money to stay in that city for months? Surely you don't expect Jamila to host us as well? We would be mad to even consider the idea.'

'If you're not going to come to London, then maybe I should take the next flight to Multan.'

She meant it in jest, but her mother was quiet for a long moment. When she spoke, her voice was almost a whisper. 'Listen to me, Ayesha. This is not a time to joke. I am fifty years old. *Beta*, I have seen the world. This man will not rest until he's destroyed you or, I don't know, made you his mistress or something. We honestly don't know what he wants. We didn't tell you this before, but after you left, every single day, his goons would come banging on our gates asking that we "hand you over". The harassment has stopped now, since your father used some of his police contacts, but he's still asking around, desperate to find out where you are. I am so glad we sent you to London when we did.'

Ayesha watched the wall in front of her with the afternoon sunshine slowly creeping across it. She felt like the room was closing in around her. She was a fool to ever think that Raza Masood would stop looking for her. 'Do you think he could be in London? I mean, if he's that desperate, anything is possible?' Her legs shook as she spoke, the hand gripping the cell phone clammy with sweat.

'You haven't told anyone that you're in London, have you? Nobody must find out. When you return, we will figure out what to do. Maybe we will all move to Lahore, but for now, you must remain there. You don't need me to tell you what happens to girls who challenge the status quo in Pakistan.' She paused before adding, 'They die, Ayesha, and I am not losing my only daughter. So, I ask you again, have you told anyone you're in London?'

Ayesha ignored her trembling knee. 'Of course not. Who would I tell? All I said to Shugufta and my friends was that I was going out of town to recuperate.'

Her mother sighed with relief. 'Good girl. Keep your head down, but don't forget to enjoy yourself. We'll take care of the rest. And remember, tell no one.'

'You make it sound like a horror story.'

'It is a horror story.'

Ayesha didn't have the heart to tell her that she had seen someone who looked like Raza Masood and how much that had rattled her. Ending the call, she opened WhatsApp to see the countless messages from Kamil waiting for her. What was she supposed to say to him – that she was in hiding, scared at the prospect of Raza finding her? It sounded so ludicrous.

Was she going to let that bastard rule her? Was she going to be that terrified girl he had thrown acid on forever? Was she going to let him win? Although there was no one to see her in the room, she shook her head.

Raza Masood was not going to win. She was going to step out of the house, and once back in Pakistan, she was going to expose him. Reaching into her purse, she pulled out something she had always held on to. Flipping over the card, so that she could see the number, she dialled DSP Amna Habib.

She picked up at the first ring. 'DSP Amna Habib speaking.'

'This is Ayesha Safdar, the daughter of Safdar Khan.'

There was a sharp intake of breath. 'Ayesha, it ... it's good to hear from you. How may I help you?'

'How is the investigation going?'

There was a pause before DSP Amna said, 'I think you know full well how the investigation is going, and you know who attacked you – as do I. It was Raza Masood.'

Ayesha didn't miss a beat. 'It was.'

DSP Amna swore. 'I knew it. But why are you calling me now? Have you changed your mind? I was removed from the investigation and transferred by the powers that be, which you won't find surprising, knowing yourself how corrupt the system is, but listening to you now, my blood is boiling. That man cannot escape justice forever. He shouldn't.'

Her mother's warnings rang in her head, but she shrugged them off. She was done being scared. It was time to take control of her life. 'You're right. He shouldn't. I will testify against him.'

Kamil

People at work were beginning to notice how glum he seemed. His productivity had increased recently, because he'd thrown himself headfirst into work, but for some reason, he felt as if his mind was swimming when he wasn't working. To his surprise, it was Angela who was the first to notice. Judgemental Angela, who never missed an opportunity to remind him what a horrible place Pakistan was, had wheeled her chair over to his station to have a 'chat' with him.

'I know you think I'm a bitch,' she said, 'and maybe I am. God knows I am. I love to torment you and occasionally insult your country—'

'My country is Britain,' Kamil interrupted her, already getting annoyed. 'How many times do I have to tell you? I was born and bred here.'

Angela held up a hand. 'Let me finish, will you? I was simply saying that as much as I like to poke fun at you, and while I never imagined that I'd feel the least bit sorry to see you down, now that you are, I feel terrible. What's happened? Is there any way I can help?'

Kamil couldn't help but laugh. 'I don't know how you do it, Angela, but you've just managed to both insult me and show concern for me at the same time. It's a unique skill.'

Angela looked at him unfazed. 'Look, I know I'm a bit of a bitch, but I just wanted you to know that I kind of like you. We all do, and it makes me sad to see you so depressed. I hope it isn't something we've done.'

Kamil had to admit he was touched. Who would have thought that someone like Angela had a heart? After reassuring her that he wasn't the least bit depressed, he sent her back to her cubicle.

The reason that he was out of sorts wasn't anything to do with work. It had everything to do with Ayesha. She had been ignoring him for days now, ever since that night in Euston, and it had made him realise just how desperately he craved her company. Nothing seemed to make him happy, not even the salary bonus he'd just been promised.

Somewhere down the line, he'd fallen in love with her, and now, with her ignoring him like this, it felt like his life was falling apart. Was she punishing him for overstepping? It was even worse at night, when he didn't have anything to do except let his mind run wild.

His phone pinged with a new message from Angela:

Hope is a wonderful thing. Believe in it.

He looked up and gave her a smile, which she returned with a thumbs-up. It was strange how people continued to surprise you. He got himself a coffee from the small room that served as a kitchen, then sat back down behind his desk and took a deep breath. He scrolled through Ayesha's messages again, the latest one asking if she'd be joining them at the Pakistani expat dinner. His mother had been badgering him about the event for ages, no doubt planning to introduce him to another British Pakistani girl, but she might want him to come just so Ayesha had some company at dinner. Shar straight out refused to attend these events, as she always got saddled with some random aunty's son and then had to spend weeks trying to infuriate him enough to give up on her.

He felt like a balloon that had been pierced by a hot needle, all deflated and useless. How could he face Ayesha at this event and not say how he really felt about her? How could he just let her go without putting up a fight?

It was as if he'd sent his thoughts as a text to her, because as he looked at his phone a message appeared. He was so surprised he dropped the phone on the floor, as if it were burning his hands.

So sorry for the silence, Kamil. I can't wait to see you at the charity event x

He didn't know how long he stared at the message, especially the kiss she had signed off with. After some hesitation, he texted her back:

No worries. I can't wait to see you too ☺

Not too bad, he thought. At least it didn't reek of desperation, because that was how he actually felt.

❧

The event was being held in a swanky hotel on Park Lane. *Never let it be said that Pakistani expats don't have money to throw away*, he thought as he stepped through the revolving doors, to see the opulent flower arrangements in the hotel lobby, and his reflection in the marble floor, which was polished to perfection. This was his favourite hotel in London, but he didn't pause once to look around. The event was supposed to be a fundraiser for whatever charity the expat community was supporting at the time. He'd barely had time to change his clothes at home before his mother's calls and voice notes had started arriving.

'Ayesha and I are already here, Kamil. *Ya Khuda*, where are you? I swear to God, it's as if you have something against your own mother.'

He'd heard this particular statement so many times that it made him laugh now. He picked up when another one of his mother's calls arrived while he was walking through the foyer.

'Will you ever arrive? Even your sister is here, and we both know she hates these events.'

That was indeed a surprise. Shar had never attended the charity fundraiser before. Had she fallen out with Juan?

'You just want your mother to suffer,' his mother continued.

'I'm sorry, Ammi. I just left work. I'll be there in a couple of hours.'

He had to hold the phone a foot away from his ear as his mother screamed at him. 'You will be the death of me, I tell you.

Are you coming here to wash the dishes, because that's all that would be left to do in two hours.'

Kamil laughed. 'Relax, Ammi. I'm already here.'

'*Badtameez.* You'll give me a heart attack one of these days. Have you brought your ID? Ayesha here had to bring her passport.'

He laughed. 'Ammi, I'm not a child. Of course I have.'

Kamil didn't even need to ask which hall the event was being hosted in. He chose the one that seemed the noisiest, and sure enough, as soon as they'd checked his ID, the doors opened to the Pakistani expat community of the United Kingdom. It seemed like the entire city had descended upon the event. It wasn't anything less than a super-sized Pakistani wedding, with women glittering in their finest and men in sherwanis or smart tuxedos. His eyes scanned the crowd and found his mother sitting at one of the round tables, breathing heavily, staring daggers at him.

Before he could go and make amends, someone threw their arms around him, hugging him close. He didn't need to see who it was. He recognised Ayesha from her familiar perfume. He blinked, too shocked to return the hug.

'It is so nice to see you here, Kamil,' she whispered, breaking their embrace after one long minute. 'I've missed you. I promise you that I haven't been avoiding you. It's just that I had some thinking to do.'

For a moment, Kamil didn't know what to say. The first thing he noticed was that Ayesha wasn't wearing her scarf. She'd let her brown hair down, and it warmed his heart to see that true to her word, she had made no attempt to hide her scars. She wore them proudly. He couldn't help but feel proud of her. He could tell she was a bit self-conscious as her fingers kept reaching for her face, but removing the scarf itself was a huge leap. Ayesha was finally embracing who she was. She wore a white shalwar kameez with silver embroidery paired with silver heels that he thought might be Shar's. Noticing his gaze, she told him that they were indeed his sister's, and that her outfit was borrowed from his mother.

'Jamila Aunty absolutely insisted that I wear one of her formal outfits as I hadn't brought any with me.' She twirled around. 'She altered it for me herself, which means she can't wear it again. So much for borrowing it. I love it, though.'

'Ayesha,' he began, raising his voice in the noise, 'I also wanted to apologise. I should have known that you needed some time—'

'Kamil, I've made the decision to bring my attacker to justice,' she said, breaking him off. 'I have been afraid for too long, but coming here, spending time with you, has given me strength. Everyone – from your family, to Saeeda, to our support group – has just cemented my belief that it is time to stop hiding.'

'Are you going to leave us, then?'

Examining her nails, she said, 'It's complicated. I've been doing a lot of thinking. I don't want to endanger my family, but I can't rest until that person is brought to justice. But I won't be leaving just yet. We need to finish that conversation you started in Euston.'

Hope really was such a funny thing. He felt his world light up immediately. 'I've missed you too this past week.' Stepping forward, he added, 'Would you like to go somewhere quiet after this. We could definitely continue that particular discussion then.'

Ayesha raised an eyebrow. 'I think I like what you're suggesting, Kamil Akbar, but are you prepared to spend your time listening to me? I always have plenty to say.'

He didn't let his gaze falter. 'I'd listen to anything you have to say. And I'd like nothing better than to spend all my time with you, Ayesha.'

'In spite of my changed appearance? What you see is what you get from now on, you know.'

'Because of that. You're a beautiful woman, Ayesha. Inside and out.'

She finally smiled, her hand resting on his cheek for a moment. 'What would I do without you, Kamil? You know, after the attack, I had promised myself that I would never speak of it again, but now, I know that if I don't, I will be doing other girls like me a huge disservice.'

Kamil took a deep breath. 'Will you tell me about the guy who did this to you? Raza Masood?'

Her eyes narrowed a fraction, and she seemed about to say something when someone behind her called her name.

'Ayesha!'

Ayesha

Raza Masood's name was on her lips when she heard the familiar voice behind her.

'Ayesha, *mera bacha*! It's so nice to see you here. How we've missed you in Pakistan.'

Neelam Khala. What was she doing here, and why hadn't her mother warned her? Ayesha reached for her dupatta, intending to cover her face and neck, but then she let her hand drop to her side. This wasn't who she was anymore. She was not going to hide from anyone, least of all this woman. Taking a deep breath, she turned around and grinned at her aunt. '*Assalam Alaikum*, Neelam Khala,' she said, embracing her. 'Lovely to see you, as always. What are you doing here in London?'

Neelam's eyes narrowed as they parted from the embrace. 'London is like the second home of the rich in Pakistan, Ayesha. Ahh ... I see that you're wearing the latest fragrance from Balenciaga. Very posh, my dear. It was a gift from your hosts, I'm sure.'

Ayesha didn't even blink. Neelam's little jibes meant nothing to her anymore. 'Actually, I bought it with the money I earned volunteering at Saeeda Aunty's charity.'

Neelam snorted. 'I bet she makes you wash all the dishes, the old fraud. Look at your hands. As rough as sandpaper.' She shook her head. 'What will your poor mother say? They've been sitting in Multan thinking you're living like a queen, away from Raza's clutches, and here you've been washing dishes like a common maid.'

'How did you know I would be here, or that I'm in London for that matter?' Ayesha knew that nothing was ever straightforward with Neelam.

Neelam threw her head back and laughed, clutching her diamond choker as she did so. 'Your dear mother never could stay mad at me for long. It took all of a week for her to call me and spill the beans about your visit.' Raising her eyebrows in Kamil's direction, she lowered her voice and added, 'You don't waste time, do you? The man's quite a catch, but has he said something about the ... you know?' Ayesha must have looked confused, because Neelam laughed again. 'Your scars, my dear. Did you have to make me say it?'

Ayesha had promised herself that she would never again let Neelam's words affect her, but it was still an effort to appear unperturbed. Ayesha held her head high. 'I am not going to dignify that with an answer, Khala. You ought to be nicer to me. I'm your niece by blood.'

She watched her aunt's face redden as she inflated like a hot-air balloon. 'You never were one for manners. You've always resisted my love – and my concern for you.'

'Is something the matter here?'

It was Kamil, always trying to rescue her.

'You're better off with a British girl than my heartless niece.' Neelam almost spat the words.

Ayesha noticed Kamil's eyes widen as he cast a glance at her and then at Neelam. 'Excuse me? Are you seriously saying this stuff about your own niece?'

Ayesha touched his arm. 'Forget it, Kamil. She's no aunt of mine.'

'Of course,' Neelam sneered. 'Why would I want to be related to someone like you? You've got none of your mother's grace and poise. You've always been brash and unkempt, just like your blundering father.' She turned to Kamil. 'The bloody nerve of this girl, and she has the audacity to denounce me? Her family has lived off me for decades, and this is the repayment I get. Well, I tell you that this little *gushti* is no niece of mine.'

Before Ayesha could stop herself, she'd raised her hand and

slapped Neelam across the face. The sound of the slap rang across the hall, and plenty of heads turned in their direction.

Ayesha clapped her hands over her mouth, stunned at what she'd just done, but she didn't apologise. Somewhere deep inside, she knew that her aunt deserved it. Her heart swelled with happiness. 'That was a long time coming.'

Neelam's face was as red as beetroot as she touched her cheek. The slap had left its mark. Spit drooled out of the side of her mouth as she said, 'You'll pay for this, Ayesha. All I have ever done is to make your life better, and you resist me at every turn? I am your Khala, your mother's sister!'

'And, I was all of ten years old, Khala. I'm sorry the stitches ruined Sabeena's cheek, but I didn't do it on purpose. How long must you punish me for something I had no control over?' Ayesha exhaled.

'You ruined her face, Ayesha. And just now, you slapped your own aunt across the face. I have only ever wanted what was good for you, but now, I wonder if you deserve what you got in life.' Her eyes suddenly widened as the realisation of what she'd just said dawned on her. 'What I mean is...'

Ayesha felt Kamil touch her shoulder. 'Do you want to leave? Let's just leave.'

She backed away. Wherever she went, destruction followed. She noticed Jamila Aunty rising from her seat and walking towards her, concern etched on her face. Behind her, Saeeda and Moeeza followed.

'Come on, let's go,' Kamil told her, taking her hand. She closed her eyes, grateful for his support, but she didn't need to take him down with her. Maybe Neelam Khala was right, after all. Perhaps someone as twisted as her deserved what she had got. She certainly didn't deserve someone as pure-hearted as Kamil. She pulled her hand away from his and looked up at him. There was only kindness in his eyes. He truly cared for her.

It was too much for her to handle; she needed to get out of

here. But just then a large group of people arrived, milling about and blocking the entrance. Then one of the organisers proceeded to close the doors behind them, ushering them forward and pointing at the stage.

'The ceremony is about to begin,' he announced.

Ayesha's hands felt clammy. What was she doing, standing here, being gawked at by people she didn't even know? Backing away, she shook her head at Kamil. She needed space.

Kamil understood. He nodded and put a hand on his mother's shoulder, whispering in her ear. Jamila Aunty looked worried, but at this moment Ayesha didn't have it in her to console anyone. She felt unmoored. Neelam's words had unlocked a deep fear in her. She touched the ridged scar tissue on her face and neck, feeling it burn her, a pain she was so familiar with by now that it felt like a part of her.

Perhaps the man standing guard at the door saw something in her expression, because he promptly opened the door for her.

Kamil

What was supposed to have been a charity dinner had turned into a bit of a circus. His mother stood facing Neelam, panting slightly. 'You were here as a guest, and you wrecked the entire event to settle scores. Ayesha is my responsibility. How dare you insult her like this? You are her real aunt. Did your blood not go cold at the mere possibility of maligning your niece like this? What would your sister say?'

'This is a family matter,' Neelam snapped. 'You stay out of it. You don't know what this girl is like.'

For the first time that evening, Shar strode forward and past the cluster of people that surrounded Jamila and Neelam. Back at the stage, the organisers were still going on about charity, but a lot of people's attention had wavered. Shar came within inches of Neelam, and Kamil had to strain to hear what she was saying.

'This isn't Pakistan, where you can say whatever you want and get away with it. There can be consequences for your behaviour, so if I were you, I'd be very careful.'

'Stay out of Ayesha's life,' Kamil found himself saying to Neelam. He hated public confrontations, and yet, here he was, speaking out for Ayesha. What did that make him?

Neelam's eyes were bloodshot, her immense body quivering with humiliation. She leaned against a chair for support, running her gaze over him. 'You are so in love with her, it's sickening.' She smiled, but it wasn't a kind smile. It was all teeth. 'It's so obvious. Your face is showing it, plain as day.'

'And what if I am?' he asked, surprising even himself.

His mother gasped, clapping her hands together. 'Oh, you are? How wonderful! *Haye*, I've never been so happy.'

Neelam hacked up phlegm in her throat and spat it at their feet. 'There, I need to get out of this place. I'd like to hear your opinion about her when you get slapped by her. I thought I could improve her life, but she doesn't want it. She's not like my Sabeena, who turns heads wherever she goes, and that too after pushing a child out into the world.'

'God, this event has turned into a disaster,' Shar said, pushing past Neelam. She looked pretty in her yellow shalwar kameez today, but the expression on her face was murderous. She took hold of his elbow and steered him away from the small crowd that had formed around them.

'I've suspected that you might be in love with Ayesha,' she said, as they paused near an empty roundtable. 'I could see it in your eyes when you looked at her, but as much as I love Ayesha, I don't know if she's in love with you.'

'You're right.'

Shar's eyes widened. 'Then why did you just declare your love for her just now?'

Kamil thought for a moment. What was he supposed to say – that he had the worst luck when it came to love, that either he fell in love with women who would ultimately betray him or women who he wasn't sure loved him back?

He ran a hand over his face. 'I don't know why I said it. All I know is that something's changed over these last few weeks. I finally feel happy in a way I never did with anyone. Not Arooj, not even Madiha.'

Shar winced at Arooj's name, opening her mouth to say something, but Kamil cut her off.

'We shouldn't fear saying her name, Shar. It only gives her more power over us. I am done thinking about what she did to me and what could have been. All I know is that at this point in my life, I deserve to be happy.'

Shar wiped a tear from her cheek. 'In that case, what the hell are you standing here for? Go and tell this to Ayesha. Maybe she likes you just as much as you like her.' She gave him a small push. 'Go! I'll handle Ammi and that Neelam. What a way to ruin a perfectly good event. Thank God Juan isn't here or he'd have dumped me, seeing how crazy Pakistanis can be.'

Without a backward glance, he walked out of the hall. Maybe Ayesha was still around, waiting for a taxi or something. Pulling out his cell phone, he dialled her number.

It went straight to voicemail.

'Damn it,' he muttered, looking around the entrance. She'd probably just gone into Central London to blow off some steam, or maybe she'd taken the train to Whetstone? He pulled out his cell phone again and wrote a text message.

Where are you? Hope you're okay! You know me, chronic worrier.

He pressed send before he could reconsider the tone of the message. He didn't care if he sounded paranoid or weird. Right now, all he wanted was to have her standing in front of him, so that he could tell her how he really felt.

Where are you, Ayesha? he wondered as his feet took him in the direction of Hyde Park Corner station.

Ayesha

Exiting Totteridge and Whetstone Station after midnight, she realised she should have taken a taxi home. Not only had it taken almost an hour to get here from Central London, a signal failure on the Northern Line had meant another hour of waiting. Generally, she'd found people in London to be aloof but respectful, but everyone's true nature came out on the Underground. People had pushed past her, some elbowing her hard in the chest and back to get on the packed trains, and it wasn't until several had passed that she was able to get on. Under normal circumstances, it would have made her laugh, but now that she had missed the last bus to Whetstone, it wasn't funny anymore. She pulled her shawl tight across her shoulders, hoping the glittering outfit was obscured as much as possible. She didn't want to stand out like a beacon in the darkness in Jamila Aunty's festive outfit. There were no taxis to be had, so she doubled down against the cold, and headed towards Jamila Aunty's house, a good twenty-minute walk from the station.

Neelam Khala had no right to talk to her the way she had tonight, especially in front of Kamil and Jamila Aunty. It wasn't Neelam who had suffered an acid attack and permanent disfiguration. It was Ayesha. She was the one who had to contend with it her entire life. How could anyone dare tell her to forget about it and move on? Let Raza Masood go free? If she had remained in Pakistan, she may have done that, but something had awakened inside her in London, and she knew what it was.

The thirst for justice – not just for herself, but for those countless other women who suffered in silence just like her. She was going to go to Pakistan and expose that bastard, no matter what happened. And she was going to make sure she never saw Neelam's face again. Her parents could move to Lahore if they wanted, but she was done being afraid. She was done looking over her shoulder.

Lost in thought, she turned into a side street off the main road, realising only later that the houses around her were all unfamiliar. It was her first time walking in Whetstone so late at night, and since the street was not well-lit like the main road, there were shadows everywhere. The hair on the back of her neck stood up. She looked back to see if she could return to the main road, and her stomach did a somersault. There were four men behind her, a dozen or so metres away. They didn't seem to be in a rush, but in the dark, it was impossible to tell what they looked like. It was only when they passed under a streetlight that she noticed black surgical masks over their faces and their heads wrapped in scarves. She increased her pace, hurrying towards the intersection where she could see more cars. Her heart raced, but she forced herself to be practical. There was no reason for them to be following her, especially not in a safe neighbourhood in North London. She looked straight ahead and tried to seem relaxed, glancing at the houses on either side, hoping to see a lit window, someone standing at their door. The purr of a car made her shiver. It was behind her, moving slowly. Why didn't it pass? Was it stopping at one of the houses? No. It seemed to be keeping pace with her. Unable to resist, she snuck a look at it. A black van with tinted windows, creeping along, the men beside it. Alarm bells suddenly rang in her head, and without thinking, she broke into a run, desperate to get somewhere with people around. The clothes she wore were not made for running, and neither were the heels. She flung them off and ran barefoot, not paying attention to her shawl, which caught in the wind and flew away.

'Help!' she screamed, but it was as if nobody lived on the street. Were the people inside the houses mistaking her for a drunk person, or did they just not care? Over the sound of her blood whooshing in her ears, she could hear boots hitting the pavement behind her, growing ever closer. She made the mistake of looking back, and that's when she stumbled. There was only time for her to scream once before the men caught up with her, one of them slapping a damp cloth against her mouth.

'Some chloroform... just to get you to relax,' one of the men panted in a Russian accent.

That was the last thing she heard before her body grew slack and the world went dark.

When she came to, she wasn't gagged anymore, but was slumped in an armchair. She attempted to rise, but her legs were like jelly and wouldn't support her weight. It took her a moment to realise that she was in someone's bedroom. Before she could properly observe her surroundings, there was a rustle of clothing behind her as the overpowering smell of men's cologne filled her nose.

'Boo,' someone whispered in her ear.

An involuntary gasp escaped her. As soon as she'd seen the van, she'd known who was behind this, but the sound of his voice still sent terror shooting through her. Ignoring the numbness in her legs, she lunged out of the armchair, holding on to the nearby chest of drawers for support.

Raza Masood stood before her, the same insufferable smirk on his face that he had worn the last time she'd seen him in the hospital. 'So, we meet again.' His smirk widened as he watched her almost lose her balance. 'That's exactly the kind of reaction I was hoping for.'

Raza had cinched his dressing gown at the waist, but left it open around the chest for effect. Lowering himself into an armchair, he gestured for her to take the one opposite to him.

Over my dead body, she thought, staying rooted to the spot. His bare chest made her skin crawl. The day of the assault flashed before her eyes, the scars on her face and neck starting to burn suddenly. She jerked her head, trying to banish the images from her mind. She needed to have a clear mind to deal with him.

'How did you find me?' she asked Raza, facing him head on, not breaking eye contact even though she wanted to. She looked straight into the depths of those malevolent black eyes, determined to not give an inch. 'After doing what you did, why would you want to find me anyway? To kill me so I took this incident to my grave?'

Raza held a hand at his heart in mock horror. 'Mademoiselle, you wound me. Why on earth would I go to all this trouble just to kill you? Where's the fun in that? Do you honestly think I've spent all this money on hiring goons from the dark web just to have you killed? God, no. Those Russians cost good money, although they were easy enough to get in touch with.'

'The dark web?'

'Who knew the dark web could be so much fun?' Raza laughed then, a distasteful sound. Waving a hand around the room, he continued, 'This is my London home. Do you like it? Don't get any ideas of running away, Ayesha, because the doors are automatic and I hold the key.' He held up a small remote.

Tears threatened, but she swallowed them. This was not the time to display weakness. One sign of it, and there was no telling what Raza might do. What she wouldn't give to be back at Jamila Aunty's place.

As if reading her thoughts, Raza held up her cell phone. 'It was fairly easy to unlock your phone and send a flurry of messages to your lovely Jamila Aunty, saying that you were staying with a friend for a couple of days. That woman sure asks a lot of questions, though.'

Ayesha kept holding on to the chest of drawers, leaning against it. All she knew was that she had to keep talking. She didn't want to think what would happen if they stopped. 'But why?' she began. 'I don't understand why you won't leave me alone, especially after throwing acid on my face. What more could you possibly want from me? Why travel to London for me?'

Raza raised an eyebrow as he rose from the armchair, taking a step towards her. 'Revenge, Ayesha.' He bared his teeth. 'You cheated on me with that good-for-nothing Saqib. It almost drove me insane. Did you not expect the jealousy and hurt you might cause? By the time I got my bearings, your parents had squirrelled you off to God knows where. Nobody knew where you'd gone, not even your colleagues.' Drawing even closer, he added, 'Yes, I contacted everyone. We had almost given up hope, when that aunt of yours let it slip in front of my mother. Neelam, is it? Blurted everything out about you being here. And that is when I knew that the time had arrived for me to plan my revenge. I would destroy you just like you destroyed me.'

Ayesha swore under her breath. 'Haven't you destroyed me enough, Raza?'

He shook his head. 'I tried to move on, but it was as if an obsession had gripped me. I couldn't get you out of my head. And then, word of your shenanigans with Saqib spread to my friends. And that's when I knew that I had to punish you.' He spread his arms. 'You made me look like a fool, and Raza Masood is no fool.'

Ayesha took a step back. 'Raza, listen—'

'Your useless father was once an influential man – not so much now, but, if he could send you to London, who knew where he'd send you next? Perhaps he would never have let you return to Pakistan. No, once I knew you were in London, I had to act. Burning you with acid wasn't enough. My revenge was still incomplete. So ... what to do?' He tapped his finger on his chin, inching closer to Ayesha as he did so. 'I wanted you to break into a thousand pieces and watch you admit defeat. But when I arrived in London, I realised that you were blossoming instead. It pissed me off so much that I grew reckless. You caught a glimpse of me at Euston Station, didn't you?' Another smile. 'You weren't sure, though. I could see it on your face. I could also see that the guy with you was desperate to kiss you. I bet you didn't notice *that.*'

Ayesha was breathing hard. Her legs gave way and she slumped back into the armchair. She should have run for it when she had a chance. That sighting of Raza in Euston was a warning, and she'd ignored it. What had she been thinking? That she could fight this man? Expose him? She was like an animal to him. Worse than that, she was like a thing he wanted to own and destroy. And Kamil ... she struggled not to think about him, what she could have had with him.

'You...' Raza breathed. 'You've tormented me, Ayesha. More than anyone in my life. I would spend hours wondering why you left me for that piece of shit, Saqib, who couldn't wait to help himself to some of my money. I screamed at the walls in frustration, but there was no reply.' He had come impossibly close to her now, close enough for her to count the hairs on his chest. 'And then the answer came to me. You see, you were never marriage material at all. I should have treated you like the whore you are from day one. That was my biggest mistake – giving you respect. But no matter, now that you're here, I will finally treat you the way a whore ought to be treated.' Winking at her, he added, 'I will finally make you pay for cheating on me and then leaving me. I will have my revenge. Today, you are mine.'

Ayesha gasped. She couldn't help it. For a moment, her mind refused to accept what she'd just heard. Her eyes darted to the door as she shrank away from Raza, away from the cloying smell of his aftershave. 'If you think you'll be raping me in this, or any other country, you're sadly mistaken. I'm going to call the police.'

'With what? I have your phone.' Raza folded his arms around his chest, the smirk back on his face. 'And let's say you do manage to call the police, what do you think will happen to your parents back in Multan? Two fifty-something has-beens. They would be easy to kill? No one would even bother investigating. Your father isn't that important.'

Ayesha stared at him. 'You wouldn't. You're bluffing. You bastards are all the same. Your mother was the same as well. Idle threats.'

In a flash, Raza had pushed her against the mantelpiece, his fingers around her throat. 'Don't you dare bring my mother into this, you filthy *kanjari*!' And just like that, his rage subsided, and once again, a smile played on his lips. 'I am really going to enjoy kissing every part of you.' Leaning closer, he whispered, 'Even your ugly scars.'

'You bastard!'

Raza's entire body shook with laughter. He loosened his grip on her neck slightly, stroking her chin with a thumb. 'You are going to be so much fun.'

Ayesha was still groggy from the chloroform, and knew that she would soon be overpowered, but Raza's phone began ringing and he turned his head, so she used every bit of her strength to kick him straight in the balls. He squealed like a dying pig, clutching his groin. 'You bitch! Wait till I—'

She didn't wait to listen. Turning on her heel, she made a beeline for the stairs. She'd break a window if she had to, but she was getting out of this place. There was no way Raza was going to have her parents killed.

Hurrying down the stairs, she tried the main door, but it was locked. Looking around for something heavy enough to break the large window next to it, her eye caught a large pewter-coloured vase full of fresh flowers. Pulling the flowers out, she wrapped her fingers around the handles, and banged it against the window.

The vase shattered into a million pieces, but the window remained intact.

What the hell?

As she stood there panting, she realised that Raza hadn't come rushing down to stop her. It was almost as if he was convinced that she couldn't leave. Was she really trapped? She wrapped her arms around herself. She wasn't going to let Raza touch her, no matter what. The very thought nauseated her.

And then, she heard it. The soft sound of footsteps on carpet. He was coming downstairs. She looked around, for something, anything strong enough to break glass. In the fireplace, there were a bunch of large stones. They might be able to do the trick.

Grabbing one, she hurled it at the window with all her strength.

The stone hardly made a dent.

'You could keep trying, but I'm afraid failure is inevitable,' Raza said. He sounded amused. He showed her his cell phone. 'Shall I call my people in Multan and tell them you're being troublesome?'

'You evil bastard! You will not get away with this. My ... my father has connections.'

'I have more.' She could see the anger building in Raza's eyes, but that infuriating smile remained on his face. 'Your father is an old fool. My men can barge into your house right this moment and gun both your parents down. Nobody will bat an eye. But, if that's not enough' – his eyes gleamed – 'What if I told you that right at this moment, one of those men I hired is watching Kamil Akbar walking down Warwick Road towards his little studio? Knife crimes are pretty common in London. Imagine the drawings my man would carve on beautiful Kamil's pathetic face. You know he will. They kidnapped you, didn't they?'

As she watched the lunatic in front of her give her a wink, she realised that there was no way out. His threats were real. The stone dropped from her hand, landing on the carpet with a thud, and rolling underneath a sofa.

'Good girl,' Raza whispered. 'Very good girl.'

Kamil

'Sometimes, acceptance doesn't happen immediately. It takes time,' Matt said as Kamil sat with the support group.

Everyone was there except for Ayesha. The same Ayesha who had told him that she missed his presence had now ghosted him completely. He'd sent her a bunch of texts only to be met with a wall of indifference. Those blue ticks on his Whatsapp glared at him as if blaming him for putting himself out there like that.

I never do learn my lesson, he thought. *After Arooj, I'd vowed never to fall for someone so completely, and yet, here I am.*

'But love doesn't take time.' Shabbir remarked. 'Love in itself is such a beautiful feeling. My wife and I haven't been in love for ages. Perhaps we never were. It's not something you can force on the other person.'

Sandra scoffed. 'Pfft. There is nothing beautiful about love. It only gives you pain. The pain of seeing the person you love in someone else's arms, the pain of wanting to end things, but never quite managing it, and most of all, the pain of seeing them happy without you.'

Matt attuned, as always, to everyone's mood turned to Kamil as he took a sip of his coffee. 'Why so glum? Are you missing Ayesha? Was she too busy to be here?'

Kamil didn't reply. It was strange, but he felt as if something bad had happened. Ayesha hadn't responded to his texts, but she'd informed his mother that she was staying with some friends. What friends? He hadn't realised she'd made any in London.

'Yeah,' he said, at last. 'Maybe she's busy.' He hated the looks of sympathy he got from everyone around the table, but it was hard to mask his feelings from them now. Somehow, this motley collection of people had become his family. Through thick and thin, wasn't that what they said about family? Kamil had been there for them too when they needed him. He'd taken Sandra out shopping when she'd been suicidal. They'd taken turns to watch over her, so she wouldn't attempt anything foolish. Although Matt liked to consider himself the leader of this group, his struggle was there for everyone to see as well. He'd told everyone how much he'd suffered in his first marriage, and that the group was sometimes the only thing that kept him sane and out of trouble.

Yes, they were family.

But sitting there, among people Ayesha had embraced too, it hit him again. Why hadn't he heard from her?

'*Haye*, why did I ever let the girl out of my sight?' his mother wailed, beating her chest. 'Why didn't I ask her the address of the friends she's staying with? What will I tell Ishrat when she asks me about her daughter? This is a travesty.'

'Now, now, Jamila. There's no point in crying, is there?' Akbar Khan said, patting his wife on the shoulder. 'I'm sure there's nothing to worry about. Ayesha is a spirited girl. She will turn up. It's only been a day or so.'

'Spirited? Her phone is switched off, and all the while I've been planning kitty parties. I swear I will kill Moeeza with my bare hands. She had the audacity to say that it was good riddance that Ayesha has disappeared.' Another sob escaped Jamila. 'Oh, the shame. The girl was under my supervision.'

'Ammi, she's twenty-seven years old. Not exactly a child. Wherever she is, it's not your fault.'

'*Bas karo*, Sharmeela. You know nothing about the world. I don't know how you've managed to breeze through life like this. Ayesha is a young woman alone in London. Why, anyone could have taken advantage of her.'

'I bet she would give them a piece of her mind.'

'You don't know that,' Kamil told her. 'She could be in grave danger.'

She threw up her hands. 'I think we're all overreacting.'

'Her phone is off, Shar! We're not overreacting.' He hadn't told his family that he'd had a call from Saeeda Aunty earlier as well, who'd told her that Ayesha had missed her shift at the charity centre, but it was time to tell them now.

'The girl's no fool,' Saeeda had told him. 'But I can't understand why she can't see love staring at her. I was hoping to have a word with her yesterday, but I didn't manage to get a hold of her. God knows where she is.'

'I think we need to notify the police,' he announced now. 'Ayesha missed her shift at the charity centre yesterday as well.'

His mother paled. 'Police?' She turned to her husband. 'Can't you use your past connections in the police force to ask around? You used to be a detective. A formal inquiry will mean word getting out, and her parents finding out. *Haye*, they will be so disappointed in me.'

'Ayesha is missing, Ammi. I think their disappointment should be the least of your worries.'

His mother flapped a hand in his direction. 'You don't know Pakistani society the way I do. They'll make me a pariah.'

'Ammi, are you honestly worried about that at the moment?' Shar piped in. 'Besides, you have your kitty, don't you?'

'Uff! Are you my children or my enemies? May God never give anyone such ungrateful children.'

Kamil looked up to meet his father's gaze, and could tell that things were dire – he uncharacteristically looked troubled. 'A day without a word is not as concerning as her phone being off, but the fact that she failed to turn up for her shift is certainly alarming. I think Kamil is right. We must involve the police.' He patted his wife's shoulder again. 'You must be strong now, Jamila. It's not your fault, but still, you must be strong. Our first and foremost priority must be to find out where Ayesha is. I'll make some enquiries in the morning, and we will take it from there.'

'*Haye*.'

After their parents had settled in for the night, Shar padded over to the living room with two mugs of coffee. 'So, what do you think has happened?'

Kamil checked his watch. It was past midnight. 'I don't even want to think about it right now, Shar. It's all too much. Let's allow Abbu to make some enquiries first. After all, he used to be in the police force.'

'Poor Ayesha.' Sipping at her coffee, she added, 'Ammi will have to tell her parents as well. Ugh, I can't believe she'd just disappear like that. It has really put everyone in a difficult situation. I hope it doesn't have anything to do with that guy who attacked her.'

Kamil's blood froze. He hadn't even thought of that. 'Why do you say that?'

Shar shrugged. 'Just a thought.'

From what Kamil knew, the man was very rich, but could his influence extend all the way to London? He found it very unlikely. Surely, there had to be another reason. Noticing his sister watching him, he looked away. 'None of your pity, Shar. I never really stood a chance.'

'That's not true. I saw the way she looked at you sometimes. There was definitely something there. I think she is in love with you, Kamil, but she doesn't know it yet.'

Putting his mug down on the table, Kamil rose from the sofa. Hope and guilt pierced him in equal measure. 'Why didn't I say something when I had the chance?' he murmured to himself.

Ayesha

She wished she could have talked to her parents, seen their faces just one more time. She wished that she could have told Kamil how she really felt about him, how he lit up her whole world, how she couldn't envisage a life without him by her side. People said that a person's life flashes before their eyes before death. For Ayesha, it was happening now as Raza shrugged off his dressing gown.

She looked away, tears leaking out of her eyes. She wished he'd just get it over with.

As if reading her thoughts, Raza laughed. 'This won't be a quickie. I have waited way too long for this.'

If Ayesha had the strength, she'd have flung the armchair at him. She wouldn't have hesitated in shooting him if she had a gun.

Her body stiffened as Raza climbed into the bed. He'd made her put on some tacky lingerie beneath a nightgown he claimed was worth hundreds of pounds. Nausea crept up her throat at the smell of his familiar cologne, his nose brushing against her cheek. Every part of her body screamed in protest, but she couldn't move. She couldn't push him away. If she did, who was to say what he'd do to Kamil and his family – to her family? She used to think her father was a man of influence despite their obvious penury, but now she knew otherwise. Nobody had the means to stand against the great Masood empire. Raza was right. It wouldn't take two seconds for him to kill her parents. If he was capable of burning her face and abducting her, he was certainly capable of murder too.

Their bodies were touching, one big hand resting on her stomach. 'I'm going to take you to Pakistan and get you a nice flat in Lahore,' he whispered in her ear. 'You can live there in luxury. Appealing, isn't it?'

'As your *rakhail*?' The words were out of her mouth before she could stop herself.

But far from enraging him, her words made Raza laugh. 'Of course, you'll be my mistress, Ayesha. Did you have dreams of becoming my wife? You have a reputation for having sex with the first available man, for God's sake. You are not fit to be anyone's wife. All you're fit for' – his fingers dug into her breast – 'is this. You deserve to be ravaged like this. It's what you were born for.' Hoisting himself up, he closed his fingers around her neck. 'Now stop being a bloody tease and show me what you've got.'

She glared at him, not trusting herself to speak. There was nothing she could say that would deter this dog.

'I like the fire in your eyes,' he panted, tearing away her nightgown in one single jerk. He forced her legs open with his knee. 'Good girl. I've been wanting to do this for a very long time.'

Ayesha didn't close her eyes or retreat into her mind. She wanted to be fully present for every slight, every humiliation this man levelled against her.

She bore it all silently, his large paws as they grabbed at every part of her body, his damp breath on her face as he tried to split her into two.

She endured it all.

As his thrusts gained momentum, Ayesha bunched the bed sheet in her fists, trying not to scream. Instead, as their eyes met, she vowed that someday, she would wreak her revenge.

For everything.

However, Raza Masood was cleverer than she gave him credit for. He violated her three times that day, and although she expected him to do the same the next day, he didn't. He didn't even touch her. Instead, he began making arrangements for them to fly back to Pakistan.

Whatever semblance of hope that had survived in her heart was snuffed out. The longer he kept her in London, the more likely it would be that Jamila Aunty and Kamil would report her missing. She counted on her fingers and felt her stomach fall. She'd only been out of touch with them for two days, and Raza had already told Jamila Aunty that she would be staying with friends for a few days.

Presently, he was shouting on the phone at his travel agent. 'Yes, the passports are ready, *bhenchod*. Why aren't you issuing the tickets?' A pause. 'Didn't I just tell you I had the passports? Hers was in the bag.'

Ayesha swore under her breath. If the charity event hadn't required proof of identity, this bastard wouldn't have had access to her passport. He seemed to have thought of everything, knowing exactly when to strike. She wanted to scream for help, but there was nobody to listen to her.

Closing her eyes for a moment, she opened them again with force. She couldn't afford to lose control now. She searched the room for something – anything – she could use to call the police, but there was nothing. Even the windows were sealed shut. This place was almost like a tomb. Looking at the morning sunshine filtering in the room, she wondered when she'd be able to be in London again.

Probably, never. Who knew what Raza had in mind for her.

Ideas of escape were swirling in her head when Raza came back into the room, his expression stern. He made a face. 'This room reeks of sex. Are you so used to this smell that you don't even notice it? Get in the bloody shower, woman. Clean yourself up.' He collapsed into an armchair, holding his head in his hands. 'I'll probably have to burn these sheets. This room is drenched in your smell.'

'You couldn't seem to get enough of it last night.' *Kanjar*, she added as an afterthought.

The smirk was back on his face. 'Liked it, did you? First time with a real man, eh? I'm sure you'll never look at another man the same way now that you've been with me.'

'Truer words were never spoken,' she shot back, packing as much bile into her words as possible.

'You're a dirty little slut, Ayesha. I love it.'

In the bathroom, with the shower turned on, she finally let herself cry. Big, wracking sobs. She scrubbed herself raw in a bid to get every bit of him out of her, but the more she scrubbed, the worse she felt. He had permanently soiled her, and no amount of washing or cleaning would ever get the filth out.

He'd left his razor blade on the counter next to the washbasin. She imagined how it would feel to slit her wrists and let the blood mix with water as it drained down London's gutters. A part of her claimed by this city forever. Instead, she looked at the burnt skin on her face, and grazed the razor along it, letting it catch a scar. She gasped as a single drop of blood trickled down her neck. She forced herself to remember what this man had done to her.

No. This was not going to be her end. She wasn't going to be found dead in the bathroom like a common criminal, and allow Raza to get off scot-free. He had to pay for everything he'd put her through. Maybe not today, but someday, she would get her revenge.

How many times will you allow him to rape you before you gather the courage? a voice in her head said, but she knew the answer to that.

Revenge took time, especially when it came to people like Raza. Wiping away the mist that had gathered on the mirror, she attempted to smile at herself.

'You can do this,' she told herself. 'Even if he takes you to Pakistan, it won't be the end.'

Her spirits lifted, she pulled the price tags from some clothes he'd left for her in the bathroom and pulled them on. The shirt was a bit loose, but the pants were a perfect fit. By the time she opened the door of the bathroom, she was feeling a little optimistic about the future.

Her heart fell as soon as she stepped back into the bedroom, though. Raza had his cell phone in front of him and he beckoned her to join him. 'Look,' he said as she approached. 'See if you can guess what I'm looking at.'

It was a live feed of the exterior of her house in Multan. The gate was open and her parents were standing in the porch, gesticulating wildly. If the situation hadn't been so dire, she'd have laughed, but she knew what this meant. It was a threat.

Raza swiped at the screen. 'Now, look here. This seem familiar to you?'

She only had to glance at it to understand what he was showing her. She'd spent enough time there over the past few months. It was Jamila Aunty's house.

'Like I said, it is surprising how efficient the dark web is, so I'd advise extreme caution as we make our way to the airport.'

Ayesha stared at him, her heart rate picking up. 'We're going today? I can't go. I'm not ready.'

'We're actually leaving shortly. You don't need anything. I'll take care of all your needs. Just remember one thing: you put one toe out of line and the first thing I'll do is have your parents killed, and the next thing will be to have my men torture your Jamila Aunty and her beautiful daughter. Sharmeela, is it?' He looked amused, but his tone brokered no argument. 'That girl is a marvel, I tell you. She's got spice.'

'They've got nothing to do with this,' she whispered, pleading with her eyes, hoping he'd understand. 'All they did was open their home to me during my visit. Please keep them out of this. Don't harm them.'

'Oh, I forgot to say: young Kamil will face the same fate.'

'Raza, please!'

His eyes gleamed. 'Look at you, with those tears brimming in your eyes and bottom lip quivering as if I'm some sort of a villain.' He put the phone away and grabbed her face, his fingernails digging into her cheeks. 'These people joined my hit list the moment they offered you refuge. If you'd stayed in

Pakistan, I wouldn't have had to spend all these millions of rupees searching for you. What a colossal waste of money.' Releasing her face, he began rummaging in his shoulder bag. 'Come and sit on my lap.'

'Excuse me?'

Raza rolled his eyes. 'I'm not about to have sex with you, idiot. I'm a man, not a machine. Even I have limitations. Now, come here before I lose my temper again.'

Sitting on his lap, she felt her humiliation was complete. She'd finally reached a point of no return. She looked at herself in the full-length mirror in front of her. She looked like a zombie.

Raza took in a deep breath. 'Not bad, Ayesha. You smell pretty nice. Now be a good girl and roll up your sleeve.'

He tugged at her arm, but she jerked it away. 'Why?'

He brandished a syringe at her. 'This will help you relax while we're travelling. You may be a good actress, but nobody is that good. I don't want people noticing anything. You'll be in a wheelchair, and so out of it that nobody will notice a thing. I'll just tell them you're my cute, injured girlfriend who is on pain meds.' He pulled a piece of paper from the inside pocket of his jacket. 'I've got a prescription too. Now pull up your sleeve. I won't ask again.'

Her mind must have gone numb with the shock, because she barely felt the needle pierce her skin.

'There you go. Now, you'll be nice and pliable throughout the entire process.'

All her early bravado from the bathroom vanished into thin air. This, here, was the end.

Her life was over.

The feeling was entirely foreign for her. She felt her head drooping to her chest, and it was an effort to keep it upright. The terror she'd been feeling just a while ago had dissolved, replaced by emptiness.

She felt nothing. It seemed to her that nothing could go wrong in the world, and if it did, she couldn't care less.

'What on earth did you give me?' she murmured to Raza, slurring her words slightly. They were in a chauffeur-driven car that was taking them to the airport. To her surprise, his aftershave, which usually made her nauseous, now had no impact on her. 'I feel like I could dance and sleep at the same time, and for a thousand years.'

Raza frowned at her. 'You're a lightweight, aren't you? I didn't think such a small dose would have this huge impact on you. You're as high as a kite.' Edging closer, he gripped her upper arm – hard. 'Pull yourself together. I wanted you happy, but not this happy. If you give anyone cause to suspect us, I promise you that your parents will soon be taking their last breaths. Them and your darling Kamil, along with his family. I will have them all killed.'

The familiar terror reared its head, but whatever Raza had given her kept it at bay. 'Do me a favour and kill my old boyfriend, Saqib, too.' She laughed at her own joke.

Without warning, Raza angled her face towards him, and slapped her. 'Pull yourself together. Now!'

If the driver noticed it, he didn't bat an eyelid. Even in her muddled state, Ayesha couldn't help but marvel at the power Raza and his family seemed to wield everywhere.

Her thoughts remained cloudy all the way to Heathrow, to the point that none of her surroundings registered. She failed to feel the cold when Raza had to lower the window for something. Most of all, she didn't even feel the ridges of her scar tissue. It all felt like smooth skin to her.

What had he done to her? Since when had she become so powerless?

By the time they arrived at Heathrow Terminal Three, some of the effects of the drug had started to wear off, but she still remained oblivious to her surroundings and to what was happening to her. As much as she hated it, she had to lean on Raza to get into a wheelchair.

Strapping a belt across her belly, he drew close to her, his breath tickling her ear. 'No funny business, Ayesha, or your parents die. Guns are aimed at their house as we speak, and I'll make sure death doesn't come easily to them. I'll make them suffer for it. Plenty of sexually frustrated people in Multan who would be more than happy to unleash their demons on your parents.' He kissed her on the mouth. 'It doesn't matter if they're a bit, you know, mature. There are plenty of takers for that in Multan, so behave, won't you?'

She still held the hand he'd used to help her into the wheelchair. She curled her fingers around his wrist and dug her fingernails into his bare skin with as much strength as she could muster. He simply laughed, jerking his hand away. 'Once a lightweight, forever a lightweight. I can't wait to have you as my mistress in Lahore. We'll spend many happy years together, and once I've sucked all the juice out of you, I'll hand over your remains to some thirsty brothel.'

'One day, I'll get you back for this,' she whispered, slurring slightly.

'What was that? I'm sorry, I didn't quite catch it.'

With all her strength she pushed herself forward by a few inches so that they were face to face. 'I said, that someday, when you least expect it, I will get back at you for this. For everything. I will kill you, Raza Masood.'

Raza held a hand to his heart in mock horror. 'Consider me duly warned, mademoiselle. I shall breathlessly await that day.'

And with that, he tipped the chauffeur and wheeled her into the terminal.

It was odd, but the same place that had seemed so full of promise just a few months ago was now making her feel as if her life was ending. The sight of the check-in area alone brought tears to her eyes.

She would now travel to Pakistan and remain there forever as his mistress, or whatever it was he had in store for her. Her entire body hurt, her muscles coiled with tension. Last night, it was as if a demon had been unleashed in him. His eyes were crazed, almost terrifying, making her close her own to the entire ordeal. She shuddered as she imagined being put through that kind of torture every day.

The lady at the check-in counter glanced at her as she flipped through her passport, and for a moment, Ayesha almost cried out for help, but then the image of her parents appeared before her eyes, and she hung her head again, watching her hands, the nail polish she had painted on so long ago now chipped. The hands seemed foreign to her. When she tried to lift them up, she couldn't. What had he done to her? The more she tried to concentrate, the harder it became, the words she wanted to say swimming in her head.

Before long, the wheelchair started moving again, Raza leaning forward to whisper in her ear. She tried to jerk her head away, but discovered that she didn't possess the strength.

'Well done for keeping quiet,' he murmured, squeezing her shoulder. 'If you keep this up, then I may not rape you repeatedly like I did last night. I might actually make it pleasurable for you. Believe me, you might even enjoy being my mistress.' Releasing her shoulder, he straightened up. 'And your good-for-nothing parents will also stay alive.' Laughing, he added, 'Maybe I'll throw a few crumbs at them.'

Ayesha closed her eyes. She hoped someone would see. She loved her parents more than anything in life, but what kind of existence would she be leading? And Kamil, who had been nothing but kind to her, who had included her in every part of his life as if she truly belonged with him – could she put his life in danger like this?

She shook her head. No, this was going to be her sacrifice. Her ultimate sacrifice. All her life, people had done things for her. It was now time to return the favour, and if living with Raza Masood meant that her people stayed alive, then so be it.

'Now, when we're being checked, I want you to act perfectly normal,' Raza told her as they approached security. 'I'll tell the officer that you're in significant pain, and hopefully that will be enough to make them feel sorry for you and wave you through.' Touching her shoulder again, he added, 'Any funny stuff and you know what will happen.'

Ayesha opened her mouth to say something, but her tongue didn't seem to cooperate. She sputtered, holding her throat.

Raza smiled as he knelt in front of her. 'Yeah, you see this is one of the effects of the drug I gave you. Couldn't have you yapping away to the airport officials like there's no tomorrow, could I?' He reached out a hand to wipe the dribble from her mouth. 'Ugh! So disgusting, but I'll enjoy seeing you kneel before me.'

'That's – funny – s – since you're – the – one kn – kneeling.' It was a struggle to get the words out, but it was worth seeing Raza's face change.

'Why, you little *gushti*. You've still got a metal rod up your ass, don't you?'

At that moment, she thought she saw something in the distance, something that looked like a gathering of officials in uniform. A few of them seemed to be walking in their direction. She watched them, every cell in her body telling her to scream, to gesticulate, to basically do anything to save herself. She knew that as long as she was on British soil, she'd be treated fairly. This wasn't Pakistan, where money governed everything. But then, her gaze slid to the phone in Raza's hand. The fate of her parents and the fate of Kamil was contained in that small device. One message was all it would take for Raza to destroy her world – forever.

So, she watched helpless as the uniformed officers inched closer. Any moment they would pass them, and her last chance at escape would pass with them. Raza tracked her gaze and looked behind him. His head whipped back at her so fast that he wasn't able to hide the expression on his face – alarm. Raza was afraid.

Holding a finger to his lips, he held up his phone.

A warning.

Ayesha closed her eyes, and nodded. She would endure this, not for him but for her family. And then she would find a way to exact her revenge.

She played by his rules through security check and all through the flight. Raza had booked them business-class seats, and every now and then, he tried pushing food at her, but if she gave him the satisfaction of eating food he'd paid for, then what was the point of resisting him at all? This resistance was all she had left, and she clung to it fiercely.

'Still mourning your precious London? See how I whisked you out of that city? I hope you don't doubt my influence now.'

As a stewardess arrived to collect their dishes, Ayesha's stone-cold meal returning to the trolley, Raza raised an eyebrow at her. 'I paid good money for your ticket. If I'd known you'd behave like a little princess, I'd have thrown you in cargo. Bitch.'

The effects of the drugs were wearing off, so Ayesha could now speak without hindrance. 'Life doesn't begin and end with money, Raza.'

He smirked at that. 'I beg to differ. You forget that I bought your parents with money. Money is what makes the world go round.' Taking hold of her wrist, he massaged it gently before gripping it hard. 'If you keep up this behaviour, I'll make sure that you get to see precious little of both money and food. If you don't behave, I'll keep raping you, and when I'm done, I'll have my servants rape you, and then when they're done, I'll have my dog rape you too.'

Ayesha didn't flinch even though a storm was brewing inside her. A storm that made her want to scream at the top of her lungs.

'Tell me you'll behave and I might go easy on you.'

She kept looking ahead, ignoring the pain in her wrist.

Raza's grip tightened. 'Say it now or you will suffer.'

Ayesha's eyes were watering from the pain, but she still didn't respond. What more could this little man do to her that he hadn't already done before? Luckily, the pilot took that moment to ask them to fasten their seat belts, which distracted Raza. He didn't want to risk being seen by the cabin crew, so when he finally released her wrist, she saw that his fingernails had left crescent-shaped marks where they'd dug into her skin. She held her head high.

She'd wear them proudly as her battle scars.

Seated adjacent to them, a middle-aged woman kept craning to look at them, but when Ayesha caught her eye, she looked away, busying herself with her book. *That was Pakistanis in the nutshell*, she thought. They couldn't wait to catch the drama, but when it came to offering help, they were the first to look away. She wasn't surprised in the least. Besides, where she was going, this woman's pity wouldn't help her. She had to survive on her own.

Despite remaining steadfast in the face of Raza's abuse, she couldn't help but feel her spirits flagging as the plane touched down at Lahore, slowly grinding to a halt, just like her life. She watched the jungle of concrete that had begun to grow around the airport, the luxury flats looking down at the tarmac. Just to avoid thinking of the man seated next to her, she imagined what it would be like to live in a flat that overlooked the airport. She liked planes, but she didn't think she liked them enough to listen to them all day long.

'Don't get your hopes up,' Raza whispered. 'You new house is not going to be a flashy flat, my little mistress. It will be something more suited to your ... ah, humble standards.'

'*Kanjar*,' she whispered under her breath.

'What was that?'

Ayesha examined her nails. 'Nothing. Shall we get our bags?'

'Typical Pakistani bumpkin. You have to wait until the plane comes to a complete stop. Did nobody teach you that?'

'I'm sure you'll teach me plenty when I'm imprisoned.'

Raza narrowed his eyes. 'I don't know if you're being sarcastic, but if you are, I'd watch myself.'

'Duly noted, monsieur.'

She enjoyed watching him grind his teeth.

Someone from the airport protocol was waiting for them at the gate. For a city the size of Lahore, the airport was woefully small, so it wasn't surprising to see the crowds of people packed together in the small arrivals hall. Their protocol guy led them through the throngs of people, most of them watching with distaste, knowing full well that the moment rich people landed in the country, they started flexing their muscles.

If only you knew where I was headed, Ayesha thought as a woman with gold-streaked hair stared her down.

Their passports were slammed in front of the immigration officer, who was then told to hurry. Ayesha caught Raza's smirk and her heart sank lower than ever. She closed her eyes and tried to ignore the noise around her. She thought back to her life in London, to Kamil, with his earnest eyes and respectable manner. She had been such a fool for not knowing love when it was staring her in the face. What she wouldn't give to rewind time now. But that was the thing about time: you could never turn it back, and you only understood the value of it when it had passed.

As their passports were stamped, Raza looked around at the security cameras and scowled. 'We can't be seen exiting together. There will be someone waiting outside to take you to your destination, while I'll stay back.' His eyes gleamed. 'Don't worry, I will be seeing you very soon, and remember' – he pointed at this cell phone – 'one wrong move from you is all it takes.'

Although it had been frigid in London, it was still warm in Lahore, the thick smog making her head spin. As she was ushered into a waiting Toyota Corolla and driven away from the airport, she realised that she was now entirely at the mercy of Raza Masood.

Kamil

Kamil sat at home with his family in Whetstone. Guilt cut through him like glass as he thought back to the last time he'd seen Ayesha at the charity fundraiser. He should have been quicker to follow her out so he could accompany her home.

He watched his mother sitting on the sofa like a statue, dark circles under her eyes from lack of sleep. Shar had to call in sick at work because she hadn't slept a wink taking care of their mother.

The cops had been nothing but kind. Detective Inspector Clarke from Whetstone Police Station had asked all the right questions and promised them that they'd do their best, but the news that had emerged was far from encouraging.

It was devastating, in fact.

Ayesha had returned to Pakistan.

'I can't believe she's just disappeared,' his father muttered. 'Are you sure she hasn't arrived home in Multan by now, Jamila?'

Jamila Akbar was inconsolable. 'Of course she hasn't, Ji. Do you take me for a fool? I called Ishrat, and she was beside herself with worry. I wanted the earth to swallow me whole, I swear. I was responsible for that girl.'

'For the last time, you weren't responsible for her, Ammi,' Shar said, although she looked glum too. 'Whatever happened is unfortunate, but it is not your fault. You'll give yourself a heart attack at this rate.'

His mother beat her fists against her chest. 'I wish I could drop dead this instant.'

'I'm going to Pakistan,' Kamil announced. 'I'm leaving in the morning.'

Stunned silence greeted his words.

'You can't be serious, Kamil,' Shar began. 'You're going to that country all by yourself? We haven't been there in ages.'

His mother's forehead was creased with worry. 'What will you even do there, Kamil? The police will be doing all they can.'

Kamil shook his head. He was surprised it had taken him this long to decide. 'I can't rest until she's found, Ammi. What I had – have – with Ayesha is special. I cannot bear the thought of her imprisoned somewhere while I go about life like nothing has happened.'

'But what will you even do?'

'I'm going to bring that bastard to justice. She was on the same plane as him. That's what the police said. I bet you everything that he abducted Ayesha here in London, and that he's behind her disappearance.'

Shar threw up her hands. 'Then go. Do what you must.'

'But—' Jamila began, but Akbar Khan held up a hand to silence her.

'Jamila…' he said, louder this time, his gaze finding Kamil. 'Let him go.'

The smog was what hit him first when he stepped out of Multan airport – a thick wall of noxious grey fumes that made his head spin. It had been a long flight, with a layover in Lahore. From what he'd heard, the smog in Lahore was much worse than Multan's at this time of the year, so he was happy to have been spared that. At least he wasn't back in London, making that insufferable daily commute to work. His boss, Amelia, had pressed her lips together in a grimace when he'd asked her for six weeks of leave, but in the end, they agreed to make it unpaid. He couldn't say that he missed the office, but surprisingly, he did miss Angela's judgemental quips.

'Ayesha, I am in your country,' he whispered as he looked at the steel-and-glass airport building, an impressive upgrade from the bus stand of an airport Multan used to have when he'd visited as a child.

The car he had booked beforehand was waiting for him, a white Honda Civic that was thankfully air-conditioned. And his Saraiki was good enough that the driver wasn't able to tell that he was from London and not Lahore.

He was supposed to be staying with Ayesha's parents, but before that, there was something he had to see.

'Do you know where the Masood family home is?'

In the rear-view mirror, he noticed the driver arch an eyebrow. 'Who doesn't know that, Sahab,' he said. 'Everyone in the city knows where Masood Sahab lives.'

'Can you take me there?'

His fingers drummed the steering wheel as he put the car into motion. 'I could, but unless you know them personally, they're not going to let you in.'

Kamil needed to see Raza's house. He needed to be close to that son of a bitch. He wanted rage to overwhelm him. How dare he abduct her like that?

As they drove through Multan Cantt, with its wide boulevards and civilised traffic, Kamil imagined Ayesha in the city, going to work, having coffee or meeting friends. He attempted to see Multan through her eyes, but gave up. Ayesha was gone, and unless something was done to find her, she might never return. He decided to test the waters with the driver.

'Any word on what happened to the Multani girl who was abducted from London and then brought to Lahore?'

The driver grunted. 'Say what? Who is that?'

When Kamil mentioned the name of Ayesha's father, the driver grunted again. 'Who cares? There are several girls picked up in Pakistan every day. If the police were to chase after every little slut who decides to elope with her lover, that's all they'd be doing. They've got much bigger things to worry about, like terrorism and politics.'

Kamil was about to give him a piece of his mind, when the car slowed outside a monstrosity of white stone with marbled pillars and a sprawling lawn. The Masood mansion.

'Here it is, Sahab,' the driver announced. 'One of Multan's most desirable addresses.' Somewhere inside Raza Masood would be sleeping soundly, content in the knowledge that he had silenced Ayesha forever.

If Kamil knew Ayesha even a little bit, she was not the kind to be silenced. Wherever she was, he was sure she'd be fighting back.

'Give him hell, Ayesha,' he whispered.

At Ayesha's place, the mood was sombre enough to make him weep. His mother had said that Ishrat Safdar was full of life and generally very chatty, but it was obvious that the disappearance of her daughter had taken everything out of her.

'You are one of the few people who have come here to support us, Kamil,' she said, embracing him. 'You needn't have come, but you still did.'

Kamil took her hands in his own. 'I wanted to.' And he meant it.

'Please tell Jamila that I really appreciate all she did for Ayesha in London. My daughter sounded like a new person whenever I spoke to her. So happy, so full of hope.' Her face creased with emotion. 'Just when she had finally found her tribe, she's gone, and we don't even know where.'

Kamil lowered his head, looking at his shoes. 'We are very sorry we didn't take better care of her.'

'Don't be silly,' Ishrat said, hugging him again. 'Nobody could have stood between her and Raza Masood. We sent her all the way to London, and he still got her.'

Safdar Khan was seated on the sofa in the living room, gazing at nothing in particular. 'The police won't tell us anything. It's as if they've given up on our girl. The more time elapses, the less bothered they become.' When he looked at them, his eyes were ringed with red, as if he hadn't slept for days. 'The CCTV footage shows that they arrived in Lahore together, and just because they didn't leave together, the police refuse to arrest him.'

'They brought him in for questioning, Kamil. That's all. They didn't even investigate. Raza came with a legion of his lawyers, and they somehow convinced the police that he wasn't involved. I'm sure his father bought off the police. It's as if our daughter doesn't even matter, like she isn't even human.' Ishrat sobbed, collapsing on the sofa next to her husband. 'Even Neelam hasn't managed to do anything. She keeps avoiding my calls.'

Kamil didn't have the heart to tell Ishrat that her sister was the reason Ayesha had left that party early. If Neelam hadn't tormented her so much, maybe he would have been with Ayesha that night. Maybe ... that was all he was left with now: maybe.

'She's our only child,' Safdar Khan spoke up. 'Without Ayesha, nothing matters. This house' – he waved a hand in the air – 'means nothing without our daughter. We don't even know if she's alive.'

'They've even managed to have DSP Amna Habib transferred,' Ishrat said, adjusting the dupatta on her head. 'She was the one person who was sympathetic to our plight, but they've taken her off the case.'

Kamil's ears perked up. Finally, here was something he could use. 'Do you have her number, this policewoman?'

Safdar Khan shrugged. 'Yes, but what good will she be able to do? It's not in her jurisdiction anymore. I've tried everything, Kamil. What else do you think I've been doing all this time? I've used all my contacts, but it's like I keep hitting a wall.'

They had nothing more to contribute, so Kamil sat with them and nodded through their stories about Ayesha, his mind slowly accommodating all this new information about her. He felt closer than ever to her here, even though he couldn't see her. Ayesha's parents kept thanking him for coming, but how could he tell them that he had no choice? That his love for Ayesha was so intense, he would have perished in London if he hadn't come. How was he to tell them that Ayesha was all he could think of?

Once Ishrat had shown him to Ayesha's room, and he had reassured his parents back home in London that he'd reached Multan safely, he opened his laptop and created a new Facebook page. He may not know where Ayesha was yet, but that didn't mean he was completely powerless. Social media was a powerful tool, and he had been using it at work for years. Today, he was going to use the very same social media for Ayesha, and he'd be damned if the entire country wasn't talking about her within days.

Ayesha

The call for prayer woke her from a dreamless sleep, the afternoon light filtering from between a gap in the curtains. She shivered under the covers. Raza insisted that she remain naked even after sex.

It was all a ploy to humiliate her.

If it wasn't enough for him to rape her, he also brought some of his close friends to poke fun at her.

Ayesha still remembered one of them wrinkling his nose when he saw her. 'Look at the state of her, Raza. She's all damaged. How do you bang that?'

Raza had sniggered, the cigarette dangling in his mouth. 'Hands off my mistress, pal. Damaged or not, she's great in bed. Beneath all that damage lies a woman who would put Cleopatra to shame.'

She closed her eyes, willing herself to return to the land of dreams, a place where she could be with her loved ones ... with Kamil. It hurt when she thought back to her life in London, how perfect everything was, and how close she had come to finding love again. She'd always admired Kamil's lustrous brown hair, and had yearned to run her fingers through it.

Now, she never would.

Twice in her life, she had come close to real happiness, and both times, Raza Masood had taken it all away from her. Just when it seemed that everything was in her reach, Raza plucked it out of her hands.

It was impossible to tell how many days had passed since she'd arrived in Lahore. Several times a day, she wondered if Kamil had found someone else now, and if he was happy. In a strange way, she almost wished he had, because he deserved it.

Everyone did, except for her, apparently.

Taking deep breaths, she swallowed the lump down her throat, refusing to allow the tears to slide out of her eyes. They did, anyway.

It was imperative to keep a cool mind, she told herself, or she would never see the last of Raza Masood. If she'd learned one thing in all her years in Multan, it was patience.

Without patience, she was lost.

At least today wasn't a moving day. Every couple of weeks, Raza took her to a new location – generally one of his friends' places. Once there, he would stay with her for a couple of days, and after having his fill of her, he'd take off, leaving her locked in the room with a couple of his trusted servants to take care of her basic needs. So far, she had failed to convince those servants to let her go, no matter how hard she tried. Hammad, the sixty-something man who was primarily responsible for her, was like a hardened criminal. No kindness flickered in his eyes, and he always brought someone else with him when he entered her room, so that she couldn't try anything. She couldn't have done it if she tried. The man was built like an ox.

'He's one of our goons that we use to pressure people to sell their agricultural lands to us,' Raza had told her, as if snatching other people's lands against their will was something to be proud of.

At the moment, she was staying in a large bungalow that she assumed was somewhere outside Lahore because she never heard any of the sounds she had come to associate with the city. It was impossible to tell exactly where she was because she was kept blindfolded throughout the journey, but since the journeys never took very long, it was obvious that she was still near the city.

Opening her eyes, she watched Raza's sleeping form, his massive chest rising and falling rhythmically. The first night in Lahore she had tried holding a pillow to his face, but the bastard was fast. In one swift moment, he had wrenched the pillow out of her grasp, and punched her in the face.

'Don't try that again or you will fare much worse next time. You're my mistress now. Act like one.'

Now, as he slept beside her, she bunched her hands into fists to prevent herself from launching herself at him. No, there had to be another way. Her eye caught his phone charging on the side table next to him, and before she could change her mind, she quietly reached over Raza for it.

Her fingers had barely brushed the smooth screen of the cell phone before Raza's hand shot up and gripped her wrist.

His eyes crinkled when he smiled. 'Not so fast. Did you honestly think I would make it so easy for you?' His morning breath smelled rank.

'I just wanted to check the time,' she lied, not letting any of the rage she felt filter into her voice. 'And I wanted to know how long you've kept me imprisoned.'

Raza's chest rumbled with laughter. 'What do you care? You're living in all this luxury even though your real place is in the slums. You should be happy I've had a change of heart and I'm treating you like a queen and not like the dirty little *rakhail* you are.' Whipping the quilt off his body, he breathed in deeply. 'You're just torturing yourself thinking that you can escape. I've bought the local police in Multan, and the police here don't give a shit about you. Nobody does. You're old news, and since nobody has followed up on you, you've been forgotten. Even your parents have moved on.'

'Liar,' she whispered. 'My parents could never forget me.'

Raza shrugged. 'I don't know what to tell you. You're an intelligent woman, and you've worked in the charity sector for long enough. You tell me how many women get any justice in this country.' He made an O with his thumb and forefinger. 'Zilch.'

There must have been some hostility in her face, because the expression on Raza's face changed. 'Do you know what I'll do with you once I'm tired of your body?' Reaching over to slap her on the thigh, he grinned: 'I will kill you.'

His eyes told her that he wasn't joking. Nothing Raza Masood did these days was a joke. It pained her to accept it, but today had started off as one of her worst. She looked at the window, which had been bolted shut, a tight grille in place as an added security measure. Raza noticed her gaze and suddenly gripped her upper arms, pinning her to the bed. It left her blind with fear, unable to breathe. 'Raza, please,' she panted. 'I … I think I'm having a panic attack. Let me step outside for a moment, I beg you.'

In answer, Raza shifted his entire weight on her, pushing her legs open with a knee. 'Panic attacks are a luxury only the rich can afford, not damaged old relics like you, Ayesha. Don't be insufferable, and let me do this.'

It felt like a boulder had settled on her chest, and to make matters worse, Raza held his forearm against her throat, constricting her breathing further. Ayesha could hear the breath rattling out of her, her eyes almost popping out of their sockets from the effort of staying alive. She was sure this was the end. Reciting the *Kalima,* she waited for death to arrive.

But it didn't.

Raza's thrusts gained momentum, and yet she kept breathing like she always did. Her body simply refused to give up. Little by little, her breathing eased, and just as Raza shuddered on top of her, calling her a host of disgusting names, her breathing returned to normal.

She would be spending the next hour in the bathroom, scrubbing his essence away, knowing it was all in vain. Raza Masood had broken down all her defences, infiltrating deep into her soul. But he hadn't taken everything from her.

Not yet.

There had been plenty of opportunities, but she hadn't killed herself. Her will to live was something Raza Masood hadn't managed to snatch from her.

Rising from the bed, she wrapped the bedsheet around her body and padded towards the bathroom. What Raza said next caused her to stop dead.

'What?' she asked, turning back to face him.

Lying naked in bed with one arm thrown behind his back, Raza looked the picture of tranquillity. 'I said, it's moving day today.'

'But I just arrived here,' she said, unable to keep the whine from her voice.

A shadow passed over his face. 'You better get ready in ten minutes, Ayesha. I won't repeat myself. Today is moving day.'

By the time she had taken a quick shower and put her meagre possessions in a small bag, the bedroom door opened to reveal a stone-faced Hammad waiting to escort her downstairs. Ignoring her protests, he held on to her, his fingers digging into the flesh of her forearm as he steered her outside. Since the usual residents of the house were on holiday abroad – or at least that's the story she'd been told – most of the corridors lay shrouded in darkness. Their footsteps echoed in the silent building, and it was a relief when they stepped outside into the bright sunshine. There was a slight nip in the air, indicating the arrival of winter in Lahore. With a pang, she realised that it must have been more than a month since she had been picked up from the airport, because at the time, it wasn't chilly. Her parents probably thought she was dead by now. Did Kamil think that too?

This was the only time Ayesha was allowed to breathe freely in the fresh air, and she gulped in as much of the air as possible before the blindfold went on. As always, Raza drove ahead, with Hammad following in a large pickup, Ayesha bound to her seat in the back.

In the early days, she used to pray that someone would intercept them, rescuing her in the process. Her belief was so great that when she finally reached her destination, it would take her hours to accept the fact that she hadn't been freed. For some reason, she was sure it would be her father there with the police to save her, but no help came – from her father or anyone else. She was on her own, shackled to a sadist who took pleasure in hurting her both physically and mentally.

Hammad refused to say a word, so Ayesha spent the entire journey trying to guess where they were headed. She tried to count the number of the turns the van took, but soon lost track, her head spinning. Giving up, she closed her eyes behind the blindfold, and pounded her head against the headrest.

She must have nodded off, because the next moment, someone slapped her cheek, not hard, but enough to wake her.

'Wake up, sunshine,' Raza said. 'Your welcome party awaits.'

She groaned, swallowing the spit that had gathered in her mouth. Raza's welcome parties were hateful. He would invite some of his most savage friends with their prostitutes. Their biting insults about her appearance drove her silently mad.

It was still unclear why she'd been moved so soon. Most likely, the original occupants of the house were due to arrive, because like Raza had said, everyone had forgotten about Ayesha. It wasn't like anyone was going to come looking for her.

Even Kamil, for all his declarations of friendship and love, had abandoned her.

As soon as they stepped inside, the blindfold was removed, and Ayesha found herself in what appeared to be a small house. Two rooms and a kitchen opened into the living room in which they all stood.

She recognised the friend at once. It was Raheel, a particularly unpleasant man who took great joy in torturing people, but only after he had ridiculed them to his heart's content. He hadn't been present when Raza had poured acid on her, or he would have participated. He was that sort of person.

'Ayesha Safdar,' he said, giving her a mock bow. 'We meet again. You look as beautiful as ever despite your very prominent – ah – injuries.'

Ayesha closed her eyes, waiting for more of his insults.

'Thanks for opening up your spare house for us,' Raza murmured. 'Can't tell you how much it means at this time, you know...'

Raheel gave him a tight smile. 'No worries, but how long do you intend to saddle yourself with this thing? Wouldn't it be better to just get rid of her?'

Raza glanced at her. 'Not here. Come with me.'

With that, he steered Raheel away so that Ayesha couldn't eavesdrop. She had no interest in listening to their stupid banter anyway. If he wanted to get rid of her, he could try. She wouldn't make it easy for him. She looked around her new prison, wondering how long it would be until she was plucked away from this place and taken somewhere new and much more awful.

As Raza made himself comfortable on the sofa with Raheel, the person sitting opposite them caught Ayesha's attention. She'd met several women over the past few weeks, none of them familiar or friendly, but there was something about this one that told her otherwise. For starters, the girl was staring back at her, her mouth open.

'Raza, allow me to introduce you to my current flame,' Raheel said, pointing towards the woman. 'Her name is Chandni, and let me tell you something. The girl is a revelation in bed.'

It all came back to Ayesha, then. Chandni was the girl who had tried to stop Raza from throwing acid on her face. Chandni had tried to save her even though she was in no position to do so.

She looked at Raza, afraid that he had recognised her too, but Raza hadn't given her a second glance. His eyebrows were knotted together in a frown as he typed something on his phone, his friend murmuring in his ear.

Chandni, Ayesha thought. *Chandni.*

Kamil

'Have you found her yet?' his mother asked him over the phone for the umpteenth time as he sat in one of the Gloria Jean's coffee shops that were dotted around Multan. The weather was getting colder, but for Kamil, who was used to winters in London, it was almost balmy. He was waiting for DSP Amna Habib, who had travelled to Multan specially to see him. The moment he had mentioned Ayesha and his online campaign to her, she'd told him that she would meet him in Multan.

'Not yet,' he replied to his mother. 'But hopefully I'm getting close.'

'You two made the most beautiful pair,' his mother said, and after a pause added, 'Sharmeela says *Assalam Alaikum* to you as well.'

'I just said to tell him hello, Ammi. I didn't say *Assalam Alaikum*, for God's sake,' he heard Shar mutter in the background. 'You make everything so formal.'

'Being a proper Muslim won't kill you, Sharmeela. *Tauba!*'

Kamil wasn't surprised in the least to hear his mother and sister bickering. It was their favourite pastime. 'I hope you are taking care of yourself, and eating right,' he said.

His mother sighed. '*Haye*! How could you ask me that? I am worried sick about poor Ayesha, and for my son. Please do take care, *beta*. As much as I love Pakistan, I am not sure it's entirely safe.' It was obvious that his mother was trying not to sob when she added, 'You are my only son.'

'Oh God, the theatrics,' Shar said in the background.

'Enough with the drama, Ammi,' he echoed Shar, then noticed a tall woman walking towards him. He hastily said goodbye and put the phone in his pocket.

'DSP Amna Habib,' the woman said, extending a hand in his direction. She was wearing a light-blue jumper with skinny jeans and looked nothing like a policewoman. As if reading his thoughts, she added, 'Sorry, I didn't see the need to wear my uniform where I have no jurisdiction. Raza Masood's family made sure I have no power here.' Her eyes gleamed, the breeze stirring her long black hair. 'Kamil Abkar, I take it?'

He nodded, unsure of how to begin the conversation. 'Yes, I'm the one behind the digital campaign.'

DSP Amna whistled. 'That's all everyone is talking about ... a privileged, educated woman abducted in broad daylight from Lahore airport, with the police none the wiser. You've created quite a stir, Kamil. Talk about using social media for the right reasons. Even a tiny city like Sheikhupura, where I am stationed, is buzzing with the news. The police in Lahore are finally under pressure for once.'

Kamil shrugged, but inside he was proud. He had made that happen. The police in Pakistan were under pressure because of him. And it wasn't by chance, rather it was a carefully crafted social-media campaign aimed to hit the youth of Pakistan, who he knew would make the most amount of noise. Using whatever photos of Ayesha he could find, he had created a 'Free Ayesha Safdar' account on all social-media platforms and used his digital-marketing expertise to pour money into the posts. Initially it was his own money, but within days, the news spread, the younger people doing his job for him by sharing the posts widely and commenting on them. And then the donations started to come in. Last time he'd checked, the Instagram account alone had over five hundred thousand followers, and #FreeAyesha had been trending on Twitter for days. The longer Ayesha remained missing, the more shameful it was for Punjab Police. The news had taken Pakistan by such a storm that even the highest-ranking officials had to make statements assuring the public that the culprits would be found soon.

So far, nothing had happened, but at least DSP Amna Habib was here. That was a start. 'Do you think there will be a breakthrough in the case?' he asked her. 'What can you tell me?'

DSP Amna waited until the waiter had placed their coffees on the table. She took a sip, licked the froth from her lips and put the mug down. 'I came here today because I've been wracked with guilt ever since Ayesha disappeared. I knew all along that it was Raza Masood who threw acid on her, but there was no proof, no witnesses. Ayesha didn't help matters by keeping quiet about it. Even after she left the country, I tried my best to pin down Raza, but all I have to show for my efforts is my transfer to Sheikhupura.' She grimaced as she sipped on the coffee again. 'The Masood family is very powerful, but it's hard to say what will happen now.'

Kamil had been holding the mug just to be polite. His stomach was churning with anxiety. 'What do you mean?'

'You've gone and kicked the hornet's nest, Kamil. Raza Masood has disappeared somewhere in Lahore. Nobody knows where.'

'But how do you know?'

She gave him a look. 'I'm in the police force. Give me *some* credit. I've been tracking his movements for a while, but it appears that he changes vehicles when he is in Lahore, making it hard to track his movements. However, now he's just vanished, thanks to this social-media campaign.'

Kamil was beginning to feel queasy. 'Is that a good thing or a bad thing?'

'Kamil, I want you to tell me the moment you get any news on Ayesha. Any tip, and you tell me immediately. That's what I came here for, in addition to wanting to put a face to the name. It's best if information goes through me first. I don't trust our senior officers. I may not have any jurisdiction here, but I do have a few friends in the force.'

Kamil was holding his breath. 'You didn't answer my question.'

DSP Amna sighed, abandoning all pretence of drinking coffee and pushing her mug away. Rubbing her hands together, she said,

'Social media is a double-edged sword. What you've done is corner the person who has abducted Ayesha. Either he will free her, or he will...'

'Or what?' He wasn't sure he wanted to hear the answer.

DSP Amna stared in his eyes. 'I don't think you need me to spell it out for you.'

Ayesha

It was very unlike Raza Masood to spend so many days with her, and even more unlike him to not want sex. Something was eating away at him, but it was obvious that he wasn't going to share it with her. She had noticed the first day they had arrived here that he could hardly tear his eyes away from his phone, and when Raheel whispered to him, he had scowled. Raza Masood did not admit to weakness. A part of her hoped that this might mean people were looking for her, but the more realistic part of her told her not to get her hopes up.

The most probable reason was that Raza Masood was getting tired of hiding her, and once he tired of her completely, it wasn't difficult to guess what would come next.

Death.

She'd be tossed aside like a rag doll, maybe buried in a deep grave where nobody would ever find her.

A strange sense of calm descended on her mind at the thought of death. Whistling to herself, she stared at the black, mouldy spots on the ceiling. So far, she'd counted seventy of them. If she was going to die, it was better it happened sooner rather than later. There was a limit to how much trauma a person could tolerate. After a point, the human body simply gave up.

Last night, she had dreamed that she was in Euston again, hand in hand with Kamil, the fresh London breeze on her face. In front of the church opposite Euston Station, Kamil had taken her face in his hands and leaned forward. Their lips had barely touched when his face morphed into Raza's and awoke her.

It had been a week since she'd seen him. Ayesha knew, because she had been counting the days on her fingers. She had seen the sun set seven times from the small window in the basement where she was being held with just a cot and chair for company. Even Hammad didn't come in to deliver the food anymore, using a cat flap instead to throw her whatever meagre fare he'd cooked. For the first few days, she had tried to sample the undercooked potato curry and tough chapatti, but lately, she had given up. What was the point? She didn't know why things had suddenly changed, and she wouldn't have known Raza was still here if it wasn't for him shouting on the phone upstairs all day. All while she remained imprisoned in the basement.

When I tire of you, I will kill you. Despite herself, the words still sent a shiver through her. Seeing Chandni had kindled a long-lost hope in her, but a week later, even that hope had been extinguished. Besides, why would she help her? It wasn't like Ayesha had ever lifted a finger for her. She hadn't even thought of her until now.

She slumped in the chair, watching the lonely bulb dangling from the ceiling, casting shadows on the walls of her small room. If it wasn't for the window, she would have lost all sense of time. She tried not to think of her room in London, where the window afforded her a breathtaking view of the city. Not like here where all she could see was a sliver of sky.

The bulb seemed to be having a hypnotic effect on her, as her eyes drooped, the world of dreams beckoning, but before she could quite surrender herself to sleep, there was a soft knock on the door.

Had she started dreaming already? She'd fallen asleep quickly.

The knocking came again, more urgent, and then she heard it – a whisper: 'Ayesha Bibi.'

She recognised that voice. She had heard it on the day Raza Masood had disfigured her forever. Chandni was on the other side of the door.

'Ayesha Bibi!' the voice whispered again. 'Are you in there?'

She sprang from the chair and rushed to the door, pressing her ear against it.

'Chandni?'

There was a pause, before Chandni replied, 'Yes, it's me.' Without missing a beat, she continued, 'They're both drunk upstairs, and the servant is busy cooking food. However, he's sharp, so I might only have a few moments before he figures out I'm not in the living room.'

It took Ayesha a moment to realise that she was actually having a conversation with someone who didn't wish her harm. It had been weeks. The thought brought a lump to her throat, but she swallowed it. Now was not the time to fall apart. 'Why are you here? How do I know this isn't a trick?'

Chandni laughed, a deep mournful sound. 'Ah Bibi, What would I have to gain from this? I'm putting myself in danger, talking to you.'

Ayesha lowered herself until she was level with the cat flap. Lifting it up, she caught Chandni's brown eyes looking back at her. 'You can't rescue me, Chandni. They'll never let you.'

'I'm not here to rescue you. I am here to warn you,' Chandni whispered. 'Things are not looking good. The police are looking for you. You're becoming more and more famous.'

Ayesha stared at her. The girl had obviously taken leave of her senses. Chandni had probably been treated so badly that she'd lost her mind. She shook her head at the poor girl, looking at the frown lines on her forehead, the bite marks on her neck and cleavage. 'I'm sorry,' she whispered. 'I don't know what they did to you, but you're not making any sense. Why would the police be looking for me? Raza Masood has bought them off.'

Chandni looked around, checking there was nobody to hear them. 'Ayesha Bibi, I meant that you are famous on the internet. You're what everyone is talking about. I don't know much about phones, but I have heard from Raheel Sahab that you have gone viral.' She jerked her head in the direction of the living room. 'You've been brought here because Raza Sahab was getting nervous.'

Ayesha couldn't quite believe what she was hearing. Famous? How on earth could she go viral, and more importantly, who would go to all that effort for her. 'Chandni, you are not making any sense at all.' Ayesha tried to control her rapid heartbeat. 'You must be mistaken.'

'A smaller place like this will mean that you are easier to contain, much harder to find and…'

She didn't need to say more. 'Much easier to kill,' Ayesha finished for her.

Chandni closed her eyes for a second before opening them. 'This world is very unfair on us women. Rasheeda Baji sold me to Raheel Sahab months ago. He beats me and rapes me, sometimes both at the same time. He keeps me imprisoned in his house, deprived of everything … even a phone. Whenever he does let me speak to my relatives, he hovers over me, worried that I'll give him away. I am his property to do with as he pleases.' Her eyes were glassy, her voice devoid of emotion. The girl was dead inside. 'Sometimes when he thinks I'm not listening, he talks, and that's how I found out about you. I have been hoping for a long time that he'd bring me here. I wanted to see you with my own eyes.'

'Chandni, I—'

'Bibi, you need to get out of here. This man will kill you. I can already see it in his eyes. He is like a cornered animal. He will never let you go willingly. You get out of this place and find refuge somewhere.'

Ayesha would have laughed if it didn't mean alerting the men. 'I don't even know where I am. He keeps me locked in this room. I haven't held a phone in my hands for weeks.' She swallowed the sob that rose out of her. 'I haven't felt the sun on my face for over a week.'

'You may not be able to get hold of a phone, but I might. Who would you have me call?'

'Why would you help me?' she asked again, her eyes narrowed.

Chandni met her gaze, and this time, her eyes were clear and focused. 'Because I wasn't able to help you the last time, and because I want to see Raheel and his friend rot in jail. If helping you means I can help myself in the process, I would like nothing more. Maybe you will be able to take care of me once I do this.'

Ayesha didn't even miss a beat. 'I will protect you, Chandni.'

Chandni's eyes grew wide as the music in the living room dimmed. 'I need to go. Someone might walk in on us. Tell me, Ayesha Bibi. Tell me now who I should call. I can't promise that Raheel will let me anywhere near a phone, or whether the person will understand what I'm trying to tell them, but I will try my best.'

Ayesha did the only thing she could think of. She gave her the number she had memorised long ago. 'This is DSP Amna Habib's number. Make sure you know it by heart.'

Kamil

Despite the uproar on social media, nothing much had happened. The police had come up empty-handed. They'd tried to bring Raza Masood in for questioning again, but there was no sign of him. He seemed to have vanished into thin air. But that made him more suspicious – at least he hoped so. Kamil had urged the police to investigate Raza's friends, but either they didn't know anything or fear of the Masood empire prevented them from doing anything. They seemed to have left everything to the police in Lahore, who seemed to have bigger fish to fry with the political turmoil in the country.

Somewhere along the way, Ayesha was being forgotten. Kamil knew that without new information, public interest in the case would peter out and then eventually die entirely.

And Ayesha's whereabouts were still unknown.

'Do we even know if our daughter is alive?' Ishrat said. 'All this noise on social media, and yet there isn't any sign of her.' Her eyes were round with terror as she added, 'Could he have killed her already? My poor daughter. *Haye!*'

Kamil didn't know what to say. He was beginning to question the idea behind the social-media campaign himself. Had he unknowingly put Ayesha in greater danger by exposing Raza like this? He couldn't meet Ishrat's eye whenever she asked him about progress in the case.

The truth was that there was none. He checked his phone every five minutes, hoping for a sighting or an update – anything at all to reassure him that Ayesha was alive, but so far, nothing. Even the Masood family was quiet. The word on the street was that both Masood and Rabbiya had flown off to New York to avoid the press attention, leaving Raza behind.

In his desperation, Kamil had taken up smoking again, something he had avoided since his college days as it reminded him of Arooj. But sitting in Ayesha's old bedroom, among her things, he felt like she was slipping away from him. Each day that went by with no news was like a knife to his chest.

Messages arrived every day from his friends in the therapy group, from his colleagues at work, but Kamil had nothing to say to them. He had nothing to say to himself.

It was all his fault. He had stirred the pot, and now, there was the added fear of Ayesha being in mortal danger.

'She was always in mortal danger, Kamil,' Shar said over the phone. 'You ought to be commended for trying to get her back, not reproached.'

'Nobody is reproaching me, Shar.'

'I know you, Kamil. You're reproaching yourself, and you shouldn't.'

Since that evening at Gloria Jean's, he hadn't heard from DSP Amna either. Her phone went straight to voicemail, but since she was a busy police officer, he wasn't surprised.

His earlier optimism about the power of social media was fading, and it was DSP Amna's words that came back to haunt him at night: *I don't think you need me to spell it out for you.*

He'd been in Multan for three weeks now and was wondering whether he was still welcome in the Safdar house. It was lunchtime, and Ishrat's meal of white rice and daal rolled around in his stomach, making him queasy. For the thousandth time, he refreshed all the social-media apps, but the only comments he saw were from concerned people or trolls. There had been a few people who had claimed that they'd seen Raza Masood in Lahore, but when pressed, they couldn't say where.

That didn't help him. Everyone knew Raza Masood was somewhere in Lahore. The big question was where exactly?

Just as he was ready to smash his phone against the wall in frustration, it started buzzing. DSP Amna's name lit up the screen, and on the second ring, he picked up.

She seemed breathless when she said, 'Come to Lahore as fast as you can. Bring Ayesha's parents too. I'm already on my way and I am liaising with the police there.'

The room spun around him, and he had to grab the wall to stop himself from falling down. 'She'd dead, isn't she?' he croaked. 'Ayesha's gone?'

DSP Amna inhaled, the sound of cars honking in the background. 'If she was dead, I wouldn't be rushing to Lahore at the speed of light. Thanks to your social-media campaign, it seems that Raza hasn't been able to move Ayesha, and we have finally received a tip-off.' There was a pause before she added, 'Don't get your hopes up yet, but this is a major breakthrough. Depending on how this goes, we might actually be seeing Ayesha soon. Come to Lahore.'

For a moment, Kamil stood rooted to the spot, the phone in his hand, his mind unable to process what he had just heard. And then it finally hit him – Ayesha might be alive – and with that, he rushed downstairs.

Ayesha

'A woman must be strong, but above all, she must also be patient. If she isn't, life will teach her the hard way.'

Lately, not only did her grandmother's words come back to her, but Ayesha also saw her in her dreams. It was as if her grandmother was getting ready to come and get her. The words chimed in her head as she lay in the cot for the third consecutive day since speaking to Chandni. Like everything else in her life, Chandni's assurances had come to naught. No rescue had arrived for her, and none would. She would have attributed that weird meeting to a dream if it hadn't been for the razor blade tucked in her bra. Before leaving, Chandni had passed it to her from the cat flap.

'In case I am unable to help you, here's something. You shouldn't be defenceless, Bibi.'

Ayesha wasn't sure what the razor blade was for, because it only served to put ideas of suicide in her head. How easy it would be to take a clean swipe across her neck and allow her suffering to end forever. It wouldn't even take a moment. She'd seen goats sacrificed for Eid, their throats sliced with sharp knives, and knew that humans were no different. All she needed to do was close her eyes and be brave.

Unrolling the piece of butter paper to reveal the blade, she held it up to the light, wondering how something so slight could cause so much damage. The blood would be impossible to clean, but if she did this now, who was to say that Raza wouldn't just dump her here and go back to Multan.

Free forever.

The faces of her friends from the support group came into her mind, followed by Kamil and his lop-sided grin. If she did this now, she'd never see him again.

She'd never see her parents again.

She'd never see London again.

Rolling the blade in the piece of paper, she tucked it back in her bra.

She had suffered an acid attack, and lived. It would take a lot more than this to finish her. Raza Masood won't get the satisfaction of seeing her end her life.

Somewhere in the distance, a rooster crowed, making her wonder how quickly morning had arrived, but before she could think any further, the door to her room was thrown open.

In an instant, she sat up, her heart pounding. Not even allowing her a chance to reach for her dupatta, Raza Masood took a fistful of her hair and pulled her up.

She screamed, clawing at his forearm, but his grip was strong.

'You come with me right now. We're leaving.'

He didn't let go of her hair until they were in the living room upstairs. Apart from a layer of grime on all the surfaces, the place was just as she had last seen it. Standing in the middle of the room was Raheel, his chest rising and falling quickly, a gun in his hand.

The ground beneath her spun. Were they going to kill her right here?

'Raza, what's going on? Why does he have a gun?'

Finally letting go of her hair, he shifted his grip to her upper arm. 'You ruin whatever you touch, Ayesha. Like your face, your soul is damaged. Disfigured.'

Her eyes were still on the gun. 'I don't understand what you mean.'

Raheel bared his teeth at her. 'I put a bullet between her eyes. She thought she was being clever, pretending the policewoman was her mother, trying to speak in code, but I wasn't born yesterday, you know.'

Ayesha stared at him. 'You're lying. You wouldn't.' Her heart was racing a mile a minute. It couldn't be. If Chandni was dead, it would be...

'Your fault,' Raheel finished her thought, scratching his beard. 'You cost me my mistress, Ayesha. She was good in bed, and very obedient, until she met you. Who is going to warm my bed at night now? You?'

'You animal,' Ayesha whispered. 'You killed an innocent girl.' She tried to pull her arm free, but Raza's grip was too strong. 'I'm going to be sick.'

Raza looked at her, hatred etched on his face. 'Even after all this, you still have a metal rod stuck up your ass? Scheming behind my back? Maybe what you've suffered isn't enough.' All of a sudden he smiled and gave her a wink. 'And I thought you were finally falling for me.'

Ayesha curled her lips with disgust. The man was delusional. 'I could never love you,' she said, enunciating each word properly. 'Nobody could love a person like you, Raza.'

'It's all that bastard Kamil's fault,' Raheel shouted, gesticulating wildly with the gun in hand. 'He started that viral campaign, and now everyone is looking for her. You better get her out of here if you know what's good for you, Raza. I caught the little bitch, but who knows how much she had blabbed. The police could be on their way.'

'Kamil? Is he here, in Pakistan?' Once again, she tried to wrench her arm from Raza's grasp. 'This is your chance, Raza. Let me go. Put things right, for once in your life. Please.'

'This has gone on for too long,' Raza murmured, his speech slurred. Was he drunk? 'It's out of my hands now. There's nothing more I can do. You need to die, Ayesha.'

He was completely plastered. He couldn't even focus properly. 'Raza, you wouldn't dare.'

'Not here!' Raheel shouted. 'Kill her somewhere nobody will see you. Get out of here now. The police could be here at any moment.'

'Hammad, get our things,' Raza began, but as the servant had run upstairs, Raheel started speaking again.

'There's no time, Raza. Don't you understand? I've already killed one person today. I can't be seen with you guys.' Holding out the gun, he added, 'Here, take this. And use it on her. She should die from the same gun I killed the other bitch with. Now get out of here. I'll do the same. I'll take Hammad with me, but right now, you need to leave.' He pushed Raza. 'Go!'

Ayesha was almost catatonic with fright, and it took her several moments after the car had screeched out of the gate to realise that she wasn't gagged or shackled. In fact, she was sitting right next to Raza in the front seat with no sign of Hammad anywhere.

They were alone.

She glanced at him as he weaved his way through traffic, cursing everyone until finally hitting the ring road that encircled the outskirts of Lahore.

'Slow down,' she told him, watching the speedometer climb to over seventy kilometres per hour. 'You're drunk. You'll get us both killed.'

'I loved you, Ayesha,' Raza said, his eyes on the road. He gripped the wheel tightly with both hands. 'But you betrayed me the first chance you got. You've had this coming for a very long time.'

'You are ruining both our lives, Raza. Think about it. If you kill me, do you think they'll let you go? You'll rot in jail forever.'

He laughed. 'You idiot. I've kept you captive for weeks, and nobody has been any wiser. The police in this country are a joke.'

'Is that why you stopped moving me every few days? Because they're a joke, or because the noose is tightening around your neck?'

It was the wrong thing to say. Raza's hands began shaking. 'As soon as we are out of Lahore, I will kill you and bury your body in the fields. Hammad has told me of a place near the Lahore-Sialkot motorway where nobody will ever find you. You will die a nobody, just like you lived.' He wiped the sweat from his forehead with his shirt sleeve. 'I could have given you the world, Ayesha, but you chose this. When the bullet tears through your skull, you must remember that it was all your fault.'

He was serious, she could see that. If she didn't do something now, certain death awaited her. It was now or never.

Pulling the blade out of her bra, she swiped it across his forearm, going as deep as she could.

The blood spurted out of his arm like a small fountain.

'*Gushti!*' Raz screamed, taking his bleeding arm off the steering wheel and putting pressure on the wound with his other hand. 'What have you done?'

Without warning, his whole body shook, causing the steering wheel to turn right. She tried to take control of it, but before she could, the car slid off the asphalt and onto the grassy verge. The car hit a mound of earth and went flying into the air. The next few seconds almost happened in slow motion. They were tossed in the air, Ayesha's head hitting the roof of the car before they hit their seats again – hard. As the car landed on the ground, the sound of metal and plastic grinding against hard earth filled the air. She was thrown forward, her shoulder banging against the dashboard. Raza yelled as the car lost its balance, rolling once and then twice before toppling into a nearby ditch.

Her head spun, and all she could see was red. Her ears were ringing, and Raza's yelling seemed to be coming from a faraway place. A searing pain tore through her shoulder and as her vision adjusted, she saw Raza nursing his head in his hands, a trickle of blood streaming down the side of his face. A coppery taste clung to her mouth as she spat out blood, and attempted to push herself out of the shattered window of the jeep. Beside her, Raza's breathing was quick, his expression dazed as if he was seeing stars. He rubbed some of the blood between his fingers and frowned.

She paused, gazing with wonder at the man who had ruined her life. How much bitterness and bile could someone possess to change so completely someone else's life like this? What she saw before her wasn't a man of thirty-six, but a demon.

She looked into those black pupils, which had devoured her every chance they got, the hands that had pinned her down as she was raped time and again, the chest that pressed on hers, knocking the breath out of her.

Raza Masood lay beside her, utterly helpless.

As if on cue, he murmured, 'Kill me.'

Her fingers closed around the gun, which had fallen out of his pocket. She'd seen her father hunt enough times to know how guns worked. With the safety off, all she needed to do was pull the trigger, and it would be over.

Raza Masood would cease to exist.

She would be free forever.

'Do it,' he panted, his breathing ragged, blood oozing out of his forearm where the blade had slashed him. 'I have wronged you. Just end my misery.'

'You're saying this just to escape your fate, aren't you?'

He closed his eyes. 'I don't want to get caught by the police. Please. Just kill me!'

Her finger touched the trigger, and she closed her eyes. She saw Raza's dead body being lowered into the ground for a final time, his reign of terror at an end.

She also saw herself back in London, walking down Gower Street with Kamil and their friends. She saw Jamila Aunty heaping her plate with food, while kissing her on the forehead. Most of all, she saw her parents opening their arms to her – her brave parents who had done their best to raise her right, who had done whatever was in their power to ensure she had a good life. Could she do this to them?

She opened her eyes to see Raza Masood still pleading with her to kill him.

'Even now, you are putting your own needs before everyone else, Raza. It's only now you have failed that you want your misery to end.' Unlatching the seat belt, she threw the gun out of the window, as far as it would go. Then she looked him straight in the eye. 'I want you to look at my face, remember it, and know that I didn't kill you. For the rest of your life, I want you to live with the knowledge that the woman you tried so hard to finish let you live in the end. I want you to know that I choose life, Raza. I will always choose life. I am not a coward. You have not defeated me.'

Without a backward glance, she hoisted herself up out of the shattered window and landed on the grass next to the ditch, where people were beginning to gather.

'Can we get you any help?' one of them asked.

'She seems to be in pretty bad shape.'

'There's something familiar about her, but I can't say what.'

Ayesha ignored them, staggering out onto the road, breathing in the crisp morning air. Even at this distance, Raza's plaintive cries drilled into her ears. She looked back to see people helping him out of the wreckage before seating him gently on the grass as they waited for an ambulance to arrive. He would live.

Their eyes met. For the first time since she had met him, she had the upper hand, and he knew it. She could see the terror on his face, the uncertainty about the future, and it made her wonder if he wished he had died in the car crash after all.

Ayesha wished the ambulance would hurry. Sparing Raza's life was the best thing she'd ever done, and now she couldn't wait for his real punishment to begin.

Without looking back, she walked on, not knowing where she was going, but right now, she wanted to put as much distance between herself and Raza Masood as possible. The crowds that had gathered were not going to let him go anywhere, and besides, his injuries wouldn't allow him to walk, much less run.

She closed her eyes and lifted her face to let the winter sun wash over her, and then proceeded to pick her way among the asphalt and brambles. It wasn't until she stepped on a sharp stone that she realised she was barefoot.

Walking in the open air, it finally hit her that she was free.

Free from imprisonment, rape and pain.

Free from the shackles of society.

Free from Raza Masood.

The experience of walking alone in the fresh air after so long was surreal. They'd crashed somewhere in the grasslands between Lahore and Sialkot, and wherever she looked, she could see only green. In the far distance, there was a village, but right now, Ayesha felt that she could spread her arms and run for miles, the cold air whipping her face as she breathed in the delectable taste of freedom.

She was so lost in her thoughts that she didn't even hear the police sirens in the distance. In fact, she didn't pay any attention to anything, focusing on putting one foot in front of the other, each footstep taking her further from her captor and rapist.

'Ayesha!' someone called behind her. It took her a moment to place the voice. It was DSP Amna Habib. So, she had finally arrived. Chandni had been successful. None of this would have happened without Chandni.

'I'm sorry,' she whispered, not caring that Chandni couldn't hear her. She never would. Ignoring DSP Amna, she walked on, still just putting one foot in front of another.

It was only when someone else called out her name that she paused.

The voice transported her back to London, to carefree evenings full of love and laughter. Her vision blurred as she turned around, not caring if he saw that she was crying. *Let him see*, for she had nothing to hide from him.

He was running towards her, his arms thrown wide, and before she could mimic his actions, he had crashed into her, encircling her in his strong arms.

'I am never letting you go,' he panted in her ear. 'Your disappearance almost killed me, Ayesha.'

'What are you even doing here?'

Kamil's face was in her hair. 'I've been here for weeks, Ayesha, trying to find you. The moment DSP Amna got word from this woman Chandni, we rushed to the house, but you had gone.' His voice broke. 'I'm so glad we found you.'

'Kamil, you came for me.'

'Of course I did, and I am never letting you go again.'

'Promise?' Her voice was barely a whisper; she didn't think she had the strength to manage anything louder.

Kamil heard her, though. His grip intensified. 'Promise.'

Kamil

A few weeks later.
Lahore, Pakistan

'*Haye haye*, drive a bit faster,' his mother chastised the taxi driver. 'Are you even a Pakistani? You drive like a *gora*.'

Kamil slapped a palm against his forehead. 'Good God, Ammi.'

'Honestly Ammi, you are so embarrassing,' Shar said in English.

'Do be quiet, Sharmeela,' Jamila snapped at them. 'We're in Pakistan now, and you don't get to tell me how I talk to my fellow countrymen.' Turning to Shar, she added, 'And don't speak to me in English. Don't forget where you're from.'

'*Acha*, Ammi. *Maaf kar dein.* Spare me.'

'Are you Saraiki?' the driver asked.

Kamil looked back to see his mother flush with pleasure. Nothing gave her more pleasure than to be recognised for her language. Switching to Saraiki, she replied, 'I am from Multan. Why do you ask?'

'There's music in your voice,' the driver replied, smiling slightly as he picked up speed. Anywhere else in the world, this might have been mistaken for flirting, but Kamil knew better. After all, Saraiki was pretty musical – a beautiful language.

'When you say it like that, I feel I can almost forgive you for your slow driving.' Jamila said. 'You see, we need to be at court as soon as possible. I can't wait to see the person we've travelled all this way for.'

Kamil leaned back in his seat and sighed. So much had happened in these past few weeks that he was still finding it hard to wrap his head around it all. No words could describe his horror when he arrived at the ring road to find Raza Masood's car lying in a ditch with Ayesha nowhere to be found. He hadn't even glanced at Raza, his eyes searching only for the person who mattered to him the most. It was someone in the crowd who finally pointed in the distance, and he saw Ayesha.

This was where things became a bit frenetic, because around that time, the international press took hold of the story. Within days, the entire country was talking about the case again: how a Pakistani girl suffered an acid attack, and went to the UK, only to be kidnapped and brought back to Pakistan, where she was raped and imprisoned by the scion of one of the country's richest families.

If Kamil didn't have to return to the UK for work, he would have stayed in Pakistan indefinitely. It broke his heart to leave Ayesha, but if he knew anything about her, it was that she needed time alone to process things.

After her rescue, she hadn't said much to anyone, preferring to spend most of her time in her room at home, but there was a moment when things had changed. She'd emerged, joining them for lunch in the dining room, and announced what she'd decided to do about her case.

'I plan to recruit the press to expedite the charges against Raza Masood,' she said, her face devoid of any emotion. 'The time has come for him to suffer for what he did to me. I won't rest until he's behind bars forever.'

However, Kamil and Ayesha seemed to have forgotten how to talk to each other now that they weren't face to face. It had been weeks since they'd even spoken on the phone. The last time they'd talked, Kamil had once again tried to apologise, and Ayesha had cut him off.

'There's nothing to apologise for,' she'd said. 'There was no way you could have foreseen what would happen. Hell, there was no way I could have anticipated that Raza Masood would go to such lengths to destroy me. If it wasn't for your campaign, maybe

Chandni wouldn't have agreed to help me. Maybe I would never even have come across her.'

'Still, I should have been there to protect you.'

'You're not my keeper, Kamil.' Realising she'd snapped, she added, 'Listen, what we have is more than friendship, it's ... I don't know what it is yet, but it's something I've wanted to talk to you about, but have never seemed to get a chance. I still feel like my mind is in the air.' After a pause, she added, 'You mean a lot to me. Don't ruin it by apologising for things that aren't even your fault. Without you, I'd never have learned to accept my new identity. Never apologise to me, Kamil.'

'I can't wait to see you,' he'd whispered into the phone.

'I can't either. Come soon.' He thought he'd caught a hint of excitement in her voice, but there was no way to be certain. But then, why would she be thinking of him when she had so much on her mind, getting Raza Masood arrested and charged? Ayesha's testimony had been damning. There was no way Raza was getting bail after that. The evidence against him was overwhelming. His father had hired the best lawyers in the country for him, but so had Ayesha. Due to the press her case had gotten, several leading lawyers were ready to represent her, and when the case went to trial, it would be one of Pakistan's most high-profile ones. Raza's friend Raheel and the servant, Hammad, had both been rounded up as well, and it was said that Raheel would be testifying against Raza, although that was the least of his worries, because he was going to be spending his whole life in jail as well for murdering Chandni.

Emerging from his reverie, he noticed that they had already turned into Mall Road, after which it was only a matter of a few minutes before they reached the court. Kamil held on to the dashboard in front of him as the car climbed over the speed bump. A huge crowd of people had already gathered outside the court, bleeding into the gardens and almost into the road itself.

Kamil craned his neck, but there was no way to get a glimpse of Ayesha. There were too many people. He considered phoning her, but he knew her phone would be switched off. In order to pressurise the Pakistani justice system to expedite the case, Ayesha was making a speech on the court steps today.

As the car slowed down, someone tapped on his window. He didn't need to see the face to know who it was. He could tell from the hands. A smile stretched his lips.

Ayesha stood there, her head covered, but her scars on full display, grinning from ear to ear.

As soon as the car stopped, his mother hurried to get out, ran to Ayesha and collapsed into arms, sobbing. '*Haye* beta, please forgive me. I should have been a better aunt to you. I should have investigated your disappearance. I should have accompanied you to wherever it was you wanted to go. I am so sorry! We came here straight from the airport.'

Shar scoffed. 'Sure, Ammi. As if you were going to be a match for those grown-ass men.'

'Oh, Shar!' Ayesha cried, but she was smiling. 'You haven't lost any of your sense of humour, I see.'

Shar smirked. 'What can I say? My Ammi brings out the worst in me.' Reaching out to give Ayesha a quick hug, she added, 'It's good to see you looking so well. We've missed you.'

'Well, thank you for coming. I'm honoured.' Ayesha looked back at the crowd of people. 'I don't think they've noticed yet that I've slipped away. I'll need to get back soon, though.' Turning to Shar again, she asked about Juan.

Shar shrugged. 'He wanted to come, but Ammi was worried what people might say.'

Kamil watched his mother stiffen.

'Well, he's a very nice boy, I grant you,' she said. 'And I really enjoy his company. Plus, he looks Pakistani, so we can just say his name is Jamal.'

'His name is Juan, Ammi. You need to stop this.'

'Stop bickering, you two,' Kamil said, before this turned into a full-blown argument. 'Don't forget what we came here for. We came here to see Ayesha. Focus on that.'

His mother pointed at him. 'This boy hasn't slept a wink. Worrying after you is all he does. Look at him, thin as a stick, my dear boy.'

Shar jerked her head towards the court building. 'Come on, let's see the nice brick buildings, Ammi.'

Jamila was beaming. 'I'm fine here, thank you. Why would I want to see the buildings? Honestly, Sharmeela.'

'Ammi, we need to go and see the buildings. Now!'

'Oh!' Realisation dawned on Jamila, then. 'Yes, those beautiful buildings. *Haye*! Absolutely stunning. Show them to me, Sharmeela. I demand it. Let's go.'

Kamil shook his head at the pair of them, watching his mother turn around to wink at him and give him a thumbs-up. He was relieved Ayesha had her back to them.

He sensed a kind of forced cheerfulness in Ayesha's manner, as if she was hiding a great deal of pain. She masked it well, but Kamil had lived his entire life masking his own feelings, so he knew the drill.

'I'm so glad you came,' Ayesha said, her eyes shining. 'I'd hug you right now, but this is Pakistan, and my character is very much up in the air. Plenty of people call me a *gushti*.' Her voice caught when she said that word.

'Ayesha, you know that doesn't mean anything, right? People will talk.'

She waved him off. 'It doesn't matter. This is Pakistan. If men cannot face a woman head on, they resort to cheap names. Tell me how the therapy group is? Matt and the others. I really miss them. I miss working with Saeeda Aunty.'

Kamil waved a hand at her to indicate that all was good. 'I'm sorry it took a while to come back, but I'm here now, and I plan on staying with you until everything is settled.'

'Your job?'

He shrugged. 'I've taken an indefinite leave of absence now. I don't know when or if I will return.'

Ayesha stared at him with her mouth open. 'And you did it for me?'

'What do you think, Ayesha? Of course, it's all for you.'

Ayesha looked away, blinking back tears. 'That means more than you'll ever know. There are days when I win in the court of public opinion, but thanks to all the money the Masoods pour into social media, I get called an ugly whore a lot as well. A mistake of nature. A woman for hire. And you know yourself how important social media is here. Even more so than in the UK.'

Kamil folded his arms against his chest to stop himself from throwing them around her neck. She looked so small, standing there. Small, but brave. 'You've been avoiding me for weeks,' he finally said. 'Did you think you could hide your pain from me? I thought we knew each other better than that.'

'Kamil, I ... I just needed time. I've been treated like a piece of meat to be used and thrown away. Raza almost robbed me of my very being. What I felt for you in my heart was the only thing he couldn't take from me ... the only thing that has sustained me these past few weeks and months. If I had told you what had happened to me – the stuff they did to me – you'd have left and never looked back.'

His heart was breaking, not at her words, but at how much unnecessary guilt she carried. For a moment, he wished that they were back with the therapy group. There was so much to unpack here. 'Ayesha, I'd never leave you. I've been in love with you all this time. Not knowing where you were, what had happened to you, almost consumed me. I'd never leave you.'

'I'm damaged goods, Kamil. In every sense of the word.'

He didn't care what people thought now. He threw his arms around her. 'Never think, or say, that again. Nobody should have to go through what you did, but look at you now. You will nail that bastard and send his ass to jail, where he belongs.' He nodded at the burgeoning crowd. 'Don't cry. Look at them. Why do you think they're here?'

She sobbed quietly into his shirt. 'Don't stop me. Let me cry. God knows I've wanted to do this for weeks.'

'Is my company that bad that it makes you cry?'

She beat a fist against her chest, but she was laughing through her sobs.

As they walked towards the steps leading to the court building, where several media people had gathered with their cameras and mics, Ayesha took his hand and held it tight.

She climbed the steps, her flat heels clacking on the red brick as she took each one. When they finally turned, Kamil saw a sea of faces looking back at them.

'This is how it's going to be for me from now on. Do you think you can cope with it, the good and the bad?' she whispered without looking at him.

'Always,' he replied. 'I will always be at your side.'

'Tell us your story, Ayesha,' one of the journalists shouted. 'The world is listening.'

Ayesha took a deep breath and exhaled. 'My name is Ayesha Safdar. I am the survivor of an acid attack and rape. I have been bought and sold like chattels. I've been drugged and threatened. I have also known and found love. I have learned how to love myself. I have learned how to survive.' Glancing at Kamil, she gave him a winning smile. 'I am Ayesha Safdar.'

Ayesha

Six years later
Islamabad, Pakistan

Her phone started ringing the moment she landed at Islamabad Airport. Ayesha glanced at the number and smiled. 'Yes, Chandni?'

'Mama, I cannot find my doll, and Abbu isn't here to help me either.'

'That's because he is with me, my darling. Why don't you ask Nani to help you find it?'

'I don't want Nani,' Chandni whispered. 'I want you.'

Beside her, Kamil unbuckled his seat belt, stretching his legs in the aisle. 'I wonder where our daughter gets this flair for theatrics from?' Before she could reply, he laughed. 'It was a rhetorical question, Ayesha. I know she gets it from my mother.'

Her four-year-old daughter wasn't pleased to hear her mother laughing, and she demonstrated her anger by ending the call without saying goodbye.

'She's definitely a drama queen, but I'm not going to pin the blame on Jamila Aunty. No way.'

'I swear, my mother loves you more than me. After all, you gave her the grandchild she desired for so long.'

As they waited for the plane to dock at a boarding bridge, Ayesha took Kamil's hand and rested her head on his shoulder. 'Sometimes, I can't believe we ended up together. Who would have thought it would happen?'

'I did,' Kamil quipped. 'I thought it was pretty obvious. I think I fell in love with you the very first day.'

'Oh, please, we couldn't see eye to eye on the first day. We had such awkward conversations.'

'But I love you more than ever now, Mrs Ayesha Kamil.'

Before anyone could notice, Ayesha quickly planted a kiss on Kamil's lips. 'That should be enough for now.'

'To be continued in the hotel room,' Kamil said, his eyes crinkling with fine lines – which had only recently appeared on his face. Ayesha loved him all the more for them. At forty-one, Kamil could still pass for a thirty-year-old, but it wasn't his youth that she was in love with. Of all the men she had known in her life, it was only Kamil who had stuck with her. Even now, as she travelled to Islamabad, he insisted on accompanying her.

She ran a hand down the right side of her face, her fingers brushing the remnants of scars and her now-smooth nose. After a few more surgeries over the years, she had decided to call it quits. Her face wasn't perfect and would never be. She was done letting facial beauty define her. The people she loved the most in the world liked her with all her imperfections, so why should she have any more surgeries? To match society's expectations? At the age of thirty-three, she'd had enough of that. Her priority now was her work, and when women she worked with saw her face, they understood. They knew that they could confide in her. They could let Ayesha into their lives.

Seeing her lost in thought, Kamil ran a hand over the right side of her face too. 'I think I love you more every day.'

'Are you saying that so you'll get lucky in the hotel?'

Kamil sucked in a breath. 'You wound me, Ayesha.' And then, after a beat, 'Yes, that's why I am saying all this.'

They laughed together, ignoring the people hurrying to get their luggage from the overhead bins.

It had taken a few months after her imprisonment to have Raza Masood charged for all the crimes he had committed against her, but it wasn't until more than a year later that he was sentenced to ten years in prison. Although he had many of the country's best lawyers with him, thanks to Kamil's social-media campaign, she had funding and her own army of lawyers, and they had ensured that in the end, she got justice.

Raza Masood had wept like a child the day she testified against him in court. Looking at her, he'd mouthed, 'Please, Ayesha.'

If anything, it had made her angrier than before. How dare he?

She hadn't balked or hesitated. She had looked him straight in the eye and told the truth. She'd told the truth of the acid attack and disfigurement, of the kidnapping and rape, and most of all, of all his attempts to enslave her and reduce her to only a shadow of her former self.

'This happens to more women than we care to admit,' she'd said. 'Most of us don't speak about these things, allowing these animals to roam free. I know I didn't, and I regret my decision every day. If I had said something after my attack, he may not have had the guts to kidnap me.' Not breaking eye contact with Raza Masood, she had finally said, 'People like Raza Masood deserve a fate worse than death. People like him are the reason why woman can't walk freely in our country, why they feel compelled to remain silent in the face of obscene wealth and connections. People like Raza Masood are a blight on his great nation, and there is only one home for them – jail.'

Ayesha had always thought that the best day of her life was when she had married Kamil almost five years ago, but it wasn't until she had seen Raza Masood finally get dragged to the Multan jail after over a year of hearings, where he would rot for the next decade of his life, that she realised what she had been waiting for all this time.

Justice.

They were in Islamabad today so she could receive the *Sitara-e-Imtiaz*, Pakistan's third highest civilian honour for services in support of human rights. Not long after her escape from Raza Masood, Ayesha had quit Insaaniyat, and started her own charity organisation for acid victims. Her organisation was local, but with the help of her friends and family in London, she had managed to raise millions of pounds from abroad, all of which were used to improve the lives of women who had suffered heinous attacks on their faces and bodies. Not only did her charity, Jazba, offer plastic surgeries to the women, but also legal support so they could finally file charges against the men who had tried to ruin their lives. She was making a difference, and just the other day, DSP Amna, who was now SP Amna Habib and had become a dear friend, had called her to say that acid attacks in the country had reduced by about half.

'This is all down to what you're doing,' she told Ayesha. 'If it wasn't for your organisation, for the way you sent a privileged feudal lord like Raza Masood to jail, men would still be marauding around, looking for women to destroy.'

As they stepped outside the sprawling airport of Pakistan's capital city, a car from the Government of Pakistan was waiting to take her to the President House.

Her grip on Kamil's hand tightened. Here was a girl from Multan who had somehow survived impossible odds to be standing here today to get a medal from the President of Pakistan. It was an honour accorded to very few, as Shugufta Raheem, her former boss, kept telling her. She knew that her father would have the television turned on full volume to see her get the medal. Although Ayesha would have loved to have them in Islamabad, she knew they couldn't come, not with her father's heart problems flaring up again.

It kept her up at night, wondering how long her father had left with them, and she didn't know how she would have coped with everything if it wasn't for Kamil. Her Kamil, who had resigned from his job in London to move with her to Multan, who hadn't looked back once as he put all his efforts into managing Jazba with her, who was proud always to stand a step behind her, preferring to work behind the scenes while she swiftly became the face of the charity.

'Maybe you were meant to go to London,' her mother always said to her. 'If you hadn't, you would never have met Kamil.'

She was right.

It was Kamil who suggested that they name their daughter after the girl who had given up her life to save Ayesha's. 'This way, she will always stay with us, a reminder that kindness does exist in this world.'

Ayesha hadn't told Kamil yet, but she was expecting again, and there was something else she had been planning for a long time, but hadn't said a word about. Kamil thought he hid it well, but she could see how much he missed his parents, his family, how he was upset he couldn't be in London when Shar's baby was born. She saw his eyes misting up whenever the name of his city came up. So tonight, she was going to tell him that Jazba would be opening its office in London. Acid attacks weren't something that happened only in Pakistan, but the world over, and Ayesha was finally in a position to do something about that.

As they drove through the city, she pulled the coat tightly over her fancy silk shalwar kameez that she was wearing for the event. It was the middle of January, so the weather in Islamabad was chilly.

'It almost feels like London, doesn't it?' Kamil remarked as they passed the leafy boulevards of the capital, the civilised traffic here quite unlike that of Multan.

She glanced at Kamil and smiled to herself. 'It sure does.'

The President House was built on a hill that overlooked the city, and as she stepped out of the vehicle and into the bracing wind that blew in from the Margalla Hills, Ayesha knew that she had finally made it.

She was so lost in the magnificent view that Kamil had to nudge her to get her attention.

'All set for the ceremony? Shall we go inside?'

'Just a moment.' She wanted to spend a few more moments admiring Islamabad.

'It's a beautiful view, isn't it?' Kamil murmured. 'You almost feel like you're on top of the world.' Reaching for her hand, he added, 'I am so glad I get to experience this with you, Ayesha.'

She squeezed his hand in return. 'I feel the same.'

Somewhere out there, Raza Masood was rotting in prison. Was he familiar with the feeling of regret or did that emotion fail to manifest in psychopaths? she wondered. She wished that there was a television in Multan Jail where he could see her receive the medal from the president.

'Here I am, Raza,' she whispered. 'You failed to break me.'

Turning to Kamil, she wiped the tears from her cheeks, and smiled. 'Let's go inside.'

Acknowledgements

When they say that it takes a village to write a book, it's the honest truth. This was a particularly difficult book to write for several reasons, so I owe a ton of gratitude to the people who helped make it happen. My thanks to:

Amaji (my grandmother), who I miss terribly and think of everyday without fail. My parents and the rest of my family, for always rooting for me and supporting my writing career.

Sayantan Ghosh, Executive Editor at Simon & Schuster India, for your immense belief in my talent and for always ensuring that literature transcends borders. This book would not have been possible without your support and unparalleled vision to make it the best it can be for the South Asian market. Thank you from the bottom of my heart.

My thanks also to the wonderful team at Simon & Schuster India for bringing the same passion and dedication to this book that you did for my debut *In the Company of Strangers*.

Karen Sullivan, the force behind Orenda Books, for your staunch belief in me and unfailing patience as I took much more time than usual to finish this book. My thanks also to West Camel and the rest of Team Orenda.

Annette Crossland, my superstar literary agent, for falling in love with this book the moment you read the first few chapters and for encouraging me to believe in myself and finish writing it. You've stood by me since 2017 and for that I am eternally grateful.

Heleen Kist, for your friendship, honesty and immeasurable help with the South Asian edition. The kindness you've shown me over the years is nothing short of phenomenal. You're my constant in life. My thanks also to Delphi for her amazing help.

Alan Gorevan, without whom this book would never have been written. A most supportive friend, discerning first reader, and the force that stood by me and pushed me to write this book at a time when I didn't believe in myself. There will never be enough words to express my gratitude to you.

Faiqa Mansab, for your expert advice and friendship, not to mention the numerous times you reassured me when I doubted myself. Thank you for always being on my side. I value your friendship tremendously.

Alex Chaudhuri, with whom I began my publishing journey. A loyal friend, you've always been there to pick me up whenever I fell and without your help, I don't know where I would be today. Nowhere good, I wager!

Lubna Sayed, superstar friend and possibly my biggest supporter. There really are no words to thank you for all you have done and continue to do for me. Knowing you has made me realize that kindness still exists in this world. Please, never change.

Hazel Orme, for always being my first reader. You were the first person to tell me that I was talented and should never give up. I would never have achieved anything in publishing without your belief in me.

Juliet Mushens, for being a most dependable friend, keen listener and an all-round fabulous person. Your bright personality is enough to lift anyone's spirits. So grateful to have you in my corner.

Paula Robinson, for proving that good people do exist in this world. Your staunch support of my work and me is like a beacon in the darkness.

Shirin Amani Azari, for always being a kind and hospitable friend. I learn so much about kindness from you every day.

Eve Smith, for being there for me when I needed a friend, and for devoting so much of your time and energy to make my trips to Oxford fun.

Saba Karim Khan, my amazing friend, thanks to whom, Abu Dhabi feels like home.

Mehvash Amin, for your friendship and immeasurable help with the South Asian edition.

Stuart Gibbon, for giving me so much of your time to explain police procedure – something that was necessary for this book. You have my sincerest gratitude.

Liam Chennells, for being such a positive influence in my life.

You're truly a godsend.

Ali Arsalan Pasha, for bringing so much brightness and positivity in my life. It is an honour to call you a friend.

Kirstie Long, for always bringing cheer in my life.

Sabine Edwards, PR maven, true friend and always generous with your time and support.

Mushba Said, for the fabulous cover for the South Asian edition.

Paul Waters, for your undying support for everything I

write. Sarah Faichney, for your banter, friendship and expert editorial eye. Kirsten Arcadio, for being a solid friend over the years (decades?). Damien Hine, for always being there for me. Anita Chaudhuri, for always supporting me no matter what I write. Mehr F Husain, for your unfailing friendship. Zaeem Siddiqui and Shireen Quraishi, for being my home away from home. Danielle Price, for being the marketing supremo that you are. Madam Navid Shahzad, for your help, friendship and guidance.

For all their support: Nadia K Barb, Sonia Velton, Avkirat Dyal, Tony Frobisher, Sara Naveed, Hamza Azhar Salam, Sirah Haq, Naima Rashid and Jacky Collins.

And last but not the least, Dr Asaif Khan (my brother), for your help with all things medical.